MORE PRAISE FOR JONATHAN KELLERMAN AND HIS ALEX DELAWARE NOVELS

Silent Partner

"A complex and haunting story of tangled personalities, deeply buried family secrets, and of violence lying thinly under the surface . . . Hits the reader right between the eyes."
—*Los Angeles Times Book Review*

"A most intriguing read . . . compelling."
—*New York Daily News*

Time Bomb

"Though a time bomb is ticking away at the heart of this novel, readers will forget to watch the clock once they begin it."
—*Chicago Sun-Times*

"Virtually impossible to put aside until the final horrifying showdown."
—*People*

Private Eyes

"A page-turner from beginning to end."
—*Los Angeles Times*

"Spellbinding suspense . . . Unforgettable."
—*Houston Chronicle*

Please turn the page for more reviews. . . .

P9-BZT-899

And praise
for these other terrific novels
by Jonathan Kellerman

Billy Straight
"Taut, compelling . . . Everything a thriller ought to be. The writing is excellent. The plotting is superior. The characters ring true."
—*USA Today*

"Kellerman has justly earned his reputation as a master of the psychological thriller. . . . The writing is vivid, the suspense sustained, and [he] has arranged one final, exquisitely surprising plot twist to confound the complacent reader."
—*People*

The Butcher's Theater
"Crisp . . . Suspenseful . . . Intense."
—*The New York Times Book Review*

"This one is going to scare the hell out of a lot of people on its way to the bestseller lists."
—ELMORE LEONARD

BOOKS BY JONATHAN KELLERMAN

Fiction
GONE (2006)
RAGE (2005)
TWISTED (2004)
THERAPY (2004)
THE CONSPIRACY CLUB (2003)
A COLD HEART (2003)
THE MURDER BOOK (2002)
FLESH AND BLOOD (2001)
DR. DEATH (2000)
MONSTER (1999)
BILLY STRAIGHT (1998)
SURVIVAL OF THE FITTEST (1997)
THE CLINIC (1997)
THE WEB (1996)
SELF-DEFENSE (1995)
BAD LOVE (1994)
DEVIL'S WALTZ (1993)
PRIVATE EYES (1992)
TIME BOMB (1990)
SILENT PARTNER (1989)
THE BUTCHER'S THEATER (1988)
OVER THE EDGE (1987)
BLOOD TEST (1986)
WHEN THE BOUGH BREAKS (1985)

Nonfiction
SAVAGE SPAWN:
REFLECTIONS ON VIOLENT CHILDREN (1999)
HELPING THE FEARFUL CHILD (1981)
PSYCHOLOGICAL ASPECTS OF
CHILDHOOD CANCER (1980)

For Children, Written and Illustrated
JONATHAN KELLERMAN'S
ABC OF WEIRD CREATURES (1995)
DADDY, DADDY, CAN YOU TOUCH THE SKY? (1994)

With Faye Kellerman
DOUBLE HOMICIDE
CAPITAL CRIMES

JONATHAN KELLERMAN

THE CLINIC

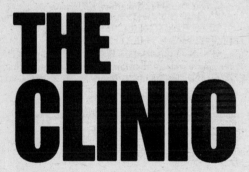

BALLANTINE BOOKS • NEW YORK

Special thanks to Dr. Michael Austerlitz

A Ballantine Book
Published by The Random House Publishing Group
Copyright © 1996 by Jonathan Kellerman
Excerpt from *Rage* copyright © 2005 by Jonathan Kellerman

Published in the United States by Ballantine Books, an imprint of The Random House Publishing Group, a division of Random House, Inc., New York, and simultaneously in Canada by Random House of Canada Limited, Toronto.

BALLANTINE and colophon are registered trademarks of Random House, Inc.

This edition published by arrangement with Bantam Books, a division of Random House, Inc.

www.ballantinebooks.com

ISBN 978-0-345-46074-5

Printed in the United States of America

First Ballantine Books Edition: April 2003

OPM   9   8   7

To Beverly Lewis

THE
CLINIC

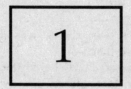

Few murder streets are lovely. This one was.

Elm-shaded, a softly curving stroll to the University, lined with generous haciendas and California colonials above lawns as unblemished as fresh billiard felt.

Giant elms. Hope Devane had bled to death under one of them, a block from her home, on the southwest corner.

I looked at the spot again, barely exposed by a reluctant moon. The night-quiet was broken only by crickets and the occasional late-model well-tuned car.

Locals returning home. Months past the curious-onlooker stage.

Milo lit up a cigarillo and blew smoke out the window.

Cranking my window down, I continued to stare at the elm.

A twisting trunk as thick as a freeway pylon supported sixty feet of opaque foliage. Stout, grasping branches appeared frosted in the moonlight, some so laden they brushed the ground.

Five years since the city had last pruned street trees. Property-tax shortfall. The theory was that the killer had hidden under the canopy, though no hint of presence other than bicycle tracks, a few feet away, was ever found.

Three months later, theory was all that remained and not much of that.

Milo's unmarked Ford shared the block with two other cars, both Mercedeses, both with parking permits on their windshields.

After the murder, the city had promised to trim the elms. No follow-through yet.

Milo had told me about it with some bitterness, cursing politicians but really damning the cold case.

"A couple of news stories, then *nada*."

"Current events as fast food," I'd said. "Quick, greasy, forgettable."

"Aren't *we* the cynic."

"Professional training: aiming for rapport with the patient."

That had gotten a laugh out of him. Now he frowned, brushed hair off his forehead, and blew wobbly smoke rings.

Edging the car up the block, he parked again. "That's her house." He pointed to one of the colonials, smallish, but well-kept. White board front, four columns, dark shutters, shiny fittings on a shiny door. Three steps up from the sidewalk a flagstone path cut through the lawn. A picket gate blocked the driveway.

Two upstairs windows were amber behind pale curtains.

"Someone home?" I said.

"That's his Volvo in the driveway."

Light-colored station wagon.

"He's always home," said Milo. "Once he gets in he never leaves."

"Still mourning?"

He shrugged. "She drove a little red Mustang. She was a lot younger than him."

"How much younger?"

"Fifteen years."

"What about him interests you?"

"The way he acts when I talk to him."

"Nervous?"

"Unhelpful. Paz and Fellows thought so, too. For what that's worth."

He didn't think much of the first detectives on the case and the common ground probably bothered him as much as anything.

"Well," I said, "isn't the husband always the first suspect? Though stabbing her out on the street doesn't sound typical."

"True." He rubbed his eyes. "Braining her in the bedroom would have been more *marital*. But it happens." Twirling the cigar. "Live long enough, everything happens."

"Where exactly were the bicycle tracks?"

"Just north of the body but I wouldn't make much of those. Lab guys say they could have been anywhere from one to ten days old. A neighbor kid, a student, a fitness freak, anyone. And no one I talked to when I did the door-to-door noticed an unusual biker that whole week."

"What's an unusual biker?"

"Someone who didn't fit in."

"Someone nonwhite?"

"Whatever works."

"Quiet neighborhood like this," I said, "it's surprising no one saw or heard anything at eleven P.M."

"Coroner said it's possible she didn't scream. No defense wounds, no tentatives, so she probably didn't struggle much."

"True." I'd read the autopsy findings. Read the entire file, starting with Paz and Fellows's initial report and ending with the pathologist's dictated drone and the packet of postmortem photos. How many such pictures had I seen over the years? It never got easier.

"No scream," I said, "because of the heart wound?"

"Coroner said it could have collapsed the heart, put her into instant shock."

He snapped thick fingers softly, then ran his hand over his face, as if washing without water. What I could see of his profile was heavy as a walrus's, pocked and fatigued.

He smoked some more. I thought again of the preautopsy photos, Hope Devane's body ice-white under the coroner's lights. Three deep purple stab wounds in close-up: chest, crotch, just above the left kidney.

The forensic scenario was that she'd been taken by surprise and dispatched quickly by the blow that exploded her heart, then slashed a second time above the vagina, and finally laid facedown on the sidewalk and stabbed in the back.

"A husband doing that," I said. "I know you've seen worse but it seems so calculated."

"This husband's an intellectual, right? A thinker." Smoke escaped the car in wisps, decaying instantly at the touch of night air. "Truth is, Alex, I want it to be

Seacrest for selfish reasons. 'Cause if it's not him, it's a goddamn logistical *nightmare*."

"Too many suspects."

"Oh yeah," he said, almost singing it. "Lots of people who could've hated her."

2

A self-help book changed Hope Devane's life.

Wolves and Sheep wasn't the first thing she published: a psychology monograph and three dozen journal articles had earned her a full professorship at thirty-eight, two years before her death.

Tenure had given her job security and the freedom to enter the public eye with a book the tenure committee wouldn't have liked.

Wolves made the best-seller lists for a month, earning her center ring in the media circus and more money than she could have accumulated in ten years as a professor.

She was suited to the public eye, blessed with the kind of refined, blond good looks that played well on the small screen. That, and a soft, modulated voice that came across confident and reasonable over the radio, meant she had no trouble getting publicity bookings. And she made the most of each one. For despite *Wolves*'s subtitle, *Why Men Inevitably Hurt Women and What Women Can Do to Avoid It*, and its indicting tone, her public persona was that of an intelligent, articulate, thoughtful, *pleasant* woman entering the public arena with reluctance but performing graciously.

I knew all that but had little understanding of the person she'd been.

Milo had left me three LAPD evidence boxes to review: her resume, audio- and videotapes, some newspaper coverage, the book. All passed along by Paz and Fellows. They'd never studied any of it.

He'd told me about inheriting the case the night before, sitting across the table from Robin and me at a seafood place in Santa Monica. The bar was crowded but half the booths were empty and we sat in a corner, away from sports on big-screen and frightened people trying to connect with strangers. Midway through the meal Robin left for the ladies' room and Milo said, "Guess what I got for Christmas?"

"Christmas is months away."

"Maybe that's why this is no gift. Cold case. Three months cold: Hope Devane."

"Why now?"

" 'Cause it's dead."

"The new lieutenant?"

He dipped a shrimp in sauce and put the whole thing in his mouth. As he chewed, his jaw bunched. He kept looking around the room even though there was nothing to see.

New lieutenant, same old pattern.

He was the only acknowledged gay detective in the LAPD, would never be fully accepted. His twenty-year climb to Detective III had been marked by humiliation, sabotage, periods of benign neglect, near-violence. His solve record was excellent and sometimes that helped keep the hostility under the surface. His quality of life depended upon the attitude of the superior-of-the-moment. The new one was baffled and nervous, but too preoccupied with a dispirited postriot department to pay too much attention to Milo.

"He gave it to you because he thinks it's a low-probability solve?"

He smiled, as if savoring a private joke.

"Also," he said, "he figures Devane might have been a lesbian. 'Should be right up your . . . ahem ahem . . . *alley*, Sturgis.'"

Another shrimp disappeared. His lumpy face remained static and he folded his napkin double, then unfolded it. His necktie was a horrid brown-and-ochre paisley fighting a duel with his gray houndstooth jacket. His black hair, now flecked with white, had been chopped nearly to the skin at the sides, but the top had been left long and the sideburns were still long—and completely snowy.

"Is there any indication she was gay?" I said.

"Nope. But she had tough things to say about men, so ergo, *ipso facto*."

Robin returned. She'd reapplied her lipstick and had fluffed her hair. The royal-blue dress intensified the auburn, the silk accentuated every movement. We'd spent some time on a Pacific island and her olive skin had held on to the tan.

I'd killed a man there. Clear self-defense—saving Robin's life as well as mine. Sometimes I still had nightmares.

"You two look serious," she said, slipping into the booth. Our knees touched.

"Doing my homework," said Milo. "I know how

much this guy enjoyed school, so I thought I'd share it."

"He just got the Hope Devane murder," I said.

"I thought they'd given up on that."

"They have."

"What a terrifying thing."

Something in her voice made me look at her.

"More terrifying," I said, "than any other murder?"

"In some ways, Alex. Good neighborhood like that, you go for a walk right outside your house and someone jumps out and cuts you?"

I placed my hand on top of hers. She didn't seem to notice.

"The first thing I thought of," she said, "was she was killed because of her views. And that would make it *terrorism*. But even if it was just some nut picking her at random, it's still terrorism in a sense. Personal freedom in this city kicked another notch lower."

Our knees moved apart. Her fingers were delicate icicles.

"Well," she said, "at least *you're* on it, Milo. Anything so far?"

"Not yet," he said. "Situation like this, what you do is start fresh. Let's hope for the best."

In the kindest of times optimism was a strain for him. The words sounded so out-of-character he could have been auditioning for summer stock.

"Also," he said, "I thought Alex might be able to help me. Dr. Devane being a psychologist."

"Did you know her, Alex?"

I shook my head.

The waiter came over. "More wine?"

"Yes," I said. "Another bottle."

*   *   *

The next morning, Milo brought me the boxes and left. On top was the academic resume.

Her full name was Hope Alice Devane. Father: Andre. Mother: Charlotte. Both deceased.

Under MARITAL STATUS, she'd typed MARRIED, but she hadn't listed Philip Seacrest's name.

CHILDREN: NONE.

She'd been born in California, in a town I'd never heard of called Higginsville. Probably somewhere in the center of the state, because she'd graduated from Bakersfield High School as class valedictorian and a National Merit Scholar before enrolling at UC Berkeley as a Regent's Scholar. Dean's list every quarter, Phi Beta Kappa, graduation with a summa cum laude degree in psychology, then continuation at Berkeley for her Ph.D.

She'd published her first two papers as a graduate student and moved to L.A. for clinical training: internship and postdoctoral fellowship, crosstown, in the Psychiatry Department at County General Hospital. Then an appointment as a lecturer in women's studies at the University and a transfer, the following year, to the Psychology Department as an assistant professor.

Next came ten pages of society memberships, scholarly publications, abstracts, papers delivered at conferences. Her first research topic had been differential achievement in girls and boys on mathematics tests, then she'd shifted gears to sex roles and child-rearing methods, and, once again, to sex roles as they affected self-control.

An average of five articles a year in solid journals—premium gas for a Ferrari on the tenure fast track. It could have been any C.V., until I came to the tail end of the bibliography section where a subheading entitled *Nonpeer Review Publication and Media Work* gave an inkling of the turn she'd taken during the year before her death.

Wolves and Sheep, along with its foreign editions, followed by scores of radio and TV and print interviews, appearances on afternoon talk shows.

Shows with titles like *FIGHT BACK! Dogging the Predator, The New Slaves, The Testosterone Conspiracy.*

The final section was *Departmental and Campus Activities* and it brought things back to dusty academia.

As an assistant professor she'd sat on four committees. Scheduling and Room Allocation, Graduate Student Orientation, Animal-Subject Safety—the kind of drudgery I knew well—then, six months before her death, she'd chaired something called Interpersonal Conduct that I'd never heard of.

Something to do with sexual harassment? Exploitation of students by faculty? That was something with hostility potential. I placed a check next to the notation and moved on to *Wolves and Sheep*.

The book jacket was matte red with embossed gold letters and a small black graphic between author and title: silhouettes of the eponymous animals.

The wolf's mouth was crammed with fangs and its claws reached out for the undersized sheep. On the back was Hope Devane's color photo. She had an oval face and sweet features, wore a beige cashmere suit and pearls and sat very straight in a brown suede chair backed by shelves of books in soft focus. Mont-Blanc pen in hand, sterling inkwell within reach. Long fingers, pink-polished nails. Honey-blond hair swept back from fine bones, the cheeks accentuated by blush. Light brown eyes clear and wide and direct, soft without being weak. A confident, possibly ironic smile on nacreous lips.

The pages were dog-eared and Milo's yellow underlining and pen scrawl were all over the margins. I read the book, drove two miles down Beverly Glen and over to the University, where I played with the Biomed library computers for a while.

Interesting results. I returned home, watched the talk-show tapes.

Four shows, four sets of noisy, giddy audiences, a quartet of smarmy, pseudosensitive, and altogether interchangeable hosts.

The Yolanda Michaels Show: What Makes a Real Woman?

Hope Devane tolerating the metal-grind rhetoric of an antifeminist woman who preached the virtues of Bible study, cosmetics, and greeting one's husband at the door in a see-through raincoat over nothing else.

Sid, Live!: Prisoners of Sex?

Hope Devane engaged in debate with a male anthropologist/ant specialist who believed all sex differences were inborn and unchangeable and that men and women should simply learn to live with one another. Hope trying to be reasonable, but the end result falling just short of shallow.

The Gina Sydney Jerome Show:

Hope Devane in a roundtable discussion with three other authors: a woman linguist who pooh-poohed psychology and recommended that men and women learn to interpret language correctly, a New York-

based syndicated columnist on women's issues who
had nothing to say but said it polysyllabically, and a
depressed-looking man who claimed to have been a
battered husband and had stretched the account of his
torment to three hundred pages.

Same old noise . . .

*Live with Morry Mayhew: Who's Really the Weaker
Sex?*

Hope Devane debating the self-styled head of a
men's-rights organization I'd never heard of who
went after her with misogynistic lust.

This one different—the hostility level ratcheted up
several notches. I rewound and watched it again.

The misogynist was named Karl Neese. Thirty or
so, lean and outwardly hip in all black and a stylish
haircut but Neanderthal in his point of view, hogging
the airtime and layering insults relentlessly—psycho-
drama parmigiana.

His target never fought back, never interrupted,
never raised her voice even when Neese's comments
drew applause from louts in the audience.

MAYHEW: Okay, Mr. Neese, now let's ask the doctor—
NEESE: Doctor? I don't see any stethoscope.
MAYHEW: She happens to be a Ph.D.—
NEESE: Am I supposed to be impressed by that? What
    does *Ph.D.* mean, anyway? "Piled higher and
    deeper"? "Papa has dough"?
MAYHEW [*Suppressing smile*]: Okay, Dr. Devane, now if
    you could please tell us—
NEESE: Tell us why feminists keep harping on about
    their problems—nag, nag, nag. But it's okay to
    abort on demand because babies are inconve-
    nient—

MAYHEW:—your theory of why women fall prey so
often to unscrupulous—

NEESE: Because they *want* unscrupulous. Bad guys.
Danger. Excitement. And they keep coming back
for more. They say they want nice, but just try to
pick up a woman using nice. Nice means weak and
weak means geek. And geek gets no peek!

[*Laughter, applause*]

HOPE DEVANE: You may actually have something there.

NEESE: Oh, I do, baby. I do. [*Leering*]

DEVANE: Sometimes we do fall into dangerous patterns. The crux, I believe, is in the lessons we learn
as children.

NEESE: Show me yours, I'll show you mine?

MAYHEW: [*Smiling*] C'mon, Karl. What kinds of lessons, Doctor—

DEVANE: The role models we learn from. The behaviors
we're taught to emulate—

Twenty more minutes of his double entendres and
her reasoned statements. Each time he got the crowd
hooting, she waited until things quieted before offering brief, precise replies that had nothing to do with
him. Sticking to her own agenda. By the end of the
show, people were listening and Neese was looking
off-balance.

I watched it again, concentrating on Hope and
what made her effective. She made eye contact in a
fearless way that established intimacy, projected an
unflappability that made the obvious seem profound.

Charisma. Calm charisma.

If the medium was the message, she was a brilliant
courier and I couldn't help thinking of what she
might have accomplished had she lived.

When the segment ended, the camera caught a close-up of Neese's face. No more wise-guy grin.

Serious. Angry?

It was a crazy idea, but could he have held on to the anger?

Why not, the case was cold and Milo had asked me to "hypothesize away." I wrote down Neese's name and reached for the homicide file.

Words, pictures. Always pictures . . .

It was close to five when I called Milo at West L.A. Detectives and told him I'd finished everything, including the book.

"That was fast."

"Easy read, she had a good style. Conversational. As if she's sitting in your living room, sharing her knowledge."

"What'd you think of the contents?"

"A lot of what's in there is hard to argue with— stick up for your rights, take care of yourself, choose your goals realistically so you can succeed and enhance your self-esteem. But when it comes to the more radical stuff she doesn't present facts to back it up. The part about testosterone and sadistic psychopathy is a pretty big stretch."

"All men are sex killers."

"All men have the *potential* to be sex killers and even consensual sex is partial rape because the penis is constructed as a weapon and penetration means invasion and loss of women's control."

"She's big on control, isn't she?"

"It's her main theme. I went to the library and checked out the studies she quoted. They don't say what she claims they do. She took facts out of context, reported selectively, played fast and loose. But unless you took the time to carefully examine each source, it wouldn't be obvious. And apart from her writing skill, I can see why the book sold so well. She had a natural constituency because women almost always *are* the victims. You heard Robin last night. When we got home she told me the murder had kept her up nights because she found herself identifying with Hope. I never knew she'd given it a moment's thought."

"What about the TV tapes?"

"She was good at that, too. Unflappable. Even when they put that moron against her on Mayhew, she never lost her cool. Remember him?"

"Skinny idiot in black? He really dumped on her, didn't he?"

"But she handled him beautifully, never let him get to her. To me, she came out the clear winner and he looked mad. What if he held a grudge?"

Silence. "You've got to be kidding."

"You said be creative. Those shows are powder kegs—dealing with sensitive issues, exploiting people on the edge. Exactly what I was trained not to do as a therapist. I've always thought it was only a matter of time before things got violent."

"Hmm," he said. "Okay, I'll look into him—what was his name?"

"Karl Neese."

He repeated it. "Wouldn't *that* be something. . . . Okay, any other thoughts about Hope?"

"That's it, so far. How about you?"

"Nothing. I get a feeling Hubby's holding something back and your buddies at the U are no help—quoting me statistics about how if it takes too long to solve a case, forget it. Also, they treat me like Joe Cretin. Talk-ing re-al slo-ow."

"Class snobbery?"

"Maybe coming in rubbing my knuckles on the ground while scarfing a banana was the wrong approach."

I laughed. "You should have dropped your master's degree into the conversation."

"Oh, sure, that would really impress a bunch of Ph.D.'s. So what do you think of the wounds? Does that groin stab make it sexual?"

"If it was intentional, it would show definite sexual hostility."

"Oh, it was intentional all right. Three clean cuts, no error wounds, no hacking around. He got her exactly where he wanted: heart, groin, back."

"When you put it that way, it sounds orchestrated," I said. "A definite sequence."

"How so?"

"Stabbing her in the heart first could be romantic, in a sick sense. Breaking someone's heart, maybe some kind of revenge. Though I guess he could have chosen the heart in order to kill her quickly. But wouldn't a throat slash have been a better bet for that?"

"Definitely. The heart's not that easy to hit, you can nick ribs, miss completely. Most quick-kill knife jobs *are* throat slashes. What about the other wounds?"

"The groin," I said, thinking of Hope's composure and impeccable clothes. Every hair in place. Left bleeding on the street. . . . "The groin could be an extension of the heart wound—love gone wrong, the sexual element. . . . If so, the back would be the coup de grâce: back stabbing. The symbol of betrayal."

"To stab her in the back," he said, "he had to take the time to flip her over and place her on her stomach. That's why I got interested when you said orchestrated. Think of it, you're standing there on the street, just killed someone. You take the time to do something like that? To *me* it says crime of passion but carried out in a calculated manner."

"Cold rage," I said. "Criminal intimacy—someone she knew?"

"Which is exactly why I'm interested in Hubby."

"But for someone like her, intimacy could mean something totally different. Her book tour took her out in front of millions of people. She could have triggered rage in any of them. Even a delusional rage. Someone who didn't like the way she signed a book, someone who watched her on TV and related to it pathologically. Fame's like stripping in a dark theater, Milo. You never know who's out there."

He was silent for a few moments.

"Gee, thanks for expanding my suspect list to infinity. . . . Here's something that never made it into the papers: Her routine was to take a half-hour to one-hour walk every night, around the same time. Ten-thirty, eleven. Usually she walked with her dog—a Rottweiler—but that day it came down with serious stomach problems and spent the night at the vet's. Convenient, huh?"

"Poisoned?"

"I called the vet this morning and he said he never worked the dog up 'cause it got better by morning, but the symptoms could have been consistent with eating something nasty. On the other hand, he said dogs eat garbage all the time."

"Did this one?"

"Not that he knew. And it's too late now to run tests. Something else Paz and Fellows never thought to ask about."

"Poisoning the dog," I said. "Someone watching her for a while, learning her habits."

"Or someone who already knew them. Wouldn't a husband fit perfectly into this love-sex-revenge orchestration thing? Someone who'd been cuckolded?"

"Had this husband been cuckolded?"

"Don't know. But assume yes. And if Seacrest was smarter than the average betrayed husband, colder, what better way to deflect suspicion than make it look like a street crime?"

"But we're talking a middle-aged history professor with no record of domestic violence. No violence, period."

"There's always a first time," he said.

"Any idea how he dealt with her fame?"

"No. Like I said, he's not helpful."

"It could have been a rough spot in their relationship: He was older, possibly more prominent academically til she wrote the book. And maybe he didn't take well to being discussed on TV. Though on the tapes I saw she talked about him fondly."

"Yeah," he said. " 'Philip's attuned to a woman's needs but he's the rare exception.' A little patronizing, maybe?"

"Another thing," I said. "I never heard any feminist outcry about her death, or the fact that it hadn't been solved. Maybe because she wasn't affiliated with any feminist groups—at least I didn't see any listed in her resume."

"True," he said. "A loner?"

"She did the usual committee things, joined academic societies. But nothing political. Despite the tone of the book. And speaking of the resume, one thing caught my eye: She chaired something called the Interpersonal Conduct Committee. It sounds like it might have something to do with sexual harassment—maybe handling complaints by students against faculty. Which could have been another source of controversy. What if she put someone's career in jeopardy?"

"Interpersonal conduct. I never noticed that."

"It was just a notation at the end."

"Thanks for paying attention. Yeah, that sounds interesting. Want to do me a favor and check it out on campus? The department head hasn't returned my calls since the first time I spoke to him."

"Ed Gabelle?"

"Yeah, what's he like?"

"A politician," I said. "Sure, I'll ask."

"Thanks. Now let me tell you what gets *me* about Professor Devane. The discrepancy between what she wrote and the way she acted on TV. In the book she basically tagged all men as scum, you'd think she was a major-league man-hater. But on the tapes she comes across as a woman who likes guys. Sure she thinks we've got some things to work out, maybe she even pities us a little. But the overall attitude is *friendliness*, Alex. She seemed *comfortable* with men—more than that. I guess to me she came across as the kind of gal you could have a couple of beers with."

"More like champagne cocktails," I said.

"Okay, granted. And not at the Dewdrop Inn. Paneled lounge at the Bel Air Hotel. But the contrast is still dramatic. At least to me."

"You know," I said, "you could say the same thing about the resume. The first half was all by-the-book academic, the second was Media Star. Almost as if she were two separate people."

"And another thing: Maybe I'm not the best judge,

but to me she was sexy on the tube. Seductive, the way she made eye contact with the camera, gave that little smile, crossed her legs, showing a little thigh. The way she said plenty by not saying anything."

"Those could have been shrinks' pauses. We learn to use silence to get others to open up."

"Then she sure learned well."

"Okay, what if she was sexy?"

"I'm wondering if she was the type to get involved in something dangerous. . . . Am I pop-psyching myself into a corner?"

"Maybe what you're really talking about is compartmentalization. Separating aspects of her life. Putting them in little boxes."

"Maybe little secret boxes," he said. "And secrets *can* get dangerous. On the other hand, could be we've got something stupid—a stone nutso who saw her on the tube and God told him to kill her. Or a psychopath out stalking blonds on the Westside and she just happened to be in the wrong place at the wrong time. God forbid. . . . Okay, I appreciate the time, Alex. Gonna be working late right here, if you think of anything else."

"I'll try Ed Gabelle on that conduct committee, call you if it gets interesting."

"It's already interesting," he said. Then he cursed.

3

Ed Gabelle was an aggressively casual physiological psychologist with a thick thatch of gray hair, a tiny mouth, and a whiny, singsong voice that sometimes veered toward an English accent. His specialty was creating lesions in cockroach neurons and observing the results. Lately, I'd heard, he'd been trying to get grant money to study drug abuse.

It was just after lunchtime and I found him leaving the faculty club wearing blue jeans, a denim shirt, and an outspoken yellow paisley tie.

His obligatory greeting faded fast when I told him what I wanted.

"The police, Alex?" he said, pityingly. "Why?"

"I've worked with them before."

"Have you . . . well, I'm afraid I can't help you on this. It wasn't a departmental issue."

"Whose was it?"

"It was . . . let's just say Hope was somewhat of

an individualist. You know what I mean—that book of hers."

"Not well-received in the department?"

"No, no, that's not what I'm getting at. She was brilliant, I'm sure the book made her money, but she wasn't much for . . . affiliation."

"No time for colleagues."

"Exactly."

"What about students?"

"Students?" As if it were a foreign word. "I assume she had some. Well, nice seeing you, Alex."

"The committee," I said. "You're telling me it was solely *her* project?"

He licked his lips.

"What was it all about, Ed?"

"I really can't get into that. It's a closed issue, anyway."

"Not anymore. Murder changes everything."

"Does it?" He began walking.

"At least tell me—"

"All I'll tell you," he said, stretching the whine, "is that I can't tell you anything. Take it up with a higher power."

"Such as?"

"The dean of students."

When I told the dean's secretary what I was after, her voice closed up like a fat-laden artery and she said she'd get back to me. Hanging up without getting my number, I phoned Milo again.

He said, "Ass-covering. I like it. Okay, I'll take on the dean myself. Thanks for reading that resume so carefully."

"That's what you pay me for."

He laughed, then turned serious. "So obviously Hope ruffled someone's feathers with this committee. And speaking of ruffling, I've got a number for the assistant producer of the Mayhew show. Want to follow through for me so I can concentrate on persecuting academics?"

"Sure," I said.

"Suzette Band," he said, reading off a Hollywood exchange. "She probably won't call back without a hassle, so feel free to be extremely annoying."

It took five times to reach Suzette Band, but when she finally came on her voice was pleasant and amused.

"The police? One Adam Twelve, One Adam Twelve?"

Committing felony impersonation of a police officer seemed easier than explaining my precise role, so I said, "Do you remember a guest you had on last year, Professor Hope Devane?"

"Oh . . . yes, of course, that was terrible. Has her murderer been caught?"

"No."

"Well, please tell us when he is. We'd love to do a follow-up. I'm serious."

Bet you are.

"I'll do my best, Ms. Band. In the meantime, maybe you can help us. There was another guest on with Professor Devane, a man named Karl Neese—"

"What about him?"

"We'd like to speak to him."

"Why—oh, no, you *can't* be serious." She laughed. "That's a scream. No, I can see why you'd—but don't waste your time with Karl."

"Why not?"

Long pause.

"Is this on tape or something?"

"No."

Silence.

"Ms. Band?"

"You're sure this isn't being taped?"

"Positive. What's the problem?"

"Well . . . the person you really want to speak to is Eileen Pietsch, the producer. But she's traveling. I'll have her office call you when—"

"Why waste time if Karl's someone we shouldn't worry about?"

"He really isn't. It's just that we . . . our show . . . Karl's a . . ."

"Professional guest?"

"I didn't say that."

"Then why shouldn't we worry about him?"

"Listen—I shouldn't be talking to you at all but I don't want you making a big deal about this and getting the show bad exposure. Lord knows we've had plenty of that with all the bluenoses in Washington hunting for scapegoats. We feel we provide a bona fide public service."

"And Karl was part of that?"

I heard a sigh on the other end.

"Okay," I said. "So he was paid to come on and be the professor's foil."

"I wouldn't put it that way."

"But he's an actor, right? If I go through the SAG book or the agent rosters I can probably find him."

"Look," she said, louder. Then she sighed again. "Yes, he's an actor. But for all I know he really does hold those views."

"Then why shouldn't I worry about him? Things got pretty nasty between him and Professor Devane."

"But that was . . . boy, you don't let up . . . okay, to be perfectly honest, Karl *is* a pro. But he's a really nice guy. We've used him before and so have other shows. We bring guys like him on to spice things up. Especially with professors because those types can be dry. All the shows do it. Some of the others even salt the audience. We *never* do that."

"So you're saying he *wasn't* really hostile toward Professor Devane."

"Of course not, he's mellow. In fact I think we had him on our Nice Guy show a year ago—you know, finishing last and all that. He's quite good. Adaptable. One of those faces you forget."

"So no one remembers they've seen him before?"

"We stick a beard on them, or a wig. People aren't that observant, anyway."

"I'd still like to speak to him. Do you have a number handy?"

Another pause. "Tell you what, I'll make you a deal."

"Do I get to choose between the money and what's behind Curtain Number Three?"

"Very funny," she said, but the friendliness was back in her voice. "Here's the deal: Call me as soon as you get a solve on the murder so we can have first dibs on a follow-up show, and I'll give you Karl. Okay?"

I pretended to deliberate. "Okay."

"Excellent—hey, maybe you can come on, too. Ace detective and all that. Do you photograph well?"

"Camera lights turn my eyes red but my fangs stay white."

"Ha ha, very funny. You'd probably do real well.

We've had cops on before but most of them are pretty wooden."

"Like professors."

"Like professors. Most *people* are wooden without help. Or some big story to tell."

"I watched Professor Devane's tape," I said. "She seemed pretty good."

"You know, she was. Class act. Really knew how to work the audience. It's really terrible about what happened to her. She could have become a regular."

Karl Neese's number was out in the Valley but his machine said to reach him at work if it was about a part. Bo Bancroft's Men's Fashions on Robertson Boulevard.

I looked up the address. Between Beverly and Third, right off Designer Row. At this hour, a twenty-minute drive.

The store was closet-sized, full of mirrors, weathered Brazilian antiques painted with roses and religious icons, and racks of three-thousand-dollar suits. Disco-remixed easy listening on the sound system, two people working, both in black: a blond girl with bored eyes behind the register and Neese folding cashmere sweaters.

Since the show, the actor had let his hair grow to his shoulders and raised a prickly beard. In person, he looked younger. Pale and hungry-looking. Very long, very white fingers.

I introduced myself and told him why I was there.

He finished folding and turned around slowly. "You're kidding."

"Wish I was, Mr. Neese."

"You know, right after it happened I wondered if someone would call me."

"Why's that?"

"Because the show got nasty."

"Nastier than it was supposed to get?"

"No, they paid me for nasty. 'Go out and be an asshole.' " He laughed. "How's that for artistic direction?"

"What else did they tell you?"

"They gave me her book, told me to read it so I'd know what she was about. Then come on like a schmuck, get on her case to the max. Not a bad gig, actually. Six months ago I was on *Xavier!* as an incestuous father with no remorse. Cheap beard and sunglasses and a shirt I wouldn't be caught dead in, but even with that I kept worrying some idiot would see me on the street and take a punch."

"You do a lot of this?"

"Not as much as I'd like to. It pays five, six hundred a throw but there're only so many openings a year. Anyway, I'm not saying it's weird for you to come by, see if I'm the big bad wolf, but I'm not. The night she was killed I was doing dinner theater out in Costa Mesa. *Man of La Mancha.* Four hundred senior citizens saw me." He smiled. "At least fuzzily. Hell, some of them might even have been sober. Here's the producer's number."

He read off a 714 exchange, then said, "Too bad."

"About what?"

"Her being killed. I didn't like her but she was sharp, really handled my bullshit beautifully. You'd be amazed how many can't cope, even when they know what's going down."

"So she knew?"

"Of course. We never had a formal rehearsal but they did get us together before the show. In the green-room. I told her I'd be coming on like Frankenstein with a militia card, she said fine."

"So why didn't you like her?"

"Because she tried to psych me out. Right before we went on. Acted friendly to me when the producer was there, all through makeup. But the minute we were alone she sidled in close to me, talking in my ear—almost seductively. Telling me she'd met plenty of actors and every one of them was screwed up psychologically. 'Uncomfortable with their identities' is the way she put it. 'Playing roles to feel in control.' " He chuckled. "Which is true, but who the hell wants to hear it?"

"Think she was trying to intimidate you?"

"She was definitely trying to intimidate me. And what was the point? It was all phony bullshit. Like TV wrestling. I was the bad guy, she was the good guy. We both knew she'd be tossing my ass on the mat. So why gild the lily?"

Playing roles to feel in control.

Little boxes.

Maybe Hope had *seen* herself as an actress.

Returning home, I called the producer of the Costa Mesa production. His assistant checked her logs and verified that Karl Neese had, indeed, been onstage the night of the murder.

"Yeah, that was one of our better ones," she said. "Good ticket sales."

"Still on?"

"Hardly. Nothing lasts long in California."

*   *   *

Milo checked in at ten to five. "Any protein in the house?"

"I'm sure I can find something."

"Start looking. The thrill of the hunt is ripe in my nostrils and I am hungry."

He sounded exhilarated.

"The visit to the dean was productive?" I said.

"Feed me and I'll tell you. I'll be over in half an hour."

No shortage of protein. Robin and I had just shopped and the new refrigerator was double the capacity of the old one.

I made him a roast beef sandwich. The white kitchen seemed vast. Too big. Too white. I was still getting used to the new house.

The old one had been eighteen hundred square feet of silvered redwood, weathered shingles, tinted glass, and half-mad angles, built from antique materials and recycled wood by a Hungarian artist who'd gone broke in L.A. and returned to Budapest to sell Russian cars.

I'd bought it years ago, seduced by the site: Deep in the foothills north of Beverly Glen and separated from neighbors by a wide patch of thickly wooded, high-table public land, it afforded a privacy that had me encountering more coyotes than people.

The seclusion had proved perfect for the psychopath who burned the house down one dry summer night. *Tinder on a foundation*, the fire marshal had called it.

Robin and I decided to rebuild. After a couple of

false starts with miscreant contractors, she began supervising the construction herself. We ended up with twenty-six hundred square feet of white stucco and gray ceramic roof, whitewashed wood floors and stairs, brass railings, skylights, and as many windows as the energy-conservation regulations would allow. At the rear of the property was the workshop where Robin went happily each morning, accompanied by Spike, our French bulldog. Several old trees had been immolated but we craned in boxed eucalyptus and Canary Island pines and coast redwoods, dug a new Japanese garden and a pond full of young koi.

Robin loved it. The few people we'd had over said it had come out great. Milo's appraisal was *"Tray chick,* but I like it anyway."* I nodded and smiled and remembered the slightly moldy smell of old wood in the morning, arthritic casement windows, the creak of foot-polished pine floorboards.

Adding a pickle to Milo's sandwich, I put the plate back in the giant fridge, brewed some coffee, and reviewed the notes on my most recent custody consultation to Family Court: both parents engineers, two adopted sons, ages three and five. The mother had fled to a dude ranch in Idaho, the father was furious and ill-equipped for child care.

The boys were painfully polite but their drawings said they had a good fix on the situation. The judge who'd referred the case was a capable man but the dolt to whom it had been transferred rarely read reports. Lawyers on both sides were miffed that I didn't agree with their respective party lines. Lately, Robin and I had started talking about having children of our own.

I was working on a final draft of the report when the bell rang.

I went to the front, looked through the peephole, saw Milo's big face, and opened the door. His unmarked was parked crookedly behind Robin's pickup. From the rear came the buzz of a power saw, then Spike's *help-I'm-choking* bark.

"Yo, pooch." He looked at his Timex. "How's that for time? Five minutes from campus."

"You really should set a better example."

Grinning, he wiped his feet on the mat and stomped in. The new Persian rug was soft, with a silky sheen, and I supposed I liked it just fine. None of my art had come through the fire and the walls were bare as fresh notepaper.

Old house or new, the kitchen remained Milo's magnet. As he continued toward it, light shot in from above and bleached him. Giant snowman.

By the time I got there, he had the sandwich out with a carton of milk and was sitting at the table.

He ate it in three bites.

"Want another?"

"No thanks—yeah, why not." Raising the carton to his lips, he drained it, then patted his gut. This month he was cutting back on alcohol and his weight had dropped a bit, maybe to 240. Most of it saddled his middle and swelled his face. The long legs that stretched him to six-three weren't particularly thin, but the contrast made them seem that way.

He wore a pale green blazer over a white shirt and black tie, brown pants and tan suede desert boots. He'd shaved closely except for a small gray patch behind his left ear, and the lumps on his face stood out like unfinished clay modeling. Static made his hair dance.

As I prepared a second sandwich he began pulling papers out of his briefcase.

"Spoils of the hunt: potential enemies list." He wiped his lips with the back of his hand. "Nixon had nothing over Professor Devane."

I brought him the food.

"Delicious," he said, chomping. "Where do you get the meat?"

"At the supermarket."

"You do the shopping, now? Hey, you can run for president. Or do you and the little lady take turns?"

"The little lady," I said. "Care to call her that to her face?"

He laughed. "Actually, this case has gotten me thinking. Used to consider myself excluded from the whole gender-bender thing but the truth is, all of us with Y chromosomes were brought up as little savages, weren't we? Anyway, the dean turned out to be fun. Nice and squirrelly when I finally got in to see him. Which wasn't easy til I started flashing the badge and talking media exposure of the conduct committee. Then all of a sudden I'm ushered into the sanctum sanctorum and he's offering me coffee, shaking my hand. Telling me there's no reason to bring up the committee, it was 'inconsequential.' Not to mention 'provisional' and 'of short duration.' The whole thing was disbanded because of 'constitutional and free-speech concerns.' "

He pulled a folder out of his briefcase. "Luckily, he's assuming I know more than I did. So I bluff, say I've heard differently around campus. He says no way, it's a dead issue. I say Professor Devane's dead, too. Why don't you just start from the beginning, sir. Which he does."

He shook the carton. "Any more milk?"

I got him some and he gulped and wiped his lip.

"You were right about it being a sexual-harassment

thing. But not between students and faculty. Between students and students. Professor Devane's idea. They heard three cases, all girls who'd taken her class on sex-roles and complained to her. Devane didn't go through official channels, just winged it. Notifying the complainants and the accused, setting up a little tribunal."

"The students had no idea it was unofficial?"

"No, says the dean. Really ethical, huh?"

"Oh boy," I said. "Constitutional and free-speech concerns—more like financial concerns, as in lawsuit."

"He wouldn't admit that, but that's the picture I got. Then he tells me the committee couldn't have had anything to do with the murder but when I asked him why not, he didn't have an answer. Then he says it would be a grave error to go public, one that could cause problems for the police department, because all the participants—accusers and defendants—had demanded strict confidentiality and they might sue us. When I didn't answer, he threatened to call the police chief. I sat there and smiled. He picked up the phone, put it down, started begging. I said I understand your position and I don't want to make problems, so give me all your written records without a hassle and I'll exercise maximum discretion."

He waved the folder. "Transcripts of the three sessions. Hope taped them."

"Why?"

"Who knows? Maybe she was planning another book. Incidentally, the dean said she put up a fuss about having the committee kiboshed. Academic freedom and all that. Then *Wolves and Sheep* came out and she lost interest."

"Maybe she intended to use it as material for the publicity tour."

"The dean suspected that, too. He said he warned her that she'd be putting herself in a dangerous position legally. That according to the University lawyers, since she hadn't gotten official approval, she'd been functioning as an independent psychologist when she chaired the committee, not as a faculty member. So if she divulged information she'd be violating patient confidentiality and putting her license in jeopardy. She took issue with that and threatened to hire her own lawyer, but apparently changed her mind because that was the end of it."

"It's amazing none of this ever came out after the murder."

"Everyone had a vested interest in keeping it quiet. Administration, students—especially the students."

He gave me the file. "Read it when you have a chance, let me know what you think. I can't close my eyes to this even though I still like Hubby. Even better, now, because I just got a look at her tax returns."

"The book made her rich?"

He nodded. "But even before then she had some interesting extracurricular activities. Ever hear of Robert Barone?"

I shook my head.

"Big-shot lawyer, does criminal defense, porn and censorship, some racketeering cases, some entertainment work—same thing, right? Last year, he paid her forty grand in consulting fees, year before that, twenty-eight."

"Diminished-capacity reports?"

"Probably something like that. Barone has offices here in Century City and up in San Francisco. He isn't returning my calls."

Drinking more milk, he said, "Her other consulting client is a Beverly Hills doctor named Milan Cruvic. He's listed in the directory as an OB-GYN and fertility expert. Any idea why a fertility expert would pay a psychologist thirty-six grand a year? Two years in a row?"

"Maybe she screened candidates for fertility treatment."

"Is that Standard Op?"

"The procedures can be grueling. A thoughtful doctor might want to see which patients could handle them. Or provide counseling for those who couldn't."

"So why not just refer to her? Why pay her directly out of his pocket?"

"Good question."

"When I called Cruvic's office his nurse said he was doing public service at some women's clinic. Which could mean abortions—another potential point of hostility if Hope got involved in that, too. Abortion violence hasn't come big-time to L.A. but we get everything, eventually. And that creep on TV—Neese— threw the issue around, pegged her as Ms. Slice-the- Fetus Radical Feminist. Who knows, maybe some nut got mad."

"Not Neese, himself," I said. I told him about confirming the alibi.

"One down," he said. "He thought she was psyching him out?"

"Neese's term. Trying to control him."

"So maybe she tried to psych out the wrong person . . . you think the abortion angle's worth pursuing?"

"Not really," I said. "Hope was no standard-bearer for the cause and a political killer would have gone public in order to make some kind of statement."

"Yeah . . . but I do want to know what she did for Cruvic and Barone. We're talking over a hundred grand in two years. Though after the book, she didn't need it."

He pulled photocopied tax returns out of his brief-case.

"Her last filing. Gross income of six hundred eighty thousand dollars, the bulk of it from advances and royalties and public speaking. The after-tax came out to almost half a mil and it's sitting in a money-market account at Merrill Lynch jointly registered to her and Seacrest. No real debts, she had the Mustang before, and Seacrest inherited the house from his parents. Another half a mil. Not a bad investment to cash in on, especially if the marriage is sour."

"How long were they married?"

"Ten years."

"How'd they meet?"

"Seacrest says at the University rec center, swim-ming."

"Was he married before?"

"Nope, he told Paz and Fellows he'd been one of those 'stodgy confirmed bachelors,' unquote. In addi-tion to the five hundred grand, there's more coming to him. Her literary agent wouldn't give me numbers but she did say substantial royalties were likely to come in over the next year or so. Book sales were brisk before the murder, the publisher was about to offer her a deal on a sequel. Hope and Seacrest did estate planning a few years ago, established a marital trust to avoid estate taxes, so Seacrest gets to keep all of it. *His* income last year was sixty-four gees, all from his University salary. His Volvo's eight years old and he's managed to put away some cash in his faculty pension plan. Plus there's the house. He's written some books, too, but they don't pay royalties. Guess romantic elements of the medieval age can't compete with penis-as-lethal-weapon."

"Ten-to-one income ratio," I said.

"Another kind of jealousy angle. What if she was going to leave him just as she struck it big? For another guy—your love-sex-betrayal thing, plus all that money sitting there. A temptation, right? And who'd be in a better position to know her habits? To poison the dog? Hope did have one thing right: More women are killed by so-called loved ones than by all the scumbags combined."

"Seacrest went all these years without big bucks," I said. "Has he turned into a high liver recently?"

"No, on the contrary, *nothing's* changed about his life: He goes to work each day and comes home. Weekends he stays home. Says he reads and watches TV. Doesn't even rent videos. But if she was cheating on him, no telling what that could do to an old-fashioned confirmed bachelor. Someone who studies romance—don't forget that stab in the heart. The guy's fifty-five, Alex. Maybe he had a midlife crisis. And like I said, I keep thinking he's hiding something."

"Why?"

"Nothing I can put my finger on, that's the problem. He answers questions but volunteers no info. He never called Fellows and Paz once, to find out how their investigation was going. When I got assigned I phoned him right away and got the feeling I was taking up his precious time. Like he was off somewhere else."

"Maybe he's still in shock."

"No, this was more like he had better things to do. If someone you loved got sliced up, how would you react? Tell you what, how about I give you a firsthand look? I'm planning to drop in on him tonight, late. Not that I'm out to exploit a pal—if you've got some serious time to invest on the case, I can actually"—he panted—"*pay* you."

He drew a folded form out of his jacket pocket. "Surprise from Uncle Milo."

Police ID badge and a consultant contract in triplicate, my name typed on the dotted line. The department was willing to engage me for no more than fifty hours at less than a quarter of my private hourly fee. Small print limited LAPD's liability: If I tripped on a banana peel or got shot, they'd be sympathetic but stingy.

"It ain't filthy lucre," he said, "but by department standards it's *Supermarket Sweep*."

"How'd you pull this off?"

"Lied and told the loo I'd heard radical-feminist-butch-lesbian grumblings about the slow progress of the case. If we didn't make it look like we were doing all we could, we might end up being called before the Police Commission. Told him radical-fem-butch-lesbo types liked shrinks, would take your involvement as proof of expanded sensitivity."

"Very creative."

"I asked him for a new computer, too, but you were cheaper. You on?"

"Fifty hours," I said. "Does that include feeding you?"

"What do you think?"

Returning to the fridge, he came back with a slab of brownie.

"Despite your suspicions of Seacrest," I said, "I still think you have to seriously consider a delusional stranger."

"Why?"

"There's a cold craziness to that wound pattern. Someone with a deep hatred for women. And we know from the way she set up the committee that Hope could be heavy-handed, so who knows who she offended? In real life or on the screen. Have you checked for murders with similar wound patterns?"

"I've gone through three years of Westside cuttings and nothing matches. Tomorrow I try Wilshire Division and whoever else I can finagle into remembering. I also sent out teletypes to other jurisdictions, but so did Paz and Fellows and that brought in nothing. So are you up for meeting Seacrest, tonight? That is, if you and the little woman don't have plans—speaking of which, let me pop back and say hi to her and the pooch. I am neither sexist nor speciesist."

4

As we walked through the garden to the shop, Milo stopped to look at the fish in the pond, then trudged on. His back was bowed and his arms dangled heavily. I wondered when he'd last slept well.

Robin was at her bench shaping the rosewood sides of a flattop guitar. The new maple floors were spotless except for a pile of shavings swept into one corner. Spike had been sleeping at her feet and he looked up and cocked his broad, flat head.

Milo gave him a mock-hostile look. Spike came over for a rub.

Robin held up a finger and continued clamping the sides to a mold. A dozen other instruments in various stages of repair were arranged around the room, but the project she was working on had nothing to do with business. The fire had destroyed my old Martin dreadnought along with a beautiful parlor guitar she'd built for me years ago. I bought another Martin from Mandolin Brothers in Staten Island. Replicating Robin's was her New Year's resolution.

One last clamp and she was done. Wiping her hands, she stood on her tiptoes and kissed Milo's cheek, then mine. Under her apron she wore a black T-shirt and jeans and her hair was wrapped in a red bandanna. Safety goggles and a mask dangled from her neck, both coated with dust.

Spike started baying like a hound and rolled over. I kneeled and scratched his tummy and he snorted in entitlement. French bulldogs are miniature versions of the English variety but with upright bat ears, a more athletic disposition, and delusions of big-dog grandeur. The best way to describe Spike physically is a Boston terrier on steroids, but his personality's more chimp than dog. He waddled into our lives one day and stayed, deciding quickly that Robin was worth knowing and I was expendable. When he's unhappy about something he pretends to choke. Milo pretends to despise him and always brings treats.

Now he fished a sandwich bag out of his sportcoat. Dried liver.

"Canapé time, pancake-face."

Spike sat motionless, Milo tossed a nugget, and the dog caught it midair, chewed, and swallowed. The two of them glared at each other. Milo rubbed his face. Spike barked. Milo muttered and gave him more liver.

"Go away and digest."

Spike head-butted Milo's foot. Rolling his eyes and grumbling, Milo bent and petted him.

More barking and butting and feeding. Finally, Milo showed him the empty bag. Spike jumped for it, shook his head, and scattered drool.

"Enough," said Robin. "You're increasing the humidity."

Spike gazed up at her with big brown eyes. The Orson Welles look—genius disturbed.

"Stay," she commanded quietly. The dog obeyed and she added, "Darling." Slipping her arm around my waist, she said, "So what's new, Milo?"

More than just good manners. We'd talked more about the murder last night.

"Plodding along," he said. "Thought I'd borrow Alex tonight. If you don't need him."

"I always need him. Just make sure you return him in one piece."

"One piece, fueled, washed, and waxed."

After he was gone, I turned to the transcripts of the conduct committee.

The documents were red-stamped CONFIDENTIAL on each page and preceded by the University's lawyers' warning that publicizing the contents could bring civil prosecution. Next came the lawyers' assessment of blame: sole credit, Professor Hope Devane.

But two other people had sat as judges along with her: an associate professor of chemistry named Julia Steinberger, and a psychology graduate student named Casey Locking.

I turned the page. The format surprised me. Face-to-face confrontations between accuser and accused. Hope's academic version of a talk show?

Case 1:
Deborah Brittain, a nineteen-year-old sophomore French major, accused Patrick Allan Huang, an eighteen-year-old sophomore engineering major, of

following her around in the college library and making "lascivious and suggestive" expressions. Huang denied any sexual interest in Brittain and said she'd "come on" to him by requesting help operating the library's search computers and repeatedly telling him how brilliant he was.

Brittain said she had indeed asked for help from Huang because "he looked like the kind of guy who'd know about computers," and had complimented his proficiency because that was "good manners. Why can't a woman be nice without getting harassed?"

PROF. DEVANE: Any answer to that, Mr. Huang?

MR. HUANG: My answer is she's a racist, figuring an Asian guy would be a techno-geek and then taking advantage of me. *She* bugged *me*, not the opposite. Coming on all friendly, so, yeah, I asked her out. Then she shuts me down and when I don't want to be her data slave anymore she gets pissed and files on me. What a hassle and a half. I didn't come to college for this.

PROF. DEVANE: What did you go to college for?

MR. HUANG: To study engineering.

PROF. DEVANE: There's more to learning than what goes on in the classroom.

MR. HUANG: All I want to do is study and mind my own business, okay? What this is about is she's a racist.

MS. BRITTAIN: He is *lying*! He *offered* to help. All I needed was a start, I didn't know the program, I was fine after that. But every time he saw me, he'd slither over. Then he asked me out and wouldn't take no for an answer—several times. I'm empowered to say no, right? Why should I have to put up with that? It got to a point where I didn't even want to go to the library. But I had a paper to write on Molière—what's he doing there, anyway? Engineering books are in the Engineering Library. He obviously hangs around to hit on women."

More he-said, she-said, no witnesses. Devane asking all the questions, Devane summing up—pointing out that Deborah Brittain had come to her "suffering from extreme stress."

She affirmed Brittain's right to study anywhere she pleased, free of harassment, advised her gently to be aware of racial stereotypes that might "elicit miscommunication. Though I'm not saying that's what happened here, Ms. Brittain."

Then she lectured Patrick Huang about respecting women's rights. Huang said he knew all that. Devane suggested he think about it, anyway, and warned him that he'd face suspension and possible expulsion if anyone else complained about him. No disciplinary actions taken.

Case 2:

A freshman English major named Cynthia Vespucci had attended a pre-Christmas-break party at the Chi Pi Omega fraternity house where she encountered a freshman business major named Kenneth Storm Jr. Recognizing him from high school, she danced with him. "Because even though most of the other guys were getting drunk and freaking out, he was a total gentleman that night."

Vespucci and Storm began dating. Nothing sexual occurred until their fourth date, when Vespucci claimed Storm drove her to a remote spot in Bel Air, three miles above campus, and demanded intercourse. When she refused, Storm grabbed her arm.

She smelled liquor on his breath, managed to pull away, and told him to let her drive. He then kicked her out of his car and threw her purse out, breaking the strap and scattering the contents, some of which, including her spare change, rolled into a storm drain. Driving off, he left her stranded. She tried gaining entrance to a residence, but all the houses were fenced and gated and no one answered her rings. She was forced to walk home to her sorority, ruining a pair of shoes and "causing me incredible fear."

When asked to respond, Kenneth Storm refused, stating, "This is bullshit."

Further prodding from Professor Devane produced "What the hell do you expect me to say?"

At that point, the graduate student, Casey Locking, entered the dialogue: "Look, guy, I'm a man but I don't have any sympathy for men who rough up women. If what she says is true, you've got a lesson to learn and you're lucky to be learning it young. If you disagree, speak up. But if you choose not to defend yourself, don't complain later."

Storm responded with "a train of expletives."

Then, surprisingly, Cynthia Vespucci seemed to have a change of heart: "Okay, okay, let's just have nothing to do with each other. Let's just end this." [*Crying*]

Prof. Devane: Here's a tissue, Ms. Vespucci.

Ms. Vespucci: I'm okay. Let's just forget it.

Prof. Devane: Are you sure, Ms. Vespucci?

Ms. Vespucci: I don't know.

Prof. Devane: When you came to me you were very upset.

Ms. Vespucci: I know. [*Starting to cry*] But I . . . now I want to stop it. Okay? Please?

PROF. DEVANE: Of course. We're out for your best interests. You should remember, though, that a process
has been set into motion.

MR. STORM: I don't believe this! She said end it!
What're you going to do, kick me out? Fine, do it,
go ahead and fucking do it, I don't give a shit
about you or this place or—

MR. LOCKING: Take it easy, man—

MR. STORM: No, *you* take it easy, asshole! This is *bullshit*, I'm *out* of here!

MR. LOCKING: I'm *warning* you, ma—

MR. STORM: About *what*, asshole? You think I give a
shit about you and your fucking *college*? *Fuck* this
place! Fuck *you*! You, too, Cindy—how could you
do this to me? First thing I do when I'm out of here
is call your mother and—

MS. VESPUCCI: Kenny! Please—no—I'm sorry—Kenny,
come on, please!

PROF. STEINBERGER: What about her mother, Mr. Storm?

MR. STORM: Let *her* tell you.

PROF. STEINBERGER: Cindy?

MR. STORM: What a laugh! This is ancient fucking history!

MR. LOCKING: Professors, it seems to me that before we
go further, this guy's going to have to—

PROF. STEINBERGER: Is there something else going on between you two that you haven't told us about,
Cindy?

MS. VESPUCCI: [*Sobbing*] It's my fault.

MR. STORM: Damn fucking strai—

MR. LOCKING: Watch your mouth!

MR. STORM: Fu—

PROF. STEINBERGER: Please, sir, we'll hear you out. But
please let her talk. Okay? Thank you. Cindy?

MS. VESPUCCI: It's my fault.

PROF. DEVANE: What is, Cindy?

MS. VESPUCCI: I—was—I was mad at him . . . maybe *partly* because of my mom.

PROF. DEVANE: He did something to your mom?

MR. STORM: Yeah, right, I'm a rapist. Tell them, Cindy, go on. Come on—what's the matter, cat got your tongue? Bringing me here with that letter, I thought I was being *suspended.* What total and complete bull—

MS. VESPUCCI: *Stop! Please!*

MR. STORM: Then tell them. Or I will.

PROF. DEVANE: Tell us what?

MS. VESPUCCI: It's stupid.

MR. STORM: That's for sure! Her mom and my dad had a—they were dating. Til my dad shut her mom down because she was too left-wing. Her mom can't hold on to a man, Cindy probably blamed my dad. So when she saw me at the party, she decided to hit on me and get even.

MS. VESPUCCI: No! That's not true! You came up to me first! I danced with you because you were acting like a gentleman—

MR. STORM: What a crock! You were wearing that nothing little black—

PROF. DEVANE: Hold on. When you say left-wing, do you mean politically?

MR. STORM: What else? Radical feminism. Her mom's a flaming extremist. Hates men, taught Cindy to. She was just setting me up for—

MS. VESPUCCI: I *wasn't*, Kenny! You were a gentleman. Not like—

MR. STORM: Not like my dad? Don't you fucking put *him* down!

MS. VESPUCCI: I didn't mean that. I meant the other guys at the—

MR. STORM: Right.

MS. VESPUCCI: Kenny—

MR. STORM: Fuck this!

PROF. STEINBERGER: Kenny, does your dad approve of your swearing?

MR. STORM: Okay. I'm sorry. I'm just super-steamed. Because this is totally unfair. My dad and her mom had problems so she set me up. It's—

MS. VESPUCCI: I *didn't*! I *swear*!

MR. STORM: Right. You just picked me 'cause of my cute face—

PROF. DEVANE: Let's regain our focus. Whatever the motivation for your initial meeting, Mr. Storm, you did go out with Ms. Vespucci. And she claims you attempted to force her to have sex with you.

MR. STORM: Bul—no way. No . . . blanking *way*! Sure I asked her. Why not? We'd already been out a bunch of times. But I didn't touch her without permission—right, Cindy? So I asked her if she wanted to do it. Is that a crime, now?

PROF. DEVANE: Shoving her out of the car when she turned you down is, sir.

MR. STORM: Yeah, except I didn't shove her. She freaked and got out herself, fell down. Actually, I tried to stop her—that's the only time I grabbed her arm.

PROF. DEVANE: That's not what she says—correct, Ms. Vespucci?

MS. VESPUCCI: Just forget it.

PROF. DEVANE: Cindy, I really don't—

MS. VESPUCCI: Please.

PROF. DEVANE: Let's talk about that purse, Cindy. Can we agree that it got thrown?

MR. STORM: Hell, no! After she got out, I gave it to her because it was hers and—

PROF. DEVANE: So you threw it at her.

MR. STORM: Not at her, *to* her. What did *I* need a purse for? Jesus. She refused to catch it so it fell into the street.

MS. VESPUCCI: But then I told you I *did* want to get back in and you just drove away!

MR. STORM: I didn't hear you.

MS. VESPUCCI: You weren't *that* far away!

MR. STORM: Read my *lips*, Cindy: *I did not hear you*. I'd already asked you ten times and you refused so I split. This is *rank*, Cindy. You set me up and you know it and now your mom's going to know it.

PROF. DEVANE: There's no call for threats—

MR. STORM: What do you think *this* is? *Fuck* this place—

MS. VESPUCCI: I'm sorry, I'm sorry—I'm sorry, Professor Devane, but I want to stop this. *Now! Please!*

PROF. STEINBERGER: Perhaps—

PROF. DEVANE: Cindy, right now you're under a lot of stress and pressure. This isn't the right time to make important decisions.

MS. VESPUCCI: I don't care, I want to *stop* this! I'm leaving. [*Exits*]

MR. STORM: [*Laughs*] What now?

PROF. DEVANE: Is there something more you want to say for yourself, sir?

MR. STORM: Not for myself. For you—*to* you: Fuck *you*, lady! And you, *too*, clown—don't like it, man? Come on outside and get it on.

MR. LOCKING: You have no idea who you're dealing—

MR. STORM: Then come on out, brain-boy. Come on— hah, bullshit walks—fuck you, fuck this college and this bullshit left-wing garbage. I'm phoning my dad, he's in real estate, knows lots of lawyers. He's going to have your asses for breakfast. [*Exits*]

A note by the University lawyers indicated that Kenneth Storm Sr., an alumnus and member of the Chancellor's Associates, had indeed contacted an attorney, Pierre Bateman, who, four weeks later, drafted a letter of complaint to the University demanding immediate dissolution of the conduct committee, a written apology, and one hundred thousand dollars for Kenneth Storm Jr. The young man had dropped out of the University and applied for transfer to the College of the Palms, in Redlands. The University lawyers noted that his first-quarter grade point average had been 1.7 and that he'd been on academic probation. His second-quarter marks were no better and he was on the verge of flunking out. Nevertheless, it was deemed advisable to settle and a deal was worked out: The Storm family agreed to drop the matter in return for payment of Kenneth Jr.'s tuition for three and a half years at the College of the Palms.

Additionally, it was recommended that the committee be dissolved.

Bad feelings in both cases, but the rage level of the second nearly scorched the paper.

Kenneth Storm Jr. had a bad temper, even taking into account his being hauled up during an especially hard time in his college career.

Had the deal failed to appease him?

Paz and Fellows had never known about the committee. I assumed Milo had at least skimmed the transcripts, but he still preferred Philip Seacrest as prime suspect.

Because of the money and the way Seacrest twanged his antennae.

But Storm had obviously *hated* Hope.

A nineteen-year-old carrying a grudge that far?

Bicycle tracks on the sidewalk.

Students rode bikes to campus.

I wrote down *K. Storm Jr.* and turned to the third transcript, dated one week after the Vespucci-Storm debacle and three weeks before Kenneth Storm's lawyer wrote the letter that killed the committee.

Only Devane and Casey Locking sat in judgment, now. Had Professor Steinberger lost her taste for inquisition?

As I read, it became clear that this was the most serious of the three complaints.

A sophomore psychology major named Tessa Ann Bowlby accused a graduate student in theater arts named Reed Muscadine of date rape. The two of them agreed on several initial points: They'd met in the student union during lunch and had gone out on a single date that night, viewing the movie *Speed* at the Village Theater, followed by dinner at Pinocchio, an Italian restaurant in Westwood Village. Then, they'd returned to Muscadine's apartment in the Mid-Wilshire District to drink wine and listen to music. Heavy petting and partial disrobing commenced. Here their stories diverged: Bowlby claimed she wanted things to go no further but Muscadine got on top of her and entered her by force. Muscadine said intercourse had been consensual.

Ms. Bowlby: [*Crying, shaking*] I . . .

Prof. Devane: What, dear?

Ms. Bowlby: [*Hugs self, shakes head*]

Prof. Devane: Do you have any further comment, Mr. Muscadine?

Mr. Muscadine: Just that this is rather Kafkaesque.

Prof. Devane: In what way, sir?

Mr. Muscadine: In the sense of being cast under suspicion with no justification and no warning. Tessa, if what happened somehow hurt you, I'm truly sorry. But you're dealing with your feelings the wrong way. You may have changed your mind, now, but what happened then was clearly what we both wanted—you never indicated otherwise.

Ms. Bowlby: I asked you to *stop*!

Mr. Muscadine: No, you really didn't, Tessa.

Ms. Bowlby: I *asked* you! I *asked* you!

Mr. Muscadine: We've already been back and forth on this, Tessa. You feel you objected, I know I heard nothing that was even close to objection. If I had, obviously, I would have stopped.

Prof. Devane: Why is it obvious?

Mr. Muscadine: Because I don't force women to be with me. Apart from being repugnant, it's unnecessary.

Prof. Devane: Why's that?

Mr. Muscadine: Because I'm able to get women without forcing them.

Prof. Devane: *Get* women?

Mr. Muscadine: Pardon the clumsy usage, I'm a little shaken up by all this. Women and I relate well. I'm able to obtain companionship without the use of coercion. That's why this whole thing is—

Mr. Locking: You're a theater arts major, right?

Mr. Muscadine: Yes.

Mr. Locking: What speciality?

Mr. Muscadine: Acting.

Mr. Locking: So you're pretty good at disguising your feelings.

Mr. Muscadine: What's that supposed to mean?

Mr. Locking: What does it mean to you?

Mr. Muscadine: You know, I came in here determined to be calm and rational, but I'm finding it a bit difficult with things getting this personal.

PROF. DEVANE: This is a personal issue.

MR. MUSCADINE: I know, but I already told you—

MR. LOCKING: Do you have a temper-control problem?

MR. MUSCADINE: No. Never. Why?

MR. LOCKING: You sound angry.

MR. MUSCADINE: [*Laughs*] No, I'm fine—maybe a little baffled.

MR. LOCKING: By what?

MR. MUSCADINE: This process. *Being* here. Am I a little angry? Sure. Wouldn't you be? And that's really all I have to say.

PROF. DEVANE: The intercourse. Did it proceed to climax?

MR. MUSCADINE: It did for me. And I thought you enjoyed it, too, Tessa.

MS. BOWLBY: [*Crying*]

MR. MUSCADINE: Obviously, I was wrong.

PROF. DEVANE: Did you wear a condom, sir?

MR. MUSCADINE: No. It was kind of—the whole thing was spontaneous. Impetuous. We really hit it off—or at least I thought we had. Nothing was planned, it just happened.

PROF. DEVANE: Have you ever been tested for HIV?

MR. MUSCADINE: No. But I'm sure I'm—

PROF. DEVANE: Would you be willing to be tested?

MR. MUSCADINE: Why?

PROF. DEVANE: For Tessa's peace of mind. And yours.

MR. MUSCADINE: Oh, c'mon—

PROF. DEVANE: You relate well to women. You've *gotten* many, many women.

MR. MUSCADINE: That's not the point.

PROF. DEVANE: What is, sir?

MR. MUSCADINE: It's intrusive.

PROF. DEVANE: So is rape.

MR. MUSCADINE: I never raped anyone.

PROF. DEVANE: Then why all of the anxiety about a simple blood test?

MR. MUSCADINE: I—I'd have to think about it.

PROF. DEVANE: Is there some fundamental problem with it, sir?

MR. MUSCADINE: No, but . . .

PROF. DEVANE: But what, sir?

MR. MUSCADINE: I don't know.

PROF. DEVANE: These are the facts: You had unprotected sex with a woman who claims you raped her. The very least you can do is to—

MR. MUSCADINE: It just seems kind of . . . drastic. Have sex and prove yourself healthy? I've slept with lots of other women and it never came up.

PROF. DEVANE: That's the point, sir. In effect, Ms. Bowlby has now slept with every one of those other women. The precise details of what occurred that night may never be proven, but it's obvious that Ms. Bowlby is experiencing some real trauma.

MR. MUSCADINE: Not because of me.

MS. BOWLBY: You *raped* me!

MR. MUSCADINE: Tessa, I didn't. I'm sorry. You've twisted this—

MS. BOWLBY: Stop! Please! [*Cries*]

MR. MUSCADINE: Tessa, if there was some way to undo it, believe me, I would. We didn't ·*need* to make love, we could have just—

PROF. DEVANE: Please stop, sir. Thank you. Are you all right, Tessa? Casey, get her a fresh tissue . . . thanks. As I was saying, Mr. Muscadine, the precise details may never be known because there were no witnesses. But Ms. Bowlby is clearly traumatized and she's entitled to some kind of closure. Given your sexual history, she'd feel a lot better if you were tested and shown to be HIV-negative. And so would this committee.

MR. MUSCADINE: Is that true, Tessa? Tessa?

MS. BOWLBY: You just *said* you sleep around!

MR. MUSCADINE: Wow. From Kafka to Dracula—give up my body fluids. Okay, I have nothing to hide—do I have to pay for it?

PROF. DEVANE: The testing can be done at Student Health with no charge. I've got an authorization form, right here, that will release all results.

MR. MUSCADINE: Oh, boy—okay, fine, I've got nothing to hide—but she should get tested, as well.

MS. BOWLBY: I already did. Right after. So far I'm negative.

MR. MUSCADINE: You'll stay negative. At least from me—listen, Tessa, I'm really sorry this whole thing has gotten to you, but I—forget it. Sure, fine. I'll get tested, tomorrow. How's that? If that's all I have to do.

PROF. DEVANE: You should also give some serious thought to the issue of rape.

MR. MUSCADINE: I don't need to.

PROF. DEVANE: Sometimes we're not aware of—

MR. MUSCADINE: I'm telling you—okay, fine. I'll think about it. Now can I go?

PROF. DEVANE: Sign these release forms, go to Student Health, and get tested within twenty-four hours.

MR. MUSCADINE: Fine, fine. What an experience—thank God I'm an actor.

PROF. DEVANE: Why's that, sir?

MR. MUSCADINE: To an actor, everything's material. Maybe I can put this to use someday.

PROF. DEVANE: I trust not, sir. As we told you at the outset, everything that goes on here is confidential.

MR. MUSCADINE: Oh . . . yes, sure. It had better be. For my sake, too.

PROF. DEVANE: What I'm saying is you're enjoined against using it. That's part of the agreement.

MR. MUSCADINE: I didn't mean use it directly. I meant subconsciously. Never mind . . . bye, Tessa. Let's keep our distance from each other. Let's stay a *planet* away from each other.

5

That night, as Milo and I drove over to visit Philip Seacrest, I said, "Kenneth Storm."

"Thought you might like him. Ugly scene, huh?"

"Do you know if Storm actually transferred to the College of the Palms?"

"No, why?"

"What if they didn't accept him? Or he enrolled and flunked out? He'd be left with nothing but bad memories and the committee to blame for it. That would put the other two committee members at risk, too. Although going for all the members might make the motive too obvious. If I needed one victim for satisfaction, it would be the leader."

He nodded. "Which Hope sure was. And second-in-command was that grad student, Locking. He was really in step with her. The third one, Professor Steinberger, didn't say much, and she wasn't there for the third case."

"Maybe she got disillusioned," I said. "Casey Locking might not have had the luxury. He's studying psychology and I wouldn't be surprised if Hope was his supervisor or in some other position of power."

"The third session was the only one where the girl actually claimed rape. What do you think of Hope asking that acting student—Muscadine—to take an AIDS test?"

"Maybe she was convinced he'd raped her, knew there was no evidence for criminal prosecution, and decided to do what she could for the victim. The girl—Tessa—got tested, too. So she was obviously worried."

"Weird," he said. "What a scene. And it never hit the papers." He stopped at the red light at Sunset and surveyed the cross traffic.

"But you still like Seacrest better than Kenneth Storm."

"I'm open-minded, but yeah. Half a million's one hell of a motive. And Seacrest has the sophistication and the opportunity to set it up—the poisoned dog. Granted, of the three students, Storm's our best bet, but he's only nineteen and from his academic record, no genius. Does that orchestrated wound pattern seem like the work of a kid with a short fuse and a dirty mouth? Fifty wounds would fit that better. Or bashing her head in. Plus Storm went through channels to vent his spleen, got his revenge through Daddy's lawyer."

"That's why I asked if he's still in school. Maybe going through channels didn't prove satisfying. And don't forget the bike tire marks."

"Boy on a ten-speed." The light changed and he turned east, drove slowly til the traffic thinned, then made a quick right south of the boulevard. We were close to the murder street. By L.A. terms, Hope had been my neighbor. Robin had probably been thinking about that.

We sailed through the cold, black privacy of Holmby Hills, past high walls and old trees; small, hostile signs reminding us of the presence of an armed patrol. Milo rolled through a boulevard stop and continued south. The estates gave way to houses as we entered residential Westwood.

"I'll follow up on Storm Junior," he said. "On all three of them. Going to be making a lot of people who thought they'd put the committee behind them very unhappy."

We sat parked near the big elm for a while, talking about the murder and other things before sinking into an aspic of silence. No movement behind the amber-lit curtains. No signs of life.

"Ready to meet him?"

"Thrilled."

"Yeah, he's a thrilling guy."

Just as we were about to get out, headlights came at us and a car stopped in front of the Devane/Seacrest house, turned up the driveway, and parked behind the Volvo.

Red Mustang.

"There you go," I said. "He does go out. Took a spin in the sports car."

"Her sports car." Milo stared, mouth tight, eyes tuned.

The headlights shut off and a man got out of the red car and walked up to the front door.

"That's not Seacrest. Seacrest is taller."

The man rang the bell. It was too dark to make out details but he was short—maybe five seven—and wore a long coat. Hands in pockets, his back to us.

A house light went on downstairs and the door opened partially. The man slipped inside.

"A pal?" I said. "Someone Seacrest lent the car to?"

"Long as he's being hospitable, let's partake."

It took a lot longer for our ring to be answered. Finally from behind the door came a "Yes?"

"It's Detective Sturgis, Professor."

Another partial opening. Philip Seacrest was indeed taller than the man in the coat. Close to Milo's six-three but sixty pounds lighter, with narrow shoulders and a drawn, squarish face turned grubby by a poorly trimmed gray beard. His nose was small and wide and might have been broken once. His hair was gray and unruly, puffing over his ears but skimpy on top. He wore a gray-and-green plaid shirt, gray twill slacks that had once been expensive but were shiny at the knees, felt bedroom slippers. The shirt was rolled to his elbows, exposing hairless, soft-looking arms.

One incongruity: a small anchor tattoo on his left forearm, pale blue, crudely done, probably a Navy souvenir. I knew he was fifty-five but he looked older. Maybe it was grief. Or bad genes. Or going to work every day and doing the same thing over and over without distinction.

"Detective." He took hold of the doorpost. Quiet voice, just above a mumble. If he lectured that way the back rows wouldn't hear him.

Behind him I could see old, clumsy furniture, floral wallpaper, a grandfather clock in the crook of a narrow staircase. Small brass chandelier. I smelled the not-quite-cooked odor of microwaved food.

On the far wall of the entry, a colonial eagle mirror's convex lens stared back like a giant eye. No sight of the Mustang driver.

"Professor," said Milo.

Seacrest's eyes were big, brown, two shades darker than those of his dead wife, soft as a child's. "What can I do for you, Mr. Sturgis?"

"Are we interrupting something, sir?"

The "we" made him notice me, but not for long. "No."

"May we come in?"

Seacrest hesitated for a second. "All right." Saying it louder—warning the other man? He stayed in the doorway, then stepped aside.

No eye contact. I was already picking up the evasiveness that had alerted Milo.

Then he did look at us. But not with affection.

Sometimes cops and victims' families bond, but there was none of that here. Quite the opposite. A coldness.

Maybe it was because he didn't like being dropped in on.

Or because he'd been treated as a suspect from the beginning.

Maybe he deserved that.

He remained in the entry hall, licking his lips and touching his Adam's apple, then he looked over his shoulder at the staircase. The shorter man up there?

Milo stepped closer and Seacrest retreated a step. It took him nearer the convex mirror and he became a gray smear in the silvered glass.

"So," he repeated. "What can I do for you?"

"Just checking in," said Milo.

"No progress."

"I'm afraid not, sir."

Seacrest nodded, as if bad news were to be expected.

I took in the house. Center hall plan, the entry modest, floored in vinyl tiles that simulated white marble, the staircase carpeted in faded green.

Living room to the right, dining room to the left. More fusty furniture, not quite old enough to be antique. He'd inherited the house from his parents. Probably the stuff he'd grown up with. Disparate throw rugs spread limply over brown wall-to-wall plush. Beyond the stairs was a small pine-paneled room lined with books. Books on the floor, too. A plaid couch. The grandfather clock hadn't been set and its pendulum hung inertly.

Footsteps thumped from the second floor.

"One of Hope's students," Seacrest said, fingering his beard. "Retrieving some research material Hope left behind. I finally had the gumption to go through Hope's things after the police took everything apart, and repack them. Those first two detectives just threw everything around—one second."

He climbed halfway up the stairs. "Almost through?" he called. "The police are here."

A voice from above said something. Seacrest came back down slowly, like an unwilling bride.

"Research material," said Milo. "It belongs to the student?"

"They were working together. It's the norm at the doctoral level."

I said, "How many students did she have?"

"I don't believe many."

"Because of the book?" said Milo.

"Pardon?"

"The time demands."

"Yes, I suppose so. But also because Hope was particular." Seacrest glanced toward the stairs. "It's still a mess—Hope's approach to things was . . . she wasn't overly . . . compulsive. Which is not to say her mind wasn't organized. It *was*. Exceptionally so. One of her many talents. Perhaps that was the point."

"What was, Professor?"

Seacrest pointed up the stairs, as if at a chalkboard. "What I mean to say is I always wondered if the reason she could afford to work in disorder was because she was so *internally* tidy—so beautifully schematized—that she had no *need* for external order. Even as a graduate student she'd study with the radio on, the television. I found that unbelievable. I need absolute solitude."

He sniffed. "She was much smarter than I." His eyes got wet.

"You're not getting much solitude tonight," said Milo.

Seacrest tried to smile. His mouth wouldn't go along and it came out a pig's-tail of ambivalence.

"So, no new ideas," he said. "I wish I had some of my own. But madness is just madness. So banal."

"Coming down," said a voice from the stairs.

The shorter man descended, a cardboard box in both hands.

He was in his twenties with long, dark, straight hair slicked back from a face so angular it made James Dean's look pudgy. He had full, dark lips, hollow cheeks, smooth skin, and heavy black eyebrows. The long coat was a scuffed black leather trench and under the hem was an inch of blue denim cuff. Black boots with thick soles and heavy chrome buckles.

He blinked. Long, curving lashes over dark blue

eyes. Upstairs, where the bedrooms were. I thought about Seacrest's possible warning and wondered about whether he'd come for something other than data.

Driving Hope's car . . . quite a privilege for someone else's student. But for a new friend . . .

I glanced over at Milo. He hadn't budged.

The young man reached the bottom, holding the box out in front of him like an offering. Neat writing in black marker on the side said SELF-CONTROL STUDY, BATCH 4, PRELIM. He put it down. Half-open flaps revealed computer printouts.

He had long, slender hands. On the right index finger was a big silver skull ring. Red glass for the skull's eyes. The kind of thing you get in a Hollywood Boulevard schlock shop.

"Hi, I'm Casey Locking." His voice was deep and liquid, relaxed, like that of an all-night DJ.

Milo identified himself.

Locking said, "I spoke to two other detectives right after it happened."

Milo's jaw twitched. Nothing about the interview in Paz and Fellows's files.

"Have you learned anything yet?" said Locking.

"Not yet."

"She was a great teacher and a fantastic person." Seacrest sighed.

"Sorry, Professor," said Locking.

"Your name rings a bell," said Milo. "Got it. You sat on the conduct committee, right?"

Locking's black eyebrows became tiny croquet wickets. "Yes, I did."

Seacrest turned toward the conversation with sudden interest.

Locking touched a leather lapel and a crescent of

white T-shirt became visible. "You're not thinking the committee had something to do with . . . what happened?"

"You don't think that's possible?"

Locking rolled his fingers. "God, I never really considered that."

"Why not?"

"It just didn't seem—I guess to me all those guys seemed like cowards."

"I'd say Professor Devane was killed in a cowardly manner."

I tried to observe Seacrest without being obvious. Still looking at the floor, arms loose and limp.

"I guess so," said Locking. "You're the detective, but . . . did you know that the dean sent down a directive? Everything associated with the committee is confidential. So I can't talk about it."

"Things have changed," said Milo.

"Yes, I guess they have. But that's really all I have to say." Locking picked up the box. "Good luck."

Milo edged closer to him. Milo's height and bulk often cause people to retreat. Locking didn't.

"So you did research with Professor Devane?"

"She was my dissertation advisor. We did some work together."

"Have you found a new advisor yet?"

"Not yet."

"How many other students was she supervising?"

"Just me and one other."

"What's the other's name?"

"Mary Ann Gonsalvez. She's been in England for a year." Locking turned to Seacrest. "The car's fine, Professor Seacrest. Just needed an oil change and a new air filter. I left the keys upstairs."

"Thank you, Casey."

Locking walked to the door, freed one hand to open it while keeping the box up against his chest.

"Nice ring," said Milo.

Locking stopped, gave a slow abdominal laugh. "Oh, that. Tacky, isn't it? Someone gave it to me. I guess I should get rid of it."

6

Milo closed the door after him.

"Nice of him to get your car fixed, Professor."

"A barter," said Seacrest. "I searched for his data and he took care of the car. Is there anything else, Mr. Sturgis?"

"No, just checking to see if you've thought of anything. And I wanted to introduce you to Dr. Delaware. He's our consulting psychologist."

The soft eyes squinted. "Oh?"

"Given your wife's background I thought Dr. Delaware might be able to help us."

"Yes, I suppose that's a good idea."

"By the way, where's the dog?"

"Pardon?"

"Your Rottweiler."

"Hilde? I gave her away. She was Hope's dog."

"Not a dog person, yourself?"

Seacrest hadn't stopped staring at me. "The truth

is, I'm tired. Can't seem to get my energy back. Can't give Hilde the attention she deserves. And I don't need yet another reminder of the way things used to be."

"Who'd you give her to?"

"An organization called Rottweiler Rescue."

"What kind of dog was Hilde?"

"Nice, a bit rambunctious."

"Was she protective?"

"Seemed to be, though that's not why Hope bought her. She wanted companionship. When she walked."

Seacrest wiped his eyes.

"Did the two of you never walk together?" said Milo.

"No, I'm not one for exercise. Hope loved physical activity and Hilde was an active dog. Always had her eyes on Hope. That's why it was terribly . . . ironic. Hilde not being there." He scratched his beard. The eyes were wide, again. Very bright, as if backlit by hot, white metal.

"After Hope's death, the dog was miserable," he said. "I was depressed, not equipped."

"Who took care of Hilde during Professor Devane's book tour?"

"Oh, I did, but Hope never stayed away long. Two, three days on the road, back for two or three, then out again."

"Did Hilde have a history of stomach problems?"

"No." Seacrest's eyes left mine reluctantly. "The first two detectives wondered if she'd been poisoned by the murderer. Had I thought of that I would have had her tested. Not that it would tell much, I suppose."

"Why not?"

"Let's say she *was* given something. We'd still have no idea by whom."

Seacrest looked at me again. "A police psychologist. That's a job Hope would never have taken."

"Why not?" said Milo.

"She distrusted authority. I'm from a different generation."

"She didn't like the police?" said Milo.

"She felt all organizations were inherently . . . inefficient."

"And you disagreed."

"I have a certain . . . arm's-length respect for law enforcement," he said. "Perhaps because I'm an historian."

"Have you studied crime history?"

"Not per se. My chief interest is the medieval period, but I'm also interested in Elizabethan history and one account of that age sticks in my mind. During the Elizabethan age, capital punishment was meted out for a wide variety of crimes. Even pickpockets were hanged. Then kinder, gentler souls had their way and the noose was eliminated for less serious offenses. Care to surmise what happened?"

"More crime," said Milo.

"You get an A, Detective."

"Do you advocate capital punishment, Professor?"

Seacrest touched his beard. "I don't know what I advocate, anymore. Losing my wife has shaken up all my preconceptions—what exactly will you be doing to help find Hope's killer, Dr. Delaware?"

"Analyzing the file," I said. "Perhaps talking to some of your wife's colleagues. Anyone in particular I should start with?"

He shook his head. "Hope and I kept our professional lives separate."

"You don't know anyone she associated with?"

"No, not professionally."

"What about friends?"

"We really didn't have any. I know that's hard to believe, but we both led very insular lives. Work, writing, Hilde, trying to steal bits of privacy."

"Must have been harder after the book came out."

"For Hope it was. She kept me out of the lime-light."

Insular. Little boxes . . .

"Professor," said Milo, "is the name Robert Barone familiar?"

Slow headshake.

"What about Milan Cruvic?"

"No. Who are they?"

"People your wife worked with."

"Well, there you go. I wouldn't know about that."

"Totally separate, huh?" said Milo.

"It worked best for us." Seacrest turned to me. "When you do speak to Hope's colleagues, I'm willing to bet what they tell you."

"What's that, Professor?"

"That she was brilliant but a loner. A first-rate scholar and teacher." His hands balled. "Gentlemen, pardon me for saying so, but I don't believe this approach will prove useful."

"What approach is that, sir?" said Milo.

"Examining Hope's academic career. That's not what killed her. It was that *book*. Getting out into what's known laughably as the *real* world. She had the courage to be controversial and that controversy inspired some schizophrenic fiend or whatever. Dear God . . ."

Rubbing his forehead, he stared at the floor. "Give

me the ivory tower any day, Detective. Spare me *reality*."

Milo asked if we could see Hope's study.

"As you like. Do you mind if I stay down here and have some tea?"

"Not at all."

"Up the stairs and take the first room to your left. Look anywhere else you please."

At the top were three smallish bedrooms and a bath off a central landing. The room to the left was walled with budget Swedish-modern cases jammed top to bottom with journals and books, the shelves bowing under the weight. Venetian blinds shielded two windows. The furniture looked strewn rather than placed: two mismatched chairs, a desk, and a workstand with PC, printer, modem, software manuals. The American Psychological Association's Style Guide, dictionary, thesaurus.

Next to the computer were several copies of an article Hope Devane had authored last year in *The Journal of Personality and Social Psychology*. Coauthor: Casey Locking. "Self-Control As a Function of Gender Identity."

I read the abstract. No significant differences between men and women in the ability to control nail-biting using a behavioral technique. No relationship between success and subjects' views on sex-role behavior and equality. In *Wolves and Sheep* Hope claimed women were superior to men in breaking bad habits because estrogen had an "impulse-suppressing" role. The sole exception: compulsive overeating, because societal pressure created body-image conflict in women.

The article said just the opposite. I turned to the Discussion section at the back. Hope and Locking hedged their results by stating that their sample was too small.

As Milo opened drawers and read the spines of shelved books, I inspected the rest of the room. Loose journals and books covered half the floorspace. A red wool throw was tossed carelessly over a box. Just like the carton Locking had carried out, the same neat black lettering.

Five sealed cartons from Hope Devane's publisher stamped WOLVES AND SHEEP, COMP. COPIES were shoved into a corner. Unopened reams of computer paper.

The lettered box contained more of Hope's published papers, Locking the coauthor on two of them. No authorship for the other student, Mary Ann Gonsalvez.

Teacher's pet?

Judging from the conduct-committee transcripts, Locking had been a kindred spirit.

More than that?

He was young, bright, good-looking if you like the brooding underwear-ad type.

Younger man, older woman.

First I'd wondered about Locking and Seacrest, now I was speculating about a heterosexual affair.

Sin on the brain, Delaware?

But the wound pattern connoted sin—someone's idea of transgression made good.

Heart, vagina. Stabbing in the back.

The heat of passion buttressed by cold planning.

Seacrest *seemed* the bloodless type.

Had he shed blood?

*   *   *

Milo fished some more, then said, "Anything?"

I told him about the discrepancy between the self-control article and the book.

"Like you said, she fudged." He looked through the office door, across the landing, and cocked his head. I followed him out to Seacrest's office.

Also book-lined and furnished with aesthetic apathy, but pin-neat.

Next, Seacrest's bedroom. Now that he had it all to himself, the historian kept his sleeping space tidy. Queen-sized brass bed, floral coverlet tucked so tight it looked painted on the mattress.

We went downstairs. Seacrest was nowhere in sight.

Milo said, "Professor?" and Seacrest came into the dining room from the kitchen, mug in hand. The tag and string of a tea bag dangled over the side. University mascot on the mug.

"Anything else you'd like to see?"

"Where are Dr. Devane's professional records—patient files, things like that?"

"Anything not here would be in her campus office."

"I've been through that and there are no patient files."

"Then I don't know what to tell you."

"Did she have a private office?"

"No."

"Did she see patients here?"

"No."

"Did she see patients at all?"

"She never discussed her work."

"I'm not talking specifics, Professor Seacrest. Just if she saw any patients."

"If she did she never mentioned it. We didn't talk about our jobs. Only . . . scholarly issues."

Seacrest touched his tattoo.

"Navy?" said Milo.

"Coast Guard." Seacrest smiled. "A moment of poor judgment."

"Where'd you serve?"

"Off Catalina Island. More of a vacation, I'm forced to admit."

"So you're from California."

"Grew up right here. In this house. Campus brat. My father was a chemistry professor."

"And Hope's?"

"Hope's parents are both deceased. As are mine. Neither of us had siblings. I suppose I'm all that's left of both families."

I knew what Milo was thinking: *sole heir.*

"What did her father do?" he said.

"He was a sailor. Merchant marine. He died when Hope was very young. She didn't talk much about him."

"And her mother?"

"Her mother worked in a restaurant." Seacrest headed for the door. "As I told the first detectives, she's also deceased and Hope had no other family."

Milo said, "Quite a skill."

"What is?"

"Keeping your professional lives separate. Keeping things separate, in general."

Seacrest licked his lips. "Not at all. Quite the opposite, actually."

"It was easy?"

"Certainly. Because we respected each other."
Opening the door, he extended an arm outside.

"Warm night," he said. "The night it happened
was much cooler."

Milo drove Wilshire Boulevard through the corridor of high-rise condos that made up L.A.'s nod to
Park Avenue.

"Diagnosis?" he said.

"He's not Mr. Warmth but he's got reason to
be depressed. He could be hiding something or really not know much. Bottom line: nothing earth-
shattering."

"And Mr. Locking?"

"The skull ring was cute. First I found myself wondering about a relationship between him and Seacrest,
then between him and Hope."

"Him and Seacrest? Why?"

"Locking driving that car seemed awfully personal, though Seacrest's barter explanation could
cover that. Also, Seacrest seemed to be delaying letting us in and once he did, he called upstairs to say
the police were there. Which could have been his way
of warning Locking. Giving him time to get his
clothes on? All of which is pure supposition."

"Okay . . . why Locking and Hope?"

"You've wondered all along about her having an
affair. Most affairs begin at work and Locking was the
guy she worked with. And after marriage to someone
like Seacrest, she might have been ready for a little
excitement."

"Black leather and a skull ring," he said, drum-
ming the steering wheel and heading into Westwood
Village. Like so much else in L.A., the district had

been intellectually downscaled, the bookstores of my college days surrendering to games arcades, gyro shacks, and insta-latte assembly-line franchises.

"What I found interesting," he said, "was the way Seacrest suggested the murder could be blamed on the book. Insisting it had nothing to do with her academic life. Which distances it from *him*. I've seen killers who think they're smart do that—give out alternative scenarios. That way they can look helpful while thinking they're steering us away from them. And that dog. Who better to slip her a nice big steak laced with God-knows-what. And now he's given her away."

"Getting rid of the reminders."

He made an ugly sound and loosened his tie. "Locking and Hope, Locking and Seacrest. Guess I'll make use of some of my homo*sexual* contacts. Maybe the lieutenant was right and I am the perfect guy for the case."

"I wonder," I said, "why it took so long for Locking to come get his data. Hope's been dead three months. That's a lot of time when you're working on your dissertation. Then again, Locking hasn't found a new advisor so maybe he's having trouble adjusting to Hope's death. Maybe because they had more going than a student-teacher thing. Or, he's just a hang-loose guy in no great hurry to finish. You see that in grad school. Though his go-round with Kenneth Storm was anything but mellow."

"What do you think of Hope appointing her own prize student to the committee?"

"Packing the jury. She could have justified it in the name of efficiency. Seacrest said she distrusted organizations, and everything else tells us she wasn't much of a team player."

"That's why I'm interested in meeting people she did work with. Lawyer Barone's still ignoring me but Dr. Cruvic left a message saying he'll see me briefly at ten-thirty tomorrow morning. Care to come, psych him out?"

"Sure."

"Not a team player," he said. "Cowgirl with a Ph.D. Sometimes cowgirls get thrown."

7

The following day I met Milo for breakfast at Nate 'n Al's on Beverly, then we drove to Dr. Cruvic's office on Civic Center Drive.

Interesting location for a private practitioner. Most of Beverly Hills's medical suites are housed in the stylish neo-Federal buildings that line North Bedford, Roxbury, and Camden, and in the big reflective towers on Wilshire.

Civic Center was the northern edge of the city's meager industrial district, a few nondescript blocks that paralleled Santa Monica Boulevard but were blocked from motorists' view by tall hedges and eucalyptus. Unused railroad tracks cut diagonally through the street. Past the tracks were a pink granite office complex, the frosted-glass headquarters of a record company, and the neo-retro-post-whatever-revival municipal center that contained Beverly Hills's city hall, library, police and fire departments.

Development hadn't come yet to the other side of the tracks, where Cruvic's pink stucco Spanish building shared space with an assortment of narrow, shabby/cute single- and double-story structures dating from World War I and earlier. The doctor's immediate neighbors were a beauty parlor, a telephone answering service, and an unmarked building with a loading dock. The pink building had no front windows, just a massive wood-and-iron door like those you see in Spain and Italy and Greece, leading to courtyards. A ring-in buzzer was topped by a tarnished bronze sign so small it seemed intent on avoiding discovery. M. CRUVIC, M.D. etched shallowly.

Milo punched the buzzer and we waited. But for the hum of the cars on Santa Monica, the street was sleepy. Geraniums grew out of boxes in the beautician's window. In all my years in L.A., I'd never had a reason to be here.

Milo knew what I was thinking. "Looks like someone else likes privacy."

Rubbing his lip with his lower teeth, he pushed the buzzer again.

Electric bee-buzz response, the click of release. He shoved at the heavy wood and we stepped in.

On the other side was a courtyard. Flagstone-floored, open to the sky, set up with potted bananas, flax plants, azaleas. A small iron table and two chairs. Ashtray on the table. Two lipsticked butts. The interior building was two stories with barred windows and hand-wrought balconies. Two doors. The right one opened and a woman in a light blue uniform came out. "Right here." Throaty voice. She pointed to the left.

She was around fifty, trim and brunette with a very large bust, a tight, shiny, tan face, and dancer's calves.

"Detective Sturgis? I'm Anna, come on in." She gave a one-second smile, led us to the left, and opened the door. "Dr. Cruvic will be right with you. Can I get you some coffee? We have an espresso machine."

"No, thanks."

She'd taken us into a short, bright hallway. Dark wood doors, all closed, and dense tan carpeting that smothered our footsteps. The walls were white and looked freshly painted. She opened the fourth door and stepped aside.

The room was small with a low ceiling. Two beige cotton armchairs and a matching love seat sat on a black area rug. A chrome-and-glass coffee table separated them. A pair of high windows exposed the brick wall of the beauty-parlor building. No desk, no books, no phone.

"Dr. Cruvic's offices are on the other side but he'd like you to remain here so as not to upset the patients. You're sure you don't want coffee? Or tea?"

Milo declined again and smiled.

"Okay, then. Make yourselves comfortable, he should be right in."

"Nice old building," said Milo. "Must be good to have this kind of space in Beverly Hills."

"Oh, it is neat," she said. "I think it used to be some kind of stable—they ran horses around here back in the old days. I think Mary Pickford kept her horses here, or maybe it was another of those old-time stars."

I said, "Does Dr. Cruvic do his operating right here or does he go over to Cedars or Century City?"

Her taut face turned glassy. "Mostly we do outpatient procedures. Nice to meet you."

She left, closing the door. Milo waited several moments, then opened it and looked out. Four long strides took him to the end of the corridor and a door marked TO WEST WING. He tried the knob. Locked. On his way back, he jiggled others. All bolted.

"Is my paranoia kicking in 'cause I don't like doctors' offices or did she not like your question about where he operates?"

"It did seem to throw her," I said. "Sorry to put a stress on her face-lift."

"Yeah, she *is* glossy. I thought she might have been recuperating from a sunburn, but with that chest you're probably right. . . . *Did* you want coffee? Far be it for me to speak for the entire class."

"No, this room is stimulating enough."

He laughed. "Warm and cozy, huh—could you do therapy, here?"

"I can do therapy anywhere but I'd prefer something a little less stark."

"Maybe this was Hope's therapy room."

"Why do you say that?"

"Because it's separate from the west wing. No *upsetting* the patients. Assuming she worked here. Which isn't that big of a stretch: He paid her almost forty grand, we haven't found patient files anywhere else."

The door opened and a very broad-shouldered man about five-nine gusted in wearing a very wide frown.

He was around forty with thick gray hair styled in a long, spiky crew cut, the sideburns clipped high above small, close-set ears. Dark, extremely alert eyes studied us. Slanted—five degrees short of an Asian tilt.

His face was round with pronounced, rosy cheekbones, a straight nose with flared nostrils, and a strong chin already shadowed with morning growth.

He wore a tailored white double-breasted jacket over a spread-collar blue shirt and a black silk crepe tie hand-painted with crimson and gold swirls. Black slacks broke perfectly over two-tone black-leather-and-gray-suede wing tips. He stuck out his hand and revealed a French cuff held together by a gold-barrel link. His wrist was thick and coated with straight black hair.

"Mike Cruvic." Nodding, as if we'd just come to a consensus. Even when he stood still he seemed to bounce.

"Doctor," said Milo. They shook, then I got Cruvic's hand. Muscular grip but soft palm. Buffed nails.

"Thanks for taking the time, sir."

"Happy to, though I really don't know how I can help you find Hope's killer." He shook his head. "Let's sit, okay? Got myself a heel spur from running in old shoes. You'd think I'd know better." He knuckled his forehead three times and sank into the love seat.

"You know what they say," said Milo. "The doctor's kids go barefoot."

Cruvic smiled and stretched his arms. "In this case the doctor gets sore feet. I never thought I'd be talking to the police about murder, let alone Hope's."

Tucking his finger into a wing tip, he rubbed the side of his foot and winced.

"Creak, creak," he said, rolling his shoulders. Their bulk wasn't due to padding. His posture was perfect, his belly board-flat. I pictured him in his home gym at daybreak, bouncing and pedaling and pumping. One of those early risers just waiting to take on the day and knock it out in two rounds.

"So," he said, finally sitting still. "What would you like to know?"

"We have on record that you paid Dr. Devane thirty-six thousand dollars last year," said Milo. "Did she work for you?"

Cruvic floated a palm over the spikes of his crew cut. "I never tallied it up but that sounds right. She consulted to the practice."

"In what capacity, Doctor?"

Cruvic touched a finger to a broad, pale lip. "Let's see, how can I be forthcoming without compromising my patients . . . are you aware of what we do here?"

"Obstetrics-gynecology and fertility."

Cruvic produced a business card from an inner pocket of the white jacket. Milo read it, then handed it to me.

MILAN A. CRUVIC, M.D., FACOG
PRACTICE LIMITED TO PROBLEMS OF FERTILITY

"I used to do OB-GYN but for the last few years I've been doing just fertility."

"The hours?" said Milo.

"Pardon?"

"Delivering babies. The hours can be rough."

Cruvic laughed. "No, that never bothered me, I don't need much sleep. I just *like* doing fertility. People come in, sometimes there's absolutely no medical reason they can't conceive. It tears them apart. You analyze it, come up with a solution." He grinned. "I guess I fancy myself a detective of sorts." He looked at his watch.

"What was Professor Devane's role in all of that, sir?"

"I called Hope in when I had doubts."

"About what?"

"Patients' psychological preparedness." Cruvic's brow creased and the gray spikes tilted down. "Fertility enhancement's an exhausting process. Physically *and* psychologically. And sometimes nothing we do works. I warn patients beforehand but not everyone can handle it. When they can't, it's best not to start. Sometimes I can judge who's likely to have problems. If I can't, I call in experts."

"Do you use other psychologists besides Professor Devane?"

"I have in the past. And some patients have their own therapists. But after I met Hope she became my preferred choice."

He put both hands on his knees. "She was terrific. Very insightful. A great judge of people. And excellent with the patients. Because unlike other psychologists and psychiatrists she had no stake in sucking people into long-term treatment."

"Why's that?"

"She was busy enough."

"With her book?"

"Her book, teaching." He clapped his hands. "Quick, to the point, the least amount of treatment necessary. I guess that appealed to the surgeon in me."

His ruddy cheeks were almost scarlet and his eyes had turned distant. Rubbing his foot some more, he leaned forward. "I—the practice misses her. Some of these shrinks are weirder than the patients. Hope talked plain English. She was fantastic."

"How many cases did you refer to her?"

"I never counted."

"Were there any patients who weren't happy with her?"

"Not a one—oh, come on, you can't be serious. No, no, Detective, not a chance. I deal with civilized people, not nutcases."

Milo shrugged and smiled. "Gotta ask. . . . Is it my imagination, Doctor, or is there more infertility, nowadays?"

"It's not your imagination at all. Some of it's probably due to people waiting longer to start. The ideal conception age for a woman is early to mid-twenties. Tack on ten, fifteen years and you've got an aging uterus and diminished probability."

He put a hand on each knee and his slacks stretched over thick, muscular thighs. "I'd never say this to a patient because they've got enough guilt, but some of it's also due to all the messing around people did in the seventies. Promiscuity, repetitive subclinical infections, endometriosis—that's internal scarring. That's also part of what I used Hope for. The guilt."

"Why'd you pay her directly instead of having her do her own billing?"

Cruvic's head moved back. The hands came off the knees and pressed down hard on the love-seat cushion.

"Insurance," said Cruvic. "We tried it the other way and found out it was easier to recover payment for a gynecologic-behavioral consult than for psychotherapy."

Another stroke of the crew cut. "My CPA assures me it's all on the up-and-up. Now, if that's all—"

"Did she work well with the husbands, too?" I said.

"Why wouldn't she?"

"Her opinions about men were controversial."

"In what sense?"

"Her book."

"Oh, that. Well, she was never controversial here. Everyone was very satisfied with her work. . . . Not that it's my place to tell you how to do your job, but it seems to me you're barking up a completely wrong tree. Hope's murder had nothing to do with her work for me."

"I'm sure you're right," said Milo. "Where'd you meet her?"

"At another health facility."

"Where?"

"A charity clinic in Santa Monica."

"Name?"

"The Women's Health Center. I've been active there for a while. Once a year they throw a fundraiser. Hope and I sat next to each other on the dais and we began talking."

He stood. His tie had ridden up and he pulled it down. "If you'll excuse me, I've got some ladies out there who want to be mommies."

"Sure. Thanks, Doctor." Milo stood, too. Blocking the door. "One more thing. Did Professor Devane keep her patient files here?"

"She had no files of her own. Made notes in mine. That way we could communicate easily. My files are kept strictly confidential, so it wasn't a problem."

"But she did see patients here."

"Yes."

"In this room, by any chance?"

"You know," said Cruvic, "I believe she may have. I don't assign rooms, the staff does."

"But she stayed in this wing," said Milo. "The privacy issue."

"Exactly."

"Nice setup for privacy. Location-wise, I mean. Off the beaten path."

Cruvic's bulky shoulders rose, then fell. "We like it."

He tried to sight around Milo.

Milo seemed to move aside, then his notepad came out. "This Women's Center, you do fertility work there?"

Cruvic inhaled, forced a smile. "Fertility is rarely an issue for the poor. At the center I donate my time to general women's health care."

"Does that include abortions?"

"With all due respect, I don't see that that's relevant."

Milo smiled. "It probably isn't."

"I'm sure you know I'm not free to discuss any of my cases. Even poor women have a right to confid—"

"Sorry, Doc. I wasn't asking about specific cases, just a general question about what you do there."

"Why raise the abortion issue at all? What's the point, Detective?"

"Abortion's legal but it's still controversial. And some people express their opposition to it violently. So if you do perform abortions and Professor Devane was involved in that, as well, it might give us another angle."

"Oh, for God's sake," said Cruvic. "I support a woman's right to choose and so did Hope, but if anyone would be targeted it would be the person actually performing the procedure." He tapped his chest. "And I'm obviously here."

"Obviously," said Milo. "Once again, I have to ask, Doc."

"I understand," said Cruvic, but he didn't look

mollified. "I'm sure my opinion doesn't mean much but I think Hope was murdered by some psychotic who hates women and chose her because she'd achieved fame. A nut. Not a patient here or at the Women's Center."

"On the contrary, Doctor. Your opinion does matter. That's exactly what we need. Opinions of people who knew her."

Cruvic colored and he touched his tie. "I only knew her professionally. But I think her death represents so much that's wrong with our society."

"How so, sir?"

"Success and the malignant jealousy it evokes. We adulate talented people, put them on a pedestal, then enjoy knocking them off. Why? Because their success threatens us."

The cheeks bright red now.

He walked around Milo. Stopped at the door and looked back at us.

"The losers punish the winners, gentlemen. If it keeps going that way, we all lose. Good luck."

Milo said, "If you think of anything, Doc," and gave him a business card. The straight version, not the one the detectives pass among themselves that reads ROBBERY-HOMICIDE: OUR DAY BEGINS WHEN YOURS ENDS.

Cruvic pocketed it. Charging into the hallway, he unlocked the door to the west wing and was gone.

"Any hypotheses?" said Milo.

"Well," I said, "he blushed when he said he only knew her professionally, so maybe it was more. And he got a little antsy talking about his billing, so there could have been something funny about that—taking a cut of her fee, kickbacks for referrals, billing for gynecology instead of psychology to up the reimbursement, whatever. The abortion question got his dander up a bit, meaning he probably does them at the center. Maybe here, too, for the high-priced crowd. If so, he wouldn't want it publicized, apart from the controversy. Because a pro-life fertility patient might find it difficult to submit to the care of someone who also destroys fetuses. But he made a good point about his being the target. And I stick with what I said about a political murderer going public."

When we got to the exit door, he said, "If he was sleeping with her the consultant thing could have been a way of shunting money to a girlfriend."

"She didn't need his forty. She made six hundred grand last year."

"He knew her before the book. Maybe it's been going on for years. And Seacrest found out. I know I'm reaching but we keep talking about that heart-genitals-back thing. Revenge. Some kind of betrayal. Cruvic did get a little passionate talking about her, wouldn't you say?"

"He did. Maybe he's just a passionate guy."

"Dr. Heelspur. Saying the same thing Seacrest did: 'It had nothing to do with me.' "

"No one wants to be close to murder," I said.

He frowned and pushed the door to the courtyard. Tight-faced Nurse Anna was at the courtyard table, smoking and reading the paper. She looked up and gave a small wave.

Milo gave her a card, too. She shook her head.

"I only saw Dr. Devane when she came to work."

"How often was that?"

"It wasn't regular. Every so often."

"Did she have her own key?"

"Yes."

"And she always worked out of that room we were just in?"

Nod.

"Nice lady?" said Milo.

Split-second pause. "Yes."

"Anything you want to tell us about her?"

"No," she said. "What could there be?"

Milo shrugged.

Returning the gesture, she stubbed out the cigarette, collected her paper, and stood up.

"Break's over, better be getting back. Have a nice day."

She headed back to the building as we crossed the flagstone. As we opened the big door to the street, she was still watching us.

8

Milo put the key in the ignition but didn't turn it.

"What?" I said.

"Something about Cruvic . . ." He started the car. "Maybe I've been on the job too long. Know what came into the station this morning? Newborn baby mauled to death by some dogs. Seventeen-year-old unwed momma weeping, tragic accident, right? Then the detectives find out the dogs were in the next-door neighbor's yard, separated by an eight-foot fence. Turns out Momma killed the kid, tossed it over to destroy the evidence."

"Jesus."

"No doubt she'll be claiming she was the victim, going on TV, writing a book." He gave a terrible smile. "So am I excused for negative thinking?"

Reaching under the seat, he pulled out a portable cellular phone and punched numbers. "Sturgis. Anything? Yeah, I'll wait."

"Mr. Information Highway," I said, struggling to erase the image of the savaged infant. "Since when does the department issue cell phones?"

"Oh, sure. Department's idea of the information highway is two extra-*large* tin cans and heavy twine. This here is a hand-me-down from Rick, he's got a new one, does all sorts of paging tricks. I don't like going through the department radio without a tactical band, and pay phones are a hassle. But so is applying for reimbursement, so I write off the calls to Blue."

Blue Investigations was his evening moonlight: after-hours surveillance jobs, mostly nailing insurance scammers. Mostly he hated it. Lately he'd been turning down referrals.

"If it's reimbursement you're after, maybe you should bill it as gynecology," I said.

He cracked up. "Uh-huh," he said, into the phone. "Yeah, yeah—where? Okay, got it. Thanks."

Backing out onto Civic Center, he drove west. "Cindy Vespucci—the girl Kenny Storm threw out of the car—just returned my message. She'll be lunching at the Ready Burger in Westwood in a quarter hour. Willing to talk if we show up before her next class."

The restaurant was on Broxton, on the west edge of the Village, where the streets knot up and walking can be faster than driving. Plastic yellow sign, sweating glass window, two rickety tables on the sidewalk, one occupied by two girls drinking Cokes with straws. Neither acknowledged us and we went inside. Three more tables, yellow tile walls also sweating. Lettuce shreds and straw wrappers flecked the red-brick floor; the smell of frying meat was everywhere. A quartet of Asian countermen with Ferrari hands chopped, flipped, wrapped, and played cash-register arpeggios. A numb-looking queue, mostly students, curved from the door to the counter.

Milo studied the interior tables. The lunchers who noticed him didn't do so for long. Same for the kids in line.

We went back outside and he checked his watch. One of the girls put her drink down and said, "Officer Sturgis?"

"Yes, ma'am."

"I'm Cindy."

She was a college freshman but looked like a high-school sophomore. Barely five feet tall, maybe ninety-five pounds, borderline beautiful in an elfin way, with long, straight blond hair, the expected wide sky-blue eyes, an upturned nose, and a cupid's bow mouth. I felt immediately protective and wondered if I'd ever have a daughter.

She wore a gray University sweatshirt over tight black leggings and white running shoes. Book bag by her chair. The nails at the end of her fingers were gnawed. The girl with her was also pretty and blond, a bit chubby. The table was littered with greasy paper and miniature foil packets of ketchup and mustard.

Milo held out his hand. Cindy swallowed and proffered hers. As she looked up at him her mouth lost resolve. He hunched a bit and made his voice gentle. "Good to meet you, Cindy. We really appreciate your talking to us."

"Oh, sure." She looked back at her friend and nodded. The chubby girl stared at us then got up, slinging her bag over her shoulder.

"Cin?"

"I'm okay, Deb. See you at two."

Deb nodded and walked up the street, peering

over her shoulder a couple of times before crossing and entering a record store.

Cindy said, "Do you—should we just talk here?"

"Whatever you like."

"Um—I'm sure someone will want to use the table. Can we walk?"

"Sure."

She retrieved her book bag, tossed back her hair, and gave a smile so effortful it must have burned calories.

Milo smiled back. Cindy turned away from him and saw me.

"This is Alex Delaware."

"Hi." She flinched and shot out her hand. I took it and received a sudden, hard squeeze from cold, child-sized fingers.

The three of us headed west to the end of the block. Across the street was a vast stretch of asphalt—one of the University's off-campus parking lots serviced by shuttles. An idle blue bus was stationed near the entrance. Thousands of spaces, every one filled.

Milo said, "How about we walk through here? Should be pretty private."

Cindy thought, gave three rapid nods. Her mouth had set grimly and her hands were closed tight.

As we entered the lot, she said, "When I was a little kid a policeman came to our school and warned us about darting out in front of parked cars."

"Good advice," said Milo. "We'll be sure to look both ways."

The girl's laugh was constricted.

We strolled a bit before Milo said, "I'm sure you know why we want to talk to you, Cindy."

"Of course. Professor Devane. She was—I'm really

sorry what happened to her but it had nothing to do with Kenny and me."

"I'm sure it didn't, but we have to check out everything."

Suddenly, the girl's eyes grew merry. "That sounds just like on TV."

"Then it's got to be real, right?"

She gazed up at Milo, then back at me. "I've never met an actual detective."

"Oh, it's a real big deal. Somewhere between the Pulitzer and the Nobel."

The girl squinted at him. "You're funny. What do you want me to tell you about Professor Devane?"

"Your experience with the Interpersonal Conduct Committee."

The narrow mouth twisted.

Milo said, "I know it's hard to talk about, but—"

"No, it's not really hard. Not anymore. 'Cause it's over. Kenny and I have resolved things."

We kept walking. A few steps later, she said, "Actually, we're dating."

Milo made a noncommittal sound.

"No doubt it sounds bizarre to you, but it's working for us. I guess there was some . . . chemistry between us. Maybe that's what caused all the initial conflict. Anyway, it's all worked out."

"So Kenny knows you're talking to us."

"Sure, actually he—" She stopped herself.

"He asked you to talk to us?"

"No, no. It's just that I'm here in town and he's down in San Diego, so we thought I could clear things up for both of us."

"Okay," said Milo. "What's to clear?"

She shifted her book bag to another shoulder. "Nothing, really." Her voice had risen in pitch. "It was a mistake. Filing a complaint. I should never have made such a big deal, but there were complications. Between Kenny and me—it's a long story, not really relevant."

"Your mom and his dad," I said.

She looked at me. "So that came out, too."

"There are transcripts of the sessions," said Milo.

"Oh. Great." She looked ready to cry. "I thought everything was supposed to be kept confidential."

"Murder changes the rules, Cindy. But we're doing all we can to keep it quiet."

She exhaled and shook her head. "How blown-up is this going to get?"

"If it had nothing to do with Dr. Devane's death, hopefully not at all."

"It didn't. At least Kenny's and my thing didn't." She punched her chest. "*God*, I was an *idiot* for going along with it!"

I said, "Someone reading the transcript could get the impression you had a valid claim against Kenny."

"Well, I didn't. I told you, it was complicated. Yes, because of our parents. Not that Mom asked me to be her . . . defender. I just . . . I misread some cues. That's all. Kenny didn't behave himself perfectly, but he's no animal. We could have worked things out. Proof is, we *have*."

She shifted the bag again.

Milo said, "I'd offer to carry that for you but it's probably not PC."

She started to say something, then shot him an amused look and handed over the bag. In his hands it looked like a lunch sack.

Rolling her shoulders, she glanced back at the Village as we continued to stroll between the parked cars. "Is this going to take much longer?"

"Not much. Your mom and Kenny's dad, how are *they* getting along?"

"Fine."

"Dating again?"

"No! They're just friends. Thank God. That would be—incestuous. That was a big part of the initial problem. Kenny and I didn't realize the extent of the baggage. Plus his mother died a year ago. He's still hurting."

"What about his kicking you out of the car?"

Cindy stopped. "Please, Detective, I'd know if I was a victim."

Milo didn't answer.

She said, "That night, he—it was stupid. I demanded to get out, he opened the door for me, and I tripped."

She laughed but she looked as if someone had died. "I felt like such a spaz. We needed to work on our communication, that's all. The proof is empirical: we're fine."

"You're a good student, aren't you, Cindy?"

The girl blushed. "I work hard."

"Straight A's?"

"So far, but it's just two quarters—"

"Kenny's not much of a student, is he?"

"He's *very* bright! It's just that he has to find something that inspires him." Licking her lips. "Some focus."

"Motivation."

"Exactly. People move at different paces. I've always known what I want to be."

"What's that?"

"A psychologist or an attorney. I want to work for children's rights."

"Well," said Milo, "we can sure use people doing that."

We walked past three more aisles. A car pulled out, the driver a girl no older than Cindy. We waited til it sped away.

"So Kenny's in San Diego," said Milo. "Thought he was at the College of the Palms in Redlands."

She shook her head. "He decided not to go."

"Why?"

"He needed to get his head straight."

"So he's not in school in San Diego?"

"Not yet. He's interning at a real-estate office in La Jolla. Friend of his dad's. So far he likes it a lot. He's good at selling things."

"I'll bet."

Cindy stopped again and snapped her head up at him. "He didn't sell anything to me, if that's what you're implying! I'm not some gullible jerk and I wouldn't settle for a relationship without equity."

"What do you mean by equity, Cindy?"

"Balance. Emotional fairness."

"Okay. Sorry if I offended you." He scratched his chin and we reached the rear of the lot. The fence was backed by tall trees and a soft breeze blew through them.

Cindy said, "I feel good about Kenny and me. The whole reason I agreed to talk to you is because I wanted to do the right thing. Professor Devane's murder was horrible, but you're really wasting your time with me. She wasn't a significant part of my life. Or Kenny's. He only met her that one time and I just sat in on her class a couple of times before we talked about filing a complaint. She was nice, but even then I was ambivalent. The moment I got in there I knew it was a mistake."

"Why?"

"The atmosphere—the three of them sitting there at a long table. Tape recorder and pens and paper. The whole thing was . . . inquisitional. Not at all what Professor Devane led me to believe—look, I'm sorry she's dead and I admired her a lot, but I have to say she was . . . misleading."

"How so?"

"She made it sound like it would be a counseling session. Everyone communicating their feelings, trying to reach a resolution. More like a discussion group. The moment I saw that table, I knew that was wrong. Kenny said there should have been black candles and he was right. They were clearly out to judge men."

"Which of Professor Devane's classes did you sit in on?"

"Sex-Roles and Development. I wasn't even enrolled but some of my friends were taking it, they kept coming back to the house—the sorority—and telling everyone how great it was. How they were learning all about gender and human behavior. All about men. I had a free period on Tuesday so I figured why not."

"Was Professor Devane a good teacher?"

"She was a fantastic teacher. Riveting. The lecture was in Morton Hall 100—that's a huge room, six hundred seats. But she made you feel she was talking right to you. Which, believe me, is rare, especially when it comes to freshman classes. Some of the faculty just go through the motions."

"She had a way of personalizing things," I said. Just as she did on TV.

"Exactly. And she knew her stuff. Really a great lecturer."

"And you sat in two, three times," said Milo.

"Yes."

"How'd you come to complain about Kenny?"

"The—what happened—the incident was on a Monday night and I was still very upset on Tuesday when I went to class." She wet her lips with her tongue. "Professor Devane was lecturing on domestic violence and I started to feel like a victim. It was one of those stupid, impulsive things you do when you're stressed-out. I went up to her after class, said I had a problem. She took me to her office and just listened, made some tea for me. I cried a little and she gave me a tissue. Then, when I calmed down, she told me she might have a solution for me. That's when she described the committee."

"What'd she say about it?"

"That it was brand-new. Important—in terms of women's rights on campus. She said I could play a significant role in countering women's helplessness."

She looked at the book bag. "I had doubts but she seemed so caring. I can take the bag, now."

"Don't worry about it," said Milo. "So you feel she deceived you."

"Not—I can't call it deliberate deception. Maybe I just heard what I wanted to because I was upset."

"Sounds like you had good reason to be upset, Cindy," I said. "Walking back to campus alone at night must have been scary."

"Very. You hear all sorts of stories."

"About crime?"

She nodded. "Weirdos stalking the hills—look what happened to Professor Devane!"

Milo said, "You think a weirdo killed her?"

"I don't know, but a woman in my sorority works on the student paper and she was doing some research over at the campus police station. They told her there are lots of rapes and attempted rapes that never make the news. And there I was—it was pitch-black. I had to find my way back."

"Not fun."

"Not much." Suddenly, she was crying, hands snapping across her face.

Milo shifted the bag from hand to hand several times, hefting it as if it were a ball.

Wiping her eyes with her fingers, she said, "Sorry."

"Nothing to be sorry for," he said.

"Believe me, I'm sorry about plenty. Maybe even about talking to you. 'Cause what's the point? College is rough enough without this kind of shi—mess." She wiped her eyes again. "Excuse my language. I just never thought I'd know anyone who was murdered."

Milo pulled a small plastic-wrapped package from a pocket and gave her a tissue. Had he come prepared for tears?

She took it and dabbed, looked around the parking lot. "Can I go, please? I have a two-o'clock all the way on North Campus and my bike's parked over on Gayley."

"Sure, just a couple more questions. What'd you think of the other members of the committee?"

"What do you mean?"

"Were they inquisitional, too?"

"*He* was—the guy, the grad student—I forget his name."

"Casey Locking."

"I guess so. He had a real attitude. Clear agenda."

"Which was?"

"Being Mr. Feminist—probably kissing up to Professor Devane. He impressed me as one of those guys who tries to prove how unsexist he is by dumping on other guys."

She smiled.

"What, Cindy?"

"The funny thing is, when he and Kenny started sounding off against each other it was typical male stuff—no offense. Locking was trying to be Mr. Nonsexist but his style was still male—hostile, aggressive, competitive. Maybe some things are unchangeable. Maybe we should just learn to live with each other."

"As long as the strong don't pummel the weak," said Milo.

"Yes, of course. No one should stand for being victimized."

"Professor Devane was victimized."

She stared at him. A moist streak remained under one eye. "I know. It's terrible. But what can *I* do?"

"Just what you're doing, Cindy. What about the other woman on the committee, Professor Steinberger?"

"She was okay. She really didn't say much. It was clearly Professor Devane's show. I got the feeling she had a personal stake in it."

"Why's that?"

"Because afterward, when I said I wanted to forget the whole thing, she told me I shouldn't retreat from my position, she would support me all the way. And when I said no, she got a little chilly. Distant. As if I'd let her down. I felt rotten on so many levels, just wanted to get out of there and be by myself."

"Did you and she have any contact after that?"

"She called me once at the Theta house. Nice again, just wanting to know how I was doing. She also offered to send me a reading list of books that might help me."

"Feminist books?"

"I guess so, I wasn't really listening. I kind of cut her off."

"Because you didn't trust her?"

"She was using all the right words but I'd had enough."

"What about Kenny?"

"What about him?"

"Did she call him, too?"

"Not that I know. No, I'm sure she didn't because he would have told me. He—" She stopped herself.

"He what, Cindy?"

"Nothing."

"What were you going to say?"

"Nothing. Just that he didn't mention her calling."

"Were you going to say Kenny hated her?"

She looked away. "If you've read the transcripts, I guess that's no big shock. No, he didn't like her one bit. He said she was a—she was manipulative. And a radical feminist—Kenny's kind of conservative politically. And I can't blame him for feeling railroaded. He was already having a hard time at the U, thinking about transferring out. The committee was the final straw."

"Did he blame Dr. Devane for having to transfer?"

"No, he was just generally down on everything."

"Life, in general?" I said. "Or something specific?"

She looked up with alarm. "I know what you're getting at, but it's ridiculous. He'd never touch her. That's not Kenny. And he wasn't even in L.A. the night she was killed. He's in San Diego except on weekends when he drives in to see me. He's working hard to get his life together—he's only nineteen."

"He comes in every weekend?" said Milo.

"Not every, most. And she was killed on a Monday. He's never in town on Monday."

Milo looked down at her and smiled. "Sounds like you've been thinking about his schedule."

"Only after you called. We were really surprised, then we figured you'd learned about the committee and we said, Oh my God, unreal. Because you know, the system. You can get caught up in it, people get abused. I mean, it's so absurd that anyone would connect us to what happened. We're kids, basically. The last time I had anything to do with the police was when that guy came to class and told us about parked cars."

She smiled.

"He had a parrot, that policeman. A trained parrot that could talk. Like, 'Stop, you're under arrest!' and 'You have the right to remain silent.' I think he called him Officer Squawk, or something. Whatever. I really can take that bag."

Milo handed it to her.

"I really need to forget all this, Detective Sturgis. I have to concentrate on my grades because my mom makes sacrifices for me. That's why I didn't go to private college. So, please."

"Sure, Cindy. Thanks for your time." He gave her a card.

"Robbery-homicide," she said, shivering. "What's this for?"

"In case you think of something."

"I won't, believe me." Her small face puckered and I thought she'd cry again. Then she said, "Thanks," and walked away.

* * *

"Cutie pie," said Milo. "I just want to give her milk and cookies, tell her Prince Charming is coming soon and he doesn't have a rap sheet."

"She feels she's found him already."

He shook his head. "She's a little intrapunitive, wouldn't you say?"

"Very. Blaming herself for what happened between her and Kenny Storm, then for complaining."

"Storm," he said. "Smart kid like her hooking up with a dumb guy. What is it, low self-esteem?"

"More interested in Storm, now?"

"Why?"

"His academic career *hasn't* gone well. Meaning he never got to receive the U's concession money. Meaning he could still be angry and unresolved."

"And maybe she's willing to lie for him. Maybe despite what she said, he stayed over one weekend."

"He could have borrowed Cindy's bike," I said. "Or he has one of his own."

"Neither he nor his daddy have returned calls . . . selling real estate in La Jolla. Should be easy enough to find out which company, see if the alibi checks out."

His eyes drifted upward. "Little Cindy. She looks like a fourteen-year-old but talks like an adult. Then again, the sweetheart who threw her baby to the dogs was pretty adorable, too."

9

We drove out of the Village, hugging the eastern edge of the campus and cutting past Sorority Row. Students jogged and strolled and jaywalked with abandon. The spiked tops of the cactus in the Botanical Garden stuck over the iron fence like supplementary security.

I said, "A picture of Hope seems to be taking shape. Brilliant, charismatic, good with people. But able to bend the rules when it suits her, and from what Cindy said, to change faces pretty quickly. Consistent with the little boxes."

A laughing couple around Kenny and Cindy's age darted across the street, holding hands, wrapped up in each other. Milo had to brake hard. They kept going, unaware.

"Ah, love," I said.

"Or too many years on Walkmans and video games. Okay, I'll drop you at home."

"Why don't you let me off here and I'll try to see Professor Steinberger."

"The quiet one?"

"Sometimes the quiet ones have the most to say."

"Okay." He pulled over next to a bus bench. Two Hispanic women in domestic's uniforms were sitting there and they stared at us before looking away.

"Gonna walk home after that?"

"Sure, it's only a couple of miles."

"What an aerobicon . . . listen, if you have time and inclination, I don't mind you talking to the other students involved in the committee, too. Maybe you won't scare them as much as I scared Cindy."

"I thought you did fine with her."

He frowned. "Maybe I shoulda brought a parrot. You up for student interviews?"

"How do I locate them?"

Reaching over to the backseat, he grabbed his briefcase and swung it onto his lap, took out a sheet of paper, and gave it to me.

Xeroxed photo-ID student cards and class schedules. The reproductions were dark and blurred, turning Cindy Vespucci into a brunette. Kenneth Storm had a full face, short hair, and a sad mouth, but that's about all you could say about him.

I folded and pocketed it. "Any rules about how I present myself?"

He thought. "Guess the truth would be fine. Anything that encourages them to talk. They'll probably relate to you better, professorial demeanor and all that."

"Maybe not," I said. "Professors are the ones who fail them."

*   *   *

The tall, white Psychology Tower was on the outer edge of the Science Quad—maybe more than architectural accident—and the brick cube that housed Chemistry was its next-door neighbor.

It had been a long time since I'd been inside the chem building and then only to take an advanced psychopathology course in borrowed classroom space; back when I'd been a grad student, psychology had been the U's most popular major and the lecture halls had overflowed with those seeking self-understanding. Twenty years later, fear of the future was the dominant motive and business administration was king.

Chemistry's halls still oozed the vinegary reek of acetic acid and the walls were toothpaste-green, maybe a bit grimier. No one was in sight but I could hear clinking and splashing behind doors marked LABORATORY.

The directory listed two Steinbergers, Gerald and Julia, both with offices on the third floor. I took the stairs and found Julia's.

The door was open. She was at her desk grading exams with radio soft-rock in the background, a nice-looking woman around thirty wearing a black scoop-necked sweater over a white blouse and gray wool slacks. An amber-and-old-silver necklace that looked Middle Eastern rested on her chest. She had square shoulders, an earnest face that surprised itself by bottoming out in a pointed chin, a serene mouth glossed pink, and shiny brown hair ending at her shoulders, the bangs clipped just above graceful eyebrows. Her eyes were gray, clear and unbothered as they looked up. Beautiful, really. They made her beautiful.

She marked a paper and put it aside. "Yes?"

I told her who I was, trying without success to

make it sound logical, and that I'd come to discuss Hope Devane.

"Oh." Puzzled. "Might I see some identification?" Pleasant voice, Chicago accent.

I showed her the badge. She studied my name for a long time.

"Please," she said, handing it back, and pointing to a chair.

The office was cramped but fresh-smelling, gray-metal University issue brightened by batik wall hangings and folk-art dolls positioned among the books on the shelves. The radio rested on a windowsill behind her, next to a potted coleus. Someone singing about the freedom that love brought.

The exams were stacked high. The one she'd put aside was filled with computations and red question marks. She'd given it a B–. When she saw me looking at it, she covered it with a notebook and turned the stack over just as the phone rang.

"Hi," she said. "Actually not right now." Looking at me. "Maybe in fifteen. I'll come to you." Pretty smile. Blush. "Me, too."

Hanging up, she pushed away from the desk and rested her hands on her lap. "My husband's down the hall. We usually have lunch together."

"If it's a bad time—"

"No, he's got things to do and this shouldn't take long. So, run that by me again, I'm still intrigued. You're on the faculty but you're working with the police department on Hope's murder?"

"I'm on the faculty crosstown, at the med school. I've done forensic work and occasionally the police ask me to consult. Hope Devane's murder is what they call a cold case. No leads, a new detective starting from scratch. Frankly I'm a member of the court of last resort."

"Crosstown." She smiled. "The enemy?"

"I got my doctorate here so it's more of a case of split allegiance."

"How do you cope at football games?"

"I ignore them."

She laughed. "Me, too. Gerry—my husband—has become a football fanatic since we arrived. We used to be at the University of Chicago, which believe me is no great seat of athletic achievement. Anyway, I'm glad the police are still looking into Hope's murder. I'd assumed they'd given up."

"Why's that?"

"Because after the first week or so there was nothing in the news. Isn't it true that the longer a case goes unsolved the less chance there is of success?"

"Generally."

"What's the name of the new detective?"

I told her and she wrote it down.

"Does the fact that he's chosen not to come himself mean anything?"

"It's a combination of time pressure and strategy," I said. "He's working the case alone and he hasn't fared well with the faculty people he's interviewed so far."

"In what way?"

"They treat him as if he's a Neanderthal."

"Is he?"

"Not at all."

"Well," she said, "I suppose as a group, we tend to be intolerant—not that we're really a group. Most of us have nothing in common beyond the patience to endure twenty-plus years of schooling. Hope and I are prime examples of that, so I don't think I'll be of much help."

"She knew you well enough to ask you to be on the Interpersonal Conduct Committee."

She placed her pen on the desk. "The committee. I figured it had to be that. In terms of our relationship, we'd spoken a few times before she asked me to serve but we were far from friends. How much do the police know about the committee?"

"They know its history and the fact that it was disbanded. There are also transcripts of the three cases that were heard. I noticed you didn't participate in the third."

"That's because I resigned," she said. "It's obvious now that the whole thing was a mistake but it took me a while to realize it."

"Mistake in what way?"

"I think Hope's motives were pure but they led her somewhat . . . far afield. I thought it would be an attempt to heal, not create more conflict."

"Did you voice your concerns to her?"

She tightened her lips and gazed up at the ceiling. "No. Hope was a complex person."

"She wouldn't have listened?"

"I don't really know. It was just . . . I don't want to demean the dead. Let's just say she was strong-willed."

"Obsessive?"

"About the mistreatment of women, definitely. Which is fine with me."

Lifting the pen, she tapped one knee. "Sometimes passion blocks out contradictory information. So much so—and this is more your area than mine—that I found myself wondering if she had a personal history of abuse that directed her scholarship."

The quiet one.

"Because of the extent of her passion?" I said.

She shifted in her chair, bit her lip, and nodded. Placed an index finger alongside one smooth cheek.

"I must say I feel uncomfortable suggesting that, because I don't want to trivialize Hope's commitment—to bring it down to the level of personal vindication. I'm a physical chemist, which is about as far as you get from psychoanalysis."

She wheeled back, so her head was inches from the bookshelves. A brownish rag doll's legs extended past her right ear. She pulled it down, sat it in her lap, and played with its black string hair.

"I want you to know that I thought highly of her. She was brilliant, and committed to her ideals. Which is rarer than it should be—maybe I should explain how I got involved with the committee. Because clearly it's not going to just go away."

"Please," I said. "I'd appreciate that."

Taking a deep breath, she stroked the doll. "I began college as a premed and in my sophomore year I volunteered at a battered-women's shelter on the South Side of Chicago. To get brownie points for med school and because both my parents are physicians and old-style liberals and they taught me it was noble to help people. I thought I'd heard everything around the dinner table, but the shelter opened my eyes to a whole new, terrible world. Putting it simply, I was terrified. It was one of the reasons I changed my mind about medicine."

Her fingers parted the doll's hair. "The women I worked with—the ones who'd gotten past the fear and the denial and were in touch with what was being done to them—had the same look I sometimes saw in Hope's eyes. Part injury, part rage—I can only call it ferocious. In Hope's case it was strikingly discrepant from her usual manner."

"Which was?"

"Cool and collected. Very cool and collected."

"In control."

"Very much so. She was a leader, had tremendous force of personality. But when we discussed abuse, I saw that look in her eyes. Not always, but frequently enough to remind me of the women at the shelter."

She gave a shy smile. "No doubt I'm overinterpreting."

"Did she ask you to serve because of your experience at the shelter?"

She nodded. "We first met at a faculty tea, one of those dreadful things at the beginning of the academic year where everyone pretends to get acquainted? Gerry had gone off to talk sports with some guys and Hope came up to me. She was also alone."

"Her husband wasn't there?"

"No. She said he never came to parties. She certainly didn't know me, I'd just arrived. I didn't know who she was but I had noticed her. Because of her clothes. Expensive designer suit, good jewelry, great makeup. Like some of the girls I'd known from Lake Forest—heiresses. You don't see much of that on campus. We got to talking and I told her about the shelter."

She moved in a way that pinched the doll's soft torso and caused its head to pitch forward.

"The funny thing is, all those years I hadn't talked about it. Even to my husband." Smile. "And as you can tell, I have no problem talking. But there I was at a party, with a virtual stranger, getting into things I'd forgotten about—horrendous things. I actually had to go into a corner to dry my eyes. Looking back, I think Hope drew the memories out of me."

"How?"

"By listening the right way. Don't you people call it active listening?" She smiled again. "Just what you're doing right now. I learned about that, too, at the shelter. I suppose anyone can grasp the rudiments but there are few virtuosos."

"Like Hope."

She laughed. "There, just what you're doing: bouncing things back. It works even when you know what's going on, doesn't it?"

I smiled and stroked my chin and said, "Sounds like you think it's effective," in a stagy voice.

She laughed again, got up, and closed the door. She was shapely, and taller than I'd thought: five-eight or -nine, a good deal of it legs.

"Yes," she said, sitting down again and crossing them. "She was a brilliant listener. Had a way of . . . moving in. Not just emotionally, actually getting close physically—inching toward you. But without seeming intrusive. Because she made you feel as if you were the most important person in the world."

"Charisma and passion."

"Yes. Like a good evangelist."

The legs uncrossed. "This must sound so strange. First I tell you I didn't know her, and then I go on as if I did. But everything I've said is just an impression. She and I never got close, though at first I thought she *wanted* a friend."

"Why's that?"

"The day after the tea she called me saying she'd really enjoyed meeting me, would I like to have coffee in the Faculty Club. I was ambivalent. I liked her but I *didn't* want to talk about the shelter again. Even so, I accepted. Determined to keep my mouth shut." The doll bounced. "Unbelievably, I ended up talking again. About the *worst* cases I'd seen: women who'd been brutalized beyond comprehension. That was the first time I saw the ferociousness in her eyes."

She looked at the doll, put it back on the shelf. "All this can't possibly help you."

"It might."

"How?"

"By illuminating her personality," I said. "Right now, there's little else to go on."

"That assumes her personality had something to do with her being murdered."

"You don't think it did?"

"I have no idea. When I found out she'd been killed, my first assumption was that her politics had angered some psychotic."

"A stranger?"

She stared at me. "You're not actually saying it had anything to do with the committee?"

"We don't have enough information to say anything, but is it impossible?"

"Highly improbable, I'd say. They were just kids."

"Things got pretty rough. Especially with the Storm boy."

"Yes, that one did have a temper. And a foul mouth. But the transcripts may be misleading—make him out worse than he was."

"In what way?"

She thought. "He was . . . he seemed to me more bark than bite. One of those blustery kids who throws tantrums and then gets it off his chest? And the accounts of the murder made it sound like a stalking. I just can't see a kid doing that. Then again, I don't have kids, so what do I know?"

"When Hope asked you to serve, what specifics did she give you?"

"She reassured me it wouldn't take much time. She said it was provisional but certain to be made permanent and that it had strong backing from the administration. Which, of course, wasn't true. In fact, she made it sound as if the administration had *asked* her to set it up. She told me we'd be focusing on offenses that didn't qualify for criminal prosecution and that our goal would be early detection—what she called primary prevention."

"Catching problems early."

"Catching problems early in order to avoid the kinds of things I'd seen at the shelter." Shaking her head. "She knew what button to push."

"So she misled you."

"Oh, yes," she said, sadly. "I suppose she felt a straightforward approach wouldn't have worked. And maybe it wouldn't have. I certainly don't enjoy sitting in judgment of people."

"From the transcripts, the other member, Casey Locking, didn't mind judging."

"Yes, he was quite . . . enthusiastic. Doctrinaire, really. Not that I fault him. How sincere can any student be when collaborating with his faculty supervisor? Power is power."

"Did Hope say why she appointed him?"

"No. She did tell me one member would have to be a man. To avoid the appearance of a war between the sexes."

"How did she react when you resigned?"

"She didn't."

"Not at all?"

"Not at all. I called her office and left a message on her machine, explaining that I just didn't feel comfortable continuing, and thanking her for thinking of me. She never returned the call. We never spoke again. I assumed she was angry . . . and now we're judging her. That bothers me. Because no matter what she did I believe she had good intentions and what happened to her is an atrocity."

She got up and showed me the door.

"I'm sorry, I can't talk about this anymore." Her hand twisted the knob and the door opened. The gray eyes had narrowed with strain.

"Thanks for your time," I said, "and sorry to dredge up unpleasantness."

"Maybe it needed dredging. . . . The whole thing is *sickening*. Such a loss. Not that one person's life is worth more than another's. But Hope was impressive—she had spine. Especially impressive if I'm right that she had been abused, because that would mean she'd made it. Had summoned the strength to help others."

She bit her lip again. "She *was* strong. The *last* person you'd think of as a victim."

10

It was 2:00 P.M. when I stepped outside.

I thought of the way Hope had elicited Julia Steinberger's tears at the faculty tea by stoking old memories.

A good listener—Cindy Vespucci said the same thing.

But she hadn't handled Kenny Storm—or the other two male students—very skillfully.

Able to deal with women but not with men?

Most probably a man had executed her—I realized that's how I thought of the murder. An execution.

Which man?

Long-suffering husband pushed to the brink? A deranged stranger?

Or someone midway between those two extremes on the intimacy scale?

Crossing the quad, I sat down at a stone table and checked the class schedules Milo had given me.

Unless they were playing hooky, Patrick Huang was in the middle of a thermodynamics class, Deborah Brittain was contending with Math for Humanities Majors, and Reed Muscadine, the theater-arts grad student, was participating in something called Performance Seminar 201B a half-mile away in Mac-Manus Hall on the north end of the campus. But Tessa Bowlby's Psychology of Perception class would be letting out in fifteen minutes in the Psych Tower.

I studied the picture of the young woman who had accused Reed Muscadine of date rape. Very short dark hair and a thin, slightly weak-jawed face. Even allowing for the poor photocopy, she looked discouraged.

The drooping eyes of someone much older.

But not because of the encounter with Muscadine. The picture had been taken at the beginning of the school year, months prior. I had a quick cup of vending-machine coffee and returned to the Psychology Tower to see if life had knocked her even lower.

Her class let out five minutes early and students gushed into the hall like dam water. She wasn't hard to spot, heading for the exit alone, hauling a denim bag bulging with books. She stopped short when I said, "Ms. Bowlby?"

Her arm dropped and the bag's weight yanked down her shoulder. Despite the tentative chin and a few pimples, she was waifishly attractive with very white skin and enormous blue eyes. Her hair was dyed absolute black, cut unevenly—either carelessly or with great intention. Her nose was pink at the tip and nostrils—a cold or allergies. She wore a baggy black raglan sweater with one sleeve starting to unravel, old black pipestem jeans torn at the knees, and lace-up leather boots with thick soles and toes scuffed fuzzy.

She backed up against the wall to let classmates pass. I showed her my ID and began my introduction.

"No," she said, waving one narrow hand, frantically. "*Please.*" Pleading in a hoarse voice. Her eyes darted to the exit sign.

"Ms. Bowlby—"

"No!" she said, louder. "Leave me alone! I have nothing to say!"

She shot for the exit. I hung back for a moment, then followed, watching from a distance as she hurried out the main doors of the tower, racing, nearly tumbling, down the front steps, toward the inverted fountain that fronted the tower. The fountain was dry and streams of students converged near the dirty black hole before spreading out and radiating across campus like a giant ant trail.

She ran clumsily, struggling with the heavy bag. A thin, fragile-looking figure, so emaciated her buttocks failed to fill out the narrow jeans and the denim flapped with each stride.

Drugs? Stress? Anorexia? Illness?

As I wondered, she slipped into the throng and became one of many.

Her anxiety—panic, really—made me want to talk to the man she'd accused.

I recalled the details of the complaint: movie and dinner, heavy petting. Tessa claiming forced entry; Muscadine, consensual sex.

The kind of thing that could never be proved, either way.

AIDS testing for him. She'd already gotten tested. Negative. So far.

But now she was ghostly pale, thin, fatigued.

The disease took time to incubate. Maybe her luck had changed.

That could account for the panic . . . but she was still enrolled in classes.

Maybe Hope Devane had been a source of support. Now, with Hope dead and her own health in question, was she overwhelmed?

The testing had been done at the Student Health Center. Getting records without legal grounds would be impossible.

Having a look at Muscadine seemed more important than ever, but the acting seminar was one of those weekly things that lasted four hours and was only half-over.

In the meantime, I'd try the others. Patrick Huang would be free in thirty minutes, Deborah Brittain soon after. Huang's class was nearby, in the Engineering Building. Back to the Science Quad. As I started to turn, a deep voice behind me said, "Sleuthing on campus, Detective?"

Casey Locking stood several steps above me, looking amused. His long hair was freshly moussed, and he wore the same long leather coat, jeans, and motorcycle boots. Black T-shirt under the coat. The skull ring was still there, too, despite his remark about getting rid of it.

Glinting in the sunlight, the death's-head grin wide, almost alive.

In the ringed hand was a cigarette, in the other an attaché case, olive leather, gold-embossed CDL over the clasp. The fingers sandwiching the cigarette twitched and smoke puffed and rose.

"I'm not a detective," I said.

That made him blink, but nothing else on his face moved.

I climbed to his level and showed him my consultant's badge. His mouth pursed as he studied it.

So Seacrest hadn't told him.

Meaning they weren't confidants?

"Ph.D. in what?"

"Psychology."

"Really." He flicked ashes. "For the police?"

"Sometimes I consult to the police."

"What exactly do you do?"

"It varies from case to case."

"Crime-scene analysis?"

"All kinds of things."

My ambiguity didn't seem to bother him. "Interesting. Did they assign you to Hope's murder because she was a psychologist or because the case is perceived as psychologically complex?"

"Both."

"Police psychologist." He took a long, hard drag, holding the smoke in. "The career opportunities they never tell you about in grad school. How long have you been doing it?"

"A few years."

White vapors emerged from his nostrils. "Around here all they talk about is pure academics. They measure their success by the number of tenure-track types they place. All the tenure-track jobs are disappearing but they groom us for them, anyway. So much for reality-testing, but I guess the academic world's never been noted for having a good grip on reality. Do you think Hope's murder will ever be solved?"

"Don't know. How about you?"

"Doesn't look promising," he said. "Which stinks. . . . Is that big detective on the ball?"

"Yes."

He smoked some more and scratched his upper lip. "Police psychologist. Actually, that appeals to me. Dealing with the big issues: crime, deviance, the nature of evil. Since the murder I've thought a lot about evil."

"Come up with any insights?"

He shook his head. "Students aren't permitted to have insights."

"Have you found a new advisor yet?"

"Not yet. I need someone who won't make me start all over or dump scut work on me. Hope was great that way. If you did your job, she treated you like an adult."

"Laissez-faire?"

"When it was deserved." He ground out the cigarette. "She knew the difference between good and bad. She was a fine human being and whoever destroyed her should experience an excruciatingly slow, immensely bloody, *inconceivably* painful death."

His lips turned upward but this time you couldn't call the end product a smile. He put down his attaché case, and reaching under the coat, pulled out a hardpack of Marlboros.

"But that's unlikely to happen, right? Because even if somehow they do catch him, there'll be legal loopholes, procedural calisthenics. Probably some expert from *our* field claiming the prick suffered from psychosis or an impulse-control disorder no one's ever heard of before. That's why I like the idea of what you do. Being on the right side. My research area's self-control. Petty stuff—free-feeding in rats versus sched-

ules of reinforcement. But maybe one of these days I'll
be able to relate it to the real world."

"Self-control and crime detection?"

"Why not? Self-control's an integral part of civili-
zation. *The* integral component. Babies are born cute
and cuddly and *amoral*. And it's certainly not hard to
train them to be *im*moral, is it?"

He made a pistol with his free hand. "Everyone's
making such a big deal about ten-year-olds with Uzis
but it's just Fagin and the street rats with a little tech-
nology thrown in, right?"

"Lack of self-control," I said.

"On a societal level. Take away external control
mechanisms and the internalization process—conscience development—is immobilized and what you
get are millions of savages running around giving free
rein to their impulses. Like the piece of shit who
killed Hope. So goddamn *stupid*!"

He produced a lighter and ignited another cigarette. Slightly shaky hands. He jammed them in the
pockets of his coat.

"I tell you, I'd study real life if I could, but I'd be in
school for the rest of my life and that's a no-brainer.
Hope steered me right, said not to try for the Nobel
Prize, pick something doable, get my union card, and
move on."

He sucked smoke. "Finding another advisor won't
be easy. I'm considered the departmental fascist because I can't stand platitudes and I believe in the
power of discipline."

"And Hope was okay with that."

"Hope was the *ultimate* scholar-slash-good-mother:
tough, honest, secure enough to let you go your own
way once you proved you weren't full of shit. She

looked at everything with a fresh eye, refused to do or be what was expected of her. So they killed her."

"They?"

"They, he, some drooling, psychopathic, totally fucked-up savage."

"Any theories about the specific motive?"

He glanced back at the glass doors of the tower. "I've spent a *long* time thinking about it and all I've come up with are mental pretzels. Finally I realized it's a waste of energy because I have no data, just my feelings. And my feelings were knocking me low. That's really why it took so long to get back to my research. That's why I couldn't even go near my data til last night. But now it's time to get back in gear. Hope would want that. She had no patience for excuses."

"Whose idea was it to barter data for car care?" I said.

He stared at me. "I called Phil up, he said he was having trouble getting the car started, so I offered to help."

"So you knew him before."

"Just from working with Hope. Basically, Phil's asocial. . . . Well, good talking to you."

He picked up the attaché case and started up the stairs.

I said, "What's your view of the Interpersonal Conduct Committee?"

He stopped, smiled. "That, again. My *view*? I thought it was an excellent idea with insufficient enforcement power."

"Some people believe the committee was a mistake."

"Some people believe quality of life means anarchy."

"So you think it should have been allowed to continue."

"Sure, but what chance was there of that? That rich snot's father shut it down because this place operates on the same principles as any other political system: money and power. If the girl he harassed had been the one with the fat-cat daddy, you can believe the committee would be alive and healthy."

He smoked the cigarette down to the filter, looked at it, snapped it away. "The point is, women will always be physically weaker than men and their safety can't be left up to the good graces of anyone with a penis. The only way to simulate equity is through rules and consequences."

"Discipline."

"Better believe it." He smoothed a leather lapel. "You're asking me about the committee because you think it had something to do with Hope's death. One of those chickenshit little weenies getting back at her. But like I said, they were all cowards."

"Cowards commit murder."

"But I sat on the committee, too, and I'm obviously intact."

Same logic Cruvic had used, talking about abortion protest.

"Let me ask you something else," I said. "Did Hope ever mention being abused, herself?"

The lapel bunched as his hand closed tight around the leather. "No. Why?"

"Sometimes people's work is directed by personal experience."

The black brows dipped low and his eyes got cold. "You want to reduce her achievements to *psychopathology*?"

"I want to learn as much as I can about her. Did she ever talk about her past?"

Uncurling his fingers, he let his arms drop very slowly. Then he raised them very quickly, almost a martial-arts move. Folding them across his chest, as if warding off attack.

"She talked about her work. That's all. Whatever personal things I was able to infer came from that."

"What did you infer?"

"That she was incredibly intelligent and focused and cared deeply about what she was doing. That's why she took me on. Focus is my thing. I get my teeth in and don't let go."

He smiled, showing white enamel. "She appreciated the fact that I was willing to come out and say how I really felt. That I believed people can't just follow their impulses. Around here, that's still heresy."

"What about her other student, Mary Ann Gonsalvez?"

"What about her?"

"Is she also focused?"

"Don't know, we didn't see each other much. Good talking to you, got to run an experiment. If you ever do find the piece of shit, convict him, sentence him to die, invite me to San Quentin to jam the hypodermic into his veins."

Giving a choppy salute, he vaulted up the steps to the tower, shoved at one of the heavy glass doors. As it swung open, I caught a momentary flash of reflection. The delicate mouth curving, but hard to read.

11

Like Cruvic, he'd talked about Hope with passion. Wet eyes notwithstanding, her husband hadn't.

Leading her to turn elsewhere?

Love, sex, stab in the back.

Seacrest had no history of violence, but men who killed their wives often didn't. And like Seacrest, they tended to be middle-aged.

As for the lover being left unharmed, that was also typical: jealous husbands targeting their wives, sparing the lover unless he happened to get in the way.

But if Locking had been Hope's lover, would Seacrest have maintained any connection to him?

I thought about the interplay between the two men. No signs of hostility, but formal.

Then a discrepancy hit me: Last night, Locking had called Seacrest Professor. Today it was *Phil*.

Did any of it matter?

I bought another cup of cardboard-flavored coffee

and drank it on my way over to the Engineering Building, wondering what kind of surprises a chat with Patrick Huang would bring.

He was flustered when I showed up at his locker but offered no resistance when I suggested we talk.

We found a bench on the west end of the quad and I offered to get him coffee.

"No, thanks, I'm caffeined enough. NoDoz. Exams."

He simulated a tremoring hand and frowned.

He was five-ten and heavy-set with a smooth square face and shoulder-length hair parted in the middle. His wrinkled T-shirt said STONE TEMPLE PILOTS and he wore it over paisley cutoffs and rubber beach thongs. A couple of books were sandwiched under his arm, both on thermodynamics.

"Thanks for talking to me, Patrick."

He looked down at the bench. "I figured somebody would finally get to me."

"Why's that?"

"After what happened to Professor Devane, I figured the committee was bound to come up. I'm surprised it took this long."

He fidgeted. "Did they send a psychologist because they think I'm nuts?"

"No. I do work for the police and they thought I could be helpful on this case."

He thought about that. "I think I'll get a burger, okay?"

"Sure."

Leaving his books behind, he went to one of the snack bars and came back with a waxed-paper wad, a box of crinkled fries buried under a blob of ketchup, and a large orange soda.

"I have an uncle who's a psychologist," he said, settling. "Robert Chan? Works for the prison system?"

"Don't know him," I said.

"My dad's a lawyer." He unwrapped the wad. The paper was translucent with grease, and cheese dripped over the sides of the hamburger. Biting down hard, he chewed fast and swallowed. "My dad was mega-pissed about the committee. That I didn't tell him about it. At the time I thought it was a bad joke, why get into it? But after I heard about Professor Devane I said *uh*-oh, I'm screwed." He rolled his eyes.

"Trouble with your father."

"He's traditional—big shame on the family and all that." He took a huge bite out of the burger, and ate stoically while gazing across the quad.

"Not that I did anything wrong. Everything I said at the hearing was true. That girl's a stone racist. I never hassled her, she used me. But Dad . . ."

He whistled and shook his head. "After he chewed me out and reduced my credit-card limit for six months, he said I should expect trouble because the police were bound to look into Professor Devane's background. When it didn't happen, I thought, whew, lucky break."

Looking around some more, he dragged his eyes back to me. "Wrong again. Anyway, I've got no real problem because on the night she was killed I was at a big family get-together. Grandparents' fiftieth anniversary. We all went out to Lawry's, on La Cienega. Prime rib and all the trimmings. I was there the whole time, from eight to after eleven-thirty, sitting right next to Dad, Numbah One Son, along with about a

hundred relatives. I've even got documented proof:
My cousin took pictures. Lots of pictures, big surprise,
huh?''

He shot me an angry smile, placed his front teeth
over his lower lip, and wiggled an index finger. "Ah
so. Say cheese with *wontons, crick crick.*"

I didn't respond.

"Want some?" he said, pointing to the fries.

"No thanks."

He put his mouth to the straw and filled it with
orange soda. "You want the pictures, I'll have my dad
send them. He actually put them in his office vault."
He laughed. "Now can I go?"

"Any thoughts about Professor Devane?"

"Nope."

"What about the committee?"

"I told you, big joke."

"How so?"

"Hauling people in like some kind of kangaroo
court. One person's word against the other's. I don't
know how many other guys got hassled, but if their
cases were as stupid as mine, you've got plenty of
pissed-off people. Maybe one of them offed Professor
Devane."

"But you have an alibi."

He lowered the drink to the bench. It hit hard and
some soda splashed onto the stone. "Thank God I *do*.
Because for weeks after the hearing I was pissed at
her. But you know us good little Chinese boys—play
with computers, never get violent."

I said nothing.

"Anyway, I'm over the whole thing and to prove it,
I see that girl on campus all the time, just walk by,
shine her on. And that's the way I eventually felt

about Professor Devane. Forget about her, get on with things."

"So you felt victimized," I said.

"Yeah, but it was partly my own fault. I should have checked with Dad first before showing up. He told me she had no right to do that to me."

"Why'd you go?"

"A letter comes to you on official University stationery, what would you do? How many other guys were involved?"

"Sorry," I said, "I'm not talking to them about you, either."

He blinked. "Yeah, okay, better to forget the whole thing."

He picked up the books and stood. "That's all I've got to say. I'm probably in trouble already for talking to you without checking with Dad. You want the photos, contact him. Allan D. Huang. Curtis, Ballou, Semple, and Huang." He shot off a downtown address on Seventh Street and a phone number and I copied them down.

"Anything else you want to tell me, Patrick?"

"About the committee?"

"The committee, Professor Devane, Deborah Brittain, anything."

"What's to tell? Devane was hard as nails. Good at twisting words. And her agenda was clear: All men are scum."

"What about the other judges?"

"Mostly they just sat there like dummies. It was her show—and that's what it was, a show. Like one of those improv things where they call you up from the audience and make a fool out of you. Only this was real."

His free hand balled. "She actually *asked* me if I'd gone to college for the purpose of finding women to harass. All because I helped that girl. Sucks, huh? Well, bye, time to hitch up the ricksha."

Deborah Brittain's math class was long over and her schedule said she had nothing more today. She lived off-campus, in Sherman Oaks, so I hiked to North Campus to find Reed Muscadine.

MacManus Hall was an unobtrusive pink building with auditoriums on the ground floor. Performance Seminar 201B, now two-thirds over, was held in the Wiley Theater at the back. The blond maple double doors were unlocked and I slipped through. Lights off, maybe fifty rows of padded seats facing a blue-lit stage.

As my eyes adjusted, I made out a dozen or so people, scattered around the room. No one turned as I walked toward the front.

Up on the stage were two people, sitting on hard wooden chairs, hands on knees, staring into each other's eyes.

I took an aisle seat in the third row and watched. The couple onstage didn't budge, the sparse audience remained inert, and the theater was silent.

Two more minutes of nothing.

Five minutes, six . . . group hypnosis?

Tough job market for actors so maybe the U was training them to be department-store mannequins.

Five more minutes passed before a man in the front row stood up and snapped his fingers. Pudgy and bald, tiny eyeglasses, black turtleneck, baggy green cords.

The couple got up and walked offstage in opposite directions. Another pair came on. Women. They sat.

Assumed the position.

More nothing.

My eyes were accustomed to the darkness and I scanned the audience, trying to guess which young man was Muscadine. Hopeless. I looked at my watch. Over an hour to go and spending it in Static Heaven was threatening to put me to sleep.

I walked quietly to the front row and sat down next to the bald finger-snapper.

He gave me a sidelong look, then ignored me. Up close I saw a little patch of hair under his lower lip. What jazz musicians used to call a honey mop.

Taking out my LAPD badge, I flexed it so the plastic coating caught stage light.

He turned again.

"I'm looking for Reed Muscadine," I whispered.

He returned his eyes to the stage, where the two women continued to simulate paralysis.

I put the badge away and crossed my legs.

The bald man turned to me again, glaring.

I smiled.

He hooked a thumb toward the rear of the theater and got up.

But instead of walking, he stood there, hands on hips, staring down at me.

A few eyes from the audience drifted toward me, too. The turtlenecked man snapped his fingers and they sat straighter.

He hooked his thumb, again.

I got up and left. To my surprise he followed me, catching up out in the hall.

"I'm Professor Dirkhoff. What the hell's going on?"

His chin hairs were ginger, striped with white, as were the few left on his head. He scowled and the honey mop tilted forward like a collection of tiny bayonets.

"I'm looking for—"

"I heard what you said. Why?"

Before I could answer, he said, "*Well?*" Stretching the word theatrically.

"It's about Professor Hope Devane's murd—"

"*That?* What does Reed have to do with *that*?" One hand flew up to his face and the knuckles rested under the chin, socratically.

"We're talking to students who knew Professor Devane and he's one of them."

"There must be hundreds," he said. "What a waste of time. And it doesn't permit you to barge in here, unannounced."

"Sorry for interrupting. I'll wait til after class."

"Then you'll be wasting your time. Reed's not here."

"Okay, thanks." I turned and walked away. When I'd taken three steps, he said, "I mean, he's not here at all."

"Not in class or not in school?"

"Both. He dropped out a month ago. I'm quite miffed—more than miffed. Our acting program is extremely selective and we expect our students to finish no matter what the reason."

"What was his reason?"

He turned his back on me and headed back to the swinging doors. Placing one hand on blond wood, he gave a pitying smile.

"He got a *job*."

"What kind of job?"

Long, deep breath. "One of those *soap* operas. A serious mistake on his part."

"Why's that?"

"The boy has talent but he needs seasoning. Soon he'll be driving a Porsche and wondering why he feels so empty. Like everyone else in this town."

12

Back home a note on the fridge said, "How about we eat in? Went for provisions with Handsome, back by six."

At five-thirty Milo called and I pulled out my notes and got ready to report on the day's interviews. But he broke in:

"Got a response to my teletype. Las Vegas Homicide has a cold case that matches: twenty-three-year-old call girl, found on a dark side street near her apartment. Stabbed in the heart, groin, and back, in that order. Under a tree, no less. A month before Hope. They've been figuring it for a lust-psycho. Working girls get killed all the time there. This girl danced, in addition to hooking, had been in a topless show at the Palm Princess casino last year. But recently she'd been working the pits as a freelance. Two, three hundred a trick."

"So why was she found on the street?"

"The theory was she hitched up with the wrong john and he killed her either on the way over to party at her place or afterward. Maybe she was walking him out to his car and he surprised her with the knife. Or maybe she hadn't made him happy enough or they couldn't agree on price and he left mad."

"Any physical resemblance to Hope?"

"From the photo they faxed me, no, other than they were both good-looking. This girl—Mandy Wright's her name—looks gorgeous, actually. But dark-haired. And twenty-three makes her a lot younger than Hope. And clearly no professor. But given the wound pattern, we may have a traveling psycho, so I think I'd better concentrate on finding out if any other homicides around the country match. For all her controversy, the good professor may very well have been the victim of a nutcase stranger. I'm planning to fly out to Vegas tonight, play show-me-yours-and-I'll-show-you-mine." He coughed. "So, what were you saying?"

Before I could tell him, Robin came through the door, holding a grocery bag and Spike's leash. Her color was high and she was smiling as she waved. She put the bag down and kissed me.

I mouthed, "Milo."

"Say hi." She left to change.

I relayed the message, then told him all of it: the conversations with Julia Steinberger and Casey Locking, Tessa Bowlby's panic, Patrick Huang's anger and alleged alibi, Reed Muscadine dropping out to take the acting job.

"Bottom line: Hope made a strong impression on everyone. Though if it is a traveling serial, that's probably no longer relevant."

"The Bowlby girl—was she really scared?"

"Petrified. Pale and skinny and weak-looking, too, so I wondered if Muscadine's AIDS test might have come back positive. And if he dropped out 'cause he's sick. Or maybe it was just because he got the acting job. But what's the difference?"

"Don't go around feeling useless, yet. Mandy Wright changes things but I can't afford to eliminate anyone or anything, at this point. Just because it looks like a psycho, doesn't mean it was a stranger. Maybe Hope and Mandy knew the same psycho."

"A call girl and a professor?"

"This professor may turn out to be different," he said. "So I'm still gonna talk to Kenny Storm and I'm sure as hell gonna verify the Huang boy's alibi. And if you don't mind talking to the other two girls, I'd appreciate it. Something else: Before Vegas called I was looking into Lawyer Barone's recent cases and Hope's name doesn't come up in any of them. So what did he pay Hope for?"

"Something she didn't want publicized?"

"That's the only thing I can think of. Now, Barone does lots of porno defense, mostly out of his San Francisco office, and porno's something a call girl like Mandy could get involved with. But as to Hope's role, I just can't put it together."

"Barone could have been looking for academic and feminist credentials to shore up the defense," I said.

"Then why no record of her on the cases?"

"Maybe Barone hired her to write a report but didn't like the end product. It's happened to me."

"Could be. Whatever. I'm just about to put in my tenth call to the good barrister. And I'd still like to learn more about Dr. Cruvic. The whole consulting thing is interesting—all that money."

Robin returned to the kitchen and began heating water.

I said, "In terms of Cruvic, I can check out the Women's Health Center in Santa Monica. Got an address?"

"No, sorry. Okay, thanks, Alex. Off to Burbank airport."

"Have a good trip. Maybe you can get in some gambling."

"On the taxpayers' time? Tsk-tsk. Anyway, games of chance aren't my thing. Randomness scares me."

When I put down the phone Robin was slicing onions, tomatoes, and celery, and a pot of spaghetti approached a boil on the stove.

"Gambling?" she said.

"Milo's going to Vegas. He found a murder there that matches Hope's."

I told her the details. The knife stopped.

"If it's a nut," she said, "there could be others."

"He's checking around the country."

"So ugly," she said. "That Women's Health Center you mentioned. Holly Bondurant used to be involved in a place in Santa Monica. I know because she did a benefit concert a few years ago and I set up her twelve-string. What's the connection between the center and the murder?"

"Probably nothing, but Milo got interested because Hope met a Beverly Hills gynecologist named Cruvic there. She ended up consulting to Cruvic's private practice—counseling patients undergoing fertility procedures. We went over to see him this morning and Milo wondered if there was something going on between him and Hope."

"Why?"

"Because he spoke of her with such passion. And her marriage seems somewhat passionless, so the obvious question came up. You know how thorough Milo is. Even with this new lead, he wants to clear everything."

She put the knife down, went to the phone, and punched numbers.

"Holly? It's Robin Castagna. Hi. Yes, it has been. Fine, great. And with you? Good. How's Joaquin, he must be what—fourteen . . . you're kidding! Listen, Holly, I don't know if you can help me, but . . ."

After she hung up, she said, "She'll meet you tomorrow at nine A.M. Cafe Alligator."

"Thanks."

"It's the least I can do."

Later, during dinner, she pushed food around her plate and her wineglass went untouched.

"What's the matter?" I said.

"I don't know. All the things you've been involved in, and this one seems to be getting to me."

"There is a special cruelty to it. Someone that bright and talented, cut off like that."

"Maybe that's it. Or maybe I'm just sick and tired of women being killed because they're women."

She reached across the table, grabbed my hand, and squeezed it hard.

"It wears on you, Alex. Looking over your shoulder, being told it's your responsibility to be vigilant. I know men are the usual victims of violence but they're almost always the victimizers. I guess nowadays everyone's at risk. The world dividing up into predators and prey—what's happening? Are we returning to the jungle?"

"I'm not sure we ever got out," I said. "I worry about you all the time. Especially when you're out at night alone. I never say anything because I figure you can handle yourself and I don't think you want to hear it."

She picked up her wineglass, studied it, drank.

"I didn't tell Holly what you were up to, just that you were my guy, a psychologist, wanted to learn about the center. She's a sixties type, might have gotten scared away by the word 'police.' "

"I'll deal with it." I touched her hand. "I like being your guy."

"I like it, too."

Looking down at her untouched food, she said, "I'll refrigerate this, maybe you'll want a late snack."

I started to clear. She put a hand on my shoulder.

"If you're up for it, why don't we take Spike for a walk in the canyon. It's still light out."

13

Cafe Alligator was a storefront in an old building on Broadway, central Santa Monica, ten blocks from the beach. The bricks had been painted swamp-green and a stoned-looking saurian coiled above a black sign that said ESPENSIVE ESPRESSO. CHEAP EATS.

Inside were walls of the same algae tint, four tables covered with yellow oilcloth, a pastry case/takeout counter backed by shelves of coffee and tea for sale. A fat man with a bullet-skull roasted beans with the intensity of a concert pianist. Low-volume reggae music came from ceiling speakers.

Last night I'd played Holly Bondurant's last LP, *Polychrome.* Fifteen-year-old album but I recognized her right away.

In the jacket photo, her hair had been strawberry blond, waist-length, half-concealing a beautiful Celtic face. Now it was short and blond-gray, and she'd put on thirty pounds. But her face was still smooth and youthful.

She wore a red velvet maxidress, black vest, lace-up boots, onyx necklace. A floppy black-velvet hat rested on an empty chair.

"Alex?" She smiled, stayed seated, gave me her hand, and looked at a half-filled coffee mug. "Pardon my starting without you but I need my fix. Care for a cup?"

"Please."

She waved at the fat man. He filled a cup and brought it over. "Anything else, Holly?"

"Something to eat, Alex? Great muffins."

"A muffin's fine."

"What's good today, Jake?"

"Cranberry," said the fat man, almost grudgingly. "Orange-raisin and chocolate-chocolate-chip aren't bad, either."

"Bring an assortment, please." She faced me. "It was nice hearing from Robin, too, after all these years. She used to work on all my instruments."

Her voice was melodious and her eyes crinkled when she smiled. She talked with every muscle of her face—that animated manner you see in actresses and others who live off public adulation.

"She told me."

"She's still doing luthiery, right?"

"Very actively."

Jake brought my coffee and the pastry basket and slunk back to his beans.

She picked up a cranberry muffin and nibbled. "You're a psychologist."

I nodded.

"The center can always use mental-health people.

Times are rough financially and we get fewer and fewer volunteers. It's good of you to inquire."

"Actually," I said, "that's not what I came to talk to you about."

"Oh?" She put the muffin down.

"Sometimes I consult to the police. Right now I'm working on a murder case. Hope Devane."

She moved back. Her eyes lacked the capacity to harden, but there was injury in them—trust betrayed.

"The police," she said.

"I'm sorry," I said. "There was no intention to mislead. But the case remains unsolved and I've been asked to learn anything I can about her. We know she volunteered at the center."

She said nothing. Jake picked up the tension from across the room and stopped grinding.

"Did you ever meet her?" I said.

She studied the muffin's golden-brown surface. Turned it over. Smiled at Jake and he resumed his work.

"What do you know about the center?" she said.

"Not much."

"It was established so poor women could have access to basic health care: prenatal counseling, nutrition, breast exams and Pap smears, family planning. It used to be part of the University med school rotation but that ended a long time ago and we had to depend upon volunteers. I did a few concerts for them, helped them get stuff."

"Supplies?"

"Supplies, donations. They still think of me as someone with connections. Sometimes I can actually accomplish something. Last week I heard of an agent who's redoing his office and managed to get some of his old furniture."

She looked at the pastry case.

Jake said, "Copacetic?"

She smiled again and turned back to me. "I met Hope a couple of times, but she really wasn't involved. Though we thought she'd be. The first time I saw her was at last year's fund-raiser. We had a variety show at the Aero Theater and a buffet afterward at Le Surph. She bought a five-hundred-dollar ticket that entitled her to a whole table but she said she had no one to bring so we put her on the dais. Because of her credentials. She sounded like someone we could have used. And she impressed a lot of people, with her intelligence and her personality—very dynamic. Shortly after, someone sponsored her for the board and we voted her in. But she never ended up contributing much."

She finger-combed her hair and drummed the table.

"I guess what I'm saying is what happened to her was a horror but she had very little to do with the center and I'm worried about getting bad PR."

"No reason you should get any," I said. "It's just background stuff, trying to understand her. Why didn't she contribute more?"

She took a long time to answer. "She wasn't . . . how can I say this . . . at the fund-raiser she had ideas. Talked about bringing in other psychologists, grad students from the University, developing a volunteer mental-health program. Her qualifications were fantastic and the person who sponsored her said she was dynamite. She showed up for the next board meeting, came around for a few weeks, counseled a few patients. Then she just stopped. Her book was out and I guess she was too busy. None of the programs got activated."

She ate more muffin, chewing slowly, without pleasure.

"So she got too busy," I said.

"Look," she said, "I don't enjoy judging other people. Especially someone who's dead."

"Was the person who sponsored her Dr. Cruvic?"

"You know Mike?"

"I met him once."

"Yes, it was him. Which was another reason she had credibility. He's been one of our most active board members. Really gives his time."

"So he and Hope knew each other before the fund-raiser?"

"Sure. He brought her . . . Robin said you're a guitarist."

"I play a little."

"She said you were very good."

"She's biased."

She wiped her lips with her napkin. "I don't play much anymore. After I gave birth, nothing but my son seemed important. . . . These questions about Mike Cruvic. Do the police suspect *him* of something?"

"No," I said. "There are no suspects at all. Is there something I should know about him?"

"He's been good to the center," she said, but her tone was flat.

"And he brought her to the fund-raiser."

"Are you asking if they had something going?" she said.

"Did they?"

"I wouldn't know. And what's the difference? Hope was murdered because of her views, wasn't she?"

"Is that the assumption at the center?"

"That's my assumption. Why else? She spoke out and was silenced."

She stared at me.

"You really do suspect Mike, don't you?"

"No," I said. "But anyone with a relationship to Hope is being checked out."

"Checked out. Sounds like CIA stuff."

"Basic police stuff. I understand about Cruvic's value to the center, but if there's something I should know . . ."

She shook her head. "Their relationship . . . I feel like such a traitor . . . but what happened to her . . ." She closed her eyes, took several shallow breaths, as if practicing yoga. Opened them and let her fingers graze the muffin, then picked up her hat and traced the edge of the brim.

"I'm telling you this because it feels like the right thing to do. But it also feels wrong."

I nodded.

She breathed a few more times. "One time, after the board meeting, I saw them. It was late at night, I was measuring rooms for furniture, thought everyone else had gone home. But when I walked out to the parking lot, Mike's car was still there, way at the far end. It's easy to spot—he drives a Bentley. He and Hope were standing next to it, talking. Her car was next to his—a little red thing. They weren't doing anything physical but they were standing close to each other. Very close. Facing each other. As if ready to kiss or they'd already kissed. They heard me and they both turned very quickly. Then she hurried to her car and drove away. Mike stayed there for a second, one leg bent. Almost as if he wanted me to see he was relaxed. Then he waved and got into the Bentley."

She winced. "Not worth much, is it? And please, if you question Mike, or anyone else, don't mention my name. Okay?"

"Okay," I said. "After Hope stopped coming round, was there resentment of Mike because he sponsored her?"

"If there was I didn't hear it. As I said, Mike's our most reliable volunteer M.D."

"How often does he see patients there?"

"I don't get involved in scheduling but I do know he's been coming for years."

"Doing obstetrics-gynecology?"

She tensed. "I assume."

"Abortions?"

"I said I don't know." Her voice had risen. "And if he does them, so what?"

"Because abortion sometimes inspires violence."

"But Mike wasn't murdered, Hope was. I really don't want to get into any more of this." She stood. "I really don't."

"Fair enough. Sorry to upset you."

"It's all right," she said. "But please. I beg you. Don't draw us into the abortion thing. We've avoided problems, so far, but all we need is for this to hit the press."

"Promise," I said.

She laughed. "Boy, you really got me into a fix. When you called I thought you wanted to volunteer so I spoke to the director on your behalf, set up an appointment for you in a half hour. Now I've got to call and tell her."

"I'd still like to talk to her."

"And I can't stop you, can I?"

"I'm not the enemy, Holly."

She looked down on me. "Hold on."

She walked to the back of the restaurant, veered right, and disappeared. Jake finished with the beans and concentrated on glaring at me, til Holly came back.

"She's not happy, but she'll see you very briefly. Marge Showalsky. But don't expect to learn much about Hope."

"Thanks," I said. "And sorry."

"Forget it," she said. "I'm sure you're not the enemy. Robin's too smart for that."

14

The stretch of Olympic that housed the Women's Health Center was one of those clumsy L.A. mixes: factories, junkyards, storage barns, a trendy prep school pretending it was somewhere else by erecting a border of potted ficus.

The clinic was a single story of charmless brown brick next to a parking lot rimmed with iron posts and heavy chains. The front door was locked. I rang the bell and gave my name. A moment later I was clicked in.

Three women sat in the waiting room and none of them looked up. At the rear were swinging wooden doors with small windows. The walls were covered with posters on AIDS awareness, breast examination, nutrition, support groups for trauma. A TV in the corner was tuned to the Discovery Channel. Animals chasing each other.

One door opened and a heavy, bespectacled

woman around sixty held it ajar and stuck her head out. She had short, gray, curly hair and a round, pink face that wasn't jolly. Her eyeglasses were steel-rimmed and square. She wore a dark green sweater, blue jeans, and sneakers.

"Dr. Delaware? I'm Marge," she boomed. "I'm tied up, gimme a minute."

As the door closed, the women in the waiting room looked up.

Closest to me was a black girl around eighteen, with huge, wounded eyes, meticulous cornrows, and tightly clenched lips. She wore the uniform of a fast-food outlet and clutched a Danielle Steel paperback in both hands. Across from her were what looked to be a mother and daughter: both blond, daughter fifteen or sixteen, Mom an old forty, with black roots, pouchy eyes, sunken body and spirit.

Maybe Daughter had something to do with that. She looked me straight in the eye and winked, then licked her lips.

She had an unusually narrow face, off-center nose, low-set ears, and a slightly webbed neck. Her hair color looked natural except for the hot-pink highlights at the tips. She wore it long and teased huge and flipped back. Her Daisy Duke cutoffs barely covered her skinny haunches, and a black halter top exposed spaghetti arms, a flat, white midriff, and minimal shoulders. Three earrings in one ear, four in the other. An iron nose ring, the skin around the puncture still inflamed. High black boots reached midway up her calves. Black hoop earrings were the size of drink coasters.

She winked again. Gleefully furtive crossing of legs. Her mother saw it and rattled her magazine. The girl gave a wide, naughty smile. Her teeth were blunt pegs. One hand finger-waved. Foreshortened thumbs.

It added up to some kind of genetic misalignment. Maybe nothing with an official name. What used to be called *syndromy* back in my intern days.

Her legs shifted again. A hard nudge from her mother made her sit still and pout and look down at the floor.

The black girl had watched the whole thing. Now she returned to her book, one hand rubbing her abdomen, as if it ached.

The door opened again. Marge Showalsky motioned me in and led me down a hall of examining rooms.

"Lucky for you it's a quiet day."

Her office was large but dim with moisture stains on the ceiling. Random furnishings and bookshelves that didn't look earthquake-safe. Half-open blinds gave a striped view of the asphalt lot.

She settled behind a desk not much wider than her shoulders. Two folding chairs. I took one.

"Used to be an electronics factory. Transistors or something. Thought we'd never get rid of the metal smell."

Two posters hung on the wall behind her: Gertrude Stein and Alice B. Toklas at a cafe table, under the legend GIRLTALK. A Georgia O'Keeffe skull-in-the-desert print.

"So you work for the police. Doing what?"

I told her, keeping it general.

She righted her glasses and gave a bearish grin. "You give good bullshit. Best I've had this week. Well, I can't tell you much either. The women who come here have very little left except their privacy."

"The only person I'm interested in is Hope Devane."

She smiled again. "You think I don't know who you are. You're the shrink who works with Sturgis. Anyway, in answer to your anticipated questions: Yes, we do terminations when we can find a doctor to perform them. No, I won't tell you which doctors do them. And, finally, Hope Devane wasn't involved with us much, so I'm sure her murder had nothing to do with us."

"Not involved much," I said. "As opposed to Dr. Cruvic."

Her laugh could have corroded metal. She opened a drawer, pulled out a rough-textured briar pipe, rubbed the mouthpiece. "Mike Cruvic is an M.D. with excellent credentials willing to make a regular commitment to women in need. Want to guess how many other Hippocratic types are standing in line to do that? This place is run from month to month. Mostly it's nurses on their off-hours. A machine answers our phone and we try to listen for emergencies. Maybe next month we'll get voice mail: 'If you are *dying*, press *one*.'"

She put the pipe in her mouth, bit down so hard the bowl tilted upward.

"Money crunch," I said.

"Strangulation time." She raised a fist. "Few years ago we had government grants, staff on payroll, a damn good immunization-and-screening program. Then the government started discussing health-care reform, morons came out from Washington asking us about accountability, and things got weird."

Yanking out the pipe, she pointed it like a periscope. "So, what's it like working with Milo Sturgis? Only reason I agreed to meet with you was to ask."

"You know him?"

"By reputation. You, too—the straight shrink who hangs around with him. He's legendary."

"In the gay community?"

"No, at the L.A. Country Club. What do you think?" Her eyes twinkled. "You know, some people think you're in the closet. That if you were really a good shrink you'd realize you're in love with him."

I smiled.

"Hey, we got Mona Lisa." She smiled back around the pipestem, looking, oddly enough, like Teddy Roosevelt. "So tell me, how come he never gets involved?"

"In what?"

"Sexual politics. Putting his image to constructive use."

"You'd have to ask him that."

"Ho, ho, I've touched a nerve—well, he should. Gay cop, breaking down barriers, the way he went up against the department, what was it, five years ago? Broke that lieutenant's jaw because he called him a fag." She put the pipe back in, chewed with satisfaction. "At certain bars people still talk about that."

"Interesting twist," I said.

"You know different?"

"He broke the lieutenant's jaw because the lieutenant endangered his life."

"Well," she said, "I guess that's a reason, too—so why no social conscience? He never answers calls from fund-raisers or march organizers, never joins anything. Same with that doctor boyfriend. Studs like that, they could do some good."

"Maybe he feels he already is."

She looked me up and down. "Are you bisexual?"

"No."

"So what's the connection?"

"We're friends."

"*Just* friends, huh?" She laughed.

"Like Hope and Cruvic?"

Her laughter died.

"I understand your wanting privacy," I said. "But in a case like this everything gets examined."

"Then get a court order—look, what if they *were* doing each other three times a day on top of his desk? And I'm not saying they were. Who gives a shit? Mike didn't kill her, who cares who screws who? She got killed because she got famous and pissed off some pig to the extreme."

"Any idea who the pig could be?"

"Too many out there to count. I shall reiterate: She was minimally involved here. I'm sorry when any woman's killed but there's nothing I can tell you about this woman."

Rising with effort, she made her way around the desk to the door.

"Say hi to Mr. Legend. Tell him no matter what he does for his bosses, he'll never be anything to them but a queer."

Back in the waiting room, neither girl was there, only the little blond's mother. She looked up from her reading as I passed. The magazine was *Prevention*.

I was back at my Seville when I saw her running toward me in a pinched trot. Short and slight, she had a high waist and a hunched upper body. Her lower lip was thin, its mate nonexistent. She wore baby-blue jeans, a white blouse, flesh-colored sneakers.

"The nurse told me you're a psychiatrist?"

"Psychologist."

"I was just wondering . . ."

I smiled. "Yes?"

She came closer, but carefully, the way you approach a strange dog.

"I'm Dr. Delaware," I said, extending a hand.

She looked back at the clinic. A roar sounded overhead and she jumped. A Cessna flying low, probably a takeoff from the private airport in Santa Monica. She watched it head out over the ocean. When the noise faded, she said, "I was just—are you by any chance gonna be working here?"

"No."

"Oh." Dejection. "Okay, sorry to bother you."

She turned to go.

"Is there some way I can help you?" I said.

She stopped. One hand began twisting the other. "No, forget it, sorry."

"Are you sure?" I said, touching her shoulder very lightly. "Is something the matter?"

"I just thought maybe they were finally gonna get a psychologist here."

"For your daughter?"

Her hands kept working.

"Teenage problems?" I said.

She nodded. "Her name's Chenise," she said, tentatively, as if prepared to spell it for some bureaucrat. "She's sixteen."

She patted her breast pocket. "Quit smoking, keep forgetting—yeah, teenage problems. She drives me crazy. Always has. I—she's—I been all over with her—a million clinics, all the way to the County Hospital. They always gimme some student and they can't never handle her. Last time, she ended up in the guy's lap and he didn't know *what* to do. The schools won't do nothing. She's been on all kinds of medication since she's little, now it's gotten . . . Dr. Cruvic—he's the doctor here who operated on her—said she should see a psychologist and he brought one over. A lady. *Real* good, she had Chenise's number right away. Smart. So of course Chenise didn't like talking to her. But I made her go. Then . . ."—lowering her voice—"something *happened* to her—to the psychologist." Shaking her head. "You don't want to know. . . . Anyway, better be getting back, she's probably almost through with her checkup."

"The psychologist Dr. Cruvic had her see, was that Dr. Devane?"

"Yes," she said, breathlessly. "So you *know* what happened?"

"As a matter of fact, that's why I'm here, Mrs.—"

"Farney, Mary Farney." Her eyes opened wide. Same blue as her daughter's. Pretty. Once she might have been, too. Now she had the trampled look of someone forced to remember every mistake.

"I don't understand," she said.

"I'm a psychologist and I sometimes work with the police, Mrs. Farney. Right now I'm working on Dr. Devane's murder. Did you—"

Terror in the blue eyes. "They think it had something to do with this place?"

"No, we're just talking to everyone who knew Dr. Devane."

"Well, we didn't really *know* her. Like I said, she only saw Chenise a few times. I liked her, she took the time to listen to me, understood Chenise's games . . . but that's it. I gotta get back."

"What about Dr. Cruvic?"

"What about him?"

"Did he understand Chenise?"

"Sure, he's great. Haven't seen him since—in a while."

"Since the operation."

"No reason to, she's fine."

"Who's checking Chenise out today?"

"Maribel—the nurse. Gotta go."

"Would you mind giving me your address and phone number?"

"What for?"

"In case the police want to talk to you."

"No way, forget it, I don't want to get involved."

I held out my card.

"What's this for?"

"If you think of something."

"I won't," she said, but she put the card in her purse.

"Thanks. And if you need a referral for Chenise, I can find one."

"Nah, what's the use? She wraps people around her finger. No one catches on."

I drove away.

Surgery. Given Chenise Farney's promiscuity, it wasn't hard to imagine what kind.

Cruvic and Hope working together on abortions.

Cruvic calling for a psychological consult because he cared? Or another reason?

Promiscuous teenager with low intelligence. Minor patient below the age of consent. Maybe too dull to give *informed* consent? Cruvic covering his rear?

Cruvic and Hope . . .

Holly Bondurant had assumed the two of them had something going and Marge Showalsky's angry dismissal of the issue confirmed it.

I realized Cruvic had lied to us—implying he'd met Hope at the fund-raiser when Holly was certain they'd known each other previously.

Milo's hunch confirmed.

More than a business relationship.

But in light of Mandy Wright's murder, so what? The Vegas case pointed to a stranger homicide.

A psychopath, still out there, stalking, watching, planning. Waiting to perform a knife sonata under the cover of big, beautiful trees.

I was at Overland when I spotted a coffee shop with a lunch counter and pulled over. I bought a morning paper, read it while I had a hickoryburger and a Coke, then pulled out the list of students involved in the sexual-conduct board.

Might as well finish up.

Three who hadn't been interviewed yet—four, really, because the encounter with panicked Tessa Bowlby didn't qualify.

I called the number for Deborah Brittain in Sherman Oaks. A machine told me to wait for the beep. I decided not to.

Reed Muscadine had dropped out of school, so his class schedule was no longer relevant.

I called him. His tape said, "Hello, this is Reed. I'm either not here or I'm working out and unwilling to interrupt the burn. But I *do* want to talk to you, especially if you're my golden *opportunity*—pant pant. So *please please please* leave your name and number. Starving actors need love, too."

Cheerful, mellow, modulated. The kind of voice that knew it sounded good.

If he was HIV-positive it hadn't dampened his

spirit or his attempts to stay fit. Or he hadn't changed the tape.

Starving actor . . . even after getting the soap-opera job?

Had something gotten in the way of the job?

His address was on Fourth Street. If I was lucky, I'd catch him after the burn faded and learn about his health and his feelings about Hope Devane and the conduct committee.

If my luck really held, perhaps I could find out what was scaring the hell out of Tessa Bowlby.

15

His address matched a white stucco cottage with castle pretensions: two turrets, one oversized over the front door, the other a vestigial nipple atop the right corner. An old woman wearing a wide straw hat stooped on the sidewalk, removing weeds by hand. By the time I cut the Seville's engine, she was upright with her hands on her hips. She wore brown canvas gardening pants with rubber kneepads and had sueded skin and judgmental eyes.

"Hi, I'm looking for Reed Muscadine."

"He lives in back." Then she stiffened, as if regretting telling me that much. "Who're you?"

I got out of the car and showed her my police ID. "Ph.D.?"

"I'm a psychologist. I work with the police." I looked down the driveway. An apartment sat on top of the garage, accessed by steep, skinny front steps.

"He's not in," she said. "I'm Mrs. Green. I own the place. What's going on?"

"We're questioning him with regard to a crime. Not as a suspect, just someone who knew the victim."

"Who's the victim?"

"A professor at the University."

"And he knew her?"

I nodded.

"I lived here forty-four years," she said, "never knew a victim. Now you can't step outside without getting nervous. A friend of mine's nephew's a policeman in Glendale. He tells her there's nothing the police can do til you're hurt or killed. Told her to buy a gun, carry it around, and if they catch you it's like a traffic ticket. So I did. I've also got Sammy."

She whistled twice, I heard something slam shut, and a big, thick-set, fawn-colored dog with a sad black face ambled around from the back of the house. Bullish face—cousin to Spike? But this creature weighed at least one hundred pounds and its eyes were all business.

Mrs. Green held out a palm and the dog stopped.

"Mastiff?" I said.

"*Bull*mastiff. Only breed ever designed specifically to bring down people—they raised 'em in England to catch game poachers. Come here, baby."

The dog sniffed, lowered its head, and walked over slowly, shoulders rotating, massive limbs moving in fluid concert. Drool dripped down its dewlaps. Its eyes were small, nearly black, and they hadn't left my face.

"Hey, Sammy," I said.

"Samantha. The females are the really protective ones—c'mere, puddin'."

The dog made its way over, examined my knees, looked at Mrs. Green.

"Yeah, okay, kiss him," she said.

A big mouth nuzzled my hand.

"Sweet," I said.

"If you're right, she is. If you're wrong, well . . ." Her laugh was as dry as her skin. The dog rubbed against her thigh and she petted it.

"Any idea when Reed will be back?"

"No, he's an actor."

"Irregular hours?"

"Right now it's night hours, he's waiting tables out in the Valley."

From soap opera to that? I said, "No luck in the acting department?"

"Don't fault him," she said. "It's a tough business, believe me, I know. I did some work back a ways, mostly bit parts, but I did have a walk-on in *Night After Night*—that's a Mae West film. Classic. They made her out to be some wild hussy but she was smarter than all of them. I should've bought real estate when she did. Instead I got married."

She brushed her pants and kneaded the dog's thick neck.

"So some professor got killed. And you're talking to all the students?"

"We're trying to be as thorough as possible."

"Well, like I said, Reed's an okay kid. Pays the rent pretty much on time and always lets me know if he can't. I give him a break because he's big and strong and handy and fixes things. Real good with Sammy, too, so when I go away to my sister in Palm Springs I've got someone to take care of her. Tell the truth, he reminds me of my husband—Stan was a movie grip, know what that is?"

"They move sets around."

"They move everything around. Stan was all muscle. Did stunt work til he broke his collarbone working for Keaton. My daughter's in the business, too, reads scripts for CAA. So I have a soft spot for anyone dreamy enough to still want to be part of it. That's why I rented to Reed with just a first month down. Usually I get first and last. And he's been a good tenant. Even when he got laid up, he didn't laze around too long."

"Laid up how?"

"Few months ago. He slipped a disc, lifting those weights he's got—well, looky here, you can talk to him yourself."

A battered yellow Volkswagen pulled into the driveway. Rust fringed the wheel wells.

No Porsche, yet.

The man who got out was older than I expected—thirty or so—and huge. Six-five, tanned deeply, with very pale gray eyes and long, thick black hair brushed back and flowing over a yard of shoulder. His features were strong, square, perfect for the camera. The cleft in his chin was Kirk Douglas-caliber. He wore a heavy gray sweatshirt with the sleeves cut off to expose side-of-beef biceps, very brief black shorts, and sandals without socks. I tried to picture him with Tessa Bowlby.

He shot me a quick look, the gray eyes curious and intelligent; Tarzan with an IQ. A brown paper bag was in one hand. Handing it to Mrs. Green, he added a milk-fed smile.

"How's it going, Maidie. Hey, Sam." Stroking the bullmastiff, he looked at me again. The dog's neck bulged and furrowed as she tilted her head back at him. Her eyes had softened. A big pink tongue bathed his fingers.

"Fine as rain," said Mrs. Green. "This fellow's from the police, Reed, but no cop. A psychologist, isn't that something? He's here to talk to you about some murdered professor. What'd you go and do now, kid?"

Muscadine's thick brows curved and he squinted. "*My* professor?"

"Hope Devane," I said.

"Oh. . . . Those are fresh today, Maidie."

"From where, that health-food place?"

"Where else?"

"Organic." She snorted. "Did you ever figure maybe the reason I lived so long is all the preservatives I took pickled me like a deli cuke?"

She looked inside the bag. "Peaches out of season? Must have cost a fortune."

"I only got two," said Muscadine. "The apples were actually cheap, and look at that color." He turned to me. "A psychologist?"

"I work with the police."

"I don't understand."

"I'm looking into Professor Devane's committee work."

"Oh. Sure. Want to come up?"

"Devane," said Mrs. Green, scratching her nose. "Why is that name familiar?"

"She was murdered in Westwood," said Muscadine. "What was it, three months ago?"

I nodded.

"Oh, yeah, the one who wrote a book," said Mrs. Green. "She was your professor, Reed?"

"She taught me," said Muscadine, looking at me.

"A professor." She shook her head. "In a neighborhood like that. What a world—thanks for the fruit, Reed."

"My pleasure, Maidie."

Muscadine and I started up the driveway.

Mrs. Green said, "But don't spend like that, again. Not til you become a star."

As we reached the stairs, he said, "Guess how old she is?"

"Eighty?"

"Ninety next month, maybe I *should* take preservatives." He vaulted the steps three at a time and was unlocking the front door when I reached the top.

The apartment was a single front room with a closet-sized kitchen and a rear bath.

Two walls were mirrored, the others were painted true white. An enormous chrome weight machine took up the center, flanked by a pressing bench, a curl-bar, and, against the wall, a rack of dumbbells arranged by poundage. Iron discs for the bench-bar were stacked like giant black checkers. A double window bordered by ridiculously dainty gingham curtains looked down on blossoming orange trees. Facing the glass were a motorized treadmill, a stair-stepper, a cross-country ski machine, an exercise bike, and wedged in the corner, a double-sized mattress and box spring and two pillows. Black bed linens. I thought of Tessa and Muscadine grappling.

The only pieces of conventional furniture were a cheap wooden nightstand and dresser. A wheeled aluminum rack was hung with color-coordinated shirts, slacks, jeans, and sportcoats. Not too much of each, but the quality looked good. On the floor beneath the clothes were two pairs of sneakers, brown loafers, black oxfords, gray cowboy boots.

Nothing on the cracked tile kitchen counter but a blender and a hot plate. I'd seen bigger refrigerators in Winnebagos. A sign taped to the front said THINK POSTIVE—BUT LURN HOW TO SPEL. Two steel-and-plastic stools were up against the counter. Muscadine pulled one out and said, "Sorry, I don't entertain much."

We both sat down.

"Thanks for not elaborating about the committee in front of Maidie. She gives me a break on the rent and right now I need it."

I looked over the exercise equipment. "Nice setup."

"I used to work at a health club that went under. Got it cheap."

"Were you a personal trainer?"

"More like impersonal. One of those budget places, basically a scam. I know it looks weird having all this stuff in a place this size but it ended up being cheaper than paying my own gym fees, and right now my body's my commodity."

The room was hot but his skin was dry despite the heavy sweatshirt. Tossing his hair, he laughed. "That didn't come out exactly right. What I'm saying is no matter how intellectual you get about acting, the industry runs on first impressions and when you hit a certain age, you've got to work harder."

"What age is that?"

"Depends on the person. I'm thirty-one. So far, so good."

"First impressions," I said. "The casting couch?"

"There's some of that still going around but what I mean is the way impulse rules. I can practice Stanislavsky—acting methods—from now til tomorrow, but if the bod goes so does my marketability." He hooked his thumb downward.

"How long have you been working at it?"

"Couple of years. Got a degree in business, worked for an accounting firm for nine years. Finally I couldn't stand the sight of numbers and went back for a master's in fine arts. Can I get you something to drink?"

"No, thanks."

"Well, I'm going to." Opening the fridge, he pulled a bottle of mineral water from a grouping of two dozen. The only other thing inside was a grapefruit.

Twisting the top with two fingers, he took a long swallow.

"Why'd you drop out?" I said.

"Boy, word gets around fast. Who told you?"

"Professor Dirkhoff."

"Good old Professor Dirkhoff. The old queen on his throne. He's quite *miffed* with me, thinks I should spend two more years developing my *underlying resources.*"

Flexing one arm, he rotated the hand. "Maybe I should have brought *Dirkhoff* up before the conduct committee. That would have blown Devane's mind."

"Why's that?"

"No woman victim. Because that's really what the committee was all about: men against women. From the minute I got in there she was on the attack."

Shrugging, he poured the rest of the water down his throat. "So you're talking to everyone involved with the committee?"

"Yes."

"They said all records would be kept confidential but after the murder I wondered. But why a psychologist—what's your name, by the way?"

I showed him my ID. He read it and looked up at me. "I still don't understand what your role is."

"The police have asked me to talk to people who knew Professor Devane, to do some victim analysis."

"Analyzing *her*? That's interesting. I always figured it was some nut, maybe someone who read her book. I heard it was pretty hostile toward men."

"And she was hostile in person," I said.

"Oh, yeah. It really freaked me out being accused of rape. Being *summoned*. Maybe in the end it worked out for the best because the experience brought my ambivalence about school to a head and led me to try other alternatives—have you met the girl who accused me yet?"

"Yesterday," I said. "She seems terrified."

The gray eyes enlarged. "Of what?"

"I was going to ask you that."

"You're thinking—oh, no. Lord, no, I've kept my distance. She's bad news, I wish we lived on separate planets."

"Bad news?"

"Serious problems—she needs *you*. One night with her was enough."

"What kind of problems?"

"She's disturbed. Unpredictable."

He got another bottle. "The crazy thing is, I keep thinking maybe *that* was what attracted me to her, in the first place. The unpredictability. Because she's not the type I usually go for."

"What type is that?"

"Normal. And to be frank, a lot better looking. Generally, I like girls who take care of themselves—athletes."

"Tessa doesn't?"

"You met her. Tessa is sad."

"So you think her unpredictability attracted you?"

"That and—I don't know, a certain . . . excitability. Like she might be interesting." He shrugged. "The truth is, hell if I know. I'm still trying to understand it—did she tell you how we met?"

"Why don't you give me your version?"

"Your basic casual campus pickup. So normal, at first. We were in the student union, studying, eating, our eyes met and—boom. She was intense. Hot eyes, very soulful. And on some level she *is* attractive. Whatever it was, *something* clicked. For both of us."

He shook his head and black hair streamed then fell back in place. "Maybe it was purely biochemical. I've read about certain chemicals that influence sexual attraction. Pheromones. So maybe the two of us were in chemical harmony that day, who knows? Whatever it was, it was one thousand percent mutual. Every time I looked at her she was staring at me. Finally, I went over and sat down next to her and she moved herself right up against me, hip-to-hip. Two minutes later, I'm asking her out and she's saying yes, as if what took so long, guy. I picked her up at her dorm that night. Movie, dinner, more small talk, but it was clear we were both just going through the motions, to make it seem . . . polite, before getting into the inevitable. And she was the one who suggested we come back here. I wasn't too keen on it, this place isn't exactly the Playboy Mansion, but she said there was no privacy in the dorms. I brought her back, fixed her a drink, went to the bathroom, and when I came out she was right there."

He pointed to the mattress in the corner.

"Wearing one of those little black slips and her pantyhose were off, balled up, on the floor. When she saw me, she smiled and spread her legs. Before I knew it . . ." He clapped his big hands together. "Like a collision. And both of us came. In fact, she finished first. Then all of a sudden she rolls out from under me and starts to cry. I try to hold her, she shoves me away. Then the crying gets intense and takes on a sound that spooks me—over-the-edge—hysterical. And loud. All I need is for Mrs. G. to hear and come up, maybe with Sammy—Sammy doesn't like strangers. So I put my hand over her mouth—not hard, just to calm her down, and she tries to *bite* me. At that point, I stand up and back off. It was disorienting. One minute you're making love, the next she's out to kill you. I'm thinking, you idiot, Muscadine, going for the casual pickup. And she's not letting up. Finally, she makes this snarling sound, gets on all fours, scrambles for her pantyhose, manages to put them on, then runs out of the apartment and down the stairs. I follow her, trying to find out what's wrong, but she won't talk, keeps heading for the street. And now Sam *is* barking and Mrs. G.'s light goes on."

"Did Mrs. Green come out?"

"No, we were moving pretty fast. Once she was out on Fourth, she headed north. I said c'mon, it's late, let me take you home, she said fuck you, I'll walk. Which is crazy, campus is five, six miles away. But every time I try to talk to her she threatens to scream, so finally I let her."

He blew out air. "Unreal. For days after I kept trying to figure out what happened and the best I could come up with was maybe she'd been raped or molested before and had a flashback. Then a month later I get the notice to show up for the committee. It was like being hit right here."

He pressed his solar plexus. "Later I found out I

was never obligated to show up. But the letter sure made it sound that way."

"How'd you feel about getting tested for HIV?"

"You know about that, too?"

"There are transcripts of the committee sessions."

"Transcripts? Oh, shit. Are they going to be made public?"

"Not unless they turn out to be relevant to the murder."

He rubbed his forehead. "Jesus . . . there's a school of thought in the industry says there's no such thing as bad publicity, just get your name out there. But that only applies to people who've already made it. I'm a peasant. The last thing I need is for people to think I'm a rapist or infected."

"So you're HIV-negative."

"Of course I am! Do I look sick?"

"How's your back?"

"My back?"

"Mrs. Green said you'd been laid up."

"Oh, that. Ruptured disc. My own fault. Felt feisty one morning and decided to go for three-twenty on the bench press. Spasmed, like a knife going right through me. Couldn't get up off the floor for an hour. The pain laid me up for a month, Mrs. G. brought me groceries. That's why I buy her stuff when I can. Even now I still get a twinge, but other than that I feel great. And I'm totally, one hundred percent negative."

I repeated the question about being tested.

"How did I feel? *Intruded* upon. Wouldn't you? It was outrageous. I think I said something at the hearing about it being Kafkaesque. Did they make everyone at the hearings go through it?"

"I'm not at liberty to say."

He stared. "Fair enough—anyway, that's my sum total contact with Professor Devane. Do you think any of this is going to hit the papers?"

"I guess that depends on who the killer turns out to be."

He turned contemplative. "You really think there's a chance the committee had something to do with her death?"

"Would that surprise you?"

"Absolutely. The process was nasty but in the end it didn't amount to much. I can't see murdering anyone over that. Then again, I can't see murdering anyone over anything." He grinned. "Except maybe a juicy part. Just kidding."

He yawned. " 'Scuse me. If there's nothing else, I'd like to catch a nap, have to be at work by six."

"Where's work?"

"Delvecchio's in Tarzana." He bowed and flourished. " 'And how would you like your steak done, sir? Rare? But what's my motivation?' "

"Professor Dirkhoff said you'd gotten an acting job."

The handsome face darkened. "Ouch."

"What hurts?"

"Failure. Yes, that was true—Hollywood-true—when I told him I was dropping out. But I would have left, anyway. The classes were too theoretical. Waste of tuition."

"What's Hollywood-true?"

"An air sandwich on imaginary bread."

"The job fell through?"

"It never got far enough to fall through. I allowed myself to be naively optimistic because my audition went great and my agent told me I was a shoo-in."

"What happened?"

"Someone else got the job and I didn't."

"Why?"

"Hell if I know. They never tell you."

"What show was it?"

"Some soap opera, independent deal for cable."

"Did it go into production?"

"Everything was really preliminary. They didn't even have a name for it, something about spies and diplomats, foreign embassies. The casting director told me I was up for the James Bond part. Wear a patch on one eye and sweep ladies off their feet. Then she pinched my ass and said, 'Yum, grade-A, prime.' Where are those conduct committees when you need them?"

16

Milo came to the house from the airport, arriving at eight and looking disheveled.

"Where are the white shoes?" I said.

He flexed a scuffed desert boot. "Decided to go formal." He sat down at the kitchen table and took an eight- by twelve-inch photo out of his briefcase.

Torso-length color promo shot of a stunning young woman with long, silky, dark hair, feather-blushed cheekbones, bite-me lips slightly parted, amazed oblong eyes the color of espresso.

She wore a white-sequined, strapless dress and leaned forward, offering full, surging breasts split by deep cleavage. A wide diamond choker circled her neck. Diamond clips on each ear. Too many carats to be real. Some sort of wind machine had been used to gently blow the hair back from her face. Her smile was inviting yet mocking.

At the bottom:

AMANDA WRIGHT
ACTRESS AND DANCER
REPRESENTED BY ONYX ASSOCIATES

"Her agents?" I said.

"Vegas PD says they're a defunct slick-sleaze outfit, used to do casino booking for topless acts. Mandy had no criminal record, which isn't unusual for the high-class honeys who show up when the chips start piling and do the old thigh-rub. Other vital statistics: She was single, liked to party, did grass, pills, coke. Her last boyfriend was a blackjack dealer named Ted Barnaby, also a cokehead, moved to Reno soon after the murder. Vegas interviewed him the day after, he was cooperative and had an alibi: working all that night, verified by the pit boss. Also, he seemed genuinely torn up about her death."

"But he moved."

"It didn't set off any alarms because casino people are transient. A detective took me over to the crime scene last night. Middle-class condos, quiet. Not a lot of trees like Hope's street, but there was a huge eucalyptus growing right in front of Mandy's building and that's where he got her. Vegas and I have both been calling all over the country and no other matches have turned up yet, but there's plenty to do."

"Any record of Mandy living in L.A.?"

"Not so far. She'd been leasing the same apartment for almost three years, grew up in Hawaii, no police record there, either. Wouldn't surprise me if she came down to L.A. at one time or another, but her credit-card receipts don't show it and they do show other travel."

"Where?"

Reaching into the briefcase again, he produced a

thick black binder that he flipped open and placed next to the photo. Wetting his thumb, he turned to a page that showed two years of Visa and MasterCard summaries reduced to tiny print, three statements per page.

Mandy Wright's monthly bills ranged from five hundred dollars to four thousand. Plenty of overdue notices and interest charges. A couple of defaults. Both times she'd been cut off and switched companies.

I ran my finger down the itemized expenditures. Mostly clothes, cosmetics, jewelry, and restaurants. The travel information had been circled. A dozen flights: two each to Aspen and Park City, Utah; six to Honolulu; one to New York; one to New Orleans.

"Well-traveled lady," I said. "Business trips?"

"Hawaii might have been personal, she's got a brother there, but yeah, the rest could be work: the ski places for the winter—working the lodges as a snow bunny. New Orleans was during Mardi Gras and that's a big-time hooker scene. New York could be anything any time of the year."

"But no L.A.," I said. "Isn't Vegas to L.A. a big hooker run? Don't you find it odd that she flew everywhere *but* here?"

"Maybe she doesn't like smog," he said. "Maybe she drove down. But you're right, lots of girls do make the desert run regularly. Last year we had some married women from the Westside picking up change by giving head in motels, back home in time to serve dinner. So maybe Mandy had a regular client in L.A. who didn't want records kept." He tapped the photo. "A girl who looked like that, you could see some rich guy paying her to come down regularly, keep it from the wife."

He got a beer and I examined the rest of the folder, starting with the summary of Ted Barnaby's interview. A single paragraph written by a Detective A. Holzer, who'd spoken to the boyfriend before he left for Reno. Barnaby had shown "tears and other evidence of grief. Subject professes no knowledge of any motive for the homicide. Says he knew victim did 'some call-girl' work, 'that's why we didn't live together. She needed her own place.' Subject also says he didn't like the fact that victim engaged in prostitution and that he and victim had argued about this in the past but he'd come to accept it. 'You've got to accept people on their terms.' His alibi checks out, verified by Franklin A. Varese, casino pit supervisor, and fellow dealers Sandra Boething and Luis Maldonado."

Next, autopsy and lab reports:

The toxicology screen showed a moderate amount of cocaine in Mandy Wright's blood the night of the murder.

Midnight murder. Hope had been stabbed just after 11:00 P.M.

I flipped a page.

The wound pattern, described almost word-for-word as in Hope's file.

The initial blow to the heart had collapsed the organ, death resulting from exsanguination and shock. Prior to that, Mandy Wright's cardiovascular system had been in excellent condition, the arteries clear and unobstructed. No venereal disease, including HIV. No evidence of any outstanding illness or infection other than minor nasal erosion probably due to cocaine abuse.

The final paragraph cited significant expansion of the anal opening and fibroid scarring of the rectum indicating a history of anal sex, but vaginal sexual intercourse had not taken place within the past twenty-four hours. Postmortem examination of the pelvic region revealed no tumors or other pathology; however, changes related to past pregnancy were noted.

That made me think. As did the last line:

"The fallopian tubes have been ligated; from the degree of atrophy, probably within a year or two."

"Sterilized? Any record of her having a child?"

Milo shook his head.

"And she'd been pregnant before," I said. "Meaning an abortion—unless she miscarried. Either before the ligation or at the same time. It's a long shot, but that kind of surgery is Dr. Cruvic's specialty. What if he was her L.A. connection?"

He put the beer down. "There are lots of obstetricians. That's some leap."

"Just throwing out ideas. Should I stop?"

"No, go on."

"Cruvic has money," I said. "Drives a Bentley. Those clothes we saw weren't Kmart. Not inconsistent with the kind of guy who might fly down a party girl and pay for her ticket in cash."

"First he's her doctor, now he's her party pal?"

"He could be both. Maybe that's why he performed the ligation rather than having a doctor in Vegas do it. Hell, maybe he was even the father of her child—who'd be in a better position to get himself out of a mess than an OB? We've got him in at least one fib—not knowing Hope before the fund-raiser. Why try to mislead us? Probably because your hunch was right: Their relationship had been more than friendship. And I've got additional support for that."

I told him what Holly Bondurant had seen in the

parking lot, Marge Showalsky's protest-too-much denials. "Then there's the matter of his direct billing for Hope's services. It just doesn't smell right. Plus, I learned something today that tells me he may skirt other ethical boundaries."

I repeated my conversation with Mary Farney. "Operating on a mentally deficient minor and knowing she probably couldn't give informed consent. Maybe he used Hope for backup. Maybe they were involved in other iffy things."

"Like what?"

"Who knows? Financial shenanigans. Or maybe they did something really ugly, like take eggs out of one fertility patient and sell them to another."

"So where would Mandy fit in?"

"Wild guess? She could have been an egg donor—young, healthy girl. And she learned something she wasn't supposed to. Or tried to blackmail Cruvic. Or maybe Cruvic's just the kind of guy who loves 'em and kills 'em. Hell, I can go on all day but the bottom line is my gut tells me Dr. Cruvic is worth looking into, despite the sex-killer scenario."

He got up and walked around. "We both noticed how hyper Cruvic was, bouncing all over the place. He tried to tell us it was fitness, but maybe it was coke, and *there's* our link with Mandy. Though Hope's autopsy showed no dope in her system and nothing indicates she ever used. Bringing me full circle: If she *was* cheating with Cruvic—or Locking, or anyone else—Seacrest could have found out and decided she'd rubbed his face in it long enough."

"But what connection would Seacrest have to Mandy Wright?"

He paced some more. "It's not just flashy guys who fool with girlies. A quiet middle-aged professor might want a hot little playmate, too. And a quiet middle-aged professor would have reason to pay cash to the playmate. And if the playmate realized how vulnerable the professor was and decided to blackmail him, the professor could decide to end his problems: heart, vagina, back. And after succeeding at that, why not go after the wife who's become such a pain in the ass?"

"Creative," I said.

"You're a good influence."

"Okay, as long as we're screenwriting, how about this: a threesome. Cruvic, Hope, and Mandy. Or Seacrest, Hope, and Mandy. Or even an unknown guy. Flying down a call girl to spice up a tired relationship. Then, for whatever reason, the guy decides to call it quits. Permanently. Gets rid of Mandy first because murdering a call girl three hundred miles away won't attract attention in L.A. But Hope's a different story. She's prominent, local, smarter. So he waits, planning, waiting for the right time. Then Hope helps him by getting notorious with her book. Which sets up a perfect cover: some nut acting out because of the controversy she generated."

He thought about that. "But if Mandy and Hope knew each other, wouldn't Mandy's murder have alerted Hope?"

"If they'd parted ways, how would she know Mandy'd been killed? Did Mandy's murder get any media coverage?"

He shook his head. "Just one small blurb in the *Sun* the same day. Still, if Hope had been engaged in a three-way with Mandy, wouldn't she be likely to find out?"

"Okay," I said. "Let's say she knew Mandy'd been

murdered but didn't connect it to herself. Like you said, prostitutes get killed all the time."

He drank, looked out the kitchen window. The sun was small and pale, silvering the tops of the pines, turning them as shiny as Mandy Wright's dress.

"Great screenplays," he finally said. "It would sure be nice to have some facts."

"At least," I said, "I can look into Cruvic's credentials, see if anything funny shows up."

"Do that. My next stop's a chat with Kenny Storm. I want to clear the whole committee angle. I'll also check with Vegas to see if Mandy had health insurance, maybe her sterilization was documented and we can find out who did it. The boyfriend, Barnaby, might know about that, so we'll put out the word for him, too. Anything else occur while I was gone?"

"I found Reed Muscadine. Like Kenny, he dropped out of school, but for another reason. He was up for a soap-opera part, thought he had it, but it fell through. He denied raping Tessa Bowlby, repeated the same story he told at the hearing."

"Credible?"

"No alarm bells went off, but he's an actor. Take it for what it's worth."

"What do *you* think it's worth?"

"I don't know. Tessa looked extremely traumatized. I'd like to know what's eating at her. Maybe I'll give her another try."

"What's Muscadine like physically?"

"Very big and muscular, good-looking, body-conscious. His place is basically a gym."

"The kind of guy who could overpower a woman and hold her still in order to stab her in the heart."

"Easily. He could have subdued her with two fingers. But he seemed pretty calm about being questioned, so either he's innocent or he's honed his craft and was prepared for me. His landlady likes him, says he never causes problems. He claims he's HIV-negative and if he's lying, he's not showing the effects yet. Tessa, on the other hand, looks worn-out. But now that we know about Mandy, what connection could there be to the committee?"

"Good question, but I want to finish with it, seen too many screwups that seemed perfectly logical at the time. Only one student left, right?"

"Deborah Brittain. I'll try to get to her tomorrow."

"Thanks. I really appreciate this, Alex."

He put the file back in the briefcase. "Thanks for the theorizing, too. I mean it. I'd rather have theories than nothing."

I walked him to the door. "Where to now?"

"Home for a shower and then talking to fellow gendarmes. Maybe I can turn up some other pretty ladies triple-stabbed under big trees, and retreat to the comfort of *utter* powerlessness."

Cruvic's lie about not knowing Hope before the fund-raiser stuck in my head and at 7:00 P.M., with Robin working in her shop, I took a drive over to Civic Center.

Hoping for what? A glimpse of his Bentley as he left the office? Some pretty face in the passenger window?

Futile. The pink building's windowless facade gave no indication if anyone was in.

Not exactly welcoming architecture. The same question: Why set up practice here, away from all the other Beverly Hills medicos?

Privacy alone didn't answer it. Psychiatrists and

psychologists managed to provide confidentiality in conventional office buildings.

Something to hide?

Beverly Hills streets are accompanied by parallel back alleys—part of a city plan that intended to keep garbage collection and deliveries out of sight. Hanging a U-turn, I drove back to the nearest intersection—Foothill Road—where I turned right and into the asphalt strip running behind the buildings. Rear facades, loading docks, dumpsters. Finally, a high pink wall.

Three parking spots, all of them empty. The building's back entrance was an old-fashioned wooden garage door, dark and crisscrossed by beams. Heavy hasp secured by a large padlock. More like storage space than a doctor's private entry.

No cars said *this* doctor had left for the day. Maybe for his nighttime gig at the clinic?

I reversed direction again, taking little Santa Monica to Century City, then Avenue of the Stars south to Olympic Boulevard West. Another twenty minutes and I was in Santa Monica, and by that time the sky was black.

A few lights on at the Women's Health Center, a dozen or so cars parked in the sunken lot. Mostly compacts, with the exception of a gleaming silver Bentley Turbo pulled up close to the clinic's main door.

The chain across the driveway was fastened and locked and a uniformed guard patrolled slowly. Even in the dim light I made out the holster on his hip. When he saw me, he picked up his pace. I sped away before we could read each other's faces.

17

Tying up loose ends.

The next morning I called the Psychology office and got Mary Ann Gonsalvez's number. The time difference made it 5:00 P.M. in London. No answer, no machine.

I made coffee and toast and ate without tasting, thinking of the crowd at the women's clinic last night.

The armed guard, the chain blocking the parking lot.

Dr. Cruvic operating.

On patients like Chenise Farney?

Fifteen cars. Even allowing for staff, probably ten or more procedures. And for all I knew he'd been going for hours, bringing them in in shifts.

Idealism, or profit motive?

The profit could be high if he was using the clinic's facilities at no cost, and billing the state. The clinic happy to have someone volunteer services to its poor clientele.

Poor women meant Medi-Cal. Abortion funding was always subject to political fluctuations and I had no idea if Medi-Cal paid.

I made a call to the L.A. Medi-Cal office, was referred to an 800 number in Sacramento, put on hold for ten minutes, and cut off. Trying again, I endured another hold, got through, and was transferred to another 800 number, more holds, two shell-shocked-sounding clerks, and finally someone coherent who admitted that Medi-Cal did indeed reimburse for both terminations and tubal ligations, but that I would need procedure codes, too, in order to obtain specific reimbursement allowances.

I phoned the med school crosstown and used my faculty status to get the business office at Women's Hospital. The head clerk there referred me to the billing office, which referred me to the direct Medi-Cal billing office. Finally, someone whose tone implied I should have known without asking informed me that abortions were indeed reimbursable by the state at nine hundred dollars per procedure, not including hospital costs, anesthesia, and other incidentals.

I hung up.

Nine hundred per procedure. And if you were a canny biller, as Cruvic seemed to be, you could throw in things like nursing charges, operating-room costs, supplies, anesthesia, and jack up the reimbursement.

Twenty abortions a week added up to just short of a seven-figure income.

Nice little supplement to the fertility practice.

Implanting fetuses in the rich, removing them from the poor.

There were risks, of course: an antiabortion fanatic

lashing out violently. And if the papers got hold of it, bad press: BEVERLY HILLS FERTILITY DOCTOR RUNS NIGHTTIME ABORTION MILL. Pro-lifers would excoriate Cruvic for murdering babies and liberals would wax indignant over class inequality.

And whatever their political bent, Cruvic's fertility patients would shrink from that kind of publicity. And from the fact that their doctor's activities weren't limited to abetting pregnancy—despite the claim on his business card.

But with that kind of money, Cruvic probably figured the risk was worth it.

Off-the-path medical building.

Chains around the clinic parking lot, armed guard.

Had he been greedy and wanted even more?

Bloated billing? Cooking the books?

Hope going along with the fraud?

But Cruvic had paid her only thirty-six thousand a year, a very small chunk of a million-dollar business.

Maybe the thirty-six represented only what she'd reported on her tax returns and there'd been other payments, in cash.

Or had Hope not been a willing partner to fraud and, learning the truth, quit, or threatened to expose Cruvic?

And died because of it?

Then what about Mandy Wright? Her only link to obstetrics, so far, was a terminated pregnancy and a tubal ligation.

Far-fetched, Delaware.

The most likely scenario was that she and Hope had been murdered by a psychopathic stranger and Cruvic, however mercenary and ethically slippery, had nothing to do with it.

Still, I'd promised Milo to check out his credentials,

Deborah Brittain would be in class for the next few hours, and the panicked Tessa Bowlby had a day off. Lots of days off, as a matter of fact: enrolled in only two classes, both on Tuesday and Thursday.

Reduced academic load.

Trouble coping?

I'd give her another try, too, but first things first.

Calling the state medical board, I found out no malpractice complaints had been lodged against Milan Cruvic, M.D., nor was his license in jeopardy.

Farther fetched.

I got dressed and drove to school.

At the Biomed Library, I looked Cruvic up in the *Directory of Medical Specialists.*

B.A., Berkeley—Hope's alma mater, another possible link. They were the same age, too, had graduated in the same class.

Old friends? I read on. M.D., UC San Francisco— once again, studying in the same city as Hope.

Then, she'd come down to L.A. for her clinical training and he'd moved to Seattle for a surgery internship at the University of Washington.

By the book, so far.

But then it got interesting.

He completed only one year of his surgery residency at U of W before taking a leave of absence and spending a year at the Brooke-Hastings Institute in Corte Madera, California.

Then, instead of returning to Washington, he'd transferred specialties from surgery to obstetrics-gynecology, signing on as a first-year resident at Fidelity Medical Center in Carson, California, where he'd finished, passed his boards, and gotten his specialty certification in OB-GYN.

No listing of any postgraduate work in fertility.

That wasn't illegal—an M.D. and a state license allowed any physician to do just about anything medical—but it was surprising, even reckless, because fertility techniques were highly specialized.

Where had Cruvic learned his craft?

The year at the Brooke-Hastings Institute? No, because he'd been just a first-year resident at the time and no reputable institution would take someone for advanced training at that point.

Self-taught?

Cutting corners in a daring and dangerous way?

Was that the real reason he practiced away from the other Beverly Hills doctors?

If so, who sent him referrals?

People who also wanted to skirt the rules?

But maybe there was a simple solution: He'd undergone bona fide training but the fact had been accidentally left off his bio.

Still, you'd think that was the kind of thing he'd be careful to correct. And the directory was updated each year.

Freelance fertility cowboy?

Cutting corners?

Taking on cases no one else would go near?

Something on the fringe . . .

Perhaps a daring nature was what had *attracted* Hope to Cruvic.

So different from the stodgy, routine-bound Seacrest.

Old Volvo versus shiny Bentley.

Something on the fringe . . .

Something gone bad?

Now Hope was dead and Cruvic, as he himself had pointed out, was alive, busy, bouncy, doing God knew what.

But what of Mandy Wright?

What did a scholar and a call girl have in common but gruesome death?

Nothing fit.

I stayed with it, plugging Cruvic's name into every scientific and medical data bank the library offered. No publications, so his year at Brooke-Hastings probably hadn't been for research.

The institute wasn't listed anywhere, either.

By the time I finished, my gut was tight with suspicion, but there was nothing more to do and it was time to find Deborah Brittain.

I spotted her leaving Monroe Hall and heading toward a bike rack.

The photo ID had given no indication of her size.

Six feet tall, lean and big-boned with long, dirty-blond hair and sharp cheekbones. She wore a white polo shirt bearing the University seal, navy shorts, white socks and sneakers, a red mountaineer's backpack.

Her racing bicycle was one of a dozen two-wheelers hitched to a rack in back of the ruby-brick structure. I watched her slip an elastic sweatband over her forehead then remove the chain lock. As she rolled the bike out, I stepped up and introduced myself.

"Yes?" Her blue eyes switched channels, from preoccupied to alarmed. I showed her my ID.

"Professor Devane?" she said in a husky voice. "It sure took a long time." Her hands tightened around the handlebars. "I've got volleyball practice in half an hour but I want to talk to you—let's walk."

She guided the bicycle up the walkway, fast enough to make me lengthen my stride.

"I want to tell you," she said, "that Professor Devane was a truly great woman. A wonderful person. The sicko who killed her should get the death penalty but of course he won't."

"Why's that?"

"Even if you catch him and he gets convicted they never enforce the law fully."

She glanced at me without breaking step. "Want to know about Huang?"

"I want to know anything you can tell me."

"Are you thinking Huang did it?"

"No. We're just talking to everyone associated with the conduct committee."

"So you think the *committee* had something to do with it?"

"We don't know much, period, Ms. Brittain."

"Well, I'm sure people have been bad-mouthing the committee but I think it was a great idea. It saved my life—not literally, but Huang was making my life miserable until Professor Devane put an end to all that."

She stopped suddenly. Her eyes were wet and the sweatband had slipped down. She shoved it higher and we started moving again. "He used to come up behind me in the library. I'd turn to get a book and he'd *be* there. Staring, smiling. Suggestive smiles—do you understand?"

I nodded. "Was this after he asked you out or before?"

."After. The creep. It was obviously his way of getting back at me. Three separate times he asked me, three times I told him no. Three strikes and you're out, right? But he wouldn't accept it. Everywhere I'd go I'd turn around and he'd be *looking* at me. A creepy look. It was really starting to get to me."

"Was this all over campus?"

"No, only the library," she said. "As if the library was his little den. He probably stayed down there looking for women to spook, because there was no other reason for him to be there. He's an engineering major and engineering has its own library."

She wiped her forehead with the back of her hand. "I'm not paranoid, I've always been able to take care of myself. But this was horrible. I couldn't concentrate. School's tough enough without getting so distracted. Why should I have to deal with that, too? But I wouldn't have had the courage to do anything about it without Professor Devane."

She bit back tears. "It's such an incredible loss! So unfair!"

She rolled the bike faster.

"Has Huang stopped bothering you?"

"Yes. So God bless Professor Devane and to hell with the administration for caving in."

"Who'd they cave in to?"

"What I heard was there was a rich alumnus who ordered them to shut it down." She thrust her jaw out. "Is Huang dangerous?"

"Not that we've learned so far."

Her laugh was unsteady. "Well, *that's* really comforting."

"So you're still worried about him."

"I really wasn't—we pass each other on campus sometimes and I feel empowered. But then I start thinking about Professor Devane's murder. *Could* it have been something to do with the committee? And I just get sick."

We walked a bit before she said, "When I start to get anxious, I think back to something Professor Devane told me: Harassers are underassertive cowards, that's why they sneak around. The key is to face up to them, show your inner strength. Which is what I do when I see Huang. But look what happened to her."

The bike came to a skidding halt so sudden she had to pull back to maintain balance. "The fact that *she* could become victimized *enrages* me! I've got to find a way to make something good out of it—is there *any* chance it could *be* Huang?"

"He seems to have an excellent alibi."

"So at least you took him seriously enough to investigate him. Good. Let *him* know what it feels like to be under scrutiny. But if you don't suspect him, why are you talking to me?"

"I'm after any information I can get about Professor Devane. People she was close to, her activities, anyone she might have angered."

"Well, we weren't close. We only spoke a couple of times—before the hearing and after, when she coached me on how to handle myself. She was incredibly kind. So understanding. As if she really *knew*."

"About harassment?"

"About what it felt like to be the victim."

"Did she talk about having been a victim?"

"No, nothing like that. Just empathy—genuine empathy, not someone trying to fake it."

The blue eyes were unwavering.

"She was an amazing woman. I'll never forget her."

*   *   *

Tessa Bowlby's dorm was one of several six-story boxes propped at the northwest edge of the U's sprawling acreage. A big wooden sign on posts said STUDENT HOUSING, NO UNAUTHORIZED PARKING. The landscaping was rolling lawn and bearded coco palms. Just down the road was the cream-stucco-and-smoked-glass recreation center where Philip Seacrest and Hope Devane had met, years ago.

I parked in a loading zone at the side of the building, entered the lobby, and walked up to the front desk. A black woman in her twenties sat underlining a book with a thick pink marker. Her lips were the same shade of pink. Behind her was a switchboard. It blinked and beeped and as she turned to take the call she noticed me. Her book was full of fine print and pie graphs. I read the title, upside down. *Fundamentals of Economics.*

Plugging the board, she faced me. "Can I help you?"

"Tessa Bowlby, please."

She slid over a sheaf of papers. Typed list of names. The B's began on the second page and continued onto the third. She checked twice before shaking her head.

"Sorry, no one by that name."

"Tessa might be a nickname."

She inspected me and looked again. "No Bowlbys at all. Try another dorm."

I checked all of them. Same results.

Maybe Tessa had moved off-campus. Students did it all the time. But combined with the fear I'd seen in her eyes, plus her reduced workload, it added up to escape.

I used a pay phone in the last dorm to call Milo, wondering if he had her home address and wanting to tell him about the holes in Cruvic's training. He was away and the cell phone didn't answer, either. Maybe he'd found another three-stab murder or something else that would make my train of thought irrelevant.

Driving away from the U, I pulled into the first filling station I found in Westwood Village. The phone booth was a tilting aluminum wreck, but a Westside directory dangled under the phone, coverless and shredded, lots of pages missing. The page with all the Bowlbys was there.

All two of them:

Bowlby, T. J., Venice, no address listed.

Bowlby, Walter E., Mississippi Avenue in West L.A.

L.A.'s a random toss of residential pickup sticks, and with a dozen directories covering the county, the odds of either Bowlby being related to Tessa were low. But I went with what I had, starting with Walter on Mississippi because he was closer.

Very close. Between Santa Monica Boulevard and Olympic, just a mile or so south of the University, in a district of small postwar homes and a few much larger fantasy projects.

Garbage day in the neighborhood. Overflowing cans and corpulent lawn bags shouted out pride of consumption. Squirrels scavenged nervously. At night, their rat cousins would take over. Years ago the people of California had voted to reduce predatory property-tax rates and the politicians had meted out punishment by eliminating rodent control and other services. Like tree trimming. Money seemed to be available for other things, though: Last year after a storm I'd watched a thirteen-man city crew take four entire days to chop down and haul half a fallen pine.

Walter Bowlby's residence was a tan bungalow with a black shingle roof. The lawn was shaved close as a Marine recruit, more gray than green. A wide front porch played host to potted plants, an aluminum chair, and a small blue bike with training wheels. An old brown Ford Galaxie sat in the driveway. I walked up a strip of cement to the door. An enamel plaque, the kind you get at a carnival or an amusement park, said THE BOWLBYS! No one answered the bell or my knock.

I was back in the Seville and about to drive away when a blue-and-white van approached from Olympic and pulled in behind the Ford. Two bumper stickers: GO DODGERS. BUY UNION. It came to a smoking, shuddering stop and the driver's door opened.

A dark-mustachioed, bowlegged man in his forties got out. He wore a white nylon polo shirt with a horizontal green stripe that Milo would have liked, pleated off-white pants, and black work shoes. His arms were thick and sunburned but his frame was narrow. The beginnings of a gut swelled the green stripe and a cigarette pack pouched his shirt pocket. Twirling his car keys, he stood there examining the lawn, then he touched the cigarettes, as if to make sure they were still there, and turned as Tessa Bowlby came out of the front passenger door.

She looked to be wearing the same dark, baggy sweater and pipestem jeans I'd seen her in at the Psych Tower, and her complexion was even chalkier. She kept her back to the mustachioed man and slid open the van's rear door, allowing a pleasant-looking gray-haired woman in a red tank top and jeans to climb out. The woman looked tired. Gray hair but a young face. In her arms was a black-haired boy around four.

The child appeared to be sleeping but suddenly he squirmed and kicked, throwing the gray-haired woman off-balance. Tessa braced her and said something. The mustachioed man had pulled out a cigarette and now he just stood there as the gray-haired woman handed the child to Tessa.

Tessa broke into a smile so sweet and sudden it chilled me painfully, like ice cream eaten too fast.

She hugged the boy tight. He was giggling and still squirming. Tessa looked too frail to handle him, but she managed to hold on to him, planting her feet, tickling, laughing. His sneakered feet churned air and finally stopped. She nuzzled him and cut across the grass, carrying him to the porch.

All four of them went up the steps and the man put a key in the door. The little boy started squirming again and Tessa put him down. He ran straight to the blue bike and tried to get on, nearly falling. Tessa put him on the seat, held him, removed him. He tried to climb atop the porch rail and began laughing as Tessa rushed to hold his hand.

The man and the woman entered the house, leaving the door open. The boy was walking atop the rail, holding Tessa's hand. Suddenly, he jumped off. She caught him. He shimmied down her leg and he ran for the door. As she turned, she saw me.

That same look of panic.

She stared as the boy ran inside. Touched her cheek, stood there for a second, and ran in, herself.

The mustachioed man had come out a second later. Reminding myself I was legit, I stayed there.

He came toward me, swinging thick arms. When he was ten feet away, he stopped and surveyed the Seville from grille to taillight. Then he walked around the front of the car, stepping out into the street and making his way to the driver's window.

"I'm Walt Bowlby. My daughter says you're the police."

No challenge in his voice, just the weak hope that maybe it wasn't true. Up close his skin was leathery. A thin gold chain circled his neck. Chest hairs sprouted around it.

I showed him my ID. "I'm a police consultant, Mr. Bowlby."

"A consultant? Is there a problem?"

"I came here to talk to Tessa."

"Could you tell me about what, sir?"

"There was a crime near campus involving a professor of Tessa's. We're talking to anyone who knew the victim."

His shoulders dropped. "The lady professor. Tessa really doesn't know nothing about that and she's pretty—you know—upset."

"About the murder?"

He touched the cigarette pocket again, pulled out a softpack of Salems, then patted his pants for matches.

I found a book in the glove compartment and lit him up.

"Thanks. Not exactly about the professor. She . . ." He looked back at the house. "Mind if I get in your car, sir?"

"Not at all."

He walked around the back and took the passenger

seat, touching the leather. "Nice shape, always liked this model—seventy-eight?"

"Nine."

He nodded and smoked, blowing it out the window. "GM built it on a Chevy Two chassis, which lots of people thought was a mistake. But they hold up. This belong to the city, one of those impounds?"

"No, it's mine."

"Had it long?"

"A few years."

Another nod. He looked at the floorboards. "Tessa had a problem. Do you know about that?"

Not knowing if Tessa had told him about the rape, I said, "A problem Professor Devane helped her with?"

"Yeah. She . . . she's very bright. Tessa. Almost a genius IQ. When she wanted to drop out we asked why but she wouldn't tell us, just said she wanted to move back home. We were surprised, my wife and me, because she'd been the one made such a fuss about living on her own. Finally she broke down and cried and told us about the—you know. The assault. And how the professor hauled the guy up on charges. And then she got murdered. At first it sounded so wild we didn't know what to believe. Then we saw the news about the murder."

"What was wild, the murder or the rape?"

He inhaled a lot of smoke and held on to it for a long time. "Tell the truth, sir, all of it."

"Did you have doubts Tessa had been attacked?"

He stuck his arm out the car and flicked ashes. "How do I put this—I love my daughter a lot but she's . . . she's really smart, always was. Right from a baby. But different. She gets in these low moods. Depression. Since she's been little, always moody.

And then she goes into her own little world—a real good imagination. Sometimes . . ." He shrugged and smoked. The cigarette was nearly down to the filter.

"Her imagination can get wild," he said.

"Has she accused others of raping her, Mr. Bowlby?"

He sighed, took another drag, looked at the butt, and squeezed it out between his fingers. I slid open the ashtray and he dropped it in.

"Thanks. Mind if I light up another?"

"Go ahead."

"Disgusting habit. I quit every day." He laughed.

I smiled and repeated my question.

He said, "We used to live out in Temple City, the police there probably still got records. Though maybe not, 'cause the boy was a minor, I heard they don't keep records on minors."

"How long ago was this?"

"Tessa's almost twenty and she was twelve at the time, so eight years. The boy—we knew his family, I worked with his father at Ford, back when they had a plant in Montebello—the boy was a little older. Thirteen, I think. The families were close. We were all camping at Yosemite. Supposedly it happened in a tent, the two of them stayed behind while the rest of us went to the dump looking for bears. But the thing was, Tessa never said nothing til we got back home. Three or four days later. The Temple City police said it was really the park rangers' jurisdiction but they brought the boy in anyway for questioning. Then they said they thought he was innocent but we could pursue it if we wanted. They also said we should have a psychiatrist see Tessa."

Hollowing his cheeks, he sucked hungrily on the second cigarette and let the smoke trail out of his mouth. His teeth were brown, widely spaced. Veins bulged in the heavy, sunburned arms, and the tips of his nails were coal-black.

"She's—the thing is, sir, Tessa's smart, even with her problems, she always did great in school. Straight A's. Great imagination . . . we were hoping . . . I'd really prefer if you don't talk to her, sir. She's such a nice kid but delicate. Raising her's like walking a tightrope. One of her doctors said that to us. Said she's fragile. I can't see what good it would do to talk to her."

"So you do have doubts. About both stories."

He flinched. "I honestly don't know what to believe. The boy denied it completely and he never got in any other trouble that I know of. Joined the Navy last year, doing beautifully, got married, had a kid."

He looked miserable. I thought of Reed Muscadine's assessment of Tessa: *serious problems.*

"Has Tessa made other accusations, Mr. Bowlby?"

Another very long pause. He picked something out of his teeth and flicked it out the window.

"I guess you'll find out anyways, so I might as well tell you."

He started to smoke but instead made a gulping sound that caught me off-guard. A hand shot up and visored his eyes.

"She accused me," he said, in a shaky voice. "Two years later, when she was fourteen. We already had her to a psychiatrist because she was talking about hurting herself, not eating—you see how skinny she is. She used to have that disease, anorexia. Thinking she was fat, doing jumping jacks all day. She started that at around fourteen, was down to fifty pounds. The psychiatrist put her in a hospital and they fed her with an IV, gave her some counselor to talk to and that's when she started claiming she remembered."

The hand pulled away. His eyes were moist but he looked right at me.

"She said it happened when she was little—a baby, two or three." He shook his head. "It's not true, sir. They believed me—the hospital and the police and my wife. The law said they had to investigate and I went through the whole thing. It was pure hell. Temple City police, again. A Detective Gunderson. Nice guy, maybe he's still there. Anyway, the bottom line was that it was Tessa's imagination. It just runs away with itself. When she was a real little kid she'd watch something on TV, then wanna *be* it—cartoon characters, whatever. You understand? Flying around being Supergirl, whatever. So all I can figure is she musta saw some movie and started to believe something had happened to her."

He smoothed his mustache. "Before I got married I was a rough kid, spent a little time at the Youth Authority for burglary. But then I accepted my responsibilities, learned mechanics—I'm telling you all this so you see I'm straight. Know what I mean?"

"Yes."

"The thing is, with Tessa, you can never be sure *what* she's gonna do. After the investigation, she admitted she was wrong, said she felt guilty and wanted to kill herself. Her mom and I told her that would be the worst thing and we still loved her. To make matters worse, the insurance money for the hospital ran out and we had to take her home just then, when things were bad. The hospital said watch her closely. We didn't let her out of our sight. Then we did family counseling at a county clinic and she seemed to take to that, we thought she was okay. And to show you how smart she is, she got good grades through all of it, got accepted to the U. We thought *everything* was okay. Then, this year, she announces she's coming home. *Then* she breaks down and tells us about the rape thing. Some guy on a date. I told her I believed her but . . ."

He stubbed the second butt out in the ashtray. "If I was sure it was true, I'da looked for the guy, myself. But I know she falsely accused me. And that boy. So what was I to think? And she never complained right away, not til she heard that professor lecturing. Then the professor gets murdered. I heard that, I got scared."

"Scared in what way?"

"Guy like me, high-school dropout, I used to think college was safe. Then you hear about something like that."

"Did Tessa tell you anything about Professor Devane?"

"Just that she liked her. For believing her. She never thought anyone would believe her again. Then she got into what she'd said about me and started crying real hard. Saying she's sorry, doesn't want to be the girl who cried wolf. I told her, honey, what's past is past, you tell me this happened, I believe you, let's go to the police and nail the sucker. But she got *really* scared about that, said no, no one would believe her, it was a waste of time, there was no evidence, it was date rape, anyway, and no one took that seriously."

"Except Professor Devane."

"Except her. Yeah. I think that's the only reason she brought it up to us—the professor had been killed, she was scared. I said, are you telling me you think the guy who . . . assaulted you mighta killed her? But she wouldn't answer that, just kept saying the professor had believed her, treated her good and now she was dead, life sucked, the good die young, that kind of stuff. Then she said, I changed my mind about coming home, Daddy, I'm going back to the dorm. And she left. We let her go but we called her the next day and she didn't answer. So we went over there and found her lying in bed, staring at the ceiling. All this food all around her—trays of food, but she hadn't eaten any of it. She was just staring at the ceiling. We'd seen her that way, before. When she stopped taking her medicine."

"What medicine is that?"

"Used to be Nardil, then Tofranil, then Prozac. Now she's on something else—Sinequan? When she takes it, she does pretty good. Even with all the problems she's still pulling B's, which is amazing in my opinion. If she didn't have problems, she'd be straight A's. She's a smart girl, always was. Maybe too smart, I don't know."

He held his hands out, palms up.

"So you found her in bed," I said. "Not eating."

"We checked her out of the dorm and took her home. She was only in two classes, anyway, 'cause her doctor didn't want her to be pressured. We said why don't you drop out for a quarter, you can always come back. She said, no, she wanted to keep going. And her doctor said that was a good sign—her being motivated. So we let her."

He turned to me. "She's enrolled but she doesn't do nothing. No reading, no homework."

"Does she still go to classes?"

"Sometimes. My wife drives her and picks her up. Sometimes she sleeps in and doesn't go. We don't like it but what can we do? You can't watch 'em twenty-four hours. Even the psychiatrist says so."

"So she's still seeing a psychiatrist?"

"Not regularly but we still call him because he's a nice guy, kept seeing her even after the money ran out. Dr. Emerson, out in Glendale. You want to talk to him, be my guest. Albert Emerson." He recited a number that I copied.

"Did he ever give you a diagnosis?"

"Depression. He says she uses her imagination to protect herself."

He rubbed his eyes and sighed.

"Rough," I said.

"Them's the breaks. My little boy's great."

"How old is he?"

"Be four next month—big for his age."

"Any other children?"

"No, just the two. We weren't sure we should have more 'cause of all the time we put into Tess. And she—my wife—has got a retarded brother, lives in an institution. So we didn't know if there was something inbred or anything."

He smiled. "Then we got surprised."

"Nice surprise," I said.

"Oh yeah. Robbie's a great little guy, throws a ball like you wouldn't believe. Being with him's about the only thing that makes Tess happy. I let her baby-sit but I keep an eye out."

"For what?"

"Her moods. He's a happy kid and I want to keep it that way. Like when we were watching the news about that professor and Tess started to scream, it got

Robbie really upset. That's how I calmed her down. Telling her, honey, get a grip, look at Robbie. After that she was okay. After that she didn't even want to talk about it. She's calmed down, so far so good. But I keep my eye out."

18

I had him write me out permission to speak to Dr. Albert Emerson and drove home. Robin's truck was gone and I found a note in the kitchen saying she'd left to do some emergency repair work for a country singer out in Simi Valley and would be back by seven or eight.

I called the psychiatrist, expecting a service or a receptionist, but he answered his own phone in an expectant, boyish voice—someone ready for adventure.

I introduced myself.

"Delaware—I know the name. You were involved with the Jones case, right?"

"Right," I said, surprised. Rich defendant and a plea bargain; it had all been kept out of the papers.

"The defense called me," he said, "when they were figuring out which place to send the bastard. Wanted me to testify on his behalf, get him a cushy bed. I said wrong number, counselor, my wife's an assistant D.A. and my sympathies tend to run in the other direction. Did they put him away for long?"

"Hopefully," I said.

"Yeah, you never know when there's money involved. So, what can I do for you?"

"I'm working with the police on another case. A psychology professor who was murdered a few months ago."

"I remember it," he said. "Near the U. You like criminal cases?"

"I like closure."

"Know what you mean. So what's my connection?"

"Tessa Bowlby. She knew the victim. Accused another student of date rape and brought him up before a sexual-conduct committee chaired by Professor Devane. We're talking to all the students involved with the committee but Tessa doesn't want to talk and her problems make me reluctant to push it."

"Sexual-conduct committee," he said. His tone told me Tessa had never mentioned it. Walter Bowlby had said Tessa's involvement with Emerson was sketchy.

"I haven't seen Tessa in a while. Which is more than I should tell you in the first place."

"I've got a signed release from her father."

"Tessa's over eighteen so that doesn't mean much. So what's the theory, one of the guys called up before this committee got mad and acted out?"

"With no evidence, theories abound," I said. "The police are looking into every possible avenue."

"A conduct committee," he repeated. "And Tessa actually brought charges?"

"Yes."

"Wow . . . it wasn't in the papers, was it?"

"No."

"Did the process get hostile?"

"It wasn't pleasant," I said. "But the committee didn't last long 'cause the U killed it."

"And then someone killed Professor Devane. Weird. Sorry I can't help you, but let's just say I don't have much to offer."

"About Tessa or her father?"

"Both," he said. "I wouldn't . . . spend much time on that aspect. Now, I've got a patient ringing in the waiting room so let's cut this short while our ethics remain intact."

So much for the conduct committee.

Back to Dr. Cruvic of the curious educational history.

That institute where he'd spent a year after he'd left Washington—Brooke-Hastings. Corte Madera—just outside San Francisco. Returning to his Northern California turf.

I called Corte Madera Information for a number. Nothing. Nothing in San Francisco or Berkeley or Oakland or Palo Alto or anywhere within a hundred-mile radius.

Next question mark: the hospital where Cruvic had resumed his training, this time as an OB-GYN.

Fidelity Medical Center in Carson.

No listing there, either.

Could the guy be a total impostor?

But UC Berkeley told me he was a member in good standing of the alumni association. Same with UC San Francisco Medical School.

So the funny stuff began after he'd received his M.D.

As I was thinking about that, Milo called. "No other murders that match, so far. Vegas is trying to get hold of Ted Barnaby, Mandy's boyfriend, to see if he can shed light on her medical history or anything else. So far it's no-go, they got him traced as far as Tahoe, then *nada*."

"The casino circuit," I said.

"Yeah. Interestingly, they know Cruvic in Vegas. Comes a few times a year, somewhat of a high roller."

"Just the kind of guy Mandy would gravitate toward."

"No one remembers them together, but I sent Mandy's picture to L.A. Vice to see if she had any kind of history here, and I'm planning to visit a few clubs tonight, places on the Strip where the high-priced girls are known to party."

"Casinos, clubs. Some lifestyle."

"Rust never sleeps, why should I? I also received a FedEx this morning, humongous packet of alibi material on Patrick Huang from his father's law firm. Photos, menus, notarized affidavits from the maitre d', waiters, busboys, family members."

"Nothing like a lawyer father," I said. "Well, that's good, 'cause Deborah Brittain still seems nervous about him."

"Why?"

"The experience unnerved her. Though she did admit he hasn't bothered her since. She adored Hope, said Hope really made a big difference in her life. I also located Tessa Bowlby and learned something interesting."

I recounted the conversations with Walter Bowlby and Dr. Emerson.

"Major psychological problems," he said. "Think

the father's being truthful about her accusing him falsely?"

"How can you ever know? Dr. Emerson implied to me there was little value looking into it. He sounded sharp, but Tessa doesn't see him regularly, hadn't told him about her connection to Hope or the committee. Mr. Bowlby did seem forthcoming. Gave me the name of the Temple City detective who investigated the accusation. Gunderson."

"I'll call," he said. "False claims . . . so Muscadine could be telling the truth."

"Even if he isn't, I can't see any link to Mandy Wright."

"Leaving only Monsieur Kenny Storm, Junior, whom I'm meeting tomorrow afternoon at *his* dad's office. Want to come along, check out *his* psyche?"

"Sure. I also learned a few more things about Dr. Cruvic."

I started with the cars in the clinic lot late at night, the armed guard. Multiple after-hours abortions at nine hundred dollars a throw.

"Something's got to pay for the Bentley," he said.

"Wait, there's more. Cruvic's card says 'practice limited to fertility' but he lacks formal training in fertility, and there are other irregularities in his bio. He left surgical residency at the University of Washington after only one year, took a leave of absence at a place called the Brooke-Hastings Institute, and switched to OB-GYN at a hospital in Carson—Fidelity Medical Center. I can't find either place."

"A phony?"

"His B.A. and his M.D. are real and there are no claims filed against him. And it's possible both Brooke-Hastings and Fidelity closed down. But going from a high-prestige teaching hospital to an obscure private place isn't exactly a horizontal transfer. So it's possible he didn't leave because of a change in interest. Maybe he was kicked out for some sort of misconduct, cooled his heels, then applied for an inferior internship in a new area. And maybe his conduct hasn't gotten any better, since. Holding himself out as a fertility expert is certainly iffy."

"Interesting," he said. "Yes, it does begin to take on a certain *smell*. And Hope was his consultant—money games gone bad?"

"Maybe *that's* what Seacrest is being evasive about. Not infidelity—something financial. That would explain his making such a point about having kept his nose out of Hope's professional activities."

"Distancing himself . . . could be."

"Want me to have another go at him?"

"Prof to prof? Sure, be my guest. . . . Dr. Heelspur . . . he's the only one we've caught in a lie."

"Like him better as a suspect?"

"Let's just say I'm developing an incipient, borderline, minor-league crush on him. If I can tie him in with Mandy in any way, I'll fall head-over-fucking-heels in *love* with him."

It was 7:10 and Robin was still out. Emergency repairs could get complicated. I phoned the country singer's recording studio and she said, "Sorry, hon, earthquake stuff. This is going to take some time—at least another couple of hours."

"Eat yet?"

"No, I just want to finish up. But don't go to any trouble, I'll probably just want something simple."

"Foie gras?"

She laughed. "Sure, go catch a goose."

*   *   *

I sat there for a while, drinking coffee and thinking. Pizza was simple.

And there was a great little place in Beverly Hills that still believed ducks belonged in the water, not on thin crust.

On the way I'd make another stop at Civic Center Drive.

This time I checked the alley first. Once again, the three parking slots behind the pink building were empty. Once again, no lights.

In front, the street was still and dark except for widely spaced streetlamps and the occasional wash of headlight. Everyone was closed up for the night. I pulled into a spot fifty yards from the pink building's entrance, kept myself alert by imagining the things an unethical doctor could do to a patient.

Cruvic's wing tips covered with blood . . .

Hyperactive imagination. When I was a kid it had vexed my teachers.

Headlights, up close. Beverly Hills patrol car cruised by from the police station on the other side of the tracks.

Beverly Hills cops were edgy about people sitting in cars without a good excuse. But the car drove on.

Suddenly, I felt foolish. Even if Cruvic showed, what would I say?

Hi, just a bit of follow-up: What exactly is the Brooke-Hastings Institute and what did you do there—and by the way, what's with the fertility BS?

I started the Seville and was just about to switch

the lights on when a grinding sound behind me drew my attention.

The corrugated door of the building next to Cruvic's was sliding upward. A car with its lights already on.

Not a Bentley. A small, dark sedan. It edged out, then turned right. Two people inside. The driver, Nurse Anna, of the tight face and lipsticked cigarettes. Next to her, a male passenger.

So the neighboring building was part of Cruvic's setup, too.

Anna drove to Foothill Road, made an incomplete stop, and turned right again.

I backed out and followed.

She made two more rights, at Burton Way and Rexford Drive—a long U-turn that took her into the flats of north Beverly Hills with its seven-figure teardowns, up to Sunset, then across to the Coldwater Canyon intersection.

Headed toward the Valley. Maybe nothing more ominous than a working woman returning home with a spouse or boyfriend.

Two cars got between us. The commuter rush out of the city was over but traffic into the Valley was still heavy enough to slow us to twenty miles an hour. I managed to keep my sights on the small sedan and when it caught a red light at Cherokee Lane I shifted to the right to get a closer look. The car was a Toyota, newish. Two heads inside, neither of them moving.

Then Anna leaned to the right and an orange ember appeared inside the car, like a circling firefly. It flew to the left, kept going as she dangled her left hand out the window and let the cigarette droop.

Sparks flicked onto the road. The man in the passenger seat still hadn't budged. Either he was sitting low or he wasn't tall.

Cruvic was no giant. Catching a lift home from his nurse? Or was their relationship more than business?

Affairs on the brain, Delaware. And I didn't even watch soap operas.

The light turned green and the Toyota shot forward, adding more speed as it took on the Santa Monica Mountains. There were no more stops til Mulholland Drive, where most of the traffic continued the northward descent to Studio City. But the Toyota hooked east on Mulholland and I found myself behind it.

I slowed down. Anna picked up speed, taking turns with the confidence of someone who knew the route. Years ago Mulholland had been undeveloped from Woodland Hills to Hollywood, miles of black ribbon affording a heart-stopping view of the glitter below. Now roadside houses and landscaping blocked most of it out.

No one behind me. I turned off my headlights. Mulholland got darker and narrower and quieter and the Toyota whipped through the curves for another couple of miles before coming to a sudden stop.

I was a ways back but still had to stop short, managing to avoid tire-squeal and skidding only slightly. The Toyota remained on the road, brake lights on. I pulled over to the right shoulder, kept the Seville in drive, and watched.

A car was coming from the opposite direction.

When it passed, the Toyota crossed Mulholland diagonally, rolling up a driveway and coming to rest on a wide concrete pad in front of a high iron gate.

Two faint lights—fixtures on brick posts. Everything else was foliage and darkness.

The Toyota's passenger door opened and the man
got out, briefly revealed by the dome light, but his
back was to me.

He walked up to one of the gateposts and touched
it. Pushing a button.

As the gate started to slide open, I edged back onto
the road and drove forward a bit.

Then the Toyota backed out and straightened and I
waited til it drove off.

The gate was open and the man was walking
through. With my lights still off, I zoomed past—just
another bad driver. The sound made the man turn, as
I'd hoped he would.

During the split second, I studied him, helped by
the gatepost lights.

A face I'd seen before.

Lean, intelligent. Full lips. Long hair slicked back.
Hollow cheeks, arched eyebrows.

James Dean with an attitude.

A short man, but not Cruvic.

Casey Locking, Hope's prize student.

He scratched his ear.

If I hadn't known about the skull ring, I wouldn't
have seen it, glinting from his delicate white hand.

I sped back toward the Mulholland intersection.

Hope and Cruvic.

Hope's student with Cruvic's nurse.

Did Locking live behind the gates?

Nice digs for a grad student. Well-to-do parents?
Or was it Cruvic's place, and time for a conference?

Stopping, I did a three-point turn and headed back

toward the house, pausing far enough from the gate-posts to make sure no one was outside, then rolling forward slowly. The address was marked by small white numbers on the left-hand post and I memorized them.

What would a psych grad student have to do with fertility or abortions?

Carrying on Hope's "consultation"?

Something corrupt in a big way? A wide enough net to snare Hope and Mandy Wright?

Or something benign—a shared academic project on unwanted pregnancies, the psychological effects of infertility, whatever.

But Locking had never mentioned anything like that and Hope hadn't published on those topics.

And scholarship didn't explain Locking getting a lift from Cruvic's nurse.

None of it made sense.

When I pulled up in front of the house Robin and Spike were climbing the steps. I'd forgotten about the pizza.

She waved and he whirled around and stacked himself, head out, feet planted, as if competing at a dog show. Glaring til he heard my "Hi!" Then he began straining at the leash and Robin let him run down to greet me.

As I rubbed his head, he bayed like a hound and butted. Finally he shook himself off and led me up to Robin.

I pulled her up against me and kissed her deeply.

"Boy," she said. "What perfume did I put on this morning?"

"Forget perfume," I said. "Eternal love." I kissed her again, then she unlocked the door and let us in.

"How'd the emergency repair go?" I said.

She laughed and bent her head forward, flexing her neck and shaking out her curls. "Guitar 911, I salvaged most of the instruments. Poor Montana. Top of that I've got more work to do, tonight. Promised to fix Eno Burke's double-neck for a recording session tomorrow."

"You're kidding."

"Wish I was. At least they're paying me triple."

I rubbed her shoulders. "All-nighter?"

"Hopefully not. I need a nap, first."

"Want me to make you some coffee?"

"No, thanks, I've been coffeeing all day—sorry, Alex, were you planning on some quality time?"

"I'm always open-minded."

She pressed her back against my chest. "How about a nap, together? You can tell me bedtime stories."

Later that night, I sat in my robe in my office and went through the mail. Bills, liars trying to sell me things, and a long-overdue check from a lawyer who collected Ferraris.

I couldn't stop thinking of Locking and Nurse Anna . . . self-control.

I'd been unable to reach Milo anywhere. Then I remembered he was visiting clubs on the Strip tonight.

Lumbering among the beautiful people.

That brought a smile to my lips.

I checked in with my service.

Professor Julia Steinberger had called just after I'd left for Beverly Hills.

Had she remembered something?

She'd left a campus number and a Hancock Park exchange.

Her husband answered at the second ring and said, "She's not home, probably won't be back for a while. Why don't you try her tomorrow at her office."

Friendly, but tired.

I left my name, put on sweats and a T-shirt, went over to Spike's resting place in the kitchen, and asked if he wanted to get a little exercise. He ignored me but when I took out his leash, he bounded to his stumpy feet and followed me to the door.

Outside, I could hear Robin hammering.

Spike and I took a long walk up the Glen, turned onto some dark side streets where the sweet smell of budding pittosporum trees was almost overpowering.

Stopping from time to time as he paused, looked around, growled at unseen things.

19

At 9:00 A.M. I tried Julia Steinberger's office but she wasn't in and the Chemistry Department office said she was teaching a graduate seminar til noon.

I had other things to do on campus.

In the Psychology office, three secretaries sat at computer screens but the receptionist's desk was empty. Mail was piled high on the counter and several students stood at the bulletin board reading employment ads.

I said, "Excuse me," and the nearest typist looked up. Young, cute, redheaded.

Showing her my faculty card from the med school crosstown, I said, "This probably makes me persona non grata, but perhaps you'll be kind enough to help me anyway."

"Ooh," she said, smiling, still punching keys.

"Treason, Doctor? Well, I don't care about football. What can I do for you?"

"I'm looking for a grad student named Casey Locking."

"He's got an office down in the basement but he isn't here too often, mostly works out of his house."

She made a trip to the back, came back empty-handed.

"That's funny. His folder's gone. Hold on."

She typed, switched computer files, brought up a list of names. "Here we go. Room B-five-three-three-one, you can use the phone at the end of the counter."

I did. No answer. I went downstairs, anyway. Most of the basement rooms were labs. Locking's was marked by an index card. No answer to my knock.

Back upstairs, I told the redhead, "Not in. Too bad. He applied for a job and I was going to set up an appointment."

"Would you like his home number?"

"I guess I could try it."

She wrote something down. Out in the lobby I read it: A 213 number with an 858 prefix. Hollywood Hills, east of La Cienega. Not the Mulholland house.

So he'd gone there to meet someone. Probably Cruvic.

His folder gone. I used a lobby pay phone and called the number. Locking's liquid voice said, "No one home. Speak or forget it." Hanging up, I left the building.

Time to visit the History Department.

Hays Hall was one of the U's oldest buildings, just behind Palmer Library and, like Palmer, yellowish limestone grimy with pollution. Seacrest's office was on the top floor, up three flights and at the end of an echoing, musty hallway lined with carved mahogany doors. His door was open but he wasn't inside.

It was a big, chilly, pale green room with a domed ceiling and leaded windows that needed washing, brown velvet drapes tied back with brass rings, built-in bookshelves, a tatty Persian rug once red, now pink.

An ugly seven-foot Victorian desk on ball feet was backed by a black cloth orthopedic chair. Facing it were three cracked red leather club chairs, one of them mended with duct tape. The desk was as neat as his home office: Arranged on the surface were a precisely cornered stack of blue-book exams, two neolithic urns, and a Royal manual typewriter. Half an egg-salad sandwich on waxed paper sat on a green blotter along with an unopened can of Diet Sprite. Not a stain, not a crumb.

Seacrest came in drying his hands with a paper towel. He had on a gray V-neck sweater over a brown-checked shirt and gray knit tie. The sweater's cuffs were frayed and his eyes looked filmy. Walking around me, he sat down behind the desk and looked at the sandwich.

"Morning," I said.

He picked up the sandwich and took a bite. "What can I do for you?"

"If you've got time, I have a few questions."

"About?"

"Your relationship with your wife."

He put the sandwich down. He hadn't invited me to sit and I was still on my feet.

"My relationship with my wife," he repeated softly.

"I don't want to intrude—"

"But you will, anyway, because the police are paying you."

He broke off a small piece of bread crust and chewed slowly.

"Good racket," he said.

"Pardon?"

"Why are you willing to intrude?"

"Professor, if this is a bad time—"

"Oh, spare me." He tilted back in the chair. "You know, it wasn't until that little nocturnal visit you and Sturgis paid me that I realized I was actually a suspect. What was the purpose of that, anyway? Trying to catch me off-guard? Hoping I'd somehow incriminate myself? Is it a *bad* time? It's *always* a bad time."

He shook his head. "This goddamn city. Everyone wants to write his own tawdry tabloid story. Tell Sturgis he's been living in L.A. too long, should learn to do some real detecting."

His face had turned scarlet. "I suppose I shouldn't have been surprised. No doubt there's some idiotic *detective* manual that says suspect the husband. And those first two stooges were hostile from the beginning. But why inject *you* into the process? Does he really think I'm going to be impressed by your psychological *acuity*?"

Shaking his head again, he ate more of the sandwich, striking at it with hard, sharp movements, as if it were dangerous but irresistible.

"Not that being under suspicion matters to me," he said. "I've got nothing to hide, so root around to your heart's content. And as far as my relationship with my wife, neither of us was easy to get along with so the fact that we stayed together should tell you something. Furthermore, what reason would I have to harm her? Money? Yes, she made a fortune last year, but money means *nothing* to me. When her estate clears I may damn well donate all of it to charity. Wait and see if you don't believe me. So what other motive could there be?"

He laughed. "No, Delaware, my life hasn't improved since Hope died. Even when she was alive I was a solitary person. Losing her has left me *completely* alone and I find I no longer want that. Now kindly let me eat my lunch in peace."

As I headed for the door, he said, "It's a pity Sturgis is so uncreative. Following the manual will only reduce whatever small chance he has of learning the truth."

"You're not optimistic."

"Have the police given me reason to be? Perhaps I should hire a private investigator. Though I wouldn't know where to turn." He gave a low, barking laugh. "I don't even have an attorney. And not for lack of opportunity. Someone must have given my phone number to the Sleazy Lawyers Club or perhaps the bastards just sniff out misery. Right after the murder I had several calls a day, then it tapered off. Even now, they occasionally try."

"What do they want from you?"

"To sue the city for not trimming the trees." He barked again. "As if *landscaping* were the issue."

"What is?"

"The total breakdown of order—too bad I can't work up a healthy lust for profit. Write a book that would sell—wouldn't that be charming? The grieving widower on the talk-show circuit. Following in Hope's footsteps."

"Hope was pretty good at it."

"Hope was good at *everything*. Do you understand that? The woman was *exceptional*."

I nodded.

"Actually," he said, "she despised the publicity game but knew it was useful."

"She told you that."

"Yes, Delaware. She was my *wife*. She *confided* in me."

Popping the top of his soda can, he peered into the opening. "Oh, Christ, why am I wasting my time with you—can you even imagine what it was like sharing my roof with someone like that? Like living with a borrowed masterpiece—a Renoir or a Degas. One knows one can never own it, or even fully understand it, but one is *grateful*."

"Borrowed from whom?" I said.

"God, the Fates, choose your superstition."

He drank soda and put down the can. "So now he thinks: Was he jealous? The answer is no, I was in awe, but a loving awe. Next question in his psychoanalytic mind: What did she see in him? And the answer is sometimes I wondered myself. And now, she's gone . . . and your boob police friend thinks *I'm* the culprit—have you studied much history, Dr. Delaware?"

"Not formally since college but I try to learn from the past."

"How admirable. . . . Have you ever thought about what history *really* is? An accounting of failure, iniquity, errors of judgment, character flaws, bloody cruelties, obscene missteps. Human beings are such *low* things. What greater support of atheism is there than the repulsive nature of those scraps of flesh and weakness allegedly created in God's image? Or perhaps there *is* a master deity and he's an incompetent boob like everyone else. Wouldn't that be a hoot—now please leave me *alone*!"

20

It was good to get back out in the sunlight.

Pretending the warmth could melt the bitterness I'd absorbed up in his office.

Real pain and anger or an act to prevent me from probing?

Confronted with a question about his and Hope's relationship, he'd never said it had been good, only that they'd both been hard to live with and their endurance proved something.

Then he'd admitted he was jealous but turned it into worship.

Living with a masterpiece . . . that could wear thin.

I thought of the sudden way he'd flushed. Short fuse.

People with severe temper-control problems often betray themselves physiologically.

Root around to your heart's content.

Secure in his innocence or a psychopath's catch-me-if-you-can challenge?

The meeting at Kenneth Storm Sr.'s office in Pasadena was at one. Julia Steinberger would be finished teaching in twenty minutes.

I used a library phone and gave Casey Locking's home another try. Same tape.

Late evening in England, but still a civil hour to call Hope's other student, Mary Ann Gonsalvez.

Once again, the phone just kept ringing.

Back to the world of real science.

Julia Steinberger was heading for her office, flanked by two male graduate students. When she saw me, she frowned and told them, "Could you give me just a minute, guys? I'll come by the lab."

They left and she unlocked the office. She was wearing a knee-length black dress and black onyx necklace and looked troubled. When the door closed behind us, she remained standing.

"I don't know if I'm doing the right thing," she said, "but the first time you were here there was something I left out. It's probably not relevant—I find the whole thing distasteful."

"Something about Hope?" I said.

"Yes. Something—remember how I told you I'd had an intuition about her possibly having been abused?"

"The fierce look."

"That was true," she said. "She had that look. But . . . I—there was something else. It was last year—at the Faculty Club. Not the welcoming tea, something else—some guest lectureship, who remembers."

Walking to her desk, she braced her palms on the top. Looked at the doll she'd fondled the first time, but made no move toward it.

"We chatted a bit, then Hope moved on to circulate and Gerry and I found someone else to talk to. Then, maybe an hour later, at the end of the evening, I went to the ladies' room and she was in there, standing at the mirror. There's an entry room before you get into the main bathroom, also mirrored, and the way it's set up, you can get a look into the bathroom as you pass. It's carpeted, I guess she didn't hear me."

She lowered her eyes.

"She was in there, examining herself. Her arms. Her dress was cut low on the shoulders but with elbow-length sleeves. I'd noticed it, very elegant, figured it had cost a fortune. She'd pulled one of the shoulders down and was looking at her upper arm. There was a strange look in her eyes—almost hypnotized—and her expression was blank. And on the arm was a bruise. A large one. Black-and-blue. Right here."

She touched her own bicep. "Several marks, actually. Dots. Finger marks. As if she'd been squeezed very hard. Her skin was extremely white—beautiful skin—so the contrast was dramatic, almost like tattoos. And the bruises looked fresh—hadn't yet turned that greenish-purple color."

She hurried back to the door, fighting tears. "That's it."

"How'd she react when you walked in?" I said.

"She yanked up the sleeve, her eyes came back into focus, and she said, 'Hi, Julia,' as if nothing had happened. Then she made happy talk and put on her makeup. Chatting on and on about how different things would be if men were expected to always be in perfect face. I agreed with her and we *both* pretended nothing had happened. What was I supposed to say? Who did that to you?"

She opened the door. "Maybe it was nothing. Maybe she just had delicate skin, bruised easily . . . but when she asked me to be on the committee, I just felt as if I owed it to her."

Dark bruises on white skin.

Seacrest's sudden anger.

I got back in the Seville and onto the 405 north.

Pasadena eats more than its share of smog but today the air was clean and the office buildings on Cordova Street shone as beautifully as a Richard Estes painting.

Storm Realty and Investment was a one-story neo-Spanish surrounded by brilliant flower beds and jacaranda trees still in purple bloom. The accompanying parking lot was pristine. I pulled in next to Milo's unmarked just as he got out. He was carrying his briefcase and a tape recorder and was wearing a gray suit, white button-down shirt, red-and-blue rep tie.

"Very GOP," I said, looking down at his desert boots and trying not to smile.

"When in businessland, do as the businessmen. Speaking of commerce, I found a couple of Sunset Strip bars Mandy Wright just might have frequented."

"Might?"

"No ID yet but a couple of promising maybes. We're talking big hair, perfect bodies, so an ugly girl would have stood out better. As is, I was lucky to find two bartenders who'd been working there a year ago. Neither would swear it was her, just that she looked familiar."

"Was she working or hanging out?"

"Her line of work, is there a difference? And if she was working, they wouldn't admit it and jeopardize the liquor license. The thing that makes me think it could be a valid lead is the places were only a block apart, so maybe she was cruising. Club None and the Pit. Trouble is, neither barkeep can remember seeing her with anyone."

"But it does put her in L.A."

He crossed his fingers. "The other thing is, I spoke to Gunderson, the Temple City detective who handled Tessa's complaint against her old man. He's an assistant chief now, barely remembered the case, but he pulled the file and said his notes indicate they never took the complaint seriously. Considered Tessa a head case. He started to remember the father vaguely. As a nice guy—admitted to a juvenile record when he didn't have to, very up-front about everything. So Muscadine is looking increasingly righteous and let's finish with the damned committee—ready for Master Storm?"

"Before we begin, I've got some evidence of Hope being abused." I told him Steinberger's story, then my few minutes with Seacrest.

"Bruises and a bad temper," he said, frowning. "What, specifically, got him so pissed?"

"He was pissed at the outset, got red in the face when I told him I wanted to talk about the relationship."

"Good. Maybe we're getting under his skin. Maybe I should work him a little more. . . . Wouldn't that be something, he roughs her up for years and she writes the book telling women how to defend themselves."

"Wouldn't be the first time," I said.

"For what?"

"Style over substance. Little boxes. But if she and Seacrest were having problems, the book, all the attention it got her, could have crystallized her dissatisfaction, made her decide to finally break away. Maybe in that sense, fame *was* her death sentence. But as to what that has to do with Mandy Wright, I still can't come up with anything. And here's another complication: Last night I took another drive by Cruvic's office. He wasn't in but Nurse Anna was. Along with Casey Locking."

I told him about the Mulholland house and he copied down the address.

"Shit," he said. "Just when you thought it was safe to go back into hypothesisland—okay, I'll find out who owns it. Meanwhile, let's go persecute a mouthy kid."

We crossed a long, quiet reception area to get to Kenneth Storm Sr.'s office, past a pair of secretaries who looked up from their keyboards resentfully, talk radio in the background.

The Storms were a testament to genetics, both bull-necked and wide-shouldered with sandy crew cuts and small, suspicious eyes that locked in place for long stretches.

Senior was fiftyish with the dissolute, puffy look of a fullback gone sedentary. He wore a navy blazer with gold buttons and a Masonic pin in the lapel. Junior's jacket was dark green, his buttons as bright as his father's.

They were both positioned behind Senior's canoe-shaped blond-oak desk, which had been cleared of everything but a cowboy bronze and a green onyx pen-and-pencil set. The office was too big for the furniture, walled in oak veneer and carpeted in beige shag. Real-estate and life-insurance achievement awards were Senior's idea of self-validation. A cigar smell filled the room but no ashtrays were in sight.

Standing in front of the desk was a rangy, hawk-nosed, gray-haired man wearing a three-piece charcoal suit, French-cuffed powder-blue shirt, and a silk tie in someone's idea of power pink. He introduced himself as Pierre Bateman, Storm's attorney, and I recalled his name from the complaint against the conduct committee. Before we had a chance to sit, he began laying down stipulations for the interview in a slow, droning voice. Kenneth Storm Jr. yawned and scratched behind his ears and stuck his index finger in and out of a buttonhole. His father stared down at the desktop.

"Furthermore," said Bateman, "with regard to the substance of this proced—"

"Are you a criminal lawyer, sir?" said Milo.

"I'm Mr. Storm's attorney of record. I handle all his business affairs."

"So you regard this as a business affair?"

Bateman bared his teeth. "May I continue, Detective?"

"Has Mr. Storm *Jr.* engaged you formally?"

"That's hardly relevant."

"It might be if you're going to stand around making up rules."

Bateman massaged a sapphire cuff link and looked at the boy. "Would you care to designate me as your attorney, Kenny?"

Junior rolled his eyes. His father tapped his sleeve with an index finger.

"Yeah, sure."

"All right, then," said Bateman, "with regard to this procedure, Detective, you will refrain from . . ."

Milo placed his tape recorder on the desk.

"I have a problem with that," said Bateman.

"With what?"

"Taping. This is neither court testimony nor a formal deposition and my client's not under any formal suspicion—"

"So why are you acting like he is?"

"Detective," said Bateman. "I insist that you stop interrupting—"

Milo shut him up with a loud exhalation. Picking up the recorder, he examined a switch. "Mr. Bateman, we drove out here as a courtesy, rescheduled several times as a courtesy, allowed your client's father to be *present* as a courtesy, even though he's reached the age of majority. We are not talking juvey traffic court here. Our interest in the lad is the fact that he had a highly hostile exchange with a woman who was subsequently stabbed to death."

Junior mumbled and Senior shot him a look.

"Detective," said Bateman. "Surely—"

"Counselor," said Milo, taking a few steps closer. "He's not a formal suspect yet, but all this shuffling and dodging is definitely firming up the picture of an individual with something to hide. You wanna sit here, play F. Lee Bombast, that's your business. But if we do conduct an interview today it's gonna be taped and I'm gonna ask what I want. Otherwise, we'll reschedule at the West L.A. substation and *you* all deal with the freeway and the press."

Junior mumbled again.

"Ken," warned Senior.

Junior rolled his eyes again and fingered a pimple

on the side of his neck. His hands were big, hairless, powerful.

Milo said, "Sorry to be taking up your time, son. Though you've got a bit of time on your hands, don't you. Being out of school and all that."

Junior's neck stretched as he jutted his lower jaw. His father tapped his cuff again.

"Detective," said Bateman, "that was a wonderful speech. Now, if you'll allow me to continue my stipulations."

Milo picked up the recorder and headed for the door. "*Sayonara*, gentlemen."

We were halfway across the reception area when Bateman called out, "Detective?"

We kept walking and the lawyer hurried to catch up. The reception area had gone quiet, the two secretaries staring. The talk jock was pontificating about athletes' salaries. The place smelled of mouthwash.

"That was intemperate, Detective," Bateman stage-whispered. "This is a kid."

"He's nineteen and more than big enough to do damage, Mr. Bateman. Expect a call."

He pushed the door open and Bateman followed us out to the parking lot.

"Mr. Storm's well-regarded in his community, Detective, and Kenny's a solid boy."

"Good for them."

"With all the gangs and the serious crime, one would think the police have better things to do—"

"Than harass law-abiding citizens?" said Milo. "What can I say, we're stupid." We reached the unmarked.

"Just wait one minute." Bateman's voice had tightened, but with anxiety, not indignation.

Milo took out his keys.

"Look, Detective, I'm here so they'll feel protected. Kenny really *is* a good kid, I've known him for years."

"Protected against what?"

"Things have been rough, lately. They're both under considerable stress."

Milo opened the car door and put his gear in.

Bateman edged closer and spoke in a lower voice. "I don't expect you to care, but Ken—Ken Sr.'s having some financial difficulties. Serious ones. The real-estate market."

Milo straightened but didn't answer.

"It's a hard time for both of them," said Bateman. "First Ken's wife died, very sudden, an aneurysm. And now this. Ken built his business from nothing. Built this *building* twenty years ago and now it's on the verge of foreclosure. And losing it won't solve all his problems, there are plenty of other creditors. So you can see why he'd be nervous about the legal process. I'm his friend as well as his lawyer. I feel obligated to protect him as much as I can."

"We're not talking real estate, here, Mr. Bateman."

The attorney nodded. "Truth is, I don't know shit from shinola about criminal law and told Ken so. But he and I go back to grade school. He insisted on having me present."

"So he thinks the boy needs legal help."

"No, no, only in general terms—not getting shafted by the system. To be frank, Kenny's no genius and he has a bad temper. So does Ken. So did *his* dad, for that matter. The whole damn bunch of them have short fuses, for all I know that's how they got the family name."

He smiled but Milo didn't return it.

"Is Kenny an only child?"

"No, there's a daughter up at Stanford Med."

"The bright one."

"Cheryl's a whiz."

"How do she and Kenny get along?"

"Fine, but Kenny's never been at her level and everyone knows it. My point is, Detective, take those tempers and add all the stress, and without some sort of structure, there's a good chance both of them would eventually get hot under the collar and pop off. Give the wrong impression."

"Which is?"

"That Kenny's capable of violence. He isn't, believe me. He played football with my kid in high school, had the speed and the muscle but got dropped from the team because he wasn't aggressive enough."

"No killer instinct, huh?"

Bateman gave a pained look. "Furthermore, he assures me that on the night of the murder he was in San Diego."

"Does he have someone to back that up?"

"No, but like I said, he's no Einstein."

"So?"

"What I read about the murder sounded thought-out: stalking the woman, leaving no physical evidence. That just isn't Kenny. He might lose his cool and run his mouth, maybe even punch someone, but he calms down fast."

"He's smart enough to get into the U," I said.

"A miracle," said Bateman. "Believe me. Ken pulled in some alumnus chits, had him tutored, the boy took the SAT four times. Then he worked his butt off, but still couldn't cut it. Couldn't hack College of the Palms either. Now this. It couldn't come at a worse time, in terms of his self-esteem. That's why that cra—your remark about his having free time was hurtful. Being interrogated by the police isn't pleas-

ant. To be honest, Detective, he's pretty scared about
today."

"He didn't seem scared."

"He puts on a show. Believe me, he's scared."

Milo finally smiled. "You like him, huh?"

"Yes, I do, Detective."

The smile widened. "Well, I don't, Mr. Bateman.
'Cause he hasn't done anything to *earn* my liking
him."

"Det—"

"I've got a brutal, unsolved murder with a lot of
angry overtones to it on my hands and what *I* see in
your client is a big, strong, aggressive kid with a very
nasty temper who's been playing hard-to-get and finally shows up with Daddy acting antsy and a lawyer
trying to block every syllable that comes out of my
mouth. What do you want me to do, serve up my
questions on a doily with parsley on the side? If I
wanted to cater, I'd learn how to cook."

Bateman bared his teeth again. The affect behind
the mannerism was hard to gauge but his body language said submission.

"Of course not, Detective. Of course not, I'm just
trying to—all right, let's give it another try. Ask what
you want, tape everything, but I'll be taking detailed
notes. And do try to remember this *is* a good kid."

When we returned to the office, both Storms were
smoking cigars and an ashtray had appeared on the
desk.

"Panamanian?" said Milo.

Senior nodded and blew enough smoke to hide his
facial features. Junior smirked.

Milo set up the tape recorder, recited the date and

place, his badge number, and Junior's name as the subject of an "in-person interview with regard to one-eight-seven PC, Coroner's Case Number nine-four dash seven-seven-six-five, Professor Hope Devane."

Hearing her name wiped the smirk off Junior's face. He smoked and fought back a cough.

Bateman and I sat down but Milo remained on his feet.

"Afternoon, Kenny."

Grunt.

"Do you know why we're here?"

Grunt.

"How many times did you meet Professor Devane?"

Grunt.

"You're going to have to speak up."

"Once."

"When was that?"

"The committee."

"The hearing of the Interpersonal Conduct Committee chaired by Professor Devane?"

Grunt.

"What's that?"

"Yeah."

"I've read transcripts of that hearing, son. Sounds like things got pretty heated."

Grunt.

"What's that?"

"She was a bitch."

Senior took his cigar out. "*Ken.*"

"Hey, tell it like it is," said his son.

"So you didn't like her," said Milo.

"Don't put words into his mouth," ordered Senior.

Milo looked down at him. "Okay, we'll stick to quotes: You think she was a bitch."

Senior's mouth got piggish and Bateman made a go-easy gesture with his hand.

Milo repeated the question.

Junior shrugged. "She was what she was."

"Which was?"

"A fucking bitch."

"Ken!"

"Mr. Storm," said Milo. "Please stop interrupting."

"He's my son, dammit, and it's my right to—"

"Ken," said Bateman. "It's okay."

"Right," said Senior. "Everything's okay, everything's just *great*."

"Counselor," said Milo.

Bateman got up and put a hand on Senior's shoulder. Senior shook him off and smoked furiously.

"What," said Milo, "made you think she was a bitch, Kenny?"

"The way she acted."

"More specific."

"The way she set me up."

"Set you up how?"

"That letter telling me we were just going to discuss things."

"At the hearing."

"Yeah. When I got there, the way she tried to get Cindy to say I was some kind of rapist, which is total bullshit." Sidelong glance at his father. "It was just a dumb hassle between Cindy and me. Later, she called me."

"Professor Devane did?"

"Yeah."

"When?"

"Afterward."

"After the hearing?"

"Yeah."

"How long after?"

"The next day. At night. I was at the Omega house."

"Why'd she call?"

"To try to freak me out."

"In what way, son?"

"She was pissed because her little game was a loser."

"How'd she try to freak you out?"

"She said even if Cindy didn't want to press charges, I had problems—impulse-control problems, some bullshit like that. She said she could make things rough for me if I didn't behave."

"She threatened you?"

The boy shifted in his seat, looked at his cigar, and put it in the ashtray. His father stared at him.

"She didn't exactly come out and say it, more like hinting."

"Hinting how?"

"I don't remember the exact words. Like I'll be watching, I'm in control, you know?"

"Did she use the word 'control'?" I said.

"No—I don't know. Maybe—it was more like how she said it, you know? Watch your step. Or something like that. She was a radical."

"Radical?" said Milo.

"Left-wing."

"She discussed her political views with you?"

The boy smiled. "No, but it was obvious. Radical feminism, trying to establish a new order, know what I mean?"

"Not really, son."

"Socialism. Central control." Glance at his father. "Communism died in Russia but they're still trying to centralize America."

"Ah," said Milo. "So you see Professor Devane as part of some kind of left-wing conspiracy."

Kenny laughed. "No, I'm no militia freak, I'm just saying there's a certain type of person likes to control things, make rules for everyone—like *Playboy* is evil and should be banned, affirmative action for everyone."

"And Professor Devane was that type of person."

Kenny shrugged. "Seemed like it."

Milo nodded and ran his hand over his face. "And she said she'd be watching you."

"Something like that."

"Watching how?"

"She didn't say. I shined her on, anyway."

"How?"

"Told her to fuck herself and hung up and went back to playing pool. I was leaving the place anyway, what did I care, fuck her."

"Leaving the University?"

"Yeah. Place sucks, waste of time. You can't learn business in school." Another sidelong peek at his father. Senior, his head in a cloud of smoke, was staring at the framed awards.

Milo said, "So you thought she was a bitch and she threatened you. Did her threat scare you at all?"

"No way. Like I said, she was full of shit and I was out of there."

"Did you ever consider taking action against her?"

"Like what?"

"Like anything."

Senior swiveled and faced Bateman. "Can he get that general, Pierre?"

"Would you care to rephrase your question, Detective?" said Bateman.

"No," said Milo. "Did you ever consider taking any kind of action against Professor Devane, Kenny?"

Junior looked from his father to Bateman.

Milo tapped a foot.

"Dad?"

Senior gave him a disgusted look.

Milo said, "Shall I repeat the question?"

Bateman said, "Go ahead, Kenny."

"We—my father and me—we talked about suing her."

"Suing her," said Milo.

"For harassment."

"Which it was," said Senior. "The whole thing was a complete outrage."

"It woulda served her right," said Junior. "But we never did anything."

"Why not?"

No answer.

"Because she was murdered?" said Milo.

"No, because Dad's got some . . . he's busy with business complications."

"So we discussed it," said Senior, loudly. "So what? Last I heard it's still a free country, or have I missed something?"

Milo kept his eyes on the boy. "Did you ever consider taking any other kind of action against Professor Devane, Kenny?"

"Like what?"

"Anything."

"Like what?"

"Like getting back at her physically?"

"No way, man. And anyway, if I would've wanted to do that it wouldn'ta been her I'd pound, it would be that wuss with her. I'd never hit a lady."

"What wuss is that?"

"The faggot with her, he really got on my case, I don't know his name."

"You considered getting back at *him* physically."

Bateman said, "Detective, that's not a—"

Kenny said, "I didn't *consider* it, but if I *did*, he would've been the one. He kept going at me, like trying to . . . outfeminist her."

"So if you would've planned to hurt someone it would have been him, not Professor Devane."

Senior said, "He never said he'd hurt anyone."

"Exactly," said Junior. "Him, I could've duked it out fair and square with. But *she* was a woman. I still open *doors* for women."

"Car doors," said Milo. "Like for Cindy?"

The boy's shoulders bunched.

Milo checked the tape.

"Okay. Now let's talk about where you were the night of the murder."

"La Jolla." Quick answer.

"Why?"

"I live there, I work there."

"Work where?"

"Excalibur Real Estate, the training program. Used to, real estate's in the dumpster."

"So you quit."

"Yeah."

"What are you doing, now?"

"Exploring."

"Exploring what?"

"My options."

"I see," said Milo. "But the day of the murder you were still in the Excalibur Real Estate training program."

"Yeah," said the boy. "But that day, specifically, I was with friends on the beach." He ticked off his fingers: "Corey Vellinger, Mark Drummond, Brian Baskins."

"Friends from La Jolla?"

"No, from here. The Omega house. They came down to see me."

"How long were you with them?"

"From around ten to five. Then they drove back up to L.A."

"What did you do at five?"

"Went driving for a while, got a video at Blockbuster, then I think the Wherehouse for some CD's."

"You bought CD's?"

"No, I just looked."

"Do you have the receipt for the video?"

"Nope."

"You pay for it with a credit card?"

"Nope, I was overdue on my card so I left them a deposit, paid cash."

"What'd you rent?"

"Terminator 2."

"You go home and watch it?"

"First I went for dinner."

"Where?"

"Burger King."

"Is there anyone who can remember you there?"

"Nope, it was drive-through."

"Where'd you eat?"

"At my place."

"An apartment?"

"Yeah."

"Where?"

"The Coral Motel, off Torrey Pines."

"Anyone see you there?"

"Don't think so, but maybe."

"Maybe?"

"I don't know anyone, it's just this dinky-shit single he was renting for me while I was in the program."

"Who's he?"

"Dad."

Senior smoked and looked at the wall. "Month-to-month rent," he said.

"So you returned with your video and your dinner to your room. What time was this?"

"Six or seven."

"Then what?"

"I watched TV."

"What'd you watch?"

"MTV, I think."

"What was on?"

Kenny laughed. "I dunno, videos, all kinds of shit."

"Did you go out again that night?"

"Nope."

"Quiet night, huh?"

"Yeah. I got sunburned at the beach, didn't feel so good." Smiling, but an uneasiness ruffled the last few words.

"You do anything that night besides watch TV?" said Milo.

Pause. "Nope."

"Nothing at all?"

"Not really."

"Not really?"

The boy glanced at his father.

"Kenny?" said Milo.

"Basically that was it."

"Basically?"

Senior turned to his son and scowled.

"Basically?" Milo repeated.

Kenny touched the pimple on his neck.

"Don't pick at it," said Senior.

"What else did you do that night?" said Milo.

Junior's answer was nearly inaudible. "Beer."

"You had a beer?"

"Yeah."

"Just one?"

"A couple."

"How many?"

Another glance at Dad. "A couple."

"Meaning two?" said Milo.

"Maybe three."

"Or four?"

"Maybe."

"You get high, son?"

"Nope." The small eyes were active, now.

"Do anything besides beer?"

"No!"

"Four beers," said Milo. "Maybe a six-pack?"

"No, there were two left over."

"So definitely four."

"Probably."

"Probably."

"Maybe I had another in the morning."

Senior stared at his son, shook his head very slowly.

"Breakfast of champions," said Milo.

The boy didn't answer.

"Dinner, TV," said Milo. "Then four beers. What time did you drink the fourth beer?"

"I dunno, maybe eight."

Leaving enough time for the two-hour ride to L.A. and an hour of stalking. But the dog had turned ill earlier in the evening.

"Then what?" said Milo.

"Then nothing."

"You went to sleep at eight?"

"No, I . . . more TV."

"TV all night?"

"Basically."

"Be nice to have someone who saw you there, son."

"It's a small room," said Kenny, as if that explained it.

"Make any phone calls?"

"Um . . . I dunno."

"Maybe?"

"I don't know."

"It's easy to get a look at your phone records."

The boy glanced at Bateman.

Bateman said, "We'll have to explore that, Detective."

"Explore away," said Milo. "But with no alibi and Kenny's hostile exchange with Professor Devane I'll have no trouble getting a warrant."

The boy sat higher, then his shoulders fell and he blurted, "I—can I talk to you in private, sir?"

"Kenny?" said his father.

"Sure," said Milo.

"No way," said his father. "Pierre?"

"Kenny," said the lawyer, "if there's something you need to—"

The boy shot to his feet, waving his fists. "*I need privacy!*"

"I'm here to safeguard your privacy and your—"

"I mean real privacy, not legal bullshi—"

"Ken!" barked Senior.

"This is a *murder*, Dad, they can do what they *want*!"

"Shut *up*!"

"It's no big *deal*, Dad! I just want some fucking *privacy*, okay!"

Bateman said, "Kenny, there are obviously some things you and I need to—"

"No!" shouted the boy. "I'm not saying I *killed* her or anything *crazy* like that! I just made a *phone* call, okay? A fucking phone call but they're gonna find out so can I have some *privacy*?"

Silence.

Finally, Senior said, "What the hell did you do, call a whore?"

The boy blanched, sat down heavily, covered his face.

"Great," said his father. "Great judgment, Kenny."

The boy began sobbing. Talking between gasps: "All . . . I . . . wanted . . . fucking . . . pri . . . vacy."

Senior ground out his cigar. "With all the diseases going around. Jesus . . ."

"That's why I didn't want to *tell* you!"

"Great," said his father. "Very smart."

Kenny lowered his hand. His lips trembled.

Senior said, "If you were so concerned about what I'd think, why'd you do it in the first place?"

"I used a *skin*!"

Senior shook his head.

Milo said, "What you do on your own time doesn't concern me, Kenny. In fact, it could help you. Who exactly did you call?"

"Some service."

"Name?"

"I don't remember." Despondent, soft voice.

"Had you used it before?"

Silence.

Senior turned away.

"Kenny?" said Milo.

"Once."

"Once before?"

Nod.

"But you don't remember the name?"

"Starr Escorts. Two *r*'s."

"Where'd you find out about them?"

"The phone book. They're all in the Yellow Pages."

"What was the girl's name?"

"I don't—Hailey, I think."

"You think?"

"We didn't exactly talk much."

"Both times it was Hailey?"

"No, just the second time."

"Describe her."

"Mexican, short, long black hair. Not bad face. Good bo . . . nice-looking."

"How old?"

"Maybe twenty-five."

"How much did she charge?"

"Fifty."

"How'd you pay her?"

"Cash."

"What time did you call Starr Escorts?"

"Around ten."

"And what time did Hailey arrive?"

"Maybe ten-thirty, eleven."

"How long did she stay?"

"Half hour. Maybe longer. After—she watched some TV with me, we had the last two beers."

"Then?"

"Then she left and I went to sleep. Next day I turn on the news and they're talking about her—Devane. Saying somebody offed her and I'm thinking, whoa, while she was getting killed, I was . . ." He looked at his father, sat up straighter. "Right around the time she was dying I was having a good time. Freaky, but kind of . . . like some kind of revenge, know what I mean?"

"Christ," said Senior. "Can we end this?"

"So I'm covered, right? Alibied?" the boy asked Milo. "She was killed around midnight and I was getting—with Hailey, so I couldn't do it, right?"

He took a deep breath and let the air out. "I'm glad it's out. Big deal, Dad. I didn't kill anybody. Aren't you happy?"

"I'm overjoyed," said Senior.

"Starr Escorts," said Milo.

"Look it up in the book. I'll take a fucking lie-detector test, if you want."

"Shut your mouth!" said his father. "No more gutter talk!" He turned quickly to Milo: "Are you happy, now? Have you squeezed enough blood out of the rock? Why don't you just leave us alone and go out and catch some gang members?"

Milo looked at the boy. "What about Mandy Wright?"

Genuine confusion on the stolid face. "Who?"

"Christ," said Senior. "Lay off!"

"Ken," said Bateman.

"Ken," Senior repeated, as if the sound of his own name disgusted him. Pointing his hand to the door, he said, "Out. All of you. This is still my office and I want privacy."

21

Back at the unmarked, I said, "Believe him?"

"The hooker thing," he said, "is exactly what a dumb, lonely kid would do. And he probably *isn't* smart enough to plan. If I can find the massage girl and she alibis him and I don't get the feeling Daddy's paid her off, there's another one off the list."

"And he seemed genuinely unfamiliar with Mandy's name."

He pulled out a cigarillo and looked at it. A warm breeze was drifting from the San Gabriels and the palm trees planted close to the building were doing a line dance.

"So, bye-bye, committee. Hope was probably killed because of something in her private life—those bruises on her arm are bringing me back to Seacrest. And/or Cruvic, 'cause *he* was probably fooling around with her. Problem is, I can't get close to either of them . . . and I can't get a clear picture of Hope.

Just polarized opinions—she was Womanhood's Great Savior, or she was a man-hating manipulator. Nothing about her . . . core."

"One of the problems," I said, "is that there's no family other than Seacrest. No one to talk about her development—her childhood, what she was like outside of her professional role."

"All I know about her childhood is she grew up in that aggie town—Higginsville. Parents dead, no sibs. And if she's got distant relatives, they must be damned distant, because after the murder, no one ever stepped forward."

He got in the car.

"Still," I said, "no family doesn't mean no family history. I could go up to Higginsville, ask around. In a small town, someone might remember her."

"Sure," he said, without enthusiasm. "I'll call the local police and let them know you're coming, see if they can get you access to records. When do you want to go?"

"No reason it can't be tomorrow."

He nodded. "Dress for the heat, we're talking farmland. Don't they grow artichokes up there, or something?"

That night, Robin and I went out to dinner. By eight, she was soaking in a bath and I was stretched out on a sofa in my office rereading the conduct-committee transcripts. Uncharacteristically, Spike had chosen to stay with me. Probably the lingering smell of steak. Now, his big, knobby head rested in my lap and he snored. The rhythm was soporific and the bitter dialogue began to blur.

I learned nothing, felt myself grow drowsy, knew it was time to stop.

Just as I put the transcripts down, the phone rang. Spike snapped upright, bounded off, and ran to the offending machine, baying.

"Doctor, this is Joyce at your service. There's a woman on the line sounds pretty distraught. A Mary Farney?"

The woman at the Women's Center in Santa Monica. Beaten-down mother of Chenise. "Put her on, please."

A strident voice said, "Hello?"

"This is Dr. Delaware. What can I do for you, Mrs. Farney?"

"You gave me your card—at the center. Said I could—you're the one with the police, right?"

"Yes. What's the matter, Mrs. Farney?"

"I—I know who did it."

"Who did what?"

"Who killed her. Dr. Devane."

I was wide-awake now. "Who?"

"Darrell. And now he's gonna kill Dr. Cruvic, maybe he already did, I dunno, maybe I shoulda called nine-one-one but I—you—"

"Darrell who?"

"Darrell . . . oh, Jesus, how could I forget his name, he's always over here. He's Chenise's latest—Darrell *Ballitser*. He did it, I'm sure."

"How do you know?"

"Because he hated Dr. Devane's guts. Dr. Cruvic too. For what they did."

"Chenise's abortion?"

"Tonight he came in all hot and crazy and stoned on something, yelling, taking Chenise with him. He said he's going over there to *get* him!"

"Dr. Cruvic?"

"Yeah, and he's got Chen—"

"Did he go to the clinic?"

"No, no, he said he was already there, they was closed, that made him madder—"

"Where'd he go, Mrs. Farney?"

"Dr. Cruvic's other office. In Beverly Hills. I tried to stop him from taking Chenise but he pushed me away—I think he's got a knife 'cause I saw it. But Chenise don't have—"

I put her on hold, called 911, told them the problem was in Beverly Hills, and got transferred.

"Civic Center Drive?" said the Beverly Hills operator. "That's right near us. We could walk there."

"Better run," I said, hanging up and trying Milo at home. Machine. I called the station, then the cell phone, where I reached him.

"Just left the Club None," he said, "and guess what—"

"Emergency," I said, telling him about Darrell Ballitser. "She says he hated Hope and Cruvic for Chenise's abortion. Probably his baby they terminated."

"BHPD on its way?"

"Yes."

"Okay, me, too. . . . Wouldn't that be something. All our theorizing and it's some crazy kid."

"She said he'd already been to the clinic but you might want to alert Santa Monica PD, anyway. Cruvic works nights there, could be on his way over."

"Will do. Meanwhile, get this lady's phone number and address, find out any details while she's still eager to help."

"Sure," I said. But when I got back on the line, it was dead.

*   *   *

I tried my service to see if Mary Farney had left a number. She hadn't. The West L.A. directory yielded only one Farney: first initial *M*, on Brooks Avenue in Venice. That sounded like a good bet, but no answer. Either she'd phoned me from somewhere else or she'd left.

Copying down the number, I put on street clothes, went into the bathroom, where Robin was still soaking, told her I'd be going out and why.

"Be careful, honey."

"No sweat," I said, leaning down to peck her cheek. "Walking distance from the police station."

BHPD had sent three squad cars the two blocks and I could see their blinking lights from Santa Monica Boulevard. The western entrance to Civic Center Drive was blocked by a sawhorse and a uniform waved me away at the east end near Foothill, but just as I turned, Milo stepped out of the darkness and told the cop to let me through.

I parked twenty yards down from Cruvic's building. Before I got out, a vehicle pulled up beside me. Big white news van from one of the network affiliates. A frantic-looking platinum-haired woman jumped out as if parachuting from a moving plane, stopped, looked around, beckoned to a sound man and a camera operator. I stayed in the Seville as the three of them sprinted toward Cruvic's building, the reporter gesticulating. When they saw Milo they stopped again.

He shook his head and thumbed them on, then came over to me. He had on the same gray suit he'd worn at Kenneth Storm's office, had replaced the shirt and tie with a gray T-shirt. His idea of an L.A. bar-crawl getup. Red lights from the nearest cruiser gave him an intermittent blush and his eyes looked hungry.

"What's happening?" I said.

"Suspect in custody."

"That was quick."

"The ominous Darrell turns out to be a skinny kid with poor reflexes. Caught Cruvic driving out of that garage next to the building, stuck a knife through the window, and ordered him out. Cruvic kicked the door, which knocked Darrell down, then he took the knife and was in the process of pounding the shit out of the kid when BH cops showed up."

"What about Chenise?"

"If she's a teeny little blond thing in a red blouse she was standing on the sidewalk screaming and they took her to the station, along with Darrell. I told BH he's a suspect in the Devane murder, to keep things quiet, but obviously someone found out. They said I can talk to him soon as they clear their paper. What about the mom?"

"Couldn't keep her on the line. She probably lives in Venice."

Another news van pulled in. And another.

"Vulture-fest," said Milo. "C'mon, let's get over there and see how our hero's doing."

The sliding metal door of the garage was open and the silver Bentley Turbo was positioned half-in, half on the sidewalk. The driver's door was still open and the dome light illuminated black leather seats, chrome knobs, polished wood.

But no driver. Cruvic was standing nearby, wearing a black suit and black turtleneck, talking to a uniform and rubbing his knuckles. A black-and-white backed out and turned left, hooking around the municipal parking lot.

The cop smiled at Cruvic, who smiled back, flexed his foot, and pointed to the Bentley. The officer trotted over, got in the big car, drove it to the corner, and let it idle. When he came back to Cruvic, the doctor shook his hand, then that of a second cop. Male-bonding smiles all around. Then Cruvic saw the press and said something to the uniforms.

As the cops held the microphones at bay, Cruvic jogged, head-down, to the Bentley. Milo and I made it over just as he touched the door handle.

"Evening, Doc," said Milo.

Cruvic turned sharply, as if ready to defend himself again. The black sweater was skintight over a broad chest. Rubbing his knuckles again, he said, "Why, hello, Detective Sturgis."

"Quite an evening, sir."

Cruvic looked at his hand and grinned.

"Sore?" said Milo.

"It smarts, but a little ice and some anti-inflammatories should do the trick. Good thing I don't have any surgery scheduled tomorrow."

He got in the Bentley. Milo positioned himself between the open door and the car.

"Nice wheels, sir."

Cruvic shrugged. "Four years old. Finicky, but overall it runs pretty well."

"Can we talk a bit, sir?"

"About what? I already gave my statement to the Beverly Hills police."

"I realize that, Doctor, but if you don't mind—"

"Actually, I do." Smile. "It was a tough day to be-gin with and this was the capper." He looked at his hand and put it in his pocket. "Got to ice up before it balloons."

"Sir—"

Shaking his head, Cruvic said, "I'm sorry, I've got to take care of my hand."

He turned a gold ignition key and the Bentley started up almost inaudibly. Country-rock music boomed from lots of speakers. Travis Tritt singing about T-R-O-U-B-L-E. Cruvic turned the volume up even higher and put the Bentley in drive.

Milo stood there. The camera crew was headed toward us.

Cruvic lifted his foot off the brake and the car be-gan rolling, the door pressing against Milo's back. He stepped away quickly and Cruvic closed the door.

"When can we talk, sir?"

Cruvic's slanted eyes tightened. "Call me tomor-row."

As the Bentley glided past smoothly, the police cleared a way for its escape.

22

Darrell Ballitser was indeed skinny. Five-ten, 117 pounds according to the booking officer. Nineteen years old, born in Hawaiian Gardens, his current address was an SRO hotel near Skid Row.

He sat in the Beverly Hills PD interrogation room holding a paper cup of Mountain Dew. Third refill. His face was long and narrow, his shaved head topped with bumps. A blond mustache and goatee weren't much more than dandelion fluff. Bloodshot blue eyes that couldn't decide if they were tough or scared looked nowhere.

A blue Harley-Davidson tattoo marked the spot where the back of his neck met his shoulder blades. Another inscription proclaiming PARTY! was a magenta smear on his right bicep. L-I-F-E on the fingers of his right hand. D-E-A-T-H on the right. A blue-and-red Gothic CHENISE across his neck. His baggy white tank top was soiled, as were low-rider jeans barely held up by a wide black leather belt. Two hoop earrings in one ear, three in the other. A nose ring. Nature had provided additional decoration: angry patches of acne, random as buckshot wounds, on his face, back, and shoulders. Cruvic had contributed a black eye, split lip, bruised chin, lumpy jaw.

He rocked in his chair, attaining as much mobility as the hand cuffed to the bolted table would allow. They hadn't cuffed him at first, but he'd screamed and thrashed and tried to hit Milo.

Milo sat across from him, placid, almost bored. Ballitser drank the rest of the sweet yellow soda. He'd finished two sugar doughnuts provided by a slim young brunette detective named Angela Boatwright, chewing painfully, each swallow marked by the rise and fall of a plum-sized Adam's apple.

Boatwright was cheerful, a few sunburns past beautiful, with a surfer-girl rhythm to her speech, faint freckles and pale eyes, a tight runner's body, and slightly oversized hands. She wore a blue-black pantsuit and black flats with stockings. When she was with Ballitser she seemed more sorry than scornful, a long-suffering big sister, but out of earshot she'd referred to him as "a sorry little asswipe."

Now she drank coffee and sat back behind the one-way glass flexing her hands. It had taken almost an hour to do Ballitser's paperwork. I was surprised at the ease with which Boatwright and her partner, a bald man named Hoppey, had relinquished control to Milo. Maybe she read my mind, because as we entered the viewing room, she said, "We booked him on attempted assault but the murder thing takes precedence. Lucky that doctor had his wits about him."

A printout of Ballitser's criminal history rested on a fake-wood table between us. Mostly blank, except for notation of a sealed juvenile record and twenty un-paid parking tickets.

"Occupational hazard," Milo had explained. "When Darrell works he's a messenger."

"Car or bike?" I said.

"Both." He gave a tired smile and I knew he was thinking, *All that time spent on another stupid one?*

Now he said, "I'm gonna get you a lawyer, Darrell, whether you ask for one or not."

No answer.

"Darrell?"

Ballitser crumpled the paper cup and threw it on the floor.

"Is there any particular lawyer you want me to call?"

"Fuck."

Milo started to get up.

"Fuck."

"Fuck, yes, or fuck, no?"

"Fuck *no*."

"Fuck no to a lawyer?"

"Fuck *yeah*." Ballitser touched his jaw.

"Aspirin didn't kick in, yet, huh?"

No answer.

"Darrell?"

"Fuck."

Angela Boatwright stretched. "Talk about your one-note solo."

Milo got up and entered the observation room. "How many public defenders do you have on call?"

"All the PD's are tied up," said Boatwright. "We've been into the private list for a while, compassionate Wilshire Boulevard guys doing pro bono. I'll go find someone."

*   *   *

Two more Mountain Dews, a hamburger and fries, and two bathroom breaks later, an unhappy-looking attorney named Leonard Kasanjian showed up with an ostrich-skin briefcase too small to hold much. He had long black hair brushed straight back, a five-day beard, and minuscule pewter-framed eyeglasses over resigned, dark eyes. He wore a tailored olive gabardine suit, tan-check snap-collar shirt, hand-painted brown-and-gold tie, brown suede loafers.

As he approached, Boatwright smiled and whispered, "Pulled him out of Le Dome."

"Hey, Angela," he said, brightening. "You in charge, tonight? How's it—"

"Evening, Mr. Kasanjian," she said in a hard tone, and the lawyer's smile died. She said, "Let me tell you about your client," and did.

He listened, said, "Sounds pretty clear."

"Maybe to you."

"Mr. Ballitser," said Kasanjian, putting his briefcase on the table.

The boy's free hand shot out, fisted, knocking the case to the floor.

Kasanjian picked it up and flicked lint from his lapel. Smiling, but his eyes were furious.

"Mr. Ballit—"

"Fuck you!"

Milo said, "Okay, we'll transfer him downtown, pull warrants on his room."

Kasanjian looked down at the booking slip. "Hear that . . . Darrell?"

Ballitser rocked and fixed his eyes on the ceiling.

"They're taking you to the county jail, Darrell. I'll come by to see you tomorrow morning. Don't talk to anyone til then."

Nothing.

Then, "*Fuck.*"

Kasanjian shook his head and stood. He and Milo headed for the door.

Ballitser said, "Spade!"

Both men turned.

"What's that, son?" said Kasanjian.

Silence.

"Spade?" said Kasanjian. "A black guy?"

"*Fuck!*" said the boy, spraying saliva and kicking wildly.

"Easy, Darrell," said Kasanjian.

Ballitser slammed his fist on the table.

His eyes shifted to the door, his torso quivered and tightened, every muscle defined beneath the damaged skin, like a frayed anatomical diagram.

"*Fu-u-uck Spa-a-ade!*"

Kasanjian said, "Spa—"

"*Spa-a-a-de! Sp-a-a-a-de! That's* fucking *why! That's fucking why!*"

Kasanjian looked shaken. "Try to calm down, Darrell."

He turned to Milo. "He's obviously in need of psychiatric attention, Detective. I'm making a formal request that you provide immedia—"

"*Spa-a-a-a-de! Spa-a-a-a-de!*"

Ballitser twisted his body, punched his own chest, kicking at the chair, pounding the bolted table, over and over.

"Spade is 'why'?" said Milo.

"*Fucking why!*"

"Why you don't like Dr. Cruvic?"

"Fucking-A!"

"Spade."

"Fucking-A! He fucking did it!" The boy began crying, then curled his free hand and ripped at his cheeks. Milo pulled him off, held him still. Darrell's blemished face was contorted in agony.

"Cruvic did it," said Milo, gently.

"Ye-e-e-s!"

"He fucking did it, Darrell."

"Y-e-e-e-s!"

"To Chenise."

"Y-e-e-s! Spa-a-a-de! Like a fucking *dog.* Woof-fucking-*woof!"*

Ballitser clawed the table, panted.

"Chenise," said Milo.

Ballitser flopped his neck hard enough to sprain it. He raised his free hand prayerfully. Nothing aggressive in the gesture.

Milo came closer. "Tell me, son."

Tears spurted from the boy's eyes.

"It's okay, tell me, son."

Darrell's stick-body shook.

"What'd he do, son?"

Darrell shot a hand into the air. Waved it. His eyes danced wildly.

"He fucking *spayed* my lady!"

23

Twenty minutes later, after conferring with his client, Kasanjian came out smiling. "Well, there's my extenuating circumstance."

Angela Boatwright was coming back from the squad room with a cup of coffee.

"Hey, Angie," he told her, "thanks for the referral. I especially liked walking out on my date."

"Always glad to help."

They shot smile-arrows at each other.

Milo said, "Where's Chenise?"

"Down the hall."

"Any sign of her mother?"

"Not yet," said Boatwright, "and still no answer at home."

I said, "If her mother had something to do with the operation she could be scared for her own safety."

"What operation?" said Boatwright. "What's going on?"

"Your doctor hero's into involuntary sterilization," said Kasanjian.

"What?"

"Seven months ago, Dr. Cruvic aborted a child Ms. Chenise Farney was carrying. My client's child. But my client had no prior knowledge of the procedure, nor was he consulted, despite the fact that Ms. Farney is a minor, leaving my client as the sole adult parent."

"Adult? You've got to be kidding," said Boatwright.

"To make matters worse," said Kasanjian, "Dr. Cruvic wasn't satisfied with a termination: He sterilized the girl without telling her. Tied her tubes. A minor, no valid consent. And guess what, folks: Mr. Ballitser has informed me that Dr. Devane counseled Chenise but never told her she was going to be sterilized. So there was obviously a conspiracy. Meaning your hero is no Boy Scout and his unprofessional conduct is obviously a significant factor in what occurred tonight. Now, in terms of your even assuming Mr. Ballitser had anything to do with Dr. Devane's murder, I must insist that you present evidence immediately or relea—"

Milo cut him off with a wave and turned to Boatwright. "Let's talk to the girl."

"Yes, let's," said Kasanjian.

"Sorry," said Milo. "Just us cop folk."

Kasanjian's mouth worked. He buttoned his suit jacket. "Detective, if she's a potential—"

"Not tonight, Len," said Boatwright, pushing hair out of her face. It sounded like something she'd said before.

She cocked a hip and clicked her tongue. The attorney gripped his briefcase. "Have it your way, police-people. But if you choose to indict Ballitser, even for a rinky-dink misdemeanor like attempted battery, we'll get to her soon enough.''

As he left, Boatwright said, "You're actually staying with the case?"

"Why not?"

Boatwright shrugged. "Nice to see you finally commit."

After ten minutes with Chenise, Milo was saying, "I'm still not sure, hon. Did you know what Dr. Cruvic was going to do or not?"

The girl shook her head miserably. She wore tight black jeans, a lacy red midriff blouse, heavy bubble-toed black boots with red soles, a red bandanna for a belt. Her makeup was thick and chalky, just like the time I'd seen her in the waiting room, but the pink highlights in her hair had been replaced by a broad black streak down the middle that turned her coif into a photo-negative skunk. A dazed look, none of the coquettishness I'd seen in the clinic waiting room. She'd spent most of the time weeping, limiting her speech to mumbles and two-word sentences.

"Did Darrell know?" said Milo.

That raised her head. "Where's Darrell?"

"On his way to jail, Chenise. He's in big trouble." Her lip trembled and she scratched her arm.

Milo was sitting next to her, hovering, one hand on the back of her chair, the other flat on the table. He shifted slightly closer, she angled away from him.

"Chenise," he said softly. "I'm not saying you're in trouble. Just Darrell. So far."

No reaction.

"Maybe you can help us. Maybe you can help Darrell."

More weeping.

Angela Boatwright walked over and touched the girl's knobby shoulder. "Can I get you something, honey?"

Chenise's mouth dropped open as she considered the offer. Her peg teeth were caramel-colored, her lips chapped and cracked at the edges.

One short thumb scratched her cheek, then the black stripe, then the arm again.

"A snack, Chenise?" said Boatwright. "Or a drink?"

"Candy?" said the girl in a very small voice.

"Sure. What kind do you like?"

"Um . . . Mounds?"

"Okay, and if we don't have that, what's your second choice?"

"Um . . . Krackel?"

"So some kind of chocolate, huh?" Boatwright smiled at her and the girl nodded. Another touch of Chenise's shoulder caused her to sink in her chair.

"Be right back, hon."

When the door closed, Chenise leaned farther away from Milo. Her small size made him look huge. He glanced at me.

"So," I said, "you and Darrell met in a class."

Nod.

"Were you both in the class?"

"Uh-uh."

"You weren't."

Headshake.

"But you met there."

"Yeah."

"Where was Darrell?"

"Leaving."

"Leaving the class?"

Nod.

"He finished the class?"

Nod. "Gradated."

"He graduated but you were still in the class."

Nod.

"Do you remember where the class was, Chenise?"

"Uh-huh."

"Where?"

"North Bower."

"Is that a street?"

Headshake.

"School. In the back."

"In the back of North Bower School," I said. "What kind of class was it?"

That seemed to confuse her.

"What kinds of things did you learn in the class?"

"Change."

"Change?"

Nod.

"How to change?"

"Like from a dollar."

"How to *make* change."

Nod.

"And other stuff?" I said.

"Uh-huh."

"Like what?"

Shrug.

"Washing up." She touched behind one ear and a tin earring shaped like a lightning bolt swung back and forth. "Food."

"Food," I repeated.

Emphatic nod.

"Making food?"

"Buying healthy food."

"Was the class called DLS?"

"Yeah!" Big smile.

"Daily Living Skills," I said to Milo. State grant for educating the borderline retarded that had run out six months ago.

Chenise said, *"Dare to live special.* It's also that."

She batted heavily mascaraed lashes, touched her hard, white tummy, pressed her knees together, then spread them slightly.

"So Darrell finished DLS," I said.

"Uh-huh."

"And you guys met at the school."

Nod. "He got a job." Pride.

"For Ready Messenger."

"He had a room."

"His own room?"

"Yeah." She winked at me. Licked her lips. "Macipated."

That took a moment to figure out. "Darrell was emancipated?"

Nod.

"Darrell was an emancipated minor?"

The full phrase went right by her.

"Emancipated," I repeated.

Her eyes narrowed. "He *hit* on him."

"Who did?"

"Lee. Her boyfriend."

"His mother's boyfriend?"

"Yeah."

"His mother's boyfriend hit on him?" I said, unsure if that meant beating or sexual abuse.

"Yeah."

"How?"

"With a belt."

"So Darrell ran away and got emancipated."

Nod.

"When?"

"I dunno."

"Must have been a while ago because he's nine-teen, now."

She shrugged and licked her lips.

Boatwright came back with a Krackel bar.

"Here you go, hon."

The girl took the candy tentatively, unwrapped a corner, and nibbled at it. "Slow," she said.

Boatwright said, "Pardon?"

"Eat slow, don't choke."

"Good advice," I said. "Did they teach you that at DLS?"

"Show up on time, napkins in lap . . . your smile is your . . ."—wrinkled brow—"is your . . . man-ner?"

"Banner?" I said.

"Yeah!"

"Anything else?"

"Yeah." Another wink.

"Like what?"

"Safe sex means life."

That line recited in a deeper, authoritative voice.

She giggled.

"What is it, Chenise?"

Harder laughter. Saucy smile. The eyelashes worked overtime.

She rubbed the chocolate against her front teeth, turned them brown, licked it away.

"Safe . . . sex," she said, unable to stop giggling.

"What does safe sex mean?" I said.

Giggle. "Skins. Darrell don't like 'em." Rolling her eyes.

"No?"

"Bad, bad boy." She wagged a finger. Giggled some more. Touched her belly.

"When did you first know you were pregnant?" I said.

She grew serious. Shrugged and nibbled.

I repeated the question.

"No period. Then my stomach puked." Giggling. "Mom said, 'Oh no, shit!' "

Giggling.

"So she took you to Dr. Cruvic."

Nod.

"Did she tell you why?"

Silence. Suddenly, she hung her head, touched her tummy again.

I leaned in, spoke very softly. "What did your mother tell you about Dr. Cruvic, Chenise?"

Silence.

"Did she tell you anything?"

Long, slow nod.

"What's that?"

"*You* know," she said.

I smiled at her.

"Can you tell me, Chenise?"

"*You* know."

"I really don't."

Shrug. "Bortion."

"She told you Dr. Cruvic would be doing an abortion."

"Uh-huh."

"Did you talk to Dr. Cruvic before the abortion?"

"Uh-uh."

"Did you talk to someone else before the abortion?"

Nod.

"Who?"

"Her."

"Who's her?"

"Dr. Vane."

"Dr. Devane?"

"Yeah."

"What did Dr. Devane tell you?"

"Good for me."

"Did you agree with that?"

No answer.

"Did you think the abortion was good for—"

"Had to," she said in a clear voice. Her eyes were clear, too. Purified by anger.

"You *had* to think it was good for you?"

Hard nod.

"Why, Chenise?"

"Mom said."

"Mom said you had to—"

" *'You can't raise it, stupid, and I'm sure as hell not raising your basta!'* "

She stared at me with defiance, then her head dropped and she began playing with the candy wrapper. The hand dropped to her tummy again. It reminded me of something. . . . The black girl in the clinic waiting room had comforted herself exactly the same way.

"So you knew you were going to have an abortion."

No answer.

"Cheni—"

"Yeah."

"Did you know Dr. Cruvic was going to do any other operation?"

Silence. Then a small headshake.

"Did he do another operation?"

No answer. She shoved the candy bar away and it

fell off the table. Milo retrieved it, turned it between his thick fingers. Angela Boatwright was in a corner, eyes alert.

"Chenise?" I said.

The girl fingered the lower lace hem of her top. Tugged down, pulled up. Slipping her hand under the lace, she began massaging her belly.

"Did Dr. Cruvic do something else to you, Chenise?"

Silence.

"Did Dr. Devane tell you Dr. Cruvic was going to do something else?"

Silence.

"Did Dr. Devane ask you to sign your name to something?"

Nod. She licked her lips and wiped them with the back of her hand. Slid sideways in the chair, putting her body in an awkward tilt.

"Chenise—"

"Spay." She gave a soft grunt, bobbed her head as if to music.

"Spay," I said.

She coughed and sniffed.

"What does 'spay' mean, Chenise?"

"Like a dog."

"Who told you that, Chenise?"

She started to answer, then her lips compressed. The hand continued to rub her abdomen, moving over the navel in rapid cycles. Stopping, pinching the skin, then resuming.

She shifted position, straightening. Slumping. Still rubbing.

Rubbing the navel . . . the entry point for tubal ligation.

"When you woke up from the abortion," I said, "was there a Band-Aid on any part of your body?"

The hand stopped. Small fingers dug into white belly-flesh. Her top rode up, revealing a shelf of rib cage above a white hollow.

Suddenly, the other hand slammed to her pubis, cupping it.

"Here," she said, arching her pelvis.

"And *here*." Standing, she arched her back, baring the umbilicus.

"Uh. Uh," she grunted, pressing both sites and showing them again in an awkward bump-and-grind. "Hurt like *shit*. Farting all *day*!"

"Cramps," said Boatwright.

"When did you find out Dr. Cruvic had done more than an abortion?"

"Later."

"How much later?"

Shrug.

"Who told you?"

"Mom."

"What'd she say?"

" '*Go ahead, screw all you want, it don't matter, we fix you, tire the tubes no bastas!*' "

Mascara running, the eyes alive with anger. "I was a *spade*!"

She stared at me, then Milo, then Angela Boatwright. Sat down, reached for the candy, began gobbling.

When the chocolate was all gone, she looked at the wrapper ruefully.

"Another one, hon?" said Boatwright.

"Sponsability," said the girl.

"Responsibility?" I said.

"For babies."

"Babies are a big responsibility?"

Nod.

"Who told you that?"

"Mom. *Her*."

"Who's 'her'?"

"Dr. Vane."

"What does 'responsibility' mean, Chenise?"

She twisted her mouth. "Show up on time."

"Anything else?"

She thought. "Wash up, say please." Big smile. "Safe sex." To Boatwright: "Got a Three Musketeers?"

"I'll check," said Boatwright and left again.

I said, "So Mom and Dr. Devane talked to you about responsibility."

"Uh-uh."

"They didn't?"

"Not before."

"Not before the operation?"

"Uh-uh."

"So what did they talk to you about?"

"Bortion. Here's a pen."

"A pen to sign—to write something?"

Nod.

"What?"

"Like this." She made aerial loops. "I can do it." Eyeing my ballpoint.

I gave it to her along with a sheet of paper. Biting her tongue, she hunched and labored, finally producing a chain of ragged peaks and troughs. I peered at it. Indecipherable.

She started to pocket the pen, stopped, giggled, and returned it.

"Keep it," I said.

She looked at it, shook her head. I took it back.

"So you wrote your name for Dr. Devane."

"Yeah."

"Before the operation."

"Yeah."

"But she didn't talk to you about responsibility til after the operation?"

"Yeah."

Her hands dropped to the surgical sites again.

"Yeah," she repeated, almost snarling it. "*A spade—* like a dog! Pain and gas, puking. Farted all *day*!"

At eleven, I phoned Robin to tell her I was all right and would be home late.

She said, "It's on the news. They're already tying it in with Hope."

I told Milo and Boatwright. He cursed and she said, "Probably Kasanjian, the idiot. Talks about Court TV all the time, wants a big case."

Mary Farney showed up just after midnight, wearing a short yellow rayon dress with wilted lapels, off black stockings, and gold backless high-heeled shoes. Caked, pale makeup and brown eye shadow, liquor and mint on her breath. Her voice so tight I imagined hands around her neck.

She said, "Is she okay?"

"She's fine," said Milo, frowning. "We've been trying to reach you for a while, ma'am."

"I was scared, so I went somewhere. A friend's."

I took in her outfit. Ready for celebrity?

"Where is she? I want to see her."

"In a minute, Mrs. Farney."

"Is she in trouble?"

"We haven't charged her with anything."

"You mean you might?" She grabbed Milo's sleeve. "No, no, I didn't call to have that—no, no, she's—she don't understand anything!"

"I need to ask you a few questions, ma'am."

"I already told—" Her hand covered her mouth.

"Told who?"

"No one."

"Who, Mrs. Farney?"

"Just some people—outside there."

"Outside the station? Reporters?"

"Just a few."

Milo forced a smile. "What did you tell them, Mrs. Farney?"

"That Darrell was a murderer. That he killed Dr. Devane."

Boatwright rolled her eyes.

"Well, he *is*! He had a knife!"

"Okay," said Milo, "let's go into a room and talk."

"About what?"

"Chenise, ma'am."

"What about her?"

"Let's go in that room."

She sat on the edge of the chair, looked around the spare room with disdain.

"Coffee?" said Milo.

"No, I don't see why I have to stay here. I didn't do nothing!"

"Just a few questions, ma'am. Chenise says she was taken to Dr. Cruvic for an abortion but he tied her tubes without telling her."

"Oh, no, don't you accuse me! She's slinging *bull*, she can lie with the best of them, believe me!"

"Was she sterilized?"

"You bet! But she knew, all right! I explained everything to her and so did everyone else."

"Everyone, ma'am?"

"The doctors, the nurses. *Everyone*."

"Doctors," said Milo. "Meaning Dr. Cruvic and Dr. Devane?"

"Right."

"Dr. Cruvic did the surgery. What was Dr. Devane's role?"

"To talk to her. Counseling. So she *would* understand! She's just saying that to get *him* off, that little bast—"

"Did Dr. Devane do anything more than talk to Chenise?"

"What do you mean?"

"Did she conduct a physical checkup?"

Hesitation. "No, why should she?"

"You're sure about that?"

"I—I wasn't in the room every second."

"Who saw Chenise after the surgery?"

"I—probably Dr. Cruvic and his nurse. I guess."

"You guess?"

"It was at night. I work days. I picked her up later. She was throwing up, still groggy. Got my car all filthy."

"Okay," said Milo, sitting back. "So this was at the Women's Health Center in Santa Monica."

"You bet."

"Who referred you there?"

She shifted in her chair, pulled at an eyelash. "No one. Everyone knows what they do there."

"Abortions and sterilizations?"

"Yeah, so what?"

"Did Chenise know what they did?"

"You bet."

"She says she didn't."

"That's a crock. She has attention problems, half the time she's in another world." A glance at me: "Attention disorder. On top of everything else. What's the big deal? Band-Aid sterilization. The next day she was walking around."

"She said she had cramps," said Boatwright.

"So? Is that some big deal? *You* don't get cramps every month? She had cramps and gas, she was . . . gassy all day. Thought it was funny. Let it out nice and loud. She had no problem with any of it til *he* got involved. Stupid *punk*. Like he's gonna be a *father*! *Right!* Telling her she'd been *spayed*. Idiot. She never even knew what the word meant! I tell you it was no big deal. Boom, boom. The gas is 'cause they fill you up with it, here,"—touching her own pubic region—"so they can see what's in there, then they go in through the belly button and boom, it's over. Like I said, she was walking around the next day."

Angela Boatwright said, "Sounds like you know other women who've had it."

Mary Farney stared at her, defensiveness giving way to pure anger. "So?"

Boatwright shrugged.

"Yeah," said Farney. "I had it, too, okay? Dr. Cruvic said it was dangerous for me to have another kid, the way I'm built. Is that okay with you, miss? Do I have your permission?"

"Sure," said Boatwright.

Mary Farney shook a hand at her. "What do *you* know? After Chenise was born and they finally figured out she wouldn't be normal, her father walked the hell out on me. You have any kids, miss?"

"No, ma'am."

Farney's smile was smug. "Don't let her tell you

she didn't know, 'cause she did. She signed consent. It's that little asshole, getting her high, convincing her they could be Mommy and Daddy. Like it was even his in the first place."

"It wasn't?" said Milo.

"Who *knows*? That's the *point*. And even if it was his, so what? He can read at second-grade level. Maybe. He's gonna take care of her and a baby?"

"Can Chenise read?" I said.

"Some."

"What's her level?"

Pause. "I haven't had her tested in a long while."

"But she signed her name to the consent form," said Milo.

"I told her what it was and she signed it."

"Ah."

Farney put her hands on her hips. "Do *you* have kids?"

He shook his head.

"No one has kids," she said. "Must be I'm the only one crazy enough. What about you?"

"No," I said.

She laughed. "Can I smoke?" Without waiting for an answer, she pulled a package of Virginia Slims from her purse and lit up.

"When's the last time Chenise's IQ was tested?" I said.

"Who knows? Probably in school."

"Probably?"

"You think they tell me what they do? All they do is file paper, make files this thick." Spreading her arms two feet wide.

"What was the last IQ score you got for her?" I said.

"What, you don't think she's smart enough to understand? Let me tell you something, I'm her *mother* and I say she can understand. When I give her five bucks for the mall and she asks for ten, she understands just fine. When she comes home late and makes excuses, she understands. When Darrell or some other punk says be ready at a certain time and she's there at the door, early, she understands. Okay? Only *some* things she don't understand. Okay?"

"Like what?" said Boatwright.

"Like how to clean her room. Like how to keep her *pants* on."

Her laugh was brutal.

"She's like a magnet for it, since she's eleven the boys been sniffing around her. She walks that walk, winks an eye. All these years I been talking myself blue, trying to get her to see where that leads. She just smiles, sticks out her tit—her chest. Like, look what *I've* got, I'm a woman. So finally she went and proved she was."

No one said anything.

"I *love* her, okay? Before she got her period she was a sweet kid! Now all I do is worry. About AIDS and stuff. Now there's one less thing to worry about." Another laugh. "Maybe she *should* be in trouble with you guys. Maybe the best thing would *be* to lock her up. 'Cause I sure can't stop her from humping around. And who's gonna help me when she humps herself straight to AIDS?"

More silence.

"You think she can raise a kid? So I protected her the best way I knew how and she understood damn good—you know what she told me once? About men? We were sitting in the car, at a Wendy's or something, and she gives this smile and I know it's trouble. I say what, Chenise. And she says, I like

when men sweat, Mom. I say, oh? Yeah, she says, like
when they sweat between their *legs*. I nearly choked,
she was only thirteen. Then she says, know *why* I like
it, Mom? I say why, Chenise. And she takes a big
deep breath, gives a great big smile, and says, I like it
'cause it *tastes* good."

24

Shortly after 1:00 A.M., Chenise was released to her mother's morose custody. A sheriff's van had come by to transport Darrell Ballitser to the county jail.

Milo and Boatwright and I watched a late replay of the eleven o'clock news in the Beverly Hills station. The antsy blond, reading copy with a smug smile.

Long-shot of Cruvic entering his Bentley. The spin: Beverly Hills doctor fends off attack by crazed skinhead, Darrell's rage fueled by the "unauthorized sterilization of his girlfriend. Police are investigating a link between the attack and the unsolved murder of feminist psychologist Dr. Hope Devane, reputed to have worked with Dr. Cruvic. Now for an update on that drive-by in East L.A.—"

Milo turned off the set. "Better get to work on that warrant before media leeches are camped out at Ballitser's flop. Thanks, Angela."

"Any time," she said. "You see Ballitser for Devane?"

"He admits going after Cruvic but denies Devane."

"Maybe 'cause Cruvic's an attempted assault and Devane's homicide. He does ride a bike."

"Yeah. Let me check out the bike, his whole place, maybe I'll be able to tell more. Thanks again."

"No problem," she said. "Apart from rich little assholes shotgunning their parents, we don't get much excitement around here."

Civic Center Drive was empty again, the steel garage door sealed tight. Milo looked tired but walked fast.

I said, "At the risk of being repetitive, what link could there be between Darrell and Mandy Wright?"

"Exactly. And on the IQ scale, Darrell makes Kenny Storm look like Einstein, so I'm not counting on this panning out. And something else, what I was telling you about Club None: A cocktail waitress who worked there also got killed. Four days before Mandy was killed in Vegas."

"Stabbed the same way?"

"No, strangled. In the alley, four in the morning, after closing. Girl named Kathy DiNapoli. Left behind the dumpster, legs spread, blouse ripped, panties down. But no sexual entry. Maybe it was a sex thing and the guy got interrupted or couldn't get it up. Or maybe someone was trying to make it *look* like a sex thing. I know the M.O.'s different and that part of Sunset has its share of crime. But four days? Bartender couldn't say if Kathy served Mandy, but she was on shift when he thinks he saw Mandy."

"So Kathy could have been eliminated because she

saw Mandy with someone. But then, the fact that she was murdered first means the killer knew what he was going to do well before."

"Exactly," he said. "A planner."

"Not Darrell."

He laughed. "The club's definitely not Darrell's venue. We're talking studs and studettes, lots of hair and teeth. On the other hand, with what I've got so far I'd be laughed out of the D.A.'s office trying to make a case for DiNapoli as part of the package. And we do have motive on the little schmuck, plus he threatened Cruvic with a knife."

"Same kind of knife used on Hope and Mandy?"

"It looked about the right size—buck with a nice sharp edge—but there are lots of those, we'll see what the wound-worms have to say. Hopefully the boys from Central Division got to Darrell's fleabag and secured it. Maybe something'll come up there."

"Still want me to go to Higginsville?" I said.

"Sure, why not? 'Cause this sterilization thing's another one of those little boxes, and I'd like to know why Hope was Ms. Control Your Own Body in public but willing to serve as Cruvic's sterilization buddy. What do you think, *did* Chenise know what they were doing to her?"

"Maybe on some fuzzy level—if she was told. Though with her intelligence true consent would be shaky. And having her sign the consent form was sleazy because she's illiterate."

"Thanks, Mom."

"Even so," I said. "Was Mrs. Farney evil in pushing through the procedure? Let the talking heads at the think tanks have fun with it. Like she said, we don't have kids and she's the one living with Chenise's promiscuity. There's no doubt Cruvic and

Hope should have known better, but there was plenty of incentive. Nine hundred bucks for the abortion, nine more for the ligation, plus Hope's fee and other charges."

"Over two grand for an hour's work. Not bad."

"And he probably did several other procedures that night."

"Maybe the two of them were partners and Hope was really getting a bigger cut—serving as his backup for slicing up minors. With all her book income she could have buried the payoffs."

"And what if Mandy was connected to it somehow. . . ." I said. "Maybe Cruvic was her doctor and they got friendly. Maybe she brought him other patients—call girls, showgirls. Lots of potential abortions, there."

"Lots of potential enemies. So why was Mandy killed?"

"She learned something she wasn't supposed to or she messed someone up."

"But, then again, why're she and Hope dead and Cruvic's back home icing his hand?"

I had no answer.

"Whatever the specifics," I said, "we've got definite evidence that Cruvic was skirting the rules. Maybe that's what got him kicked out of the U of Washington. So who knows what else he's done that might have made someone angry."

"Like what?"

"Botching someone up? Someone smarter than Darrell. He and Hope together. And in some way, Mandy was part of it."

"But the same hitch: They're dead and he's . . . tell me, did he look scared to you tonight?"

"No, but maybe he's got too much self-esteem for

his own good. Or he really doesn't realize there's someone out there waiting for the right time to pick him off—the grand prize."

"Patient killer?"

"If you're right about Kathy DiNapoli," I said, "very patient."

He pinched his lips between thumb and forefinger.

"What?" I said.

"The shape this is taking. Waiting, stalking, long-term plans. Those wounds. Goddamn choreography."

25

"Artichokes?" said the pump jockey. "Idn't that Castroville, way over the hell up by Monterey?"

He was bowlegged and potbellied, bald on top with a manila-colored braid and matching teeth. Chuckling, he said, "Artichokes," again, wiped the windshield, and took my twenty.

I'd pulled off Route 5 for a fill-up just past the Grapevine, where the traffic suddenly swells like a clogged hose and fifty-car pileups are the rule when the fog sets in. This morning it was hot and hazy but visibility was okay.

I got back on the highway and continued north. My map said Higginsville was just west of Bakersfield and due south of Buena Vista Lake. A hundred miles out of L.A. and twenty degrees hotter. The land was Midwest-flat, green fields behind windbreaks of giant blue gum trees. Strawberries, broccoli, alfalfa, lettuce, all struggling to make it in the gasoline-drenched air.

A turn on a double-lane road took me up into high-lands crowded with small ranches and shuttered roadside stands. Then down into a dry basin and a sign that read HIGGINSVILLE, POP. 1,234, over a rusting Rotary emblem. The lettering was nearly rubbed out and the sheet-metal lemon on top was corroded.

I passed a short stand of live oak and crossed a silt-filled creek bed. Then a shut-down recreational vehicle lot and a half-collapsed barn with a cracked WESTERN ATTIRE sign on the roof. One empty lot later was a two-block main drag called Lemon Boulevard filled with one-story buildings: grocery/cafe, five-and-dime, a bar, a storefront church.

Milo had called this morning and told me the local law was a sheriff named Botula. The sheriff's station was at the end of the street, pink cinder block, with an old green Ford cruiser out in front.

Inside, a heavy, pretty, dishwater-blond girl who looked too young to vote sat behind a waist-high counter, facing a static switchboard and reading intently. Behind her, a very dark-skinned Hispanic man in a khaki uniform bent over a metal desk. A book was spread in front of him, too. He didn't look much older than the girl.

A bell over the door tinkled, they both looked up, and he stood to six feet. He had unlined nutmeg skin and a wide Aztec mouth. His black hair was straight, thin, clipped at the sides, neatly parted, his eyes burnt almonds, eager to observe.

"Dr. Delaware? Sheriff Botula." He came to the counter, unlatched a swinging door, and proffered a warm, firm hand. "This is Judy, our deputy, administrator, and dispatcher."

The girl gave him a you've-got-to-be-kidding look and he grinned. "And also my wife."

"Judy Botula." She closed the book and came over.

I read the title on the cover. *Fundamentals of Evidence Collection.*

Botula said, "Come on in, we've done a little prelim work in advance of your arrival—Judy has, actually."

Judy Botula said, "Nothing earth-shattering."

He said, "We're new to this place, still acclimating."

I walked behind the counter and took a chair alongside the desk. "How new?"

"Two months," said Botula. "We're each half-time, share the job."

A mop leaned against the wall and he put it behind a file cabinet. The walls were clean and bare, free of the usual wanted posters and bulletins, and the floor was spotless, though scarred.

Judy brought her chair over and settled. She was almost as tall as her husband, with broad shoulders and a heavy bosom, the extra weight as much muscle as fat. She had on a white knit blouse, jeans, and running shoes, and a badge on her belt. Her eyes were deep blue, dramatic, a bit disapproving.

"We both graduated from the Criminal Justice program at Fresno State," she said. "We want to enter the FBI Academy but it's real competitive right now, so we figured a year or so of experience wouldn't hurt. Not that it's too exciting around here."

"Nice and quiet," said her husband.

"To say the least."

Botula smiled. "Gives us time to study. So . . . this murder case you've got. We heard a little about it right after and then there was something on it today—an arrest."

"Probably a false lead," I said.

"Yeah, that's what Detective Sturgis said. . . . A psychologist working on homicides—is that getting more common down in L.A.?"

"No. Sometimes I work with Detective Sturgis."

"I'm pretty interested in psychology, plan to hook up with the Behavioral Science Unit once we're in Quantico. Ever do any serial-killer profiling?"

"No," I said.

He nodded as if I'd said yes. "Interesting stuff. So what are you doing on this one?"

"Trying to learn as much as I can about Dr. Devane."

"Because she was a psychologist, too?"

"Mostly because we don't know much about her."

"Makes sense. . . . Okay, here's where we stand so far: After we talked to Detective Sturgis, we thought about the best way to dig something up and came up with A, town records, B, school records, and C, interviewing the old-timers. But as it turns out, all the old records were boxed and shipped up to Sacramento ten years ago and we still haven't been able to locate them. And the schools closed down around the same time."

"Did something happen ten years ago?"

"Yup, the place died," said Judy. "As I'm sure you can see. It used to be lemon groves, a few locals, but mostly seasonal migrant camps and the citrus companies who owned all the stores. Ten years ago a big frost wiped out the lemons and whatever was left was finished off by thrips, or mites, or something. The migrants moved on, the camps closed down, and instead of replanting, the companies bought land elsewhere. The locals depended on the migrants, so a bunch of them moved out, too. From what I can gather, they tried some tourist things—fruit stands,

whatever, but it didn't last long. Too far off the interstate."

"I passed a sign claiming twelve hundred people
live here," I said.

"Claim is right," she said. "The sign's an antique.
Our rough count is three hundred, and a good part of
those are just part-timers who come up summers to
fish over by the lake. The permanents all have jobs
elsewhere except for a few women who run the stores
on Lemon, and their husbands have jobs elsewhere.
Mostly, they're older, so we don't have too many
kids, and whatever ones there are go to Ford City for
primary and middle, then over to Bakersfield High.
So no schools."

Hope had gone to Bakersfield for high school, so
even back then it had probably been a sleepy town.

"In terms of old-timers from when your victim was
a kid, most seemed to have died off, but we did manage to find a lady who might have taught her when
there was a school. At least she's old enough."

"Might have?" I said.

Botula said, "She's not exactly prime interview material." He touched his temple. "Maybe it's good
you're a psychologist."

Judy said, "We'd go with you but it would probably hurt instead of help."

"You've had problems with her?"

"We went to see her yesterday," said Botula. "It
wasn't what you'd call productive."

"That's putting it mildly." Judy frowned and returned to the switchboard. It hadn't blinked since I'd
entered.

*   *   *

Botula walked me out. "Judy thinks the reason the lady was hostile was the race thing—our marriage."

"You don't?"

He looked up at the sun and put on shades. "I don't know what makes people do the things they do. Anyway, the party's name is Elsa Campos and her place is just up Blossom—left at the next corner."

My surprised look made him smile. "When I said racial, you assumed she was Anglo?"

"I did."

"Yup," he said. "Logical. But people are people. The address is eight Blossom, but you don't need it, you'll know when you're there."

Blossom Lane had no sidewalks, just brown, weedy strips bordering ravaged road. A few twiggy lemon trees grew by the curb, dwarfed by gigantic silver-dollar eucalyptus. No tree-trimming here, either.

The north side of the street was houses; the south, dry field. Numbers 1 through 7 were cabin courts in various stages of disrepair. Elsa Campos's house was larger, a two-story redwood bungalow with a screen porch flanked by a pair of massive cedars. The surrounding earth was crusted hardpan without a stitch of landscaping. Seven-foot-high chain link surrounded the small property. The BEWARE OF DOG sign on the gate was made extraneous by the pack of twenty or so barking, jumping, mewling canines lined up behind the fence.

Terriers, spaniels, a sleek red Doberman, mongrels of all shapes and sizes, something huge and black and bearish that hung back and nosed the soil.

The noise was deafening but none of them looked

mean—on the contrary, tails wagged, tongues lolled, and the smaller dogs leaped gaily and scratched at the fence.

I got out of the Seville. The racket intensified and some of the dogs ran back, circled, and charged.

At least two dozen, all decently groomed and in good health. But with that many animals, there were limits to maintenance and I could smell the yard well before I got to the gate.

No bell, no lock, just a simple latch. The dogs continued to bark and leap and several of them nuzzled the links. I could see mounds of turd forming tiny hills on the bare yard but a ten-foot radius around the house had been cleared, the rake marks still evident.

I offered my hand, palm down, to one of the spaniels, and he licked it. Then a retriever mix's tongue shot through the fence and slurped my knuckle. The Doberman ambled over, stared, walked away. Other dogs began competing for tongue space and the gate rattled. But the big black creature still held back.

As I wondered whether to enter, the front door of the screen porch opened and an old woman in a pink sweatshirt and stretch jeans came out holding a broom.

The dogs whipped around and raced to her.

She said, "Aw, get a life," but reached into her pocket and tossed handfuls of something onto the clean dirt.

"*Find it!*"

The dogs scattered and began sniffing frantically around the yard. The scene looked like an early Warner Brothers cartoon. The old woman turned in my direction and came forward, dragging the broom in the dirt.

"Hi," I said.

"Hi." It sounded like mimicry. Squinting, she continued to inspect me. Five seven and thin, she had black hair tied back in a waist-long braid; sunken, sallow cheeks that looked as dry as the dirt; claw hands barbecued brown, the nails thick and yellow. The sweatshirt said RENO! White tennies bottomed stick-legs that gave the pants no incentive to stretch.

The big black dog came over, now, in a slow, rolling gait, so hairy its eyes were hidden by pelt. Its head reached her waist and its tongue was the size of a hot-water bottle.

"Forget it, Leopold," the woman said in a sandy voice. "Go work for treats like everyone else."

The dog cocked its head just the way Spike does and looked up at her, eyes wet with melodrama.

"Nope, no way. *Find it.*"

The massive head rubbed against her belt. Reminding me of something—Mrs. Green's bullmastiff. This was my week for old women and big dogs. A deep moan escaped from beneath the hairy mouth. I could see hard muscle under black fur.

The woman looked around at the other dogs, who were still searching. Reaching into a jeans pocket, she brought out another handful—nutmeg-colored broken bits of dog biscuit.

"Find it," she said, flinging. The dogs in the yard circled faster but the big black dog stayed put. After another surreptitious glance, the woman pulled a whole biscuit out and stuck it hurriedly into the beast's mouth.

"Okay, Leopold, now *get.*"

The black dog chewed contentedly, then walked away slowly.

"What is it, some kind of sheepdog?" I said.

"Bouvier des Flandres. Belgian. Can you believe someone abandoned it?"

"Must be hot under all that coat."

She gave me a skeptical look. "They're hardy. Protective, too."

"I've got a French bulldog," I said. "A lot smaller but the same basic approach to life."

"Which is what?"

"I'm a star. Feed me."

Her face stayed impassive. "French bulldog—those are the little ones with the big ears? Never had one. That your only one?"

I nodded.

"Well, I've got twenty-nine. Counting three sick ones inside."

"Rescues?"

"You bet. Some from pounds, the rest I pick up driving around." She sniffed the air. "Pretty putrid, time to spread the enzyme—got this new chemical that eats up the poop. So who are you and what do you want?"

"I've been told you used to teach school here, Ms. Campos."

"Who told you that?"

"Sheriff Botula and his—"

She snorted. "Those two. What else did they tell you? That I'm the town nut?"

"Just that you might be able to help me find out some information on a woman who grew up here. Unfortunately she's been murdered and the L.A. police have asked me to—"

"Murdered? Who are we talking about?"

"Hope Devane."

That sucked the color out of her face. She looked back at the dogs and when she turned to me again her expression was a mixture of innocence shattered and pessimism confirmed.

"What happened to her? When?"

"Someone stabbed her in front of her house three months ago."

"Where?"

"L.A."

"Figures. Tell me, did she turn out to be a doctor of some kind?"

"She was a psychologist."

"That's almost the same thing."

"She had plans to be a doctor?" I said.

She stared past me, across the street, at the dry, empty field. Touching her cheeks with both hands, she drew back the skin, stretching it, and for a moment I saw a younger woman. "Murdered. That's unbelievable. Any idea who did it?"

"No, it's a dead end so far. That's why the police are trying to get as much background about her as they can."

"So they asked you to come up here."

"Right."

"You talk about the police in third person. Meaning you're not one of them? Or are you just pompous?"

"I'm a psychologist, too, Ms. Campos. Sometimes I consult to the police."

"Got some proof of that?"

I showed her my ID.

She studied it and handed it back. "Just wanted to make sure you weren't a reporter. I despise them because they once did a story on my dogs and painted me as a nut."

She touched her sharp chin. "Little Hope. I don't claim to remember all my students, but I remember *her*. Okay, come on in."

She began walking to the house, leaving me to open the gate for myself. The Bouvier had ambled nearly to the back of the property but as I turned the latch, it wheeled around and raced toward me.

"He's okay, Lee," said Elsa Campos. "Don't eat him. Yet."

I followed her up the porch and into a dim parlor crowded with cheap furniture and feed bowls. Shelves full of pottery and glass, the smell of wet fur and antiseptics. A cuckoo clock over the mantel looked more Lake Arrowhead than Switzerland.

Small room, the kitchen was three steps away. She told me to sit and headed in there. On the counter sat a blow-dryer, several squeeze bottles of canine shampoo, a microwave oven, and a plastic dog-crate. Inside the crate was something small and white and still. On top were glass ampules, plastic-capped syringes, rolls of bandages.

"Hey," said Elsa Campos, sticking a finger through the wire door. The little dog stuck its tongue out and whimpered.

She cooed to it awhile. "Little girl Shih Tzu, one year old. Someone cracked her head with a stick, paralyzed the rear quarters, left her on a trash heap. Her legs got infected. When I got her she was a bag of bones, the pound was ready to gas her. She'll never be normal, but we'll get her adjusted to the others. Leopold will see to that. He's the alpha—head dog of the pack. He's good with weak things."

"That's great," I said, suddenly thinking of Milo's heavy face, black brows, bright eyes, slow movements.

"Something to drink?"

"No, thanks." I sank into a gray-slipcovered easy chair. Feather cushions soft as warm tallow shifted to encompass me. Flanking the cuckoo clock were faded photos of nature scenes. The curtains were brown chenille, the overhead light fixture dusty bulbs in a tangle of yellowed staghorns.

She pulled a beer out of an old Kelvinator fridge. "Worried you're going to catch something because I run a zoo?" Popping the top, she drank. "Well, it's a clean zoo. I can't help the smell but just because I take in hurt animals, why should it mean I want to live dirty?"

"No reason."

"Tell it to those two."

"The Botulas?"

"The Botulas," she said in that same mimicking tone. "Monsieur and Madame Sherlock." She laughed. "First week they got here, they started driving around in that old car the county gives 'em, as if they had something to do. Like *Dragnet*—you're probably too young to remember that."

"Just the facts, ma'am," I said.

Her smile was briefer than an eyeblink. "What kind of facts are you going to have *here*? The weeds grew another two inches? Send samples to the FBI?" She sipped more beer. "What a pair. Driving up and down, up and down, up and down. First week they passed by here, saw my herd playing out front, stopped, got out, started rattling the gate. Needless to say, the herd got excited. I had a Golden with three legs back then, really liked to bark, what a symphony." Smiling again. "I came out to see what the ruckus was all about, there they were trying to count heads, write it down. Then she looks *me* up and down and *he* starts reciting the health code—more than such and such in one place means you need a kennel license. I laughed and went inside, had nothing to do with them since. They'll be gone soon enough, just like the others."

"How many others have there been?"

"Lost count. County sends them over from Fresno to serve a year in Oblivion. No action, no McDonald's, no cable TV, drives them crazy and they're out of here first thing." She laughed, then turned serious. "The fifty-channel generation. God help the animals and everyone else when they take over."

She peered inside the crate. "Don't you worry, baby, soon you'll be running with the best of them."

She shook her head and her braid swung. "Can you imagine anyone wanting to hurt something so harmless?"

"No," I said. "It's about as unthinkable as murder."

Straightening, she rested her hand on the counter, put her beer down, and picked up an ampule of medicine. After reading the label, she put it down and came into the parlor. Taking a ragged cane chair, she sat, planting her heels on the linoleum floor.

"Hope, murdered. Do you know what the Greeks did to bad-news messengers?" She ran a finger across her throat.

"Hope you're not Greek," I said.

She grinned. "Lucky for you, no. I used to teach all my classes about the Greeks but not in the usual way—not that they were cultured and noble and had great mythology and started the Olympics. I used them to make the point that you can be cultured and outwardly noble and still do immoral things. Because they pretty much brutalized everyone they came into contact with, just as bad as the Romans. They don't teach morality anymore in schools except how to have sex without dying from it. Which I guess is okay because what chance do you have to do any good in the world if you're six feet under? But they should also look at other things—what do you expect to learn from me?"

"Something about Hope's background that might help explain her death."

"Why would her background explain anything?"

Her black eyes were locked into mine, sharp as a falcon's.

"There's some indication she might have been abused as an adult. Sometimes that's related to abuse as a child."

"Abused how?"

"Physically. Pushed around, bruised."

"Was she married?"

"Yes."

"To whom?"

"A history professor, quite a few years older."

"Is he the one who abused her?"

"We don't know."

"Is he a suspect in the murder?"

"No," I said.

"No? Or not yet?"

"Hard to say. There's no evidence against him."

"A professor and a psychologist," she said, closing her eyes, as if trying to picture it.

"Hope was a professor, too," I said. "She'd become pretty prominent as a researcher."

"What did she research?"

"The psychology of women. Sex-roles. Self-control."

The last phrase made her flinch and I wondered why.

"I see. . . . Tell me exactly how she was killed."

I summed up the stabbing and told her about Hope's book, the publicity tour.

"Sounds like she was more than prominent. Sounds like she was downright famous."

"During the last year, she was."

Her head moved back an inch and the black eyes got narrow. I felt like corn surveyed by a crow.

"So what does her childhood have to do with it?" she said.

"We're clutching at straws. You're one of them."

She stared at me some more. "Famous. That's what I get for not reading the papers or watching the idiot box. Stopped both years ago . . . interesting."

"What is?"

"Her getting famous. When I first got her as a student, she was shy, didn't even like to read out loud. Do you have a picture of her as an adult?"

"No."

"Too bad, would have loved to see it. Was she attractive?"

"Very." As I described Hope, her eyes softened.

"She was a beautiful kid—I can't stop thinking of her as a kid. Little blondie. Her hair was almost white . . . past her waist, with curls at the end. Big, brown eyes . . . I showed her how to do all the braids and twists with her hair, gave her a book with diagrams for a graduation gift."

"Sixth-grade graduation?"

She nodded absently. The cuckoo shot out of the clock and beeped once. "Medicine time," she said, standing. "Got two others in the bedroom even worse than the Shih Tzu. Collie hit by a truck out on Route Five and a part-beagle choked unconscious and left in a field to die."

She went to the kitchen, filled two syringes, disappeared through a rear door.

I sat in the dim room until she came back looking grim.

"Problems?" I said.

"I'm still thinking about Hope. All these years I haven't thought much about her, assumed she was fine, but now her face is right here." Tapping her nose. "Thank you for brightening an old woman's day."

"You assumed she was fine," I said. "Meaning you worried she might not be?"

She sat down and laughed. "You *are* a psychologist."

Her eyes drifted to the clock and stayed there for a while.

I said, "You don't remember all your students but you do remember her. What made her stand out?"

"Her intelligence. I taught for forty-eight years and she had to be one of the smartest kids I ever had. Maybe *the* smartest. Grasped things immediately. And a hard worker, too. Some of the gifted aren't, as I'm sure you know. Rest on their laurels, think the world's lining up for them. But Hope was a good little worker. And not because of her home environment."

The skin around the black eyes tightened.

"No?" I said.

"*No*," she said, but this time it wasn't mimicry. "Not because. *Despite*."

26

She got up again. "Sure you don't want a drink?"

"Something soft, thanks."

Swinging the fridge open, she took out another beer and a can of orange soda. "This okay?"

"Sure."

Popping both tops, she sat down and immediately started tapping her feet. Then she straightened a slipcover, pulled her braid forward, unraveled it, and began to retie.

"You need to understand something," she said. "Things were different back then." She looked down at her feet, kicked aside a pink plastic feed bowl. "Hope came here with her mother when she was just a baby. I never saw any father. The mother said he was some kind of sailor, died at sea. . . . This professor husband, what makes you think he beat her?"

"We don't know that he did. It's just a possibility."

"Why's it a possibility?"

"Because husbands are usually the ones who do that."

"Does he have a raw temper?"

"Don't know," I lied. "Why?"

"I've had two husbands and neither would classify as brutal, but both had their tempers and there were times I was afraid. How much older is he than Hope?"

"Fifteen years. Why do you ask?"

The beer can rose to her lips and she took a long time drinking. "She was always mature for her age."

"Where did Hope and her mother come from?" I said.

She shook her head and took a longer swallow. I tried the orange soda. It tasted like candy mixed with cleaning solvent. I tried to produce saliva to wash away the taste but my mouth was dry.

"The mother's name was Charlotte. Everyone called her Lottie. She and the child just showed up one day with one of the migrant picking crews. Lottie was nice-looking but she had the face of an Okie, so maybe she was one. Or maybe she just had Okie heritage—know anything about the Okies?"

I nodded.

"Where are your folks from?"

"Missouri."

She thought about that. "Well, Lottie seemed like pure Okie to me—pretty, like I said, but skinny, raw-boned. Twangy accent, not much education. I know it's a derogatory term, now, but I'm too old to start worrying about shifts of the wind. Back then they seemed fine being called Okies so they're still Okies to me. My own family's part Californio but I've been called everything from taco-bender to greaser and I've survived. Know who the Californios were?"

"The original settlers from Mexico."

"The original settlers after the Indians. Before the New Englanders came out west to find gold. I've got both in me—tamales and boiled supper but I don't exactly look like DAR so I've been getting wetback comments my whole life. I learned to close my ears and go about my business. Lottie Devane was an Okie."

Two more swallows and the beer was gone.

"She was quite a nice-looking girl—slim figure, good bust, legs. But she'd seen some wear. And she could walk, make it look like a dance step. Natural blond, too. Not the platinum stuff she started using a month after she got here, wanting to match Hope. More of a honey blond. She favored blue eye shadow and false eyelashes and red lipstick and tight dresses. Everyone wanted to be Marilyn Monroe back then, whether it was realistic or not."

She looked away. "The thing with Lottie was she came with the picking crew but she never went out to *pick*. Despite that she managed to pay rent on a two-room cabin over on Citrus Street." She hooked a finger. "That's three blocks over, we used to call it Rind Street 'cause the migrants took the oversoft fruit home to make lemonade and the gutters were full of skin and pulp. Rows of cabins—shacks. Communal bathrooms. That's where Lottie and Hope lived. Except soon they got upgraded to a double cabin. When Lottie was in town, she tended to stay indoors."

"Was she gone a lot?"

She shrugged. "She used to take day trips."

"Where?"

"No car, she used to hitch. Probably up to Bakersfield, maybe all the way to Fresno, 'cause she came back with nice things. Later, she bought herself a car."

"Nice things," I said.

The skin around the black eyes tightened. "My second husband was assistant general manager for one of the lemon companies, knew everything about everyone. He said when Lottie hitched, she stood by the side of the road and lifted her skirt way up. . . . She and Hope lived here until Hope was fourteen, then they moved up to Bakersfield. Hope told me it was so she could go to high school close to home."

"All those years of paying the rent without picking," I said.

"Like I said, she knew how to walk."

"Are we talking a steady lover or business?"

She stared at me. "Why does everything nowadays have to be so *overt*?"

"I'd like to bring back information, not hints, Mrs. Campos."

"Well, I can't see how this kind of information can help you—yes, she took money from men. How much? I don't know. Was it official or did she just lead them to understand they should leave her something under the pillow, I can't tell you that, either. Because I minded my own business. Sometimes she went away for a few days at a time and came back with lots of new dresses. Was it more than just a shopping trip?" She shrugged. "What I will say is she always brought clothes for Hope, too. Quality things. She liked dressing the child up. Other kids would be running around in jeans and T-shirts and little Hope would have on a pretty starched dress. And Hope took care of her things, too. Never got dirty or mixed in with rough stuff. She tended to stay inside the cabin, reading, practicing her penmanship. She learned to read at five, always loved it."

"Was there any indication Hope knew what her mother did?"

She shrugged and passed her beer can from one hand to the other.

"Did Hope ever talk to you about it, Mrs. Campos?"

"I *wasn't* her psychologist, just her teacher."

"More kids talk to teachers than to psychologists."

She put the can down and her arms snapped across her chest like luggage straps. "No, she never talked to me about it but everyone knew, and she wasn't stupid. I always thought shame was why she kept to herself."

"Did you see her after she moved to Bakersfield?"

The arms tightened. "A year after, she came back to visit. She'd won an award, wanted to show it to me."

"What kind of award?"

"Scholastic achievement. Sponsored by a stock-and-feed company, big ceremony at the Kern County Fair. She sent me an invitation but I had the flu, so she came two days later, with photos. She and a boy student—smartest girl, smartest boy. She kept trying to tell me I deserved the award for teaching her so much. Wanted to give me the trophy."

"Mature sentiment for a teenager."

"I told you, she was always mature. It was a one-room school and with most of the older kids out working the crop, it was easy to give her lots of personal attention. All I did was keep supplying her with new books. She chewed up information like a combine."

Springing up, she left the parlor without explanation and disappeared in the back of the house again. I went over to the battered Shih Tzu's crate and wiggled a finger through the mesh door. The little dog showed me pleading eyes. Its breathing was rapid.

"Hey, cutie," I whispered. "Heal up."

Shaggy white ears managed to twitch. I put a finger through the grate and stroked silky white fur.

"Here," said Elsa Campos behind me.

She was holding a small gold-plated trophy. Brass cup on a walnut base, the metal spotted and in need of polishing. As she thrust it at me I read the base plate:

THE BROOKE-HASTINGS AWARD
FOR ACADEMIC EXCELLENCE
PRESENTED TO
HOPE ALICE DEVANE
SENIOR GIRLS DIVISION

"Brooke-Hastings," I said.

"That was the stock company."

I gave her back the trophy and she placed it on an end table. We sat down again.

"She insisted I take it. After my second husband died I put things away, had it in a closet. Forgot about it til just now."

"Did Hope talk about anything else?"

"We discussed where she should go to college, what she should major in. I told her Berkeley was as good as any Ivy League school and it was cheap. I never found out if she listened to me."

"She did, got a Ph.D. there," I said, and that brought a smile to her face.

"I was already taking dogs in, and we talked about that, too. The virtue of caring. She was interested in life sciences, I thought she might very well become a doctor or a veterinarian. Psychologist . . . that fits, too."

She began playing with her braid. "Want another soda?"

"No, thanks."

"No more beer for me or you'll think I'm an old wetback rummy. . . . Anyway, she was a polite girl, very well-groomed, used beautiful language. This was a tough town but she never seemed part of it—as if she was just visiting. In some ways that applied to Lottie, too. . . . Even with her . . . behavior, she carried herself above it all. Hope also told me what Lottie was doing in Bakersfield. Dancing. You know the kind I mean, don't make me spell it out. Place called the Blue Barn. One of those cowboy joints. They used to have a whole row of them as you left the city, out past the stockyards and the rendering plants. Pig-bars they called them. Country-and-western plus bump-and-grind for the white boys, mariachi plus bump-and-grind for the Mexicans, lots of girls dancing, sitting on laps. Et cetera. My second husband went there a few times til I found out and set him straight."

"The Blue Barn," I said.

"Don't bother looking for it. It closed down years ago. Owned by some immigrant gangster who dealt cattle with questionable brands. He opened the clubs during the sixties when the hippies made it okay to take off your clothes, raked in a fortune. Then he shut everything and moved to San Francisco."

"Why?"

"Probably because you could get away with even more up there."

"When was this?"

She thought. "The seventies. I heard he made dirty movies, too."

"And he was Lottie's boss."

"If you call that working."

"Must have been hard for Hope."

"She cried when she told me. And not just about the kinds of things Lottie was doing for a living, but because she thought Lottie was doing them for *her*. As if the woman would have been taking shorthand except for having a child. Let's face it—some women are not going to take the time to learn a real skill if they can get by with something else. The first day Lottie arrived in Higginsville, she went into her cabin and came out that night wearing a tight red dress that *advertised* her."

"Did she move to San Francisco with the club owner?"

"I wouldn't know, but why *would* he take her, with all the young hippie girls running around? By then she'd have been too old for *his* type of business."

"What was his name?"

"Kruvinski. Polish or Yugoslavian or Czechoslovakian or something. They said he'd been a foreign general during World War Two, brought money out of Europe, came to California, and started buying up land. Why?"

"Hope worked with a doctor named Milan Cruvic."

"Well, then," she said, smiling. "Looks like you've got yourself a clue. Because Milan was Kruvinski's first name, too. But everyone called him Micky. Big Micky Kruvinski, big this way." She touched her waist. "Not that he was short, but it was his thickness you noticed. Thick all over. Big thick neck. Thick waist, thick lips. Once when I went up to Bakersfield with my second husband, we ran into him eating breakfast. Big smile, nice, dry handshake, you'd never know. But Joe—my husband—warned me away from him, said you have no idea, Ellie, what this joker does. How old's Dr. Cruvic?"

"Around Hope's age."

"Then it would have to be the son. Because Big Micky only had one kid. Little Micky. He and Hope were in the same class at Bakersfield High. In fact, he was the boy who won the Brooke-Hastings Award with Hope. Everyone suspected a put-up, but if he became a doctor, maybe he was genuinely smart."

"Why'd they suspect a put-up?"

"Because Big Micky owned the Brooke-Hastings Company. And the biggest slaughterhouse in town, and packing plants, vending machines, a gas station, farm acreage. All that on top of the clubs. The man just kept buying things up."

"Is he still alive?"

"Don't know. I stay away from the city, sit right here, and mind my own business."

She picked up the trophy and tapped it with a fingernail. The plating was cheap and bits of gold flaked off and floated to the ground. "Joe, my husband, was a smoker, four packs a day, so eventually he got emphysema. The day Hope came to visit he was in the rear bedroom on oxygen. After she left I went in and showed him the trophy and the article and he burst out laughing. Wheezing so hard he nearly passed out. I said what's funny and he said, guess who won the boys'? Big Micky's kid. Then he laughed some more and said, guess the tramp worked overtime to help her daughter. It made me feel rotten. Here I was feeling proud of my teaching and he popped a big balloon in my face. But I didn't say anything because how can you argue with a man in that condition? Also, I suspected there might be some truth to it, because I knew what Lottie was like. Still, Hope *was* gifted and I'll bet she earned it. What kind of doctor did Little Micky become?"

"Gynecologist."

"Poking women? Guess the apple *doesn't* fall far. And Hope worked with him? Why?"

"He does fertility work," I said. "Told us Hope counseled patients."

"Fertility," she said. "That *is* a laugh."

"Why?"

"Big Micky's son helping get life going. Is he a decent man?"

"I don't know."

"It would be nice if he *was* decent. Both he and Hope managing to get past their origins. Helping nurture life instead of ending it the way his father did."

"Big Micky killed people?"

"That could very well be, but what I'm talking about is the way he finished those girls off spiritually. Just used them up."

She squeezed her hands together. "And his way with animals. That's always the tip-off. His slaughterhouse was a big gray place with rail tracks running in and out. They'd ride livestock in on one end, crammed into rail cars, thrashing and moaning, and out the other side would come butchered sides hanging from hooks. I saw it personally because Joe was kind enough to drive by there once after we'd gone into town for dinner. His idea of funny. Here we were, just finished a nice meal, and he drives over there."

She licked her lips as if trying to get rid of a bad taste. "It was late at night but the place was still going full-guns. You could hear it and smell it from a mile away. I was furious, demanded Joe turn right around. He did, but not before telling me about Big Micky and how he liked coming down there personally, around midnight, putting on a rubber apron and boots and grabbing himself a studded baseball bat. The workers would stop the line, hoist up some steers and porkers, and let him have a go at them for as long as he wanted."

She shuddered. "Joe said it was Big Micky's idea of fun."

27

Trudging to the kitchen, she checked the Shih Tzu, again. "Hope and Little Micky, after all these years."

Smartest boy, smartest girl.

"Hope consulted to a lawyer named Robert Barone."

"Never heard of him."

"How about these names: Casey Locking?"

Headshake.

"Amanda or Mandy Wright?"

"No. Who are they?"

"People Hope knew."

"Being famous, she must have known lots of people."

"That's part of the problem. Her book was controversial. For all we know she was stalked and killed by a stranger because of it."

"Controversial in what way?"

I told her.

"And you're saying this was a best-seller?"

"Yes."

"I'm embarrassed not to know about it." Bending, she peered into the crate.

I said, "Did Hope talk about anything else the day she visited?"

She'd countered several direct questions by changing the subject and I expected her to do it again. Instead she came back, sat, and looked right at me.

"She told me Lottie tied her up."

Her lip trembled.

I sat there, shrink-calm. My heart raced.

"When?" I said. "Why?"

"When she was little and Lottie had to leave her alone for long stretches. Also when Lottie brought men home."

"Tied her up how?"

"In her room. To her bed. The headboard. Remember I said it was a two-room cabin? One was Hope's bedroom, the other, Lottie's. Lottie used a dog leash and a bicycle lock, fastened it to the headboard, locked her in."

"How long did this go on?"

"Years. I never knew, Hope never complained. Thank God there was never a fire. When Hope told me I was outraged but she kept telling me it was okay, there was no abuse, Lottie always left her plenty of food and drinks, toys, books, a radio, a potty. Later a TV. Hope didn't seem the least bit angry talking about it. Kept telling me it was okay, Lottie had been doing what she thought was best."

"Then why'd she bring it up?"

"She said she was worried about Lottie. The things Lottie had done to support the two of them. The things Lottie was still allowing men to do to her."

"Lottie was still bringing men home?"

"Guys she met at the Blue Barn and other places. Regulars, Hope called them. She and Lottie had moved into a nice-sized house in Bakersfield by then, and the arrangement was that Lottie would hang one of those Privacy tags you get at a hotel from her bedroom doorknob when she was working. Hope was always supposed to come in through the kitchen door, check the knob. If the sign was hanging, she had to go straight to her room and stay there til Lottie told her the coast was clear."

"More confinement."

She nodded. "Even so, she could sometimes hear what was going on."

Rubbing her eyes, she said, "And I mean besides sex. Screams. Sometimes there were marks on Lottie."

"Bruises?"

"And rope burns on her wrists and ankles. Lottie used makeup to cover them but Hope saw them anyway."

"So Lottie was getting tied up, herself."

"Can you imagine? That's what I meant by *despite* her home life."

"Did Hope talk to her mother about it?"

"She said no, as if it were a ridiculous question. 'Of course not, Mrs. Campos. She's my *mother*!' "

"But she talked about it openly."

"Yes . . . but then she cut it off. I think she really wanted to unload all the way, but just couldn't. I never saw her again." Again, she looked at the cuckoo clock.

"What was her demeanor when she told you all this?" I said.

"Calm, except when she cried about Lottie. Worried about Lottie getting hurt by a . . . customer. She

rationalized what Lottie did by saying she had no education and skills and she was just trying to support
the two of them the best way she knew how. So what
could I say to that? Face it, child, Momma's a tramp? I
knew she had to be hurting. Still, a prisoner in her
own home—can you see bringing friends home to a
place like that? I tried to get her to talk about her
feelings but she wouldn't go for it.''

"Poor kid."

"Yes, but to look at her you'd never know it. Beautiful, poised, perfect hair, the right amount of
makeup. And Lottie was obviously still spending on
her clothes. Silk blouse, nice wool suit, nylons,
pumps. She could've passed for twenty. A young
lady. And she made a point of telling me she was
getting straight A's at Bakersfield, honor society every
semester.''

"School was probably the only place she felt free,"
I said, realizing how far Hope really had come.

Getting past the fear and the shame and the isola-
tion only to lose her life on a dark, empty street. I felt
a tightening in my chest, at the back of my throat.

"Probably," she said. "That's how I rationalized
it.''

"Rationalized what?"

"Not doing anything. Not reporting it. No matter
how good she looked, she was still a minor in a bad
environment and I was the one she confided in. But I
told myself she'd found her niche, why upset the
cart? And things *were* different back then. What's to
say if I had come forth she wouldn't have denied it?
Or that anyone would have listened to me? Because
Lottie worked for Big Micky and he was well-
connected with the powers that be. If Lottie asked

him to help her out, what was the chance of bucking that?"

"Was there any indication he was Lottie's pimp? Or her lover?"

She glared, as if I'd finally given her an excuse to be angry. "I told you before, I don't know those kinds of details."

"Did Hope talk about Big Micky?"

"No. The only one she talked about was Lottie. Then, as I said, she cut it off, changed the subject. I got the feeling the visit had been an experiment for her: How far was she ready to go? And I hadn't encouraged her enough. . . . I lost a lot of sleep over it, Dr. Delaware. Thinking about that poor child tied up, what I should do. Then, with all the hurt things I was taking care of, I managed to forget about it. Until you showed up."

Another glance at the cuckoo.

"And that's all I know," she said, rising and walking quickly to the door. She pushed it open and stepped out onto the porch and a tide of canine noise rose. By the time I reached her she was out in the yard, surrounded by the dogs. Leopold, the Bouvier, watched me imperiously.

I thought of Hope's Rottweiler, unable to protect her, probably poisoned.

Hope transforming herself from prisoner to guardian of other women's rights.

But no one had *ever* protected her.

Elsa Campos continued to the front gate. "If you find out who murdered her, would you take the time to tell me?"

"Yes."

"You mean it? Because I don't want to wait for nothing."

"I promise."

"All right, then . . . I'm going to force myself out of here, take a drive up to the Bakersfield library, see if I can find her book. Not too many kids from here become famous."

The last word came out strangled. Suddenly tears were dripping down her weathered cheeks. She wiped them with her sleeve.

"Good-bye," she said. "I don't know whether to thank you or punch you."

"Good-bye. Thanks for your time."

I started to go and she said, "When all this comes out, I'll be the idiot teacher who didn't report it."

"No reason for it to come out."

"No? You're here because you think it relates to her murder."

"It may end up having nothing to do with it."

She gave a short, hard laugh. "Do you know how she rationalized it? Being tied up? She said it had made her stronger. Taught her how to concentrate. I said, 'Please, child, it's one thing not to complain but don't tell me it was for your own good.' She just smiled at me, put a hand on my shoulder. As if she were the teacher. As if she pitied me for not *understanding*. I still remember what she said: 'Really, Mrs. Campos, it's no big deal. I turned it to my own advantage. I taught myself self-control.' "

28

I covered the thirty miles to Bakersfield in twenty-five minutes. But when I arrived I knew it had been a waste of gas.

How long since I'd been up here? At least a decade. The city had maintained some of its country flavor—western-wear outlets, cowboy bars too new and flashy to be the skin joints Elsa Campos had described. But it was a big city, now, any city. Steadily homogenized by Wal-Marts and fast-food stands, the cold, clean comfort of franchise.

No one I spoke to knew anything about the Brooke-Hastings Company but when I mentioned the slaughterhouses to an old man working the counter of a Burger King, he gave me a suspicious look and directions.

The northern edge of the city, melting gradually back to agriculture.

Segments of the railroad track were there—fragmented like discarded playthings.

So was the building, huge, gray, so ugly it was hard to believe anyone had actually designed it. Square holes where the few windows had been. No roof.

The Brooke-Hastings sign painted in white had eroded to wisps. Other signs: PURE PORK SAUSAGE. LIVESTOCK AND FEED. PRIME MEAT.

A high barbed-wire fence surrounded the concrete corpse.

Acres of fields in all directions were planted in tomatoes and corn.

Stoop-laborers scuttled through the fastidious rows.

One saw me and smiled.

A Mexican woman, still on her knees, swaddled in layers of clothing despite the heat, hands so dusty they looked like clay models.

Fear in her eyes as she took in my face and clothes, the Seville's polished grille.

I headed back to L.A.

Self-control.

Years later Hope had reduced it to an academic paper.

A prostitute's child. It wouldn't play at the Faculty Club. If Seacrest knew, it was obvious why he'd want to minimize her family history.

Little Micky. Little Hope.

Smartest boy, smartest girl.

Ceremony at the county fair. Smiles, flashbulbs, 4-H banners, brass bands. I could almost smell the corn dogs and horse dung.

A little girl imprisoned. A teenage honor student listening to her mother scream, nightly. Seeing the bruises.

Cruvic, smelling the slaughterhouse stench on his father?

The two of them bonded by good grades and high aspirations, the strain for respectability.

High-school pals, maybe sweethearts.

Collaborating. On fertility, abortion, sterilization. *Control.*

Big Micky moving to San Francisco. Getting into racier clubs, producing porn—Robert Barone, the lawyer, did pornography defense. From his San Francisco office.

Hope consulted to him, too.

Fertility, termination. What else?

Grown-up 4-H projects? A new slant on animal husbandry?

I'd done 4-H my thirteenth summer. Raising angora rabbits for fur because it meant shearing, not slaughtering. My teacher had been a pretty, black-haired farmer's wife, serious, with rough hands. Mrs. Dehmers . . . Susan Dehmers. She'd sat me down the first week: *Don't get attached to them, anyway, Alexander. You won't be living with them forever.*

I pictured Big Micky and his bat. The packaging and selling of women as meat.

His son leaving surgical residency after only one year.

Leave of absence at the Brooke-Hastings Institute.

Nice little in-joke.

Had Hope laughed?

* * *

I got back just after five. The house was empty and Robin had left a typed note on the dining-room table:

Darling,

Hope your trip went well. A big bargain on some old Tyrolean maple came up out in Saugus and then I've got to deliver some instruments to the HotSound studio in Hollywood. Spike and I will try to be back by 10:00 but it could be later.

Here're the numbers I'll be at. If you haven't eaten, check out the fridge. Milo called. Love you.

Inside the fridge was a hero sandwich cut into six segments. As I phoned Milo at the station, I chewed on one, wondering how the thing had gotten its name. Milo was on another line and I held and got a beer. When he got on, I said, "I know now why control was such a big issue for her."

When I finished, he said, "Nothing like mother love," very softly. "Listening through the walls . . . you think Mama got her involved with clients beyond listening?"

"Who knows."

"Tied up for her own good. Jesus."

"She convinced herself it was for her own good, Milo. Grew up and reverted to what she knew."

"Bound and hurt—so who bruised her, Seacrest or Cruvic or some boyfriend—hell, why not Locking?"

"Why not," I said. "Talk to Cruvic today?"

"No, he's avoiding me, big-time. Answering machine at the place on Mulholland—the house is his, but he rents, doesn't own. And when I called his office, old Nurse Anna came on real cold and referred me to his lawyer. Guess who?"

"Robert Barone."

"*Bing,* you get the washer-dryer. How'd you know?"

"Big Micky was a porn merchant in San Francisco."

"From that to my-son-the-doctor," he said. "How does he spell his last name?"

I told him.

"I'll see what S.F. knows about him. I did find out about that hospital in Carson where Sonny went after leaving Seattle. One of those for-profit chains, ran into financial problems and sold out to a bigger chain. The comptroller said Fidelity was one of their less profitable outlets so it got canned. Couldn't pin him down but my impression was it hadn't exactly been the Mayo Clinic. So you're right about it being a comedown for Little Micky. The burrowing bastard."

"The incident with Ballitser put him in the public eye," I said, "and he's got lots of things he doesn't want scrutinized: the way he practices medicine, his checkered academic history. Gangster heritage. And maybe Hope's murder. Anything turn up at Darrell Ballitser's place?"

"Dope—meth, that's probably what got him hyped up. But absolutely nothing to tie him to Hope, so unless he confesses, Kasanjian will be able to get him out on bail. And if Cruvic keeps low, the D.A. probably won't be interested in prosecuting the attempted battery. Which doesn't bother me, I never saw Darrell as Mr. Stalker. Herr Doktor Cruvic's looking better and better for that. It's the best explanation for her being dead and his walking around. Something real bad must have happened that Hope wanted no part of. Cruvic was worried she'd squawk, so he quieted her."

"And Mandy Wright," I said. "Who Cruvic could easily have met through Daddy's business."

"You got it. Club None's exactly the kind of place a gangster's kid would hang. And Mandy just may turn out to be the wedge that pries the shithead out from behind Barone's custom suit. Because Vegas came through, bless their souls, and located Ted Barnaby, the boyfriend. Still dealing blackjack, but not in Nevada. Right here in Palm Springs, one of those Indian-reservation casinos. I'm heading out soon as I clear some paper, gonna do a surprise shake and see what tumbles out."

"Want company?"

"No plans tonight?"

"Robin's out for the evening. Were you planning to stay over?"

"Nah, no reason to, I don't golf. Or tan. Rick took the Explorer so I've got the Porsche, which means an hour and a quarter each way and who the hell's gonna give *me* a speeding ticket?"

29

L.A. to Palm Springs is 120 miles of a single mon-ster interstate, the 10.

The first half of the trip takes you through down-town, Boyle Heights, and the eastern exurbs—Azusa, Claremont, Upland, Rancho Cucamonga—and into San Bernardino County, where the air varies from sweet to toxic depending on wind and God's whim, and the view from the freeway is a lulling homogeny of marts and malls and car lots and the kind of hous-ing you'd expect to find hugging the freeway. Then comes agriculture and rail yards near Fontana and just after Yucaipa most of the traffic drops off and the air gets dry and healthy. By the time you pass the cherry groves of Beaumont, you're rolling through a platter of gray dirt and white rock, Joshua trees and mesquite, the San Bernardino Mountains off to the right, capped with snow.

The empty road's an invitation to speed and most

people RSVP yes. During spring break, golden kids
tank up on beer and weed and delusions of immortal-
ity, whooping and high-fiving on truck beds, hanging
over the sides of little convertibles, flashing sexual
greetings. Most make it to downtown Palm Springs,
some end up roadkill. The highway patrol stays furtive and watchful and does its best to keep the death
toll within acceptable limits.

Milo got stopped only once, just before the San
Gorgonio Pass, well after darkness had set in. He'd
pushed ninety since Riverside, the Porsche barely
working. It's a white 928, five years old, in perfect
condition, and the young CHP officer looked at it
with admiration, then inspected Milo's credentials,
blinking only once when Milo said he was working a
homicide case and he needed to catch a material witness by surprise.

Handing back the papers, the Chippie recited a
warning about nuts on the road and the need to keep
an eye out, Detective, then he watched as we rolled
out.

We cruised into Palm Springs at 10:00 P.M., passing
block after block of low-rent condos and entering the
outer edges of the business district. Unlike Bakersfield, here little had changed. The same seedy mix of
secondhand shops posing as antique dealers, motels,
white-belt clothing boutiques, dreadful art. All the big
money was in Palm Desert and Rancho Mirage, along
with the streets named after Dinah Shore and Bob
Hope.

"Look for Palm Grove Way," said Milo. "The Sun
Palace Casino."

"This doesn't look like an Indian reservation."

"What'd you expect, tepees and totem poles?
These are the lucky Indians: booted into the desert but

their patch just happened to leak shiny black stuff so they got rich, learned about loopholes, figured they were a nation to themselves and sued for the right to run games. The state finally gave 'em bingo but remained penny-ante about the immorality of gambling."

"Then the state started running the lottery," I said, "so that argument became a little inconsistent."

"Exactly. Indians all around the state are catching on. There's a new casino up in Santa Ynez. State continues to screw around, taking its sweet time to grant permits, not allowing the Indians to manufacture slot machines or bring them in from out-of-state. Which is a big deal because slots are the number one moneymakers. So they smuggle the suckers in on produce trucks and once they're on the reservation, nothing anyone can do about it."

"Detective," I said, "sounds like you're condoning law-breaking."

"There's laws and there's laws."

"Palm Grove," I said, pointing to the next block.

He turned left onto another commercial street. More motels, a laundromat, a run-down spa, fast-food joints crowded with people soaking up grease and the hot night air. Then up ahead, bright, blinking turquoise and yellow lights in the shape of a cowboy hat, crowning a fifty-foot tower.

"Tasteful, huh?"

"So all of downtown's a reservation?" I said.

"Nope, it varies from lot to lot. The key is to search land records, find some square footage once owned by an Indian, go into partnership. Here we are."

He zipped into the massive dirt parking lot surrounding the casino. Behind the hat tower was a surprisingly small one-story building trimmed with

more blue and yellow lights and huge, upslanting letters that shouted SUN PALACE in orange neon surrounded by radiating fingers of scarlet.

Between the tower and the building was a brightly
lit car drop-off. A brand-new purple Camaro was
parked up against the building, a pink ribbon
wrapped around its hood. The sign on the windshield
said FOUR BLACKJACKS IN A ROW WINS THIS CAR!

Another sign leaning against the hat tower promised VALET PARKING! but no one was around and Milo
found a space in the lot. Just as we got out, a husky,
brown-skinned boy in a white polo shirt and black
slacks trotted toward us.

"Hey, I woulda taken that for you." Hand out.

Milo showed him a badge. "I woulda joined the
Beatles if my name was McCartney."

The valet's mouth closed. He stared for a second,
then ran to open the doors of a urine-yellow, boat-
sized Cadillac full of laughing, sun-broiled, silver-
haired optimists.

We walked through the casino's glass double doors
and into a wall of noise just as a very tall man in
Johnny Cash black stumbled out. Behind him was a
four-hundred-pound woman in a flowered sundress
and beach sandals. She looked ready to deliver a
speech and he kept well ahead of her.

The doors closed behind us, locking in the noise
and eye-searing fluorescence. We were on a small, ele-
vated, brass-railed platform covered with blue-green
industrial carpeting and sectioned by arbitrary columns of polished mahogany. Steps on both sides led
down to the playing room: one single space a hundred by fifty. More aqua carpeting and columns under acoustical-tile ceiling. White walls, no windows,
no clocks.

To the right was a single stud-poker game: hunched men in plaid shirts and windbreakers, black-lensed sunshades, paralyzed faces. Then row after row of slots, maybe ten dozen machines, rolling, beeping, blinking, looking more organic than the people who cranked their handles. The blackjack tables took up the left side of the room, crammed together so you had to either sit or keep circulating. Dealers in deep red polo shirts and white name tags stood back-to-back, laying down patter, scooping up ante chips, sliding cards out of the shoe.

Bings and buzzers, nicotine air, cash-in window at the rear of the room. But this early no one wanted out. The players were a mixture of desert retirees, Japanese tourists, blue-collar workers, bikers, Indians, and a few dissolute lounge bugs trying to look sharp in fused suits and long-collar shirts. Everyone pretending winning was a habit, pretending this was Vegas. Perfect-body-less-than-perfect-face girls in white microdresses walked around, balancing drink trays. Big men dressed in white and black like the valet patrolled the room, scanning like cameras, their holstered guns eloquent.

Someone moved toward us from a corner of the platform, then stopped. A gray-haired, gray-mustachioed man in a gray sharkskin suit and red crepe tie, fifty-five or so with a long, loose face and purse-string lips. Walkie-talkie in one hand, hair-tonic tracks in his pompadour. He pretended to ignore us, didn't move. But some sort of signal must have been sent because two of the armed guards strolled over and stood beneath the platform. One was an Indian, one a freckled redhead. Both had thick arms, swaybacks, hard potbellies. The Indian's belt was tooled with red letters: GARRETT.

People came in and out of the building in a steady flow. Milo moved closer to the brass rail and the gray-mustachioed man came over as Garrett turned and watched.

"Can I help you gentlemen?" Deep, flat voice. The name tag, computer-printed. LARRY GIOVANNE, MANAGER.

Milo showed his ID in a cupped hand. "Ted Barnaby."

Giovanne didn't react. The ID went back in Milo's pocket.

"Barnaby's working tonight, right?"

"Is he in trouble?"

"No, just some questions."

"He's new."

"Started two weeks ago Wednesday," said Milo.

Giovanne looked up, taking in Milo's face, then down to the green poly shirt hanging over tan chinos. Looking for the gun-bulge.

"No problems?" he said.

"None. Where's Barnaby?"

"Did you check in with the tribal police?"

"No."

"Then technically you have no jurisdiction."

Milo smiled. "Technically, I can walk around the room til I find Barnaby, sit down at his table, play *real* slow, keep spilling my drink, ask stupid questions. Keep following him when he moves tables."

Giovanne gave a tiny headshake. "What do you want with him?"

"His girlfriend was murdered half a year ago. He's not a suspect but I want to ask him a few questions."

"We're new, too," said Giovanne. "Three months since we opened and we don't want to break up the flow if you know what I mean."

"Okay," said Milo. "How about this—send him

out when he goes on break and I'll stay out of the way."

Giovanne shot French cuffs and looked at a gold watch. "The dealers do thirty-minute shifts at each table. Barnaby's set to change in five, break in an hour. If you don't cause problems, I'll give him his break early. Fair enough?"

"More than fair. Thanks."

"Five minutes, then. Want to play in the meantime?"

Milo smiled. "Not tonight."

"Okay, then go outside, over by the Camaro, and I'll send him out to you. How 'bout some drinks, peanuts?"

"No, thanks. Give any cars away lately?"

"Three so far—after you're finished with him, come back and try your luck."

"If I had some, I'd try it."

"What's your game?"

"Cops and robbers," said Milo.

A microdress girl brought out two beers anyway and we drank them standing against the cool block wall of the casino, waiting behind the purple car, watching the in-and-out, able to feel and hear the gambling inside. The outdoor lot seemed to stretch for miles, bleeding into black space and star-painted sky. Motor drone and headlights defined a distant road but for the most part all the movement was here.

Just as we emptied our glasses, a tall, thin, red-shirted man came out and looked from side to side, long fingers curling and straightening.

Barely thirty, with thick blond hair, he wore flint-colored bullhide boots under his pressed black slacks.

Thin but knotted arms. A turquoise-and-silver brace-
let circled a hairless wrist, and a gold chain seemed to
constrict a long neck with a kinetic Adam's apple.
Handsome features, but his skin was a ruin, so acne-
scarred it made Milo's look polished. A couple of
active blemishes stood out in the light, most conspicu-
ously an angry swelling on his right temple. Small,
round Band-Aid under his left ear. Deep pits ran
down his neck.

Milo put his glass down and came out from behind
the car. "Mr. Barnaby."

Barnaby stiffened and his hands closed into fists.
Milo's ID in his face made him step back.

Milo extended a hand and Barnaby took it with the
reluctance of a man with wet palms. Milo started to
draw him out of the light but Barnaby resisted. Then
he saw the valet approaching and came along.

Back at the purple car, he looked at me and the
glass in my hand. "What the hell is this all about? You
just got me fired."

"Mandy Wright."

Hazel eyes stopped moving. "What do the L.A.
cops have to do with that?"

Milo put a foot on the Camaro's bumper.

"Careful," said Barnaby. "That's new."

"So you're not too torn-up over Mandy."

"Sure I'm torn-up. But what am I supposed to do
about it after all this time? And why should I get fired
over it?"

"I'll talk to Giovanne."

"Gee, thanks. Shit. Why'd you have to come here?
Why couldn't you just call me at home?"

"Why'd Giovanne boot you?"

"He didn't but he gave me the look. I know the

look. They're bending over backward not to have problems and you just made me a problem."

He touched the Band-Aid, pressed down, winced. *"Damn.* Just signed a lease on a place in Cathedral City."

Milo cocked his head toward the casino entrance. "This ain't exactly Caesar's, Ted. Why'd you leave Vegas after Mandy was killed?"

"I got . . . I was bummed, didn't want to deal with people."

"So you took off?"

"Yeah."

"Where?"

"To Reno."

"After that?"

"Utah."

"Why Utah?"

"It's where I'm from."

"Mormon?"

"Once upon a time—listen, I already told those Vegas cops everything I knew. Which is nothing. Some customer probably killed her. I never liked what she did, but I was heavily into her, so I stuck around. Now what am I supposed to tell you? And why are the L.A. cops interested?"

"Why didn't you return to Vegas, Ted?"

"Bad memories."

"That the only reason?"

"That's enough. I was the one identified her body, man." He shook his head and licked his lips.

"You weren't avoiding anyone?"

"Who should I avoid?"

"Mandy's killer."

"A customer? Why would I avoid him?"

"How do you know he was a customer?"

"I don't, I'm guessing. But what else? Working girls get messed up all the time—who'm I telling? You know. Occupational risk. I warned her."

"She'd been roughed up before?"

"A mark here and there. Nothing serious. Until." He touched the Band-Aid again, rubbed his pitted neck.

"Any idea who roughed her up before?"

"Nah. She never gave me names—that was our arrangement."

"What was?"

"I stayed out of her face and she gave me her spare time." Twisted smile. "I was into her a lot more than she was into me. Ever seen a picture of her? From before, I mean."

"Uh-huh," said Milo.

"Gorgeous, right?"

"The two of you ever live together?"

"Never. That's what I'm trying to tell you. She wanted her own place, her own space."

"Her own place for work."

"Yeah," said Barnaby, louder. Cracking his knuckles, he looked at his fingers sadly. "She was unbelievable. Part Hawaiian, part Polynesian. They're the finest-looking people in the world. At first, I was totally nuts over her, wanted her out of the life, the whole bit. I told her, babe, learn how to deal, the way you look you'll clean up on tips. She laughed, said she had to be her own boss. She loved money, was really into stuff."

"What kind of stuff?"

"Clothes, jewelry, cars. She used to buy a new car every few months, sell it, get another one. Corvettes, Firebirds, BMWs. The last one was a used Ferrari convertible, she got it at one of those car lots outside of town where the losers dump wheels for cash. She used to tool around the Strip in it. I told her you're the first girl I know so into cars. She laughed, said I'm into big engines, Teddy. That's why I like *you*."

The hands started moving again. "So look where it got her."

A vanload of buzz-cut GIs was disgorged into the casino, laughing like schoolkids. Barnaby stood straighter and stared at the swinging glass door.

"That's all I know, okay? You had to come out here because the same fuckhead did some girl in L.A., right? Same way Mandy was done."

Milo didn't answer.

"One of those serial killers, right?" said Barnaby. "Figures."

"What does?"

"They always go after hookers." Frowning. "Which is what Mandy was, even though she thought of herself as an actress."

"She tell you she was an actress?"

"Yeah, but half-kidding." Barnaby looked down at the pavement, bounced one sharp toe against the other.

"What do you mean?"

"Like, I pretend to be what the customer wants, Teddy. I'm an actress."

"She ever do porn movies?"

"Not that I know."

"No?"

"No!"

"She ever get specific about what kind of pretending?"

"No."

"Or who she pretended for?"

"When I asked she got pissed, so I stopped asking. Like I said, she kept everything separate."

Psychic link between call girl and professor. Milo glanced at me.

"She had her place, you had yours, Ted?"

"Right."

"Where'd you and she get together?"

"Mostly my place."

"Never hers?"

"Hers on Tuesdays. Her day off." He licked his lips. "I got another girlfriend, now. She doesn't know about Mandy." Flexing his fingers. "Only thing she's gonna know now is I signed a lease, and all of a sudden no job."

"What line of work is your new girlfriend in?"

"Not Mandy's." The hands were fists again. "Cashier, okay? She works at Thrifty Drug. Not even *close* to Mandy in the looks department but that's fine with me. She lives out in Indio, we been talking about moving in together."

"Where'd you meet?"

"Here. What's it matter? At a party."

"Where'd you meet Mandy?"

"On the floor at my casino. I was good so they put me on the 500-dollar table and she used to hang around there. She played once in a while but I knew what she was after."

"What?"

"Snagging a high roller. She used to look for the highest pile of chips, edge her way over to the table wearing a low-cut dress, lean over, blow in the guy's ear, you know."

"Did it work?"

"What do you think?"

"She have regulars?"

"I don't know, man. Can I go?"

"Soon, Ted," said Milo. "So what you're telling me is in terms of your relationship she called all the shots."

"I let her," said Barnaby. "She was *gorgeous*. But I learned. Like the song. If you wanna be happy, marry an ugly girl."

"You and Mandy ever talk marriage?"

"Right. Picket fence, two kids, and a fucking station wagon. I told you—she liked *stuff*."

"Clothes and jewelry and cars."

"Yeah."

"And coke."

Barnaby's hands clenched again. He looked upward. "I am not getting into that."

"Why not?"

"You got no rights on the reservation, I'm just talking to you 'cause I cared about Mandy. I can walk anytime. It's my right."

"True," said Milo. "But what happens if I drive over to Cathedral City PD and tell them about your past?"

"What *past*?"

"Vegas cops said you and Mandy used heavily and that you were her source."

"Bullshit."

"They said after she died you used even more. That's why no one in Vegas wanted you back."

The sweat on Barnaby's creviced face gave it the look of a fresh-glazed doughnut. He turned his back on us. The scars on his neck stood out like braille. "Why're you doing this to me?"

"I'm not doing anything to you, Ted. I just want to know as much as possible about Mandy."

"And I'm *telling* you what I know!"

"I brought up the dope because I'm interested in Mandy's lifestyle."

"Her lifestyle? What do you think it was? Doing johns!"

"Dope means bad guys. Bad guys hurt people."

Barnaby didn't answer.

"Did she owe money to anyone?" said Milo.

"I never saw her bankbook."

"Any of the guys you bought coke from pissed at her?"

"*You* say I bought for her."

"Any bad guys pissed at her?"

"Not that I knew."

"She trade sex for coke?"

"Not that I knew."

"And you never set her up to do that?"

"I'm no pimp."

"Just her spare-time buddy."

"Look," said Barnaby, "it wasn't like that. I had nothing over her, she was her own boss. She liked me 'cause I listened to her. I'm a good listener, okay? Work the casinos, you hear sad stories all day long."

"What were Mandy's problems?"

"She didn't have any that I saw."

"Happy girl."

"Seemed to be."

"And you have no idea who her regulars were?"

"No."

"The night she was killed, did she say anything about who she was going to meet?"

Barnaby massaged his neck. "You're not *getting* it. She never said *anything* about work."

"You told Vegas you were working that night."

"I didn't have to tell them. Tons of people saw me. I didn't even find out about her being killed until the next day when I called her and some cop picked up the phone. They asked me to drive over to the station. Then they asked me to go to the morgue and identify her."

"Did she work anywhere else but her apartment?"

"Probably."

"Probably?"

"If she picked up some player and he had a room in the casino, they probably went upstairs."

"If?"

"Okay, when."

"She ever work the street?"

"Yeah, right. She was a hard-up, two-bit hooker."

"Any idea why she was killed out on the street?"

"Probably walking the john out and he freaked."

"Did she make a habit of walking johns out?"

"How would I know? You asked me to guess, I'm guessing."

"You never dropped in on her during working hours?"

"Yeah, right. And piss her off grandly."

"So *she* laid down the rules."

"She was the star, man." Faint smile. "One time, when we were—she was in a good mood, she said, I know you're bugged by what I do, Teddy, but try to get past it, it's no big deal, just acting. Right, I said. And the Oscar goes to. And she laughed and said, exactly. They should *give* an Oscar for what I do—best supporting actress with her legs spread. I—it, that bugged me. I didn't like hearing it. But she thought it was funny, laughed like crazy."

"When did she get sterilized?"

Barnaby's hands dropped. "What?"

"When did she get sterilized—have her tubes tied?"

"Before I knew her."

"How long before?"

"I don't know."

"So she told you."

"It only came up because I got stupid, started talking about how I liked kids, one day it would be cool to have a couple. She laughed—she laughed a lot."

He licked his lips again. "I said what's funny, babe? She said you're cute, Teddy. Go ahead, have some rug rats with some nice girl. Have an extra one for me 'cause I got fixed. I said what do you mean? And she said *fixed.* Operated on. I said what'd you go and do that for? She said no fuss, no mess, no pills to give me cancer. Then she laughed again, said I consider it a business expense, wish I coulda taken it off as a tax deduction. Big joke. I didn't like it but with Mandy, you went along or you got off the bus. When you went along with her, laughed with her, things were cool."

"And when you didn't?"

"She shut you out."

"So she got sterilized before you met her. Meaning over a year ago."

"I met her a year and a half before she died and it was before that."

"Did she say where she had the operation?"

Second's hesitation. "No."

"She ever mention the name of the doctor?"

"No."

"What, Ted?"

"She never mentioned the name."

"She tell you something else about him?"

"No, but I saw him."

"Where?"

"The casino."

"When?"

"Maybe a month before."

"Before she was killed?"

"Yeah."

"Tell me about it."

"Why, is he some kind of—"

Milo held a big hand up. "Tell me, Ted."

"Okay, okay, I was working and saw her doing her thing. Slinking around in a little black halter dress, her hair up, fake diamond earrings." He closed his eyes for a second, preserving the image, opened them, tugged at his red shirt. "I tried to catch her eye, so I could maybe get to see her later. She gave a big smile, then I saw she was smiling past me, not at me. At someone else."

"The doctor," said Milo.

"I didn't know he was a doctor. Later she told me he was. She walked right past my table, he was at another 500-dollar table, big pile of chips. She said hi to him and some other guy, hugs and kisses, like old friends. He collected his chips and they all walked off. Next day I told her nice of you to say hi. She said don't get touchy, I go way back with the guy. He's the doctor who fixed me. I owe him."

"What'd she owe him for?"

"Maybe he did it for free, who knows?"

"A trade?"

Barnaby shrugged.

"What did he look like?" said Milo.

"Nothing special. Thirty-five, forty. Short. But big

here." Touching a shoulder. "Like a gym rat. Short hair, almost skinned, kind of jap eyes. Good threads—suit, tie, the works."

"And the other one?"

"What other one?"

"You said there was another guy."

"Yeah, but he was old, no big deal. Sick-looking—yellow skin, in a wheelchair. The doctor was pushing him around. Maybe he was a big-bucks patient having a last fling. You see that all the time in Vegas. Totally fucked-up people, paraplegics, people on air tanks, losers with no legs. Getting pushed around the casino with cups full of chips. Like a last fling, you know?"

"What else did Mandy say about them?"

"She didn't say nothing at all about the old guy."

"And the doctor?"

"Just that he fixed her."

"And she owed him."

"Yeah. Is he some wacko?"

"No," said Milo. "He's a hero."

Barnaby looked confused.

Milo said, "Anything else you can think of?"

"Nope."

"Okay, thanks."

"Yeah. You're welcome."

"The address on Vista Chino your current one?"

"Yeah."

"What's the address of the place you're leasing?"

"What's the diff, you got me busted, I can't take it now."

"Just in case."

Barnaby recited some numbers and a street. Stuffing his hands in his pockets, he started to walk off.

"Want me to talk to Giovanne?" said Milo.

"It won't do any good."

"Suit yourself."

Barnaby stopped. "Hey, you wanna do it, fine. You wanna feel like a hero, too, fine."

30

We played five hands of losing blackjack, thanked the pit boss, got back on the highway, and raced through the desert. A gray moon sat low in the sky and the sand looked like snow.

"Old man in a wheelchair," I said. "Maybe Big Micky Kruvinski?"

Milo shifted his bulk in the driver's seat and rolled his neck. "Or maybe he *was* a rich patient. Getting his ashes hauled, bill it to Medi-Cal as physical therapy. Lord only knows what kinds of things Cruvic does for a buck."

"The main thing: Cruvic knew Mandy."

"Bastard. Gotta find a way to get into his records. Barone's an expert on building paper walls and all we have against Cruvic so far is suspicion, no grounds for a warrant."

"Did you ask Barnaby about dope because you think there might be a dope angle?"

"I asked him because he's still a user—did you see all that sweat, those eyes? I meant what I said about bad guys."

"Hope and cocaine? No evidence she ever used."

"No evidence on Hope, period."

"Casey Locking might be able to provide some," I said. "He has some connection to Cruvic. I keep thinking about the time we talked on campus, his taking the law-and-order line. Which is standard psychopath behavior—the rules apply to everyone but me. Maybe I can learn something about him from Hope's other student—the one in London. I'll try her again."

He pushed the Porsche over ninety. "It's weird, Alex. The case starts out all high-tone—professors, the high-IQ crowd, but now we're back on the usual terrain: dopers, dealers, hookers, characters."

"Hope's little boxes," I said.

He thought about that for a mile or two, finally said, "Yeah. But which box had the rattlesnake?"

We stopped for coffee at an all-night diner in Ontario and were back in L.A. just before 2:00 A.M. Another note had been added to the scrap on the dining-room table:

Talk about your ships in the night!
Wake me if you want.

Your pen pal. R.

Despite four cups of decaf my throat was dry from the desert air and I poured myself an iced soda water and sat drinking in the kitchen. Then I realized it was morning in England and went to the library to find Mary Ann Gonsalvez's number.

This time she answered, in a soft, curious voice. "Hello?"

I told her who I was.

"Yes." No emotion.

"Do you have time to talk about Professor Devane?"

"I suppose—it's so terrible. Have they any idea who did it?"

"No."

"Terrible," she repeated. "I didn't find out until a week after, when the department notified me by fax. I couldn't believe it. But . . . I don't know how I can help."

"We're trying to learn as much as possible about Professor Devane," I said. "The kind of person she was. Her relationships."

"That's why you're involved, Dr. Delaware?"

"Yes."

"Interesting . . . new uses for our field. I'm sorry I didn't call back, but I just didn't think I had anything to say. She was a fine advisor for me."

Dropping pitch on the last two words.

"For you but not for someone else?" I said.

Another pause. "What I meant was her style suited mine. Hands-off, she had her own life. She did help get me funding for my year in England."

"Hands-off, how?"

"She let me do my own thing. I'm kind of compulsive, so it worked out."

"A self-starter."

She laughed. "That's a nicer way to put it."

"So someone who needed more guidance might find her style difficult?"

"I suppose so, but that would just be speculation."

"What about Casey Locking? Is he a self-starter?"

"I don't know Casey." Tension in her voice.

"Not at all?"

"Not well. You're an alumnus, Dr. Delaware, you know how the program operates: three years of coursework, quals, then on to dissertation research. Some students know what they want, hook up with an advisor right away. I didn't. Between my job, my daughter, and classes, I was in a pretty severe time crunch."

"How old's your daughter?"

"Three. I just sent her off to day care. They have excellent day care here."

"Better than L.A.?"

"Better than *I* found in L.A. I wanted someplace that would provide some nurturance, do more than warehousing. Anyway, I was crunched, needed to finish, so you can see why there wasn't much time to socialize with Casey or anyone else."

"Did you have any contact with him?"

"Minimal. He—our paths were different."

"In what way?"

"I'm interested in clinical work. He didn't seem to care about that at all."

"Pure research?"

"I guess so."

"He's a little different," I said.

"What do you mean?"

"The black leather."

"Yes," she said. "He does try to project an image."

"So even though the two of you were Professor Devane's only students, you had little to do with each other."

"Correct."

"Do you know anything about his research?"

"Something about self-control. Animal studies, I think."

"Was Professor Devane hands-off with him, too?"

"Well," she said, "they published together, so they must have shared some common ground. Why? Is Casey . . . implicated somehow?"

"Would it surprise you if he was?"

"Of course it would. The thought of *anyone* I know doing something like that would be surprising. Dr. Delaware, I have to say this conversation is making me uncomfortable. I can't even know for sure you're really who you say you are."

"If you'd like, I can give you the number of the police detective assigned to the case."

"No, that's all right. I have nothing more to say anyway."

"But discussing Casey made you uncomfortable."

She gave a small, soft laugh. "That sounds like a therapeutic comment, Dr. Delaware."

"Is it an accurate comment?"

"Discussing anyone makes me uncomfortable. I don't like to gossip."

"So it's nothing to do with Casey, specifically?"

"He—I have some feelings about him but they're really not relevant."

"You don't like him?"

"I'd rather not," she said, a bit louder.

"Ms. Gonsalvez," I said. "Professor Devane was murdered very brutally. There are no leads and no way to know what's relevant and what isn't."

"So Casey *is* under suspicion?"

"No, he isn't. Not formally. But if there's something about him that upset you, I'd like to know about it. Or I can have Detective Sturgis call."

"Oh, boy," she said. "Oh, boy . . . I really can't

afford to have this getting back to Casey. He's—I'm not afraid of him but he's someone whose bad side I wouldn't want to be on."

"Have you seen his bad side in action?"

"No, but he's—I've seen his research. I wasn't being totally honest when I said I thought he was running animal studies. I *know* he was because one night I happened to be down in the basement and passed his lab. I was grading some papers and had to pick them up in the prof's basement lab. It must have been eleven o'clock, everyone was gone. I heard music— heavy-metal music—and saw light coming through a partially open door. I peeked in and there was Casey, with his back to me. He had cages of rats, mazes, all sorts of psychophysiologic equipment. The music was very loud and he never heard me. He had a rat in his hand—between his fingers. Pinching its neck. The poor thing was squirming and squeaking, Casey was clearly hurting it. Then he started dancing around. To the music—doing a little jig while he pinched the rat. Its tail was—it was horrible to watch. I wanted to rush in and stop him but I didn't. Too scared, being down there alone. Since then I guess he always *has* scared me—the leather, his manner. Have you seen that ring he wears?"

"The skull."

"Tacky," she said. "And juvenile. He saw me looking at it once and said Hope had given it to him. Which I find hard to believe."

"Why?"

"She was the epitome of class. He was just playing head games with me—anyway, it bothered me for a long time. The rat. I kept thinking I should tell someone—the department has rules about humane treatment of animals. But Hope was his advisor and I knew she liked him and . . . I know this sounds like petty sibling rivalry but he was clearly the favored child. So if I made problems for him, how would she react? Cowardly, Dr. Delaware, but my goal is to finish my Ph.D., get out in the world, make a good home for my daughter. Hope was staying out of my life and I'd adjusted to it."

"Did she stay out to the point of neglect?"

"Honestly? There were times I needed her and she wasn't available and sometimes it hung me up. Because of my tight schedule, every delay threw me back. I even tried to tell her once. She was pleasant but really didn't want to hear it so I never brought it up again. When I picked her, I thought she'd be ideal because of her feminism. My field of interest is cross-cultural sex-roles and child rearing. I thought she'd get turned on by the topic but she really wasn't interested."

"But with Casey it was different."

"Very different. She always seemed to have time for him. Don't get me wrong, when we did get together she was great—supportive, incredibly smart. And she did come through on my grant. But getting her attention was always tough and after her book came out it became impossible. By the time I left for England, I was starting to feel like an orphan."

"How do you know she had more time with Casey?"

"Because I saw them together a lot and he let me know. 'Hope and I were lunching,' 'I was over at Hope's house the other day.' Almost gloating—God, this really does sound like sibling garbage, doesn't it?"

"Grad school often works out that way."

"I guess. She even took him with her to TV shows.

He told me about sitting in the greenroom, meeting celebrities. Which isn't to say she wasn't entitled to work with whomever she preferred."

"Pinching the rat," I said. "Gloating. Sounds like he's into control in some unpleasant ways."

"Yes. I definitely see him as highly dominant. One of those people who won't have anything to do with a situation unless he can control it. But he is bright. *Very* bright."

"How do you know?"

"During the first three years of classes, he always scored high, and I remember someone saying he was at the top of his class at Berkeley."

"But no interest in clinical issues."

"Just the opposite. He used to disparage clinical work, said psychology was presumptuous because it hadn't laid enough scientific groundwork to be able to help people. That point of view goes over pretty well with lots of the department biggies, so he'll probably end up a full professor. Heck, with his brains and his dominance needs, he'll probably end up a department *chairman*."

"Chairman in black leather?"

"I'm sure it's a stage," she said. "Maybe next year it'll be tweeds and elbow patches."

I sat thinking about the rat suffering between Locking's fingers. Mr. Skull Ring.

Hope's gift.

Another Berkeley grad.

The Northern California connection. . . . Big Micky moving up to San Francisco because you could get away with more there.

How many connecting threads? How far back did it go?

I tiptoed into the bedroom, determined not to wake Robin. Eased into bed, careful not to rock the mattress.

But she said, "Honey?" and reached out to me.

I wrapped my arms around her.

31

Next morning my mind was a gun scope with Locking centered in the crosshairs.

I started phoning at nine, in my bathrobe. No answer at his home or his campus office. Down in the basement with his rats?

I had no home address because his file was missing. Had he pulled it himself? Hiding something?

Dialing the Psych department, I filled my voice with annoyed authority and told the secretary, "This is Dr. Delaware. I need to locate a grad student on a research matter. Casey Locking. Your file on him's missing and you gave me his number but I need an address."

"One second, Doctor." Click out, click in. "I have an address for him on 1391 Londonderry Place."

After she read it off, I said, "What about his lab? Is there an extension there?"

"Hold on. . . . No, there's nothing here."

"Thanks. Is there a zip code for Londonderry Place?"

"L.A. 90069."

Hollywood Hills, north of Sunset Strip. Nice address for a grad student. Thanking her again, I got dressed.

I drove Sunset through Beverly Hills and into West Hollywood, cruising by talent agencies, high-ticket defense attorneys, glass boxes filled with used Ferraris and Lamborghinis. Past the Roxy, the House of Blues, the Snake Pit, what used to be Gazzarri's before it burned to the ground. At Holloway I spied a magenta-and-brass thing that said CLUB NONE over a neon highball glass and stirrer.

So Locking lived close to the place where Mandy had plied her trade, maybe with the ultimate bad john.

Next came Sunset Plaza with its Oscar-party fashion boutiques and sidewalk cafes crowded with would-be actresses and the poorly shaved vultures who wait for them to get rich or die. If any of the women found screen work, chances are it would be with their clothes off. One way or another the men would be watching.

Londonderry Place was a block beyond the last cafe, just past Ben Franks's twenty-four-hour coffee shop, a steep, skinny, aerobic hike above the traffic. High, canted lawns, good-sized houses, most with less architecture than a bus stop.

Locking's was two blocks up, one story, white, unmodified since its fifties birthdate. This high up there was bound to be a city view but the house had low, slatted windows. Arrow plants and yuccas and gazania crowned the sloping frontage. Concrete steps led to the front door and an alarm-company sign was staked at the top.

I walked up a very long driveway that continued past the house. Space for half a dozen vehicles but only one was parked there: black BMW 530i. Through an open wooden gate I saw a blue pool and concrete decking, an outdoor lounge chair. Thick, low-hanging ficus trees cast black shade.

Nothing luxurious but, still, the rent had to be two thousand a month.

I climbed the steps to the door. No mail piled up but it was too early for today's delivery. The car said Locking might be home.

I rang the bell and waited. Music or something like it came through the door. Loud, pounding music. Screaming vocals.

Thrash metal. Locking's choice of background as he tormented the rat.

I knocked louder, rang again, still no response. Descending to the driveway, I looked back at the street. No neighbors out. In L.A., they rarely are.

I slid past the BMW, and walked along the side of the house. More slatted windows.

The pool was fifties-big, an oval that took up ninety percent of the backyard. The rest was a hill of ivy disappearing under the gloom of the ficus trees— two of them, sixty feet tall and nearly as wide, with thick roots that had worked their way under the pool decking, cracking it, lifting it up. The lounge chair was rusted, as were two others just like it. Not far away were a gas barbecue and an unfurled garden hose, kinked so badly it was useless.

The music much louder from back here.

A fiberglass roof darkened sliding-glass doors left an inch ajar.

I went over and looked in. The room looked to be a den. Well-stocked wet bar, pub mirrors with ale trademarks, hanging glasses, big plastic ashtrays. Lights out except for green numbers dancing on a black face. Six-foot stereo stack. The CD player going. The music at steam-drill level.

Trying to ignore it, I put my hand against the glass and squinted. Alarm panel in a corner. Another green light: unarmed.

The gray carpeting was grubby. Black leather couches, black-lacquer tables, Lucite sculpture of a nude woman bending submissively. One wall was taken up by a huge chrome-framed litho of a melon-breasted, rouged woman in leather tights. Motorcycle cap pulled down over one of her eyes. The other winked. Opposite stood a free-form gray-granite fireplace with ragged edges. No logs. Black beanbag chairs. A single CD case on one.

Panic-attack drumbeat, tortured bass, jet-engine guitars. Brain-scraping vocals, over and over.

No sign of Locking.

I slid the door open a few inches wider, stuck my head in. "Hello!"

Cigarettes, butts and ashes on the carpet. On one of the tables were piles of magazines.

I took a few steps closer, shouted another "Hello?"

The magazines were a mix of psychology journals I recognized and things you didn't need a Ph.D. to understand.

Full-color covers: nipple-pink, lip-red, coif-blond, pubic-hair-umber. The oyster glisten of fresh ejaculate.

The Journal of Clinical Practice and that.

Locking's idea of homework?

On another table stood a popped can of cola, a nearly empty bottle of Bacardi, and a glass filled with something diluted, barely tinted amber. Melted ice cubes, the drink poured hours ago.

One glass. Party for one.

Maybe Locking had rum-and-Coked himself into a deep enough stupor not to hear the noise.

I shouted again.

No answer.

I tried once more. The room stank of nicotine and a durable relationship with takeout food. The big black ashtrays on the bar were overflowing. Vegas casino logo on the rim of one, the place Ted Barnaby had worked.

The CD on the chair from a band called Sepultura.

Spanish for "grave."

Cute. *The image.*

I turned off the music.

Silence. No protest.

"Hello?"

Nothing.

Not the time to explore further: Half the people in L.A. own guns and Locking's connection to Cruvic plus the tough-punk image made him likely to be one of them. If he'd managed to sleep through the racket, waking him could be dangerous. At the very least, I was guilty of criminal trespass.

I turned to leave and noticed something under one of the ashtrays.

Polaroid snapshot. One corner pinned.

Aligned perfectly with the counter edge.

Positioned.

As if for display.

Photo of a woman.

Bare to the waist, arms stretched high above her head, bound at the wrists and tied to a wooden headboard. Her smallish breasts were tugged upward by the pressure, stretching pale skin over a delicate rib cage. Tight deltoids, goosebump skin.

Her face was covered by a black leather hood studded with zippers.

Two open zippers in the nasal region, zippered mouth-slit fastened shut.

The eyeholes open, too.

Two bright, brown discs shone through.

Below them, two erect nipples, pinched by a pair of hands.

Male hands.

Two different men.

The one on the left, striped with hair, connected to a bare arm.

Small anchor tattoo midway up the forearm.

The hand on the right, smooth and hairless, emerging from a ribbed black cuff.

A ring on that one. Silver skull, red glass eyes.

I inched closer to the photo.

And saw Locking.

On the floor behind the bar.

Propped in a corner, legs splayed, arms limp. One hand curled inward, the fingers of the other outstretched.

Blue nails. Blue lips.

The skull ring grinned back at me.

His head had been thrown back so that his neck arched toward the ceiling. Cheekbones in relief, long hair mussed.

A black silk bathrobe did a poor job of covering his thin, white body.

White except for the raspberry lividity splotches where the blood had settled after he'd stopped breathing.

Mouth agape.

In life he'd been smug but he'd left this world looking surprised.

Crusted hole in the center of his high forehead.

Rusty stripes on his face, trailing down to his hairless chest, browning the black silk where they hit the robe.

Blood on the carpet and on the wall behind him.

Blood under the body.

Lots of blood; why hadn't I seen it right away?

His eyes were half-shut, dry, and dull like those of a fish left on the dock. Long lashes mascaraed by gritty blood.

I'd seen plenty of death. The last time, the man I'd killed . . . self-defense.

I could hear myself breathing.

Suddenly, the room smelled sour.

The position of his head caught my attention. It should have dropped.

But it was tilted upward, leaning against the wall, as if in prayer.

Positioned?

All around him, more Polaroids.

Lots more. *Framing* the corpse.

The same woman, bound and masked.

Close shots that obsessed on her thighs, her chest, her belly and below.

Full views that exposed her entire body, long and slim and pale, spread-eagled on a white-sheeted bed.

Legs knotted to the footboard, hips thrusting upward as if trying to buck a rider.

Shots of her alone, others with the same two hands.

Pinching, squeezing, kneading, spreading, probing.

Gynecologic close-ups.

And one facial close-up, placed near Locking's right hand.

The hood removed.

Blond hair pinned tightly and pulled away from the face.

Lovely face, cultured.

The open mouth expressing fear or arousal. Or both. The brown eyes wide, bright, focused and distant at the same time.

Even exposed that way, Hope Devane's emotions were hard to read.

My eyes shifted back to Locking's corpse.

Something else on the floor.

A cardboard box. More photos. Hundreds of them.

Neat lettering on the side in black marker.

SELF–CONTROL STUDY, BATCH 4, PRELIM.

When Locking had carried the carton from Seacrest's house he hadn't even bothered to close it. Hiding the pictures under a top layer of computer printout.

Big joke on the cops.

And Seacrest had been in on it. He *had* warned Locking.

The tattooed arm. Co-players.

A buzzing sound made me jump.

A shiny green fly had entered through the open door. It circled the room, alighted on the bar, took off again, inspected an ashtray, sped toward me. I swatted it away and it veered off, studied itself in a Beck's mirror, flew back. Hovering above Locking's body, it dove and landed on a patch of abdomen.

Pausing, then climbing up to the lifeless face.

To a bloody spot.

It stayed there. Rubbed its forelegs together.

I went to look for a phone.

32

"It is not," Philip Seacrest repeated, "a crime."

He might have been lecturing to students, but Milo was no sophomore.

A West L.A. interrogation room. A video camera hummed on auto but Milo's pen kept busy. I was alone in the observation cubicle, with cold coffee and frozen images.

"No, it's not, Professor."

"I don't expect you to understand but I believe people's personal lives are just that."

Milo stopped writing.

"When did it begin, Professor?"

"I don't know."

"No?"

"It was *not* my idea . . . never my propensity."

"Whose propensity was it?"

"*Hope's. Casey's.* I was never sure which of them actually initiated it."

"When did you get involved?" said Milo, picking up one of the Polaroids on the table and flicking a corner with his index finger.

Seacrest turned away. Moments ago, his gray herringbone jacket had been off and the sleeve of his white shirt had been rolled up, revealing the anchor tattoo. Now he was fully dressed, the jacket buttoned.

He began picking at his untidy beard. His first reaction upon seeing the snapshots had been shock. Then wet-eyed resignation followed by hardened resolve. He hadn't been arrested, though Milo had offered him an attorney during questioning. Seacrest had turned him down curtly, as if insulted by the suggestion. As the interview ground on, he'd managed to build upon the indignation.

"When did you get involved, Professor?"

"Later."

"How much later?"

"How could I possibly know that, Mr. Sturgis? As I told you, I have no idea when they began."

"When did you get involved in absolute terms?"

"A year, year and a half ago."

"And Locking was your wife's student for over three years."

"That sounds right."

"So it may have been going on for two years before you started."

"*It*," said Seacrest, smiling sourly. "Yes, *it* might have."

"So what happened?" said Milo. "The two of them just walked in one day and announced hey, guess what, we've gotten into some B-and-D games, care to join?"

Seacrest flushed but he kept his voice even. "You wouldn't understand."

"Try me."

Seacrest shook his head and flexed his neck from side to side. The smile hadn't totally faded.

"Something amusing, Professor?"

"Being brought here is *perverse*. My wife's been murdered and you concern yourself with this kind of thing."

Milo leaned forward suddenly, staring into Seacrest's eyes. Seacrest startled but composed himself and stared back. "Perverse, trivial, and irrelevant."

"Humor me, Professor. How did you get involved?"

"I—you're right about it being a game. That's exactly what it was. Just a game. I don't expect you to be tolerant of . . . divergence, but that's all it was."

Milo smiled. "Divergence?"

Seacrest ignored him.

"So they asked you to *diverge* with them."

"No. They—I *happened* upon them. One afternoon when I was supposed to be lecturing. I felt a touch of something coming on, canceled class, came home."

"And found the two of them?"

"Yes, Mr. Sturgis."

"Where?"

"In our bed." Seacrest smiled. "The marital bed."

"Must have been a big shock."

"To say the least."

"What'd you do?"

Seacrest waited a long time to answer. "Nothing."

"Nothing?"

"That's right, Mr. Sturgis. Nothing."

"You didn't get angry?"

"You didn't ask me how I felt, you asked what I

did. And the answer is nothing. I turned around and walked out."

"How'd you feel?"

Another delay. "I really can't say. It wasn't anger. Anger would have been futile."

"Why?"

"Hope didn't take well to anger."

"What do you mean?"

"She had no tolerance for it. Had I displayed anger, things would have gotten . . . confrontational."

"Married people fight, Professor. Seems to me you had a damned good reason."

"How understanding of you, Mr. Sturgis. However, Hope and I never *fought*. It didn't suit either of us."

"So what did you mean by confrontational?"

"A war. Of silence. Interminable, frigid, seemingly infinite stretches of silence. Psychological exile. Even when Hope claimed to forgive, she never forgot. I knew her emotional repertoire the way a conductor knows a score. So when I saw the two of them, I maintained my dignity and simply walked away."

"And then what?"

"And then . . ." Seacrest pulled at his beard again, "someone closed the door and I assume they . . . finished. I'm sure you find my reaction contemptible. Cowardly. *Wimpish*. No doubt you think you would have reacted differently. No doubt *you'll* be going home tonight to a dutiful wife and dutiful children— probably somewhere in the Valley. A charmingly conventional 818 lifestyle."

Milo sat back and pressed a thick finger over his lips.

Looking suddenly tired, Seacrest covered his eyes

with both hands, pulled down at the lids, let the hands trail down his cheeks and fall in his lap.

"It was go along, Mr. Sturgis, or . . ."

"Or what?"

"Or lose her. Now I've lost her anyway."

He slumped. Began to weep.

Milo waited a long time before saying, "Can I get you something to drink, Professor?"

Headshake. Seacrest looked up. Then at the Polaroids. "May we end this? Have you heard enough about the sick *divergent* world of intellectuals?"

"Just a few more questions, please."

Seacrest sighed.

Milo said, "When you found your wife and Locking you didn't figure you'd already lost her?"

"Of course not. It wasn't as if it were the . . ."

"The first time?"

Seacrest's mouth shut tight.

"Professor?"

"This is exactly what I was afraid of—Hope's reputation filthied. I refuse to be part of that."

"Part of what?"

"Dredging up her past."

"What if her past led to her murder?"

"Do you know that?"

"Now that Locking's dead, what do you think?"

No answer.

"How many other men did she play games with, Professor Seacrest?"

"I don't know."

"But you do know there were others."

"I don't know for a fact, but she had owned the . . . apparatus for some time."

"By 'apparatus' you mean the hood and the bindings and those rubber and leather garments in her size that we found at Locking's house."

Seacrest gave a dispirited nod.

"Anything else other than those items?"

"I'm not aware of any."

"No whips?"

Seacrest snorted. "She wasn't interested in pain. Only . . ."

"Only what?"

"Restraint."

"Self-control?"

Seacrest didn't answer.

Milo wrote something down. "So she'd had the apparatus for some time. How long?"

"Five or six years."

"Three years before she met Locking."

"Your arithmetic is excellent."

"Where did she keep the apparatus?"

"In her room."

"Where in her room, Professor?"

"In a box in her closet. I came across it by accident, never told her."

"What else was in there?"

"Pictures."

"Of her?"

"Of . . . us. Pictures we'd taken. She'd told me she'd thrown them out. Apparently she liked to review them."

"Who moved the photos and the apparatus to Locking's house?"

"Casey."

"When?"

"The night you dropped in."

"I only saw him carry out one box."

"He came back later. I'd asked him to move them

before. Right after Hope was murdered. I was afraid
of something exactly like this."

"Why didn't he comply?"

Seacrest shook his head. "He said he would but
kept delaying."

"More games," said Milo.

"I suppose. He was a rather . . . calculated fellow."

"You didn't like him."

"Hope did, that's all that mattered."

"Your feelings didn't matter?"

Seacrest's smile was eerie. "Not one bit, Mr. Sturgis."

"If Locking was delaying, why didn't you just
throw them out?"

"They were Hope's."

"So?"

"I . . . felt they should be preserved."

He licked his lips, averted his eyes.

"Before she died they were hers, Professor.
Wouldn't that make them yours? So why give them to
Locking?"

"For safety," said Seacrest. "I thought the police
might search Hope's room."

"But still," said Milo. "You didn't want to sully
Hope's name, yet you kept a couple hundred
photos?"

"I hid them," he said. "In my University office. Not
that I needed to. Those first two detectives never even
bothered to search Hope's room. You never really did,
either."

"So you brought them to your University office,
then back home."

"Correct."

"Then you waited for Casey Locking to take them off your hands—but what role did they play for *you*?"

Seacrest gave a start. "What role should they have played?"

"I'm asking *you*, sir. All I know is you kept them instead of destroying them. That tells me you had some use for them."

Seacrest flexed his neck again. Adding a forward bend, he opened and closed his fingers. "*Because*, Mr. Sturgis, they were the only pictures I had of her, except for her book jacket. She hated the camera. Hated having her picture taken."

"Except this way."

Seacrest nodded.

"So these were mementos."

Seacrest's jaws clenched.

"But you let Locking have them, anyway."

"I . . . kept some."

"Where?"

"In my home."

"Special ones or did you just stick your hand in and grab randomly?"

Seacrest shot to his feet. "I am terminating this."

"Fine," said Milo. "I guess I'll have to get my information elsewhere. Ask around at some bondage clubs and see if anyone knew your wife. If that doesn't work, I can go to the press, see what that stirs up."

Seacrest shook a finger. "Sir, you are . . ." His hands fisted. "You said if I came down and talked to you here, you'd be discreet."

"I said if you came down and cooperated."

"That's exactly what I'm doing."

"Think so?"

Seacrest flushed deeply, the way I'd seen in his office. I watched his breathing get quicker until he closed his eyes and seemed to concentrate on slowing it down.

"What more do you want?" he finally said. "I keep telling you this had nothing to do with Hope's murder."

"Yes, you do, Professor."

"I *knew* her! Better than *anyone*. She didn't go to *bondage* clubs! She'd never have countenanced anything so . . ."

"Plebeian?"

"Vulgar—and stop looking at the pictures every time I defend her. They were private."

"Private games."

"Yes!" Striding forward, Seacrest swiped at the table, knocking most of the photos to the floor. Snapping his eyes toward Milo, as if expecting retaliation, he placed his hands on his hips and stood there.

Milo looked at him briefly, wrote something down.

Seacrest's shoe had settled near one of the pictures. He stepped on it, ground it under his heel.

"Private," said Milo, softly. "Hope and Locking and you."

"Exactly. Nothing illegal—absolutely nothing! Neither of us killed her."

I expected Milo to follow that up but instead he said, "Are you terminating this interview, sir?"

"If I stay will you promise not to expose Hope?"

"I'm not promising anything, Professor. But if you cooperate, I'll do my best."

"The first time we met," said Seacrest, "you told me we were on the same side. What a line."

"Show me we are, Professor."

"Are we?"

"I'm out to catch your wife's murderer. How about you?"

Seacrest started to lurch forward, stopped himself, his whole body shaking. "If I found him I'd *kill* him! I'm well-versed in medieval torture devices, the things I could do!"

"The rack, huh?"

"You have no idea." Seacrest placed one hand on his own wrist, steadying it.

"Any idea who killed Locking?"

"No."

"No hypotheses?"

Seacrest shook his head. "Casey was . . . I never really knew him."

"Outside of the games."

"Correct."

"The night I dropped by he returned your wife's car."

"Yes."

"Helping out?"

"Yes."

"Even though you didn't really know him."

"Hope knew him."

"So he merited driving her car."

"Yes. And I was grateful to him."

"For what?"

"The pleasure he brought Hope."

"That night, he acted formal toward you, called you Professor Seacrest. Trying to make it seem as if you two had no personal relationship."

"We didn't, really."

Milo lifted one of the photos remaining on the table.

Seacrest said, "The relationship wasn't between Casey and myself, Mr. Sturgis. Both relationships—*everything* revolved around Hope. She was the . . . nexus."

"One sun, two moons," said Milo.

Seacrest smiled. "Very good. Yes, we were in her orbit."

"Who else was?"

"No one I'm aware of."

"No other games?"

"None she told me about."

"Would she have told you?"

"I believe so."

"Why?"

"She was honest."

"About everything?"

Seacrest gave a disgusted look. "You saw the pictures. How much more honest could anyone be?"

Milo stretched a hand toward Seacrest's chair.

"I'll remain standing, Mr. Sturgis."

Smiling, Milo got up, kneeled, and began collecting the fallen photos. "Three-way game, and two of the players are dead. Do you feel threatened?"

"I suppose."

"You suppose?"

"I don't think about myself much."

"No?"

Seacrest shook his head. "I don't think much of my own value."

"That sounds kind of depressed, sir."

"I am depressed. Profoundly."

"Some might say *you* had a motive to kill both of them."

"And what motive is that?"

"Jealousy."

"Then why would I leave the pictures near Casey's body and incriminate myself?"

Milo didn't answer.

"You're wasting my time and yours, Mr. Sturgis. I

loved my wife in a way few women are ever loved—I *obliterated* myself in her honor. Losing her has sucked all the joy from my life. I appreciated Casey because *he* contributed to *her* joy. Other than that, he meant nothing to me.''

"Where did your joy come from?"

"Hope." Seacrest smoothed the lapels of his jacket. "Be logical: Casey was shot and your own tests proved I haven't fired a gun recently. As a matter of fact, I haven't touched a firearm since I was discharged from the service. And at the time Casey was murdered, I was home.''

"Reading."

"Would you like to know the title of the book?"

"Something romantic?"

"Milton's *Paradise Lost*.''

"Original sin."

Seacrest waved a hand. "Gorge yourself on interpretation—why don't you go fetch Delaware, get him into the act, I'm sure he'll have a field day. May I go, Mr. Sturgis? I promise not to leave town. If you don't believe me, have a policeman watch me.''

"Nothing else you want to tell me?"

"Nothing."

"Okay," said Milo. "Sure."

Seacrest walked shakily to the door that led to the observation room, found it locked.

"That one," said Milo, indicating the opposite door.

Seacrest stood taller, reversed direction.

Milo squared the stack of pictures. "Reading at home. Not much of an alibi, Professor."

"I never imagined I'd need one."

"Talk to you later, Professor."

"Hopefully not." Seacrest made it to the door and

stopped. "Not that you'll believe me, but Hope was never coerced or oppressed. On the contrary. *She* made the rules, *she* was the one in control. Being able to surrender herself without fear thrilled her, and her pleasure thrilled *me*. I admit that at first I was repelled, but one learns. I learned. Hope taught me."

"Taught you what?"

"Trust. That's what it's all about, Mr. Sturgis. Total trust. Think about it—would your wife trust you the way mine trusted me?"

Milo hid his smile behind a big, thick hand.

"I know," said Seacrest, "that there's very little use asking you to keep those pictures out of the police locker room but I'm asking anyway."

"Like I said, Professor, if they've got nothing to do with the murder, there's no reason to publicize them."

"They don't. They were part of her life, not her death."

33

"Yeah, it's true about the paraffin test, he hasn't fired a gun in a while," said Milo. "But he still could have hired someone to shoot Locking. Maybe someone he met through the bondage trade."

"He's got a point about not destroying the photos," I said. "If he had, you'd never have thought of him. So maybe the bondage games *were* the reason he was evasive."

"Why *did* he hold on to the photos?"

"Could be just what he said. Mementos."

"Mental or sexual?"

"Either, both."

"So you buy his Mr. Submissive routine? Hope was God, he worshiped at her altar?"

"It would explain their marriage," I said. "She was so controlled as a child, she craved someone willing to subjugate his ego totally. Despite what she told Elsa Campos, being tied up and left behind had to have been terrifying. She kept trying to work it through. And Seacrest's passivity made him a perfect mate for her. He told Paz and Fellows he'd been a confirmed bachelor for years. Maybe the reason was he'd been a moon looking for a sun."

"Working it through," he said. "So she gets herself tied up again? Manipulated, bruised."

"Restaging it," I said. "But this time, *she's* calling the shots."

"With their games, the three of them coulda gone on the talk-show circuit," he said.

"You are starting to sound," I said, "less like a West Hollywood legend than a bourgeois policeman with a dutiful wife and an 818 lifestyle."

He laughed harder than I'd heard him in a long time.

"Those guns you found in Locking's house," I said. "Heavy artillery for a grad student."

"Three pistols, one rifle," he said. "All loaded but stashed up in the closet. Too cocky for his own good."

"And all that porn he had," I said. "Locking was from San Francisco. Big Micky's city, Big Micky's business. Who owns the house?"

"Don't know yet, but a neighbor said it was a rental. Before Locking there'd been lots of other tenants."

"Be interesting if it's the same landlord who owns Cruvic's place on Mulholland."

"Cruvic pays rent to a corporation based here in L.A.—Triad or Triton, something like that, but we haven't traced it to any individual, yet. In terms of Big Micky, what I've learned so far is that he used to be a sizable sex-biz honcho—theaters, peep shows, massage parlors, escort services—but retired because of serious health problems. Heart, liver, kidneys, everything's on the fritz. Had a couple kidney transplants that failed awhile back and ended up pretty screwed-up."

"The old guy Ted Barnaby saw in Vegas with Cruvic was yellow," I said. "Meaning jaundiced, meaning liver problems. Any word on whether Mandy Wright had ever worked in San Francisco?"

"Not yet. But there's another NorCal connection: Hope's mother died up there. Stanford Medical Center, breast cancer. All bills paid by a third party, we're trying to find out who."

"It reeks of history," I said.

"Ph.D.'s with gangster connections." He scratched his jaw. "I hate this case. Too many goddamn smart people."

He walked me out of the station. As we hit the sidewalk on Purdue, someone called out, "Detective Sturgis?"

A big blue Mercedes sedan was parked in a red zone across the street. Two cell-phone antennas on the rear deck. One of those after-market custom packages that doubles the price: wire wheels, all the chrome removed, front apron, rear spoiler. Smoke puffed out the exhaust pipes, almost daintily.

The man at the wheel was in his early sixties with a shaven head and a deep tan that was probably part sun, part bottle. Black wraparound shades, white shirt, yellow tie. Gold glint of wristwatch as he turned off the engine, got out, and jogged across the street. Six feet tall, trim and nimble, probably a few face tucks, but time had tugged at the stitches and his chin flesh shook.

"Robert Barone," he said in a breathy voice. A tan

hand shot forward. "I know you've been trying to reach me but I've been out of town."

"San Francisco?" said Milo as he shook the lawyer's hand.

Barone's smile was as sudden as bad news, as warm as sherbet.

"As a matter of fact, Hawaii. Little downtime between cases." The sunglasses angled at me. "And you are Detective . . . ?"

"What can I do for you, Mr. Barone?" said Milo.

"I was going to ask you the same thing, Detective."

"You made a trip here in person to offer your services to the poor benighted LAPD?"

"The way things have been going," said Barone, "you guys can use all the help you can get—seriously, there is a matter I'd like to discuss. If I didn't find you I was going to talk to your lieutenant."

Still looking at me, he said, "I didn't catch *your* name."

"Holmes," said Milo. "Detective Holmes."

"As in Sherlock?"

"No," said Milo, "as in Sigmund. So what does Dr. Cruvic want? Police protection now that Darrell Ballitser put his name out on the airwaves, or is he ready to confess to something?"

Barone turned serious. His bald head was liver-spotted. "Why don't we go inside?"

"You're in a no-parking zone, counselor."

Barone laughed. "I'll take my chances."

"Guess that's what you get paid to do," said Milo, "but don't blame me." To me: "Catch you later, Sig. Any research you want to do on the aforementioned topic is fine."

He headed for the station's front door, leaving Barone to catch up.

*   *   *

Research. On the Kruvinski/Cruvic clan.

The family lawyer arriving in person because someone was worried.

Little Micky still the only one with a confirmed link to Hope and Mandy.

I drove to the library and looked up his father, found fifteen citations on Milan V. Kruvinski going back twenty years, all from San Francisco papers. A couple of photos showing a bull-necked, flat-featured man with slanted eyes that cemented his paternity. But cruder than his son, a less-finished sculpture.

Not a single story from any Bakersfield paper. Quieter town, quieter time? Or payoffs?

Most of the San Francisco pieces had to do with obscenity busts. The "sex impresario and reputed crime figure" had been arrested dozens of times during the seventies and early eighties. Too much flesh in the shows, too much customer-dancer contact, liquor served to underage patrons.

I thought of something Cruvic had told us at his Beverly Hills office.

The rise in infertility problems due to *all the messing around people did in the seventies.*

Firsthand knowledge.

The articles described lots of arrests but no convictions. Lots of dismissals prior to trial.

Prosecutors had even made a stab at the old crime-busting standby: a tax-evasion charge that Kruvinski beat by proving the bulk of his income came from agricultural holdings in the Central Valley, some of which had earned him federal subsidies. His theaters on O'Farrell and Polk streets had finally closed down but not, apparently, due to legal problems.

Almost no quotes, either; when Kruvinski communicated with the press, he did it through Robert Barone. But I did find one ten-year-old interview, a fawning piece by a self-consciously Runyonesque columnist who prided himself on having San Francisco's pulse in his pocket.

He'd spoken to Kruvinski at home and the piece helped explain the porn broker's business shift out of live entertainment.

"We moved into video," said the once-robust entrepreneur from his multilevel redwood/glass Sausalito-lair-with-a-bay-view. "Guys don't want to go to a theater anymore, put up with all the harassment."

Then with typical Micky K. generosity and a Slavic smile as wide as the Embarcadero, he offered me a scotch—21 y.o. Chivas in the true-blue bottle, of course—even though he couldn't partake, himself. Liver problems. Heart. Kidneys. Last year's transplant, his second, was a beacon in the fog, but it didn't take.

I refused the booze but Micky wouldn't hear about abstinence in the name of empathy. An affectionate "Honey," brought Mrs. Micky, the beauteous, tanned, and aerobi-toned former actress-and-model Brooke Hastings out from her state-of-the-culinary-art galley, smiling and reflecting Sausalito sunlight as she wiped Micky's brow and murmured soothing, wifey words.

"His favorite thing is watching the sea lions," she confided in me, while pouring a generous dollop of the divine Chiv. Bros. blended brew. "Has fresh fish brought down to them every morning. He loves animals. Anything organic and alive. That's what attracted me to him."

Then she kissed the big guy's pate in a way that went way beyond spousal duty and he smiled and looked out a picture window as big as the stage of the Love Palace Theater. Almost dreamily, and maybe he was dreaming—who's this scrivener to testify otherwise. The former Miss H. put her arm around him and he kept looking. Looking and dreaming. Like at a movie. Different from the movies he produces, but just as sensual in its own way. T.F. Miss H. crossed shapely gams and yours truly sipped Chivas, feeling the warm fire flow down ye olde deadline slave's gullet like Scottish lava. All in all, not a bad day in Xanadu. We can only hope Micky has lots more.

Brooke Hastings. An "actress" taking the name of hubby's stock-and-fertilizer company. Kruvinski's joke—had she known to what he was comparing her?

Family joke, Junior using the same name for the institute he'd supposedly attended during the year between residencies, the year after he'd left the University of Washington.

I finished the rest of the articles. No mention of the first wife, the doctor son, or any other relatives. Ending with Big Micky's health problems, enough pathos to gag a talk-show junkie.

Where was the old man, now? Moved down to

L.A., so Junior could take care of him? In the big house on Mulholland, hidden behind gates?

But no kidney function meant dialysis. Equipment, monitoring.

A home clinic?

Was that where Anna the nurse had driven, the night I saw her in the car with Locking?

Private nurse for a very private patient?

Junior doctoring Senior . . .

But Junior was a gynecologist. Was he qualified?

A gynecologist who'd started out to be a surgeon.

Why *had* he left the U of Washington residency program?

And how *had* he filled the year?

I returned home and phoned Seattle.

The head of the surgery residency program was a man named Arnold Swenson but his secretary told me he was new to the job, having arrived the year before.

"Do you recall who the head was fourteen years ago?"

"No, because I wasn't around, either. Hold on, let me ask."

Seconds later an older-sounding woman came on.

"This is Inga Blank, how may I help you?"

I repeated the question.

"That would be Dr. John Burwasser."

"Is he still in practice?"

"No, he's retired. May I ask what this is concerning?"

"I'm working with the Los Angeles Police Department on a homicide case. We're trying to get information on one of your former residents."

"A homicide case?" she said, alarmed. "Which resident?"

"Dr. Milan Cruvic."

Her silence was worth more than words.

"Ms. Blank?"

"What has he done?"

"We're just trying to find out some background information."

"He was only in the program briefly."

"But you remember him well."

More silence. "I can't give out Dr. Burwasser's number, but if you leave me yours, I'll give him the message."

"Thank you. Isn't there something you can tell me about Dr. Cruvic?"

"I'm sorry, no."

"But you're not surprised that the police would be interested in him."

I heard her throat clear. "Very little surprises me nowadays."

Not expecting any return call and figuring Milo was still with Barone, I got into jogging clothes and prepared to sweat off the frustration.

The phone rang just as I closed the door behind me and I rushed back into the house and caught it before the service picked up.

"Dr. Delaware."

"This is Dr. Burwasser," said a dry, testy voice. "Who are you?"

I started to explain.

"Sounds fishy," he said.

"If you'd like, I can have Detective Sturgis call you—"

"No, I'm not wasting any time on this. Cruvic was with us for under a year, fourteen years ago."

Not *around* fourteen. Brief but memorable?

"Why'd he leave?" I said.

"That's no one's business."

"It will be soon. He was intimate with a woman who was murdered and he's a possible suspect. The more effort it takes to get the information, the more public it'll be."

"Is that a threat?"

"Not at all, just a statement of fact, Dr. Burwasser. Did Cruvic do something to disgrace the surgery program?"

Instead of answering, he said, "I'm not impressed by murder, seen plenty of things in my day."

"What did Dr. Cruvic do?"

"He never murdered anyone here."

"Did he murder someone somewhere else?"

"No, of course not—is this being taped?"

"No."

"Not that it matters, nothing I tell you is libelous because it's true, all on the record."

"Exactly," I said.

He didn't answer.

"What'd he do, Dr. Burwasser?"

"He stole."

"From whom?"

"That I will *not* tell you because the dead are entitled to their dignity."

That took a moment to process. "He stole from a corpse?"

"Tried to."

"How much?"

He laughed shallowly, as if needing the release. "Hard to say, the market varies."

"Jewelry?"

"Of sorts." Another laugh. "Family jewels. Organs.

We caught the little bastard trying to remove a heart. The only problem was, the donor wasn't quite dead."

"My God."

"Don't get dramatic, I said it wasn't murder. The patient was terminal—flat-lining. We were getting ready to turn off the machines and pronounce but we couldn't locate next of kin."

"But the heart was still going."

"Of course it was, otherwise why bother taking it out? Nice and strong. Young fellow, head trauma—motorcycle accident. Turned out to be a tourist from Germany, the idiot could have caused an international incident."

"Who'd he try to steal the heart for?"

"Not who. *What.* Research. He'd conned us into giving him some lab space, said he wanted to practice gall-bladder resections on dogs, write a paper."

"Not true?" I said.

"Oh, he worked on a few beagles but that wasn't the *real* reason. Idiot fancied himself a transplant surgeon, future Christiaan Barnard. I put an end to that pipe dream despite the pressure."

"Pressure from who?"

"Politicians from California." The last word delivered with even more contempt than the first.

"San Francisco?"

"Yup. Lots of calls from greasy characters. Apparently his father was some sort of big shot. No matter to me. Do something like that, you're out."

"How was he caught?"

"A nurse walked in on him, got him red-handed, the fool. Middle of the night. He had a surgical kit laid out next to the patient's bed, had even made the initial incision. Lord knows how he thought he could

have gotten away with it—enough, that's all I'm saying. I don't need this grief, go bother Swenson."

Organ theft.

Sterilization without proper consent.

Smartest boy.

Making his own rules. No surprise. He'd grown up
seeing his father do a lot worse.

Years later, more surgical felonies?

What had Hope's role been in all of it?

But the same question: Why had Hope and Locking been targeted and not Cruvic, himself?

Still, Cruvic had to be at the core of it. Barone had
shown up at the police station because Cruvic *knew*
the walls were closing in.

Scared?

Not of the police . . . scared for himself. Because
Locking's murder had put Hope's into focus for him.

Told him who. Why.

But why now, and not after *Hope's* murder?

And what had brought Cruvic out in the open?

Darrell Ballitser's attack. The news reports linking
him to Hope.

First time the *murderer* had known of the link?

But how could that be, if the issue was unethical
surgery?

I went around and around with it.

Assume Ballitser's attack had focused the murderer
on Cruvic.

After that, the murderer had begun watching
Cruvic . . . seen him with Locking? At Mulholland?

Unless I was totally off, and Cruvic had killed both
Hope and Locking to keep them quiet.

But then why send his lawyer to talk to Milo?

The more I wrestled with it, the more convinced I became that Cruvic was now a target and he knew it.

Getting away with years of loose ethics until he'd finally offended the wrong person.

In *collaboration* with Hope and Locking.

Loose ethics . . . sterilization without consent . . . organ theft.

The house on Mulholland.

Private clinic.

Something Locking had been involved with, too . . .

Then it hit me.

So simple.

But where did Mandy Wright figure in? Party girl . . . *working* girl.

Days before her murder, she'd done the club scene in L.A. Before that, she'd met with Cruvic and his father in Vegas, left the casino with both of them.

Not for sex.

Another kind of freelancing.

She'd told Barnaby, *"It's like acting."*

What had Milo said about Club None—big hair and perfect bodies.

Mandy would fit in.

Her companion, too?

The poor waitress, Kathy DiNapoli. Murdered simply because she'd served drinks in the wrong place at the wrong time.

Perfect bodies.

Mandy hired to pick someone up.

A special kind of john.

Slowly, inexorably, like a snake coming alive in the heat, the chain unfolded in my head.

The chain between Hope, Locking, Mandy, Kathy. *Venomous* snake.

The Morry Mayhew show that Hope had appeared on—what was the name of that producer? Suzette Band. I'd promised to call her if I learned something.

The old information barter.

She'd have to make another payment, first.

34

Next stop: Mulholland Drive.

The road was beautiful in the daylight, the house behind the electric gate a brown-brick contemporary, sparkling with color around the borders—flowers invisible in the dark.

I'd kept my sweat-stained T-shirt on but had substituted jeans for the running shorts. In my hand was a bag picked up from a pharmacy in Beverly Hills an hour ago. I'd bought toothpaste and dental floss and vitamin C to get it. The Seville, parked just down the road, was old enough to pass for a delivery vehicle, I supposed. I was too old a delivery boy for most cities but L.A. was full of underachievers.

I rang the bell on the gatepost. After a moment's delay a voice came through the speaker, "Yeah?"

"Delivery."

"Hold on."

A few minutes later, the front door opened and a

man in a black shirt and black jeans came out, stared at me, and approached in a flat-footed, plodding walk.

He was in his late thirties, short and wide, with thinning black hair on top, the side wisps tied into a barely long-enough ponytail. Bushy sideburns longer than Milo's, oily skin that shone, wire-rimmed glasses, pummeled features.

Sleepy expression, except for little piggy eyes that never left me.

The black shirt was silk, oversized, untucked, and he kept his right hand in front of him, as if protecting something. Plainclothes cops wore their shirts out to conceal guns and I supposed thugs did the same.

"Yeah?"

"Delivery for Mr. Kruvinski."

I held the druggist's bag out.

"What's in it?"

"Medicine, I guess."

"He gets his medicine from his doctor."

I tried to look apathetic.

"Lemme see."

I gave him the bag and he pulled out a small amber bottle filled with yellow tablets. The right color, but the wrong shape. My *Physicians' Desk Reference* chart showed Imuran as a scored doublet, these were singles. Vitamin Cs. Black shirt didn't react. As I'd hoped, not observant.

The label was a work of art. I'd steamed off an old one for penicillin, whited out all the specifics but left the pharmacy's name and address and the RX, DATE, and PRESCRIBING PHYSICIAN blanks. Photocopied it, typed in the new information, put some glue on the back, stuck it back on the vial. Pretty good job, though I wasn't ready for twenty-dollar bills.

He read the label now and his mouth pursed when he got to PRESCRIBING PHYSICIAN: M. CRUVIC, M.D. Followed by Cruvic's real license number, obtained from the medical board.

Confusion seamed his meaty forehead.

"We just got a big box of this shi—who ordered this?"

Bingo.

I tried to look stupid and peeved rather than elated. "Dunno, I just go where they tell me. You wan' me to take it back?"

Dropping the bottle back in the bag, he kept it and started for the house.

"Hey," I said.

Stopping short, he looked over his shoulder at me. His shoulders were enormous, his elbows dimpled. Pink scalp showed through the hair; the ponytail was a sad thing.

"You gotta problem?"

"COD," I said. "You gotta pay for it." Keeping it going for realism; I'd already learned what I wanted to know.

Lifting his free hand, he made a skin-gun and aimed it at my face.

"Wait, bucko."

I did. Til he got inside and closed the door.

Then I ran back to the Seville and was pulling out by the time he got back. Along with Anna the tight-faced nurse.

The two of them standing behind the iron gate, perplexed, as I got the hell out of there.

35

So much to do with the movie business is bland, mundane, characterless. The casting studio said it all.

A muddy brown lump of a one-story building on Washington Boulevard in Culver City, it sat between a Cuban seafood restaurant and a Chinese laundry. The stucco was lighter where graffiti had been over-sprayed. No windows, a warped black door.

Inside was a no-frills waiting room crowded with perfect-body hopefuls of both sexes, sitting in folding chairs, reading *Variety*, fantasizing about fame, fortune, and cutting some obnoxious restaurant customer's throat.

The inner room was much larger, but all it contained was a card table and two chairs under cheap track lighting, and a rear wall of flyspecked mirror.

I sat in a tiny storage closet, behind the mirror, watching.

Two casting directors sat behind the table: a heavy,

sloppy-looking, puffy-faced man with bad skin and greasy hair, wearing a Hawaiian shirt and grubby khakis, and a thin woman with not-bad blue eyes, wearing an obvious black wig and clad in red sweats.

Nameplates in front of them.

BRAD RABE   PAIGE BANDURA

Two Evian bottles, a pack of Winstons, and an ashtray, but no one was smoking.

"Next," said Rabe.

A hopeful entered. Audition Number 6 for the male lead.

He looked at Rabe and Bandura, smiled with what he probably thought was warmth.

I saw tension, fear, and contempt.

What was he thinking?

Frick and Frack?

Hansel and Gretel?

Who were they to judge—both of them dressed like slobs—typical. Dressing down to show they had the power, couldn't give a shit.

The hopeful knew the type—God, *did* he.

Waiting out there in that zoo for three fucking hours for the privilege of being judged by eyes that never changed through the bullshit smiles and the nods and the phony words of encouragement.

The *judging.*

"Okay," said Paige Bandura, looking at her fatso partner. "How about the scene in the middle of fortysix?"

"Sure." The hopeful grinned charmingly and flipped the script's pages. "From 'But Celine, you and I?' "

"No, right after that—from 'What exactly is it you're after.' "

The hopeful nodded, took a deep breath in that covert yoga way that no one could see. Closed his eyes, opened them, and glanced down at the script before raising them. Show them he could memorize instantaneously.

Looking into little Paige's eyes, because she seemed to be on his side.

" 'What exactly is it you're after, Celine? I thought our friendship had grown to something more.' Shall I read her line, too?"

"No," said Paige. "I'll be her."

Big, warm smile. Maybe . . .

Lifting a script from the card table, she read:

" 'Maybe, Dirk. Maybe not. But the bottom line is I need a man right now and you just may fill the bill.' "

Flat voice. Ugly voice. It came out *Buddaboddomlion is I needa mayan.*

The ones who judged were inevitably ugly in some way. The hopeful hated ugly.

" 'Is that so?' " he said, softening his tone, " 'because I think you feel more than that, Celine. I feel it and I think you feel it, too. Here.' " Touching his heart.

" 'Do you, Dirk?' "

Dooyoodirk.

" 'Yes, I do, Celine.' " He smiled at her again. "The script says he puts his hand on her—"

"That's okay," said Paige. Saucy laugh. "We'll just pretend. Okay, what's Celine's next line—'But, Dirk—' "

" 'I know, you feel it *here*, Celine. From your inner being. The place where love grows.' "

He dropped his arms. Connotation of vulnerability. Stood there. Waiting.

Paige smiled at him again, turned to Fat Sloppy Brad.

Brad looked him over. Rubbed his face. Grunted.

"Not bad," he finally pronounced.

"I'd say excellent," added Paige.

Brad said, "Okay, excellent." Grudgingly.

"If you'd like I can read more," said the hopeful.

The two of them exchanged glances.

"No, that won't be necessary," said Paige. "That was really good."

The hopeful shrugged. Boyishly. He had a great boyish grin.

Another look between him and Paige.

"Onward," she said. "Some practical issues. The show is going to be fairly physical for daytime. Lots of love scenes—steamy stuff. Any problems with that?"

"Not at all," said the hopeful, but a tightening above his navel had begun—someone—some little demon screwing up his insides. Smile. *Acting!*

"We mean *skin*," said Brad. "It's cable so they're going to stretch the standards. Nothing worse than *NYPD Blue*, but there's gonna be plenty of body shots. How about taking your shirt off?"

The hopeful didn't answer. His heart rate had climbed to over 120. Despite all the cardiovascular training . . . fuck, fuck, fuck.

"Is there a problem?" said Paige.

Rooting for him. Maybe he *could* work it out.

"No problem," he said. "I've got a scar. Some people think it's actually pretty masc—"

"A scar where?" said Brad.

"No big deal—"

"Where?"

"On my back."

Brad frowned.

The hopeful had to think fast. Play to Flat-voice Paige. Look casual—acting! Brilliance!

He reached around. "Just below the waistband, so if it's only partial—"

"Let's see," said Brad. "Take your shirt off."

The hopeful looked to Paige for support.

She nodded. Sleepy-eyed. Losing interest.

Bitch!

He slipped his sweatshirt over his head.

"Turn around and pull your jeans down far enough for us to see the whole thing," said Brad.

The hopeful did.

Silence.

Long silence.

He knew why.

Both of them staring. Grossed-out.

He put his hands on his hips, trying to distract them by showing off the big, defined muscles of his shoulders and back. Flex the triceps, flex the glutes. Nice, tight butt, he could control every muscle.

"How'd you get it?" said Brad.

"Hiking. Rock climbing. I fell, tore my back up, got stitched."

"Not stitched very well," said Brad. "That's some scar."

And the hopeful knew what he was thinking. What both of them were thinking:

Ugly.

Because it was. Pink, puckered, glossy. *Keloid fibrosing.* Especially conspicuous because the surrounding skin was so smooth and bronze. So perfect.

Severe keloiding. Crappy surgical technique, the

books said. And genetics. Black people keloided a lot. In Africa it was considered a sign of beauty.

Well, I'm white!

The treatment: shots of cortisone right into the wound early on. Too late, now. The only hope, more surgery, and that was a big maybe. Not that he could afford it yet. In more ways than one. Open *that* can of worms . . .

"Must have been quite a fall," said Brad. Smugness in his voice.

It set off the feeling.

Like turning on a steam spigot.

Hot, boiling, iron-foundry rage. Foaming up from his gut and working its way to his chest. Like a heart attack, but he'd been through the nights of panics, cold sweats, knew his heart was fine. *His* heart . . .

His hands wanted to clench and he forced them to remain open. Forced the sweat to remain *inside.*

No one talked.

The hopeful kept his back to the two of them, knowing the smallest glimpse of the rage would kill any chance he had for a good-guy part.

Like there was still a chance. But keep going. In this business, you just keep going. . . .

"What mountain were you climbing?" said Paige, and he knew she was mocking him.

Okay, thanks, babe. Ciao.

Don't call us, we'll call you.

"Does it matter?" he said, slipping the sweatshirt on and turning around.

Nearly falling over in surprise.

Because Brad and Paige were holding guns and badges.

"Looks more like a surgical scar," said Brad.

"Looks more like some kind of serious operation. Isn't that part of the back where the kidney is?"

The hopeful didn't answer.

Brad said, "And the Oscar goes to . . . okay, put your hands behind your back, Mr. Muscadine, and don't move."

Smiling. Judging.

Some of the rage must have leaked through because Brad's smile died and his green eyes got even brighter. Yet colder. The hopeful had never known green could get that cold. . . . He took a step backward.

"Easy, pal," said Fat Brad. "Let's make this easy."

"Up with the hands, Reed," said Paige. Sharp voice, hostile, no longer on his side. *Never* on his side.

He stood there. Looked at them.

Poor specimens. Pathetic.

He was very big, very strong, could probably do some damage.

Not that it would make a difference in the long run.

But what the hell, might as well get something out of this shitty afternoon.

He dove for Paige.

Because he really didn't *like* women.

Tried for a jaw-breaking punch but only managed to slap her fucking face before Brad hit him on the back of his head and he went down.

36

After the uniforms took Reed Muscadine away, I came out from behind the dirty mirror.

Milo drank Evian water and plucked at his Hawaiian shirt. "Sleek, huh?"

Detective Paige Bandura said, "I think it suits you, *Brad*."

"That right?"

"Sure. Nice and *caj*. Joe Beachbum."

"Caj." He looked at me. "So what do you think?"

"I think you could have a new career. Hell, maybe *you* can be Dirk."

"Spare me."

"I mean it, I really like the shirt," said Paige. "If you don't like it you can donate it to the Ivy. The one at the beach. They've got Hawaiian shirts hanging on the wall."

"Hoo-hah," said Milo. "How do you know about such things, Detective Bandura?"

"Rich boyfriend." She grinned, removed the black wig, and fluffed her clipped chestnut curls. "Need me for anything else, Milo?"

"Nope, thanks."

"Hey, any time. Always wanted to act—how'd I do, Doctor?"

"From where I was sitting," I said, "great."

"Haven't acted since high school. *Pirates of Penzance*. Wanted to be Mabel, but they made me a pirate."

"You were terrific," I lied.

It made her smile and she walked off with a spring in her step.

"What's her usual detail?" I said.

"Car theft." Milo sat down in the same chair he'd occupied as Brad.

Just the two of us in the room now. The empty space smelled of toxic sweat.

"Good work, Sig," he said.

"Luckily."

"Hey, you had a hypothesis. I always respect your hypotheses."

A hypothesis.

About what Hope and Locking and Cruvic had in common.

Then back to square one: the conduct committee.

One particular case. Someone pressured to take a blood test.

I'd tested it out:

Confirmed Big Micky was on Imuran, the most commonly used antirejection drug. Meaning he was off dialysis. Had received yet another kidney transplant.

After that, the details had flooded my head: Reed Muscadine's clothes the day I'd spoken to him in his apartment. Short shorts, which matched the heat of the day, but a heavy sweatshirt that *didn't*. The sleeves cut off. Baring the arms, but covering his torso.

Mrs. Green the landlady telling me he'd been laid up with a bad back for over a month.

Muscadine telling me more: *Tried for three-twenty on the bench press. It felt like a knife going through me.*

A slip? Or playing with me?

Acting?

A good actor. Professor Dirkhoff's prize student. Dirkhoff had been distressed because Muscadine had dropped out to take a job on a soap opera.

A job that sounded definite.

But Muscadine had lost the part.

I can practice Stanislavsky from now til tomorrow, but if the bod goes so does my marketability.

Not remembering the name of the soap opera. Unlikely. Starving actors attuned themselves to every detail.

But giving me enough to sound credible.

Something about spies and diplomats, foreign embassies.

That had narrowed it down enough for Suzette Band to come up with a name.

Embassy Row. She'd gotten me the number of the show's casting director, a woman named Chloe Gold, and I'd called her posing as Muscadine's new agent. Asking her if Reed could get another chance because the boy was really talented.

She'd looked him up in her files and said *No, thanks, he was bumped 'cause of physical factors.*

What physical factors?

You don't know? You're his agent.

We haven't gotten into—

Ask him. Gotta go.

*   *   *

Physical factors.

The blood test, not just for HIV, but also for tissue compatibility. Hope with faculty clout, getting access to the sample.

It fit.

Not hard evidence but enough to *hypothesize.*

Cruvic's *real* clinic was the house on Mulholland Drive.

Honor thy father . . .

Milo drank the rest of the water and looked up at the track lighting. "Maybe we should throw a wrap party. Maybe the department will even compensate me for the rental and the ad in *Variety.*"

"You paid for it yourself?"

"Department doesn't authorize sting dough on the basis of *hypotheses* and I didn't want to spend six goddamn months going through channels. And what other choice was there? The wimpo judge said no warrant on Muscadine's medical records and apartment 'cause *he* doesn't like hypotheses. Meaning if I'd just walked up to the asshole and yanked his shirt up it would be no grounds, illegal search, and the scar would be excluded from evidence. Let alone forcing him to take an X ray, see if his kidney's missing."

"And not much chance the surgeon kept records."

"And as asshole Barone came to tell me, the asshole *surgeon* is out of the country. And, for the time being, with multiple murders on the agenda, busting Dr. Heelspur for malpractice isn't going to be the D.A.'s priority. But eventually, when what he did gets out, he ain't going to be working in Beverly Hills or anywhere else."

"Any chance of jail time for him?"

He shrugged.

"Forced retirement may not mean much to him," I said. "He probably doesn't need the money. Though being a doctor's a big deal to him psychologically. A *very* big deal. So maybe it'll hurt."

"Why do you say it's such a big deal?"

"He stole Muscadine's kidney but sewed him up and let him live. Fatal error for Hope and Mandy and Locking, and, if Muscadine ever learned who'd cut him, for himself. But Cruvic wanted to see himself as a healer, not a killer. Working through his own childhood, just as Hope had tried to do."

"Hope," he said, shaking his head. "Setting Muscadine up for the knife."

"Smartest girl and smartest boy, devising a project to save Big Micky," I said. "She and Cruvic went back a long way. Strong bond. Maybe because Cruvic was someone who understood what it was like to be an A student with a parent who lived on the wrong side of the law. To have a secret life. I'll bet Big Micky paid Lottie Devane's medical bills at Stanford—one of the places he'd gotten a kidney. And the consultation money Hope's been getting from Junior and Barone is probably really some kind of allowance from Senior. Before the book, forty grand would have made a lot of difference in her life."

"Payback time," he said. "And Mandy was the bait. Where does Locking fit in?"

"I don't know, but keep looking up north."

"Another smart boy," he said. "You think the entire conduct committee was just a ploy to find a donor for Daddy?"

"No," I said. "I think Hope believed in it. But she and Cruvic had probably been discussing what to do for Big Micky for some time. We know from the doctors at Stanford that he'd already tried going through channels but was unlikely to qualify for another kidney because two failures made him a very high risk for rejection and so did his poor general health and his age. Maybe Cruvic and Hope even considered using one of the women at the clinic as a donor—sterilize, then snip something extra. Maybe they were just waiting around for the right girl—someone with no family ties whatsoever. Then Hope came face-to-face with Muscadine, big and strong and healthy *and* no family ties. Plus, she believed him to be a rapist who was going to get away with it, so there was her moral justification. They tested his blood, ruled out HIV and other infections, and did a tissue match. Bingo. Not that it was any big miracle. The more compatibility factors the better, but kidney transplants are often done just on the basis of an ABO match, and both Kruvinski and Muscadine were O-positive, the most common type."

"Christ," he said. "For all we know, they *did* do some poor girl at the clinic and that failed, too. When all this comes out, we may hear about all sorts of people with scars and backaches."

"There'd be a limit for the old man. He could only tolerate so much surgery. This was probably his last chance. That's why they had to find an ideal donor."

"Muscadine . . ."

"Who Professor Steinberger never met, because she'd resigned from the committee before his case came up."

"Hope didn't like the Storm kid much, either, but he had family ties."

"The worst kind of ties: a wealthy father more than willing to make waves. And for all Kenny's obnoxiousness, his guilt was a lot more ambiguous. Maybe Hope still held on to a sense of fairness."

"Maybe." He shook his head. "Setting up Muscadine for involuntary charity. *Harvesting* him. Christ, it's an urban legend come to life. I almost feel sympathy for the bastard."

"It would be traumatic for anyone," I said, "but for someone like Muscadine—prizing his body, trying to merchandise his looks—it was so much more. When I spoke to him at his apartment, he said he'd found the blood test Kafkaesque. He also said his back injury had felt like a knife going through him. Playing with me. Or just getting it off his chest without letting on."

"Free therapy?"

"Why not?" I said. "Don't actors learn that? Seize the moment?"

37

Big Micky was anything but.

He sat facing us under a huge live oak. Nothing grew under the tree, and the ground had reverted to sand. The rest of the yard was perfect bonsai grass around a half-Olympic black-bottom pool with a spitting-dolphin waterfall, herringbone-brick hardscape, statuary on pedestals, blood-red azalea beds, more big trees. Through the foliage, a spreading, hazy view of the San Gabriels said money couldn't buy clean air.

The old man was so shrunken he made the wheelchair look like a high-back. No shoulders, no neck—his smallish head seemed to sprout from his sternum. His skin was legal-pad yellow, his brown eyes filmed, the skin around them bagged, defatted, jeweled with blackheads. A fleshy red blob of a nose reached nearly to his gray upper lip. Bad dentures made his jaws work constantly. Only his hair was youthful: thick, coarse, still dark, with only a few sparks of gray.

Milo's warrant had opened the electric gate of the house on Mulholland but no one had come up to greet us and he'd taken out his gun and let the uniforms come on like an army. Just as we'd reached the front door it had opened and the ponytailed frog I'd given the medicine vial to was leaning against the jamb, trying to look casual.

Milo put him against the wall, cuffed him, patted him down, took his automatic and his wallet, read his driver's license.

"Armand Jacszcyc, yeah, this looks like you. Who else is in the house, Armand?"

"Just Mr. K. and a nurse."

"You're sure?"

"Yeah," said Jacszcyc. Then he noticed me and his head retracted.

The uniforms went in. A sergeant came back a few minutes later, saying, "No one else. Lots of guns, we're pulling an arsenal."

Another uniform came out with Nurse Anna. Her tight face was glossy with sweat and her big chest was emphasized by an electric-blue angora sweater.

She kept her head down as they took her away.

"Okay," said Milo. "Leave me a couple of guys to tear up the place for dope."

"No dope so far," said the sergeant.

"Keep looking. And bust this one for concealed weapon."

Frog was hustled off and we stepped in. The center of the house was one sixty-foot stretch of dark-paneled space clear to the back, sparkle-ceilinged and gold-carpeted, filled with groupings of green and brown couches, ceramic lamps with fringed shades, heavy, carved tables full of souvenir-shop porcelain and crystal. Clown paintings and Rodeo Drive oils of rainy Paris street scenes said all talent should not be encouraged. The rear wall was covered by pleated olive drapes that locked out the sun and sealed in the smell of decay.

A screech-bird voice from the back yelled, "Where's that *water*, Armand!"

A wheelchair sat next to a fake Louis XIV commode with an obscenely inlaid front. The marble top was crowded with medicine bottles. Not like the vial I'd showed Jacszcyc. Big white plastic containers. No prescription blanks. Drug-company samples.

"*Armand!*"

"He had to run," said Milo. "Nurse Anna's gone, too."

The old man blinked, tried to move. The effort turned him green and he sank back.

"Who the hell are you?"

"Police." Milo flashed ID. Two uniforms came over and he told them, "Over there." Pointing to the open doorway of a big brown kitchen. The counter was piled with water bottles, soft-drink cans, takeout cartons, dirty dishes, pots and pans.

"What the fuck you moe-rons doin' here?"

His accent was interesting: the broad farmer drawl of Bakersfield tucked up at the final syllables by a hint of Eastern Europe. Lawrence Welk without the cheer.

"Gimme some water, moe-ron."

Milo filled a glass and held it out along with the warrant.

"What's that?"

"Drug paper. Anonymous tip."

The old man took the glass but ignored the warrant.

He drank, barely able to hold the glass, water dribbling down his chin. He tried to put it on the table, didn't protest when Milo took it.

"Drug paper? Wrong customer, moe-ron. But what do I give a flying? Tear up the place, it's rented anyway."

"Rented from you," said Milo. "Triage Properties. That's a medical term. Interesting choice for a doing-business-as. My-son-the-doctor's idea?"

The old man put his hands together and closed his eyes.

"Triage," repeated Milo. "DBA the Peninsula Group, DBA Northern Lights Investments. Northern Lights traces to Excalibur Properties, which traces to Revelle Recreation, which traces to Brooke-Hastings Entertainment. Your old skin biz. Before *that*, your old manure-and-meat biz. You musta really liked the name, giving it to wife number two and the so-called charitable institution you established in San Francisco: rehab for street girls. What, Junior treating their VD and doing their abortions and helping the cute ones get into dancing?"

"You prefer welfare?"

"So what else did Junior do that year? Practice his surgical technique?"

The old man's hands shook a bit. "Go ahead, moe-ron, finish. Then go back to your boss and tell him you found nothing. *Then*, go fuck yourself."

"I'd rather talk."

"About what?"

"Bakersfield. San Francisco."

"Nice towns, both. You wanna know where to eat, I got recommendations."

Milo touched his gut. "Food isn't what I need."

"No," said the old guy. "You're a fat fuck—here's a

tip: Lay off the meat. Look what happened to me." He reached up with effort, flicked a chicken-skin jowl. It fluttered as if paper.

"Big meat eater, were you?" said Milo.

"Oh, yeah. Meat, meat, meat." A purplish tongue tip cruised along a gray lip. "I ate the best. Ate the fat, too, every bit. Now my arteries and everything else are clogged and I gotta sit here and put up with moe-rons like you."

"Tough," said Milo.

The old man laughed. "You give a flying, huh?"

Milo smiled. "So. The new kidney making life any easier?"

The gray lips turned white.

"I also want to talk about Junior," said Milo. "His sudden holiday."

"Fuck off."

"We also served paper for his place in Beverly Hills. Alleged medical offices. Except the only thing we found in there were rooms full of porn videos ready for shipping." Smiling again. "And that operating room. Must have cost a fortune."

The old man pushed a button on the wheelchair's arm and the contraption began reversing slowly.

Milo held it in place and the chair whined, wheels scraping the carpet.

"We're still talking, Mr. Kruvinski."

"I want a phone. I got a right to a fucking phone."

"What rights? You're not being arrested."

"Leggo of the chair."

"Sure," said Milo. Pushing another button, he locked the tires.

"You're in big trouble, pigass," said the old man. "Lemme see that paper."

Milo gave him the warrant again and he unfolded it.

"I need my glasses."

Milo stood there.

"Gimme my glasses!"

"Do I look like Armand?"

Cursing and squinting, the old man held the warrant at arm's length with palsying hands. The arms lost their strength and the paper slipped and fell to the floor.

I picked it up and tried to give it to him.

He shook his head. "You guys are no good. Rotten, no honor."

"Oh yeah," said Milo. "Honor among thieves. Spare me."

"What do you want!"

"Just to talk."

"Then get yourself a *psychiatrist!*"

Milo grinned at me.

"Fuck off, clown."

"Why so hasty, Kruvinski? Maybe we could help each other."

"In *hell.*"

"Maybe there, too."

Milo leaned over him. "Don't you godfather types make a big thing about gratitude? You're looking at the guy who saved Junior's life."

Something flickered behind the cloudy eyes.

"Unfortunately, I couldn't save Hope Devane. Or your grandnephew, little Casey. But I did get the guy who did them. Stopped him before he got to Junior."

The clouded eyes were wide now. Unblinking.

"Who? Gimme a name."

Milo placed a finger on Kruvinski's lips, gently. "That doesn't mean I'm going to forget about what

Junior did. Which you can bet the scumbag will use as his defense. Odds are any jury's going to sympathize with him. Especially one of our idiot L.A. juries. Or we won't even have a trial 'cause the D.A. will plea-bargain it down. Meaning sooner or later the scumbag's gonna be out and guess who he's gonna be looking for? So unless Junior plans to stay on vacation forever, he's gonna be looking over his shoulder a lot."

The old man smiled. "I give a—"

"Right," said Milo. "You're Don Corleone."

Silence. "So what do you want from me?"

"I need to know if Junior operated on anyone else for your sake. And what was the connection between Hope and your family? Why'd you pay her allowance?"

Silence.

"It's gonna come out. Better we let the prosecution have it before the defense."

"Yeah," said the old man, "we're all on the same side." He tried to spit, produced only a belch.

"God forbid," said Milo.

Soft conversation drifted from the kitchen. Then loud snaps. Cops opening and closing cabinets.

"*Shaddup!*" screeched the old man, to no effect.

"Your people are all gone," said Milo. "Some people. Armand and Little Miss Anna—the former Storm Breeze. Closest she ever came to an R.N. was playing one in that movie of yours—*Head Nurse*. Junior teach her the fundamentals of renal care?"

No answer.

"Little blur between reality and fantasy, Mr. K.? Like Junior's Beverly Hills office, all those diplomas, business cards advertising fertility medicine, but no patients. Anything to make the kid feel important, huh?''

The old man spat.

Milo stretched and looked around. ''That operating room. Those dialysis machines. A clinic for one man. At least Junior had his fling at medicine over in Santa Monica. Because the chance of him ever practicing again when all this comes out is zippo. Assuming the scumbag lets him live.''

Kruvinski didn't speak for a long time.

''Push me outside,'' he finally said. ''Under that tree.''

Waving a claw hand toward the olive-green drapes.

''What tree?'' said Milo.

''Behind the curtains, moe-ron. Open 'em, get me out in the air.''

In the shade of the oak, he said, ''Gimme a name.''

''Don't know your own donor's name?''

''I don't know any donor.''

''You could be forced to submit to a checkup.''

''On what grounds?''

''I'm sure the defense will find one.''

''Good luck.'' Gnarled hands rested in his lap. The jaws worked faster.

''How many other kidneys has Junior harvested for you?''

''You're crazy.''

''Fine,'' said Milo. ''Play hard-to-get. Other victims start coming forward, Junior's going to be in the hot seat and the scumbag'll start looking like a hero. Maybe you don't care about Hope, just another hooker's kid. But little Casey—try explaining that to his grandma, your sister Sonia. San Francisco cops told me you bailed him out of those meth-manufacturing busts at Berkeley, smoothed his record, got Hope to sponsor him into grad school. Which wasn't that big of a stretch. He was a smart kid, top of his class, just like Hope. Just like Junior. But look where it got all of them.''

The old man looked up through the tree. A hairline of light had pierced the branches, creating a hot, white scar down the center of his degraded face.

''When it comes out that Casey died because of his association with Junior, how are you gonna explain that to your sister Sonia and Casey's mommy, her daughter Cheryl? They trusted their baby to you. How you gonna explain why he's cooling in the coroner's fridge instead of writing his thesis?''

The old man gazed out at the pool. The black bottom gave it a mirrored surface, no visibility of the depths. Ten years ago, black bottoms had been the thing. Then a few kids fell in and no one noticed them.

''Family ties,'' said Milo. ''But Don Corleone took *care* of his people.''

''My son is—'' said the old man. ''You'll never have such a son.''

''Amen.''

The cloudy eyes popped. ''Fuck *you!* Coming in here, thinking you know, you don't fu—''

''That's the point,'' said Milo. ''I *don't* know.''

''*Thinking* you *know*,'' repeated the old man. ''Thinking you—moe-ron—lemme *tell* you''—a finger wagged—''*she* was good *people*, Hope. And her *mama*. Don't shoot your mou—don't disrespect people you don't know. Don't—you don't *know* so *shaddup!*''

''Was she family, too?''

"I *made* her family. Who the hell you think paid for her *schooling*? Who the hell got her mama outta hooking and into managing a club, regular hours, a paycheck, goddamn *pension* plan? Who? Some fucking social worker?"

The finger curled laboriously, managed to point at his caved-in chest. "I been working my whole life helping people! And one of the ones I helped most was that girlie's mother. When she got cancer I helped with that, too. When she died, I paid for the funeral."

"Why?"

"Because she was good *people*."

"Ah."

"The girl, too. Little blondie, body like that, you think I couldn'ta got her into club work if I wanted to? But, no, I could see she was *finer*. Had a *brain*. So I told Lottie we keep her *far* from the clubs. We make sure she gets *schooling*. I figured she'd be a doctor, like Mike. Botha them did the science projects together, geniuses. She changes her mind, decides to be a shrink, okay, it's almost the same. I treated her like she was my daughter."

"Smartest boy, smartest girl," I said.

The wizened face snapped toward me. "You *bet*, pal. My Mike was the smartest thing you ever seen, you shoulda had such a kid, reading at three, saying stuff people couldn't believe. And you know where brains come from? Genes. They *proved* it. *All* the kids in my family are brains. Casey skipped two grades, got a brother studying at MIT, nuclear physics. I came to this country with *nuttin'*, no one gave me shit. Greatest country in the world, you're smart and you work, you get what you want, not like the niggers on welfare."

"Why'd you make Hope family?" said Milo. " 'Cause you liked her mama?"

The old man glared at him. "Get your mind outta the gutter. If I wanted that kinda thing, I had plenty of others. You wanna know? I tell you. She helped Mike. Botha them helped Mike. Lottie and Hope. After that . . ." He crossed his index fingers. "Family."

"Helped him with what?"

"He had a accident. Memorial Day picnic, I threw it every year for the employees—big barbecue on my land near the Kern River. Hot dogs, sausage, the best steaks from the plant." Smiling. "Like I said, I ate the best."

He licked his lips again and his head lolled as if he was dozing off. Then it snapped up. He flinched. I tried to picture him swaggering, bull-necked and muscular, into the slaughterhouse late at night. Swinging the bat at trussed hogs.

"We had races," he said, nearly inaudible. "Potato-sack, three-legged. I hired a band. Flags all over the place, best fucking party in town. Mike was thirteen, went over to the river, where the water was strong. He was a great swimmer—on the school team. But he hit his head on something, a piece of wood or something, went down, got pushed out into the white water. No one heard him yelling except Lottie and Hope 'cause they were down there by themselves, talking. They both jumped in, pulled him out. It was hard, them being girls, they almost drowned, too. He swallowed a lotta water but they gave him the respiration, got the water outta him. By the time I got there, he was okay."

Moisture in the glazed eyes.

"From that time on, *she* was a queen and *she* was a *princess*! Cutest little blond thing, coulda been a movie star but I said using the brain was better. I started this prize for science. They earned it, Mike was always straight As, never needed help on the homework, track and field, swimming, baseball, you name it—gotta fourteen hundred on his SAT test. So that's it, Mr. Cop. Nothing *dirty*. Smart kids being smart."

"Until Mike got himself into trouble in Seattle."

Healthy color finally came into the old man's face. A pinkening around the edges of his mouth. Clarity in the eyes—the health benefits of anger?

"Moe-rons! What'd he do, take some stiff and try to get something *good* outta it?"

"Minor technicality. The stiff wasn't dead."

"What, no brain waves and it's ready to get up and do the fucking *mamba*? *Bullshit!* It was dead as your dick—they do it every day—what do you think they give the medical students to practice on? Their fucking girlfriends? *Stiffs* they give 'em! They got hundreds of 'em stored, pickled like pigs' feet. They take 'em apart, throw out the crap they don't want, like garbage. So what was *Mike's* crime? Not filling out the right forms? Big fucking deal. It was a put-up job. They didn't like him from day one 'cause he was too smart for them, showed them up all the time, pointed out their mistakes. I wanted to go up there, tell 'em they better cut out the bullshit but Mike said no, he was sick of 'em anyway, fuck 'em."

"So he left and spent a year with the Brooke-Hastings program."

"Fuck you, it *was* a program. Those kids were starving junkies in the Tenderloin, getting butt-fucked in the alley by perverts and niggers. We cleaned 'em up, got 'em medical care—Mike's a *goddamn* fine doctor."

"Vocational training," said Milo. "So they could get fucked by perverts who paid *you*."

The old man made another unsuccessful attempt to spit. "You know everything, moe-ron—if they were being abused how come the city never charged us with nothing? Because the city knew we got 'em off the welfare rolls. Those with talent we encouraged to go onstage. So what? Others we sent to school—I musta sent fifteen, twenty girls to college, secretarial school. What the fuck did *you* ever do for society?"

"Nothing," said Milo, exaggerating a grimace. "Just a civil-servant leech."

"You got that right."

"Why'd Mike switch from surgery to gynecology?" I said.

"He liked delivering babies—he delivered hundreds of 'em. How many lives *you* ever brought into the world?"

"Deliveries and abortions," I said. "And sterilizations."

"So what? You don't believe a lady's got a right to choose?"

"Where'd he go after the residency at Fidelity hospital?" Milo said.

"Back to me. Helping me with the business, taking care of the girls and building up a practice. Then, when I got sick, he concentrated on taking care of me. I tried to talk him outta it, said Mike, you got your own life, let me be. He said, Dad, I got plenty of life aheada me. I'm gonna take care of *you*."

Another quick turn toward the pool.

"Fuck you," the old man said. Softly, almost genially. "Fuck you, fuck your drug paper, fuck your life. You got no right to come in here under bullshit pretenses, insult my family."

"Talk about gratitude," said Milo.

"So what? You're telling me the scumbag walks."

"If Mike has a history of stealing people's organs he sure does."

"Mike's a better man than you'll—Mike's dirty *diaper* when he was a *baby* had more class than you'll ever have. *You* say stealing. I say bullshit. Experts cut me up twice, put in kidneys that were worth shit. I was on the fucking machine, no veins left, listening to myself pee all day. One day I pass out, wake up, Mike tells me I don't need to be on the machine anymore."

"Just like that."

"Just like that."

"What did Hope have to do with it?"

"Who says anything?"

"She visit you after the operation?"

"Why not?"

"Casey, too?"

"Why not?"

"What did Casey have to do with the operation?"

"Who says anything—and that's all I'm putting up with from you, so fuck off."

Waving a hand.

"Where's Mike hiding out?"

No answer.

"The old country?"

Nothing.

"He planning on ever coming back?"

No answer.

The old man closed his eyes.

"Suit yourself," said Milo, getting up. "But you still got a problem."

The old man kept his eyes shut. Smiled. "Problems can be solved."

38

Back home I wondered how the case would resolve.

The D.A.'s office thought the casting-office thing
was cute but maybe meaningless, because all it
proved was that Muscadine had a scar on his back.
The wheels of a bicycle found in Muscadine's garage
fit the tracks at the murder scene but it was a common
tire. Muscadine's assault upon Paige Bandura was
fortunate because it gave them something to hold him
on while the search for more evidence continued.

Would he walk on four murders?

Rape, too. Because the more I thought about Tessa
Bowlby's terror and mental deterioration the surer I
was that he'd done something to her.

Hope had been there for her.

No one was now.

Had she withdrawn her complaint at the hearing?
Because Muscadine terrorized her further?

I'd called her parents' home several times yesterday and today. No one had picked up and I'd also left messages with Dr. Emerson. He couldn't talk about his patient, but I had facts for him . . .

The phone rang.

"Dr. Delaware? My name is Ronald Oster. I'm the public defender representing Mr. Reed Muscadine."

"Okay."

"Mr. Muscadine has requested to talk to you."

"Why?"

"Mr. Muscadine understands that you consulted to the police on this case and, in that capacity, you've already interviewed him. He believes your psychological knowledge will help the court understand his motivation."

"You want me to help him develop a diminished-capacity defense?"

Pause. "Not necessarily, Doctor."

"But you're looking for some kind of psychological excuse for what he did."

"Not an excuse, Dr. Delaware. Motivation. And after what was perpetrated upon Mr. Muscadine, mental anguish would be significant, wouldn't you say?"

So Oster knew about the kidney theft. Milo'd said the D.A. was holding back, waiting to see how the case shaped up, what would be used as evidence and have to be turned over under the discovery rules.

Meaning Muscadine had told his lawyer about the surgery. But Muscadine still had no idea who the recipient was, and if the D.A. chose not to use the information, keeping the old man under wraps, and if Oster didn't ask the right questions, the details might never come out.

But the defense's problem could be turned back on

the prosecution, too. Because if Muscadine didn't confess openly, direct proof of his guilt was lacking: no weapons, no witnesses, no physical evidence.

How much to use, how much to hide?

Leah Schwartz, the assistant D.A., was still going around with it. Still talking plea bargain or even dismissal. Forty-eight hours to file or release Muscadine on bail.

Did Oster's call mean he didn't yet appreciate the weakness of the case against his client?

He said, "So will you see him, Dr. Delaware?"

"I don't think so."

"Why?"

"Conflict of interest."

He'd expected the answer and his response was rich with malicious joy. "Okay, Dr. Delaware, then I seriously suggest you think about this: If I subpoena you as an expert witness, you'll get paid. If I subpoena you and you don't cooperate, I still get you deposed and in court, but as a regular witness, and you don't receive one thin dime."

"Sounds like you're threatening me."

"No, just laying out the contingencies. For your sake."

"It's good to know someone's looking after my interests," I said. "Have a nice day."

I phoned Milo and told him.

He said, "Figures. Leah said your name came up today when she was talking to Oster. Apparently Muscadine told him about your visit and Oster's making a big deal about having a psychologist investigate Muscadine as evidence that we knew all along he was under mental strain. So now he wants to use you. It's an old tactic, co-opt the other side's consultant as your own. If he can't turn you around, he tries to humiliate you on the stand and reduces your usefulness to us."

"Has Muscadine been charged yet?"

"No, but there has been progress, 'cause this morning, we found a nice big cache of steroids in his apartment. No doubt that'll be part of the defense, too, if it gets that far: drug-induced rage. But at least it buys us some more jail time. Despite that, Leah's still thinking about a plea bargain because she's worried a jury will have sympathy for Muscadine's ordeal."

"What about Kathy DiNapoli?" I said. "If he killed her just because she saw him with Mandy Wright, there wouldn't be much sympathy for that."

"Yeah, but we've got no evidence on Kathy. When I mention her name, he gives that charming actor's smile, but that's all."

"What's the plea bargain?"

"Manslaughter on Hope only. Leah'll demand voluntary, Oster will demand involuntary, they'll work something out."

"If the case is that weak, why would Oster bargain at all?"

"He might not. Leah's keeping Big Micky's identity close to the vest for now, but she may pull it out to scare Muscadine: Walk free, turkey, and the mob goes for you. She's hoping that'll convince Muscadine to accept a reduced sentence at a federal prison under protection."

"Sweet deal for four cold-blooded murders," I said. "But doesn't Oster's calling me mean he thinks the case is stronger than it is?"

"Hard to say. He's one of those brand-new hotshots, grew up on Perry Mason, thinks he's smarter than he is. What Leah's really worried about is he'll motion to get the whole thing dismissed on insufficient evidence and succeed. If we could find a weapon, anything physical . . . but so far no luck. The only knives at Muscadine's place were for spreading butter and no guns at all to match Locking. The guy's covered his tracks."

"Starving actor," I said. Then something hit me. "When I spoke to Mrs. Green—his landlady—she told me she kept a gun around the house for protection. She also told me Muscadine took care of her dog when she was gone. Meaning he had access to her house. What if instead of buying a gun he decided to borrow one?"

"Borrowed it and put it back?"

"Why not? He wouldn't want to alarm Mrs. Green. And I'll bet she registered it, so even if it's missing you could make a point for Muscadine being the only one with access. And ballistics might have something to say about the bullet pulled out of Locking's head being compatible with that model. It wouldn't convict him, but it might tenderize him a bit."

"It is a long shot, but why not—Mrs. Green. Yeah, I've got her on my to-call list."

It took fifteen minutes for him to phone back and this time there was melody in his voice.

"American Derringer, model one, takes .22 long-rifle ammo, which is *exactly* what was pulled out of Locking's head. She hadn't fired it since she took shooting lessons two years ago. And Muscadine did have a key to her house. She ran to look for the gun, found it in the kitchen drawer where she left it, *but* it looked cleaner than she remembered. Freaked her out. I told her not to touch it and she said she wouldn't touch it with a ten-foot pole."

"He cleaned it," I said. "Too smart for his own good."

"Let's not celebrate yet, but I'm going over in person to pick it up, take it to ballistics. Thank you, your excellency, salaam, salaam."

"So what do I do about P.D. Oster?"

"Shine him on."

Two hours later he said, "Ballistics match, and Deputy D.A. Schwartz would like to have a word with you."

I knew Leah Schwartz from a previous case. Young and smart, with curly blond hair, huge blue eyes, and, sometimes, a sharp tongue. She came on the phone sounding ready to run a marathon.

"Hi, again. Thanks for the gun tip, I should put you on retainer."

"Talk is cheap."

She laughed. "So's the city. In terms of Ronnie Oster, maybe you *should* talk to him. Especially now that we've got the .22."

"Why?"

"Because up to now Muscadine's refused to say a word about the crime. Maybe you can get him to spill."

"If he does, it's confidential."

"Not if Oster uses you on the stand. Or even deposes you. Because discovery goes both ways, now, thanks to the voters, so once Oster opens up the door about Muscadine's mental status, I can cross-examine you and get anything you learn out in the open."

"And if Oster doesn't put me on the stand?"

"Why wouldn't he?"

"Because I'm no fan of diminished capacity and I won't testify Muscadine was insane."

"Oster knows that, that's probably why he mentioned mental anguish, not dim cap. And I'll grant Muscadine his anguish. The bastard was *harvested*. If you get up there and talk about mental anguish, we'll have big fun on cross getting into all the details. Another thing you can do is write a report if Oster doesn't have the smarts to specifically ask you *not* to. Do it the minute you have a chance because once it's written down, it exists as discovery material. If Oster puts you on his witness list, or uses you in the preliminary hearing, let's say to get special housing for Muscadine in the psych ward, your work product is probably fair game."

"Probably?"

"We'll squabble but I've got confidence."

"I don't know, Leah."

"No one's asking you to lie. The guy *was* anguished. But not enough to excuse four murders. And the way things are going, we can only present two of them—Devane and Locking—to the jury. I don't know about you, but the thought of Mandy Wright and the DiNapoli woman never coming to light doesn't do much for my appetite. You can make a difference here. Use your therapeutic skills, open Muscadine up. It's not like you'd be forcing yourself on him, they invited you—hell, Oster *pressured* you. Open his client up wide enough, I can probably get a warrant to X-ray him."

"What if he confesses, Oster tells me to put nothing in writing and never puts me on the stand?"

"Then we lose nothing, you make some expert-witness money, we go with the bike and the gun and see how far we can take it. But I think you *can* get him to use you. Examine Muscadine and tell Oster the truth: His client's been through hell. But don't call Oster right away to say yes, that would look too cute. Wait a day or two, then be reluctantly willing."

"So I'm a pawn."

She laughed. "For justice."

39

Dr. Albert Emerson got back to me that evening, just after nine.

"Tessa tried to commit suicide," he said in that same youthful voice, now sobered. "I've got her on a seventy-two-hour hold at Flint Hills Cottages, know where it is?"

"La Canada."

"That's the one. Their adolescent in-patient unit's one of the better ones."

"How'd she do it?" I said.

"Cut her wrist."

"Serious or cry for help?"

"She really sawed, so serious. Her father stopped the bleeding."

"Damn. I called you because I was worried about her."

"I called you back because I appreciate that and so

do the parents. They like you. What'd you want to tell me?"

"That I believe Tessa about the rape. I thought she needed to hear that from someone."

"Why now?"

"I can't say. Legal complications."

"Oh," he said. "The guy got caught for another one?"

"Let's just say she's been validated."

"Okay. I'll find out from my D.A. wife."

"She may not know. It's really a ticklish situation. As soon as I can be open I promise I will."

"Fair enough—hold on, the father wants to speak with you."

A moment later: "Doctor? Walt Bowlby, here."

"Sorry to hear about Tessa."

"Thank you, sir." His words dragged. "Dr. Emerson says she'll pull through. What can I do for you?"

"I was just checking in to see how Tessa was doing."

His voice broke. "She's—I guess I should've believed her about the rape."

"No reason to blame your—"

"The funny thing is she seemed to be getting better, spending more time with Robbie, having some fun. Then she just stopped, didn't want to play with him anymore, even be with him. Started to stay in her room all day, with the door shut. Yesterday, I went in to talk to her, found her in the bathroom. Thank God . . . anyway, the reason I didn't call you is she didn't say anything more about the professor til today. I was gonna call you about that, but we've been pretty busy."

"What'd she say today?"

"That the professor was her true friend because she

was the only one who believed her. That the bastard tied her up and forced her and no one understood what she'd been through but the professor."

"He tied her up?"

"Yeah. If I find him, I'll cut his balls off."

"Mr. Bowlby—"

"I know, I know, my wife tells me I'm stupid to even talk that way and I know she's right. But the thought of his doing that to my little girl . . . maybe there's a hell . . . the main thing is Tessa's alive. I'll deal with the other stuff later. Anyway, thanks for calling, Doc."

"Would it upset you if I came to talk to Tessa?"

"For what?"

"Just to tell her that I believe her, too."

"Wouldn't upset me but you'd have to check with Dr. Emerson."

"Is he still there?"

"He went just down the hall, want me to get him?"

"Please, if it's no bother."

"No bother at all. I'm not doing much, just hanging around."

I made it to Glendale by ten-thirty that night and La Canada a few minutes later.

Flint Hills Cottages was up Verdugo Road, well into the foothills, on the outskirts of a comfortable residential neighborhood, marked only by a small white sign on an adobe gatepost. The gate was open and the man in the guardhouse wore a blazer and tie and a practiced smile.

No central building, just small hacienda-style bungalows at the end of a curving gravel drive, tucked under hundred-year-old sycamores and cedars. Soft outdoor lighting and bougainvillea trained to the walls gave the place the look of a stylish spa.

Emerson had said Tessa was in Unit C and I found it directly across the parking lot and to the left. The front door was locked and it took a while for a uniformed nurse to answer the bell.

"Dr. Delaware for Tessa Bowlby."

She gave me a doubtful look.

"Dr. Emerson's waiting for me."

"Well, he's in back."

I followed her through a butter-yellow hallway. New chocolate carpeting, framed lithos with a tilt toward flowers, a few rock-concert posters, seven doors, all locked. At the end was a nursing station where a man sat charting.

He looked up and stood. "Dr. Delaware? Al Emerson."

He was in his early thirties with wavy brown hair trailing down his back and a thick brown beard squared meticulously at the bottom. Tweed hacking jacket, brown wool slacks, chambray shirt, blue knit tie. His grip was confident and quick.

"Thanks, Gloria," he told the nurse and she left. I read Tessa's name on the chart's tab. The ward was silent.

"Peaceful, isn't it?" he said. "All the pain locked up for the night."

"How's she doing?"

"She's starting to express regret, which is good."

"Is her dad still here?"

"No, he left a short while ago. He was in with her but only for a minute or so. Tessa's pretty mad at him."

"For not believing her?"

"That didn't help but it goes a lot deeper."

"It usually does."

He nodded appreciatively. "They're very nice people. Well-meaning, sincere. But simple. Not stupid, just simple."

"As opposed to Tessa."

"Tessa's as complex as they come. Creative, imaginative, artistic temperament. Likes to deal with existential issues. In the best of circumstances, she'd be high-maintenance. With this family it's like giving a Ferrari to a couple of perfectly competent Ford mechanics."

"Fate's little tricks," I said. "I've seen my share. Will she talk to me?"

"I haven't asked her yet. Why don't we find out?"

"Just pop in on her? The two times I tried she became highly anxious."

"But now you've got something to tell her. And my wife does know what's going on, heard rumors of a student busted for the Devane murder. If he's Tessa's rapist it would be nice for her to know he's in custody."

"It would be, but the D.A.'s keeping it quiet for a couple of days."

"I could convince Tessa to stay here for more than a couple of days. She told me she likes it here, finds it restful."

"What if I talk to her and she gets agitated?"

"Better here, where I can deal with it. Worse comes to worst, she freaks and I spend the whole night here." Grinning. "My job. Sure beats sitting with your feet up having a beer, watching Comedy Central, right?"

I laughed.

He laughed, too, then turned serious. "Want to give it a try?"

"Can you keep it confidential?"

"She's got no phone and I ain't known as a blab-bermouth."

"All right," I said.

"Good," he said. "Come on, she's in Three."

Effort had been taken to make the room look homey: white wallpaper stamped with pale blue, wavelike abstractions; real wood furniture; a big window; flowers in a vase. But a closer look revealed padding under the paper, no sharp edges on the furniture, the light fixture Allen-bolted into the ceiling, external wooden bars striping the window. The vase was plastic and also bolted. The flowers were real lilies. Lilies are related to onions. Nontoxic.

Tessa sat on the bed reading *The Atlantic Monthly.* Other magazines were piled nearby. She wore a gray University sweatshirt and denim cutoffs. Both other times I'd seen her she'd been in all black. Her legs were long and skinny, nearly as white as the walls. A triangle of bandage peeked out from under her left sleeve.

She kept reading.

Hunched vulnerability. Muscadine had read it as fair game.

"Hello again," said Emerson.

She looked up, saw me, and that same look of panic filled her eyes.

"It's all right, Tessa," Emerson said, striding to her side. "Dr. Delaware's a good guy. I vouch for him."

Her lower lip shook.

I smiled.

She looked down at her magazine.

"Good article?" said Emerson.

She didn't answer. Her chest was heaving.

Emerson came closer and read over her shoulder. "Reforestation of the Eastern seaboard." He read some more. "Says here the trees are coming back on their own accord. What, they're allowing in good news for a change?"

Tessa chewed her lip. "The trees are coming back because the economy sucks. As industries close down, people move out of small towns and the land regresses to wilderness."

"Oh," said Emerson. "So it's what, bad news? Or a mixed bag?"

"You tell me."

"What do you think?"

"That I don't want to talk to *him*."

"Is it okay if he talks to you a bit?"

"About what?"

Emerson looked at me.

"About what Reed Muscadine did to you," I said. "I know it's true. Muscadine's scum and he's in jail."

Her mouth dropped open. "Why?"

"This is going to be tough to hear, Tessa, but you'll learn it soon enough. He's the prime suspect in Professor Devane's murder."

Her eyes got wild. *"Oh!"* The word was as much animal cry as human speech. *"Oh, oh, oh!"*

She sprang up, fingers in her hair, crossing the three-pace room, returning and crossing again.

Stopping, said, "Oh God . . . *God GodRobbie!"*

"What about Robbie?" said Emerson.

"Where is he?"

"Back home with your mom, Tess."

"How do I *know*?"

"Why wouldn't he be?"

She stretched her hands in front of her, fingers curled, tremoring.

"The phone!" she exclaimed.

"You want me to call home?" said Emerson. "Have your mom tell you Robbie's okay?"

"*I* want to call! *I* want to speak to him!"

"It's almost eleven, Tessa, I'm sure Robbie's aslee—"

"I *have* to, I *need* to—please, Dr. Emerson. Let me call, *please, please, please!*" Sobbing. *"Oh, please, let me speak to my little Robbie—"*

"Okay, hon." Emerson tried to put his arm around her but she backed away. Confusion tugged at his blue eyes as he unlocked the door and let her out.

At the nursing station, he got her an outside line and both of us watched as she dialed.

"Mom? Where's Robbie? You're sure? Go check . . . please, Mom. *Please*, Mom . . . just *do* it!"

She waited, pulling at her hair, blinking, rolling her shoulders, twisting the skin of one cheek, shifting her feet.

Emerson observed her with a mixture of pity and fascination.

"You're *sure*—did you check to see if he's *breathing*? What? I'm serious—from the nursing station. He let me, he's right here—yes . . . no, I'm not tired . . . I was reading. What? Soon, soon . . . yes . . . you're *sure* he's okay, Mom? I know—I know you wouldn't . . . sorry, Mom. Sorry for bothering— what? Okay, yes, thanks. Sorry to bother you. Just take care of him. Take real good care of him . . . loveyoutoo."

She put down the phone. Sighed. Buried her face. Looked up.

"I'll go back now."

In the room, I said, "Robbie was the wedge Muscadine used on you. He threatened to kill Robbie unless you dropped the charge at the hearing."

She looked at me with what seemed like new respect.

Nodded.

I didn't ask the next question: *Why didn't you tell the police?*

Because I knew the answer: She'd told the police before, had been sent away a liar.

His word against hers.

"He can't hurt Robbie, now," I said. "He can't hurt anyone." Wishing I were sure. Almost hoping Muscadine would walk so that Big Micky could apply his own brand of justice . . . God help me.

She slumped and began sobbing again.

Emerson let her go on for a while, gave her a tissue, stepped back.

Her pain was reflected in his eyes but he could tolerate it.

At the least, I might have found someone to refer to.

Finally she stopped and said, "He killed her because of me."

"Definitely not," I said. "It had nothing to do with you. It was between him and Professor Devane."

"I wish I could believe that."

"When the facts come out you will."

"Robbie," she said.

"You protected Robbie," I said. "At your expense."

She didn't answer.

"Did Professor Devane know about the threat?"

Headshake. "I couldn't—I didn't want—she understood me but I didn't want her . . . didn't want anyone in my mess."

"But you did tell her he'd tied you up."

Long silence. Long, slow nod.

Then she shocked me with a sudden, bright smile. Emerson was caught off-guard, too. He began twisting beard hairs.

"What, Tessa?" he said.

"So I'm a martyr," she said. "Finally."

I drove through quiet streets, picturing the way it had happened.

Muscadine charming her, treating her well—courtly, even, til they got to his place.

Then turning.

Overpowering her.

Tying her up.

She'd told Hope.

Hope had listened—the expert listener—cool, supportive.

But the story had meant so much more to her than just another outrage.

Hating Muscadine. Thinking about him—big, strong.

Healthy.

Nice, *big* kidney, more than adequate for filtering garbage from the shrunken body of a man who considered her family.

Sweet.

Perfect.
Being tied down.
She knew what *that* felt like.
Though she'd never tell Tessa.
Empathy had its limits.

40

Ronald Oster was too young to be that cynical.

Maybe twenty-eight, with kinky flame-red hair and rampant freckles, he was soft around the middle and wore a vested blue suit one size too small.

I met him outside the county jail, off to one side, near the long line of women that forms every morning, waiting to visit prisoners. Some of the women looked at us but Oster paid them no notice as he gave me a long, hard look and kept smoking his British Oval.

"So why'd you change your mind?" he said.

"My own lawyer said you could force me. As long as I'm going to waste my time, I might as well get paid."

He kept staring at me.

"Speaking of which," I said, "my fee's three hundred seventy-five dollars per hour, portal-to-portal. I'll send you the bill and expect you to get it paid within thirty days. I also expect a contract from you to that effect within three days."

I handed him my business card.

"So it's the money," he said, thumbing his vest pocket.

"I'd rather not do it at all but if I have to, it sure *isn't* for the love of your client."

He pressed the flat cigarette between his fingers. "Let's get one thing clear, Doctor. From this point on if you work for anyone on this case, it's *for* my client. Anything he says to you as well as anything I say to you *about* him falls under the purview of therapeutic confidentiality. Including this conversation."

"Once we have an agreement."

"We do. Though in terms of payment, I'm a civil servant. All I can do is go through channels."

"Do your best—and one other exception. If your client threatens me in any way, it'll fall under Tarasoff and I'll report it immediately."

That threw him, but he smiled. "Tarasoff applies to threats against third parties."

"No one says it can't apply to the therapist."

"I sense hostility, Doctor."

"Self-preservation."

"Why would my client threaten you?"

"They say he's murdered several times. I'm just talking theoretically, to make sure we're clear about the rules."

"Do you get this *clear* with every attorney you work for?"

"I don't work much for attorneys."

"I've heard you do lots of child-custody work."

"When I do, I work for the court."

"I see . . . so you're afraid of Mr. Muscadine. Why?"

"I have no specific fear of him but I'm careful. Let's say I don't come to the conclusions he wants me to. If he has murdered all those people, it's an indication he doesn't take well to disappointment."

"Disappointment?" He flicked away the cigarette. "That's a mild way to describe loss of a vital organ."

I looked at my watch.

He said, "Essentially, the man was raped, Dr. Delaware."

"How does he claim it happened?"

"I'll let him tell you that. If I let him talk to you at all. Even if I don't, you'll get the contract and a check for your time today."

"Meaning I already belong to you and can't cooperate voluntarily with the police."

He smiled.

"Fine," I said, looking at my watch again. "Far as I'm concerned, the less I have to do with any of this the better."

He hooked a thumb in his vest. The line of waiting women inched past us.

"This," he said, "may not work out."

"Up to you."

"I'm interested in your professional opinion because I think it's a clear case of mental anguish—like what battered wives go through. But I'm not sure, given your history with the police, that you'll render an impartial opinion."

"If I get data, I'll render. If you want someone you can play ventriloquist with, I'm not your man."

He looked at my card. "I hear a clear prosecution bias."

"Have it your way."

"You don't lean toward the other side?" he said.

"I keep an open mind. If you want a whore, drive down Hollywood Boulevard and flash a twenty."

His freckles deepened in color and the skin between them turned pink. He gave a deep laugh. "That's good, I like that. Okay, you're my guy. Because his mental anguish is so obvious even *you'll* see it. And getting someone like you to testify to that will be all the more impressive. A police consultant."

He held out his hand and we shook. Some of the women in line watched and I could only imagine what they were thinking.

"Let's go meet Reed," he said. "And don't worry, he can't hurt you."

41

"Therapy," said Muscadine, smiling and flipping his long hair. "Quite a luxury for a starving actor."

"Ever had any therapy?" I said.

"Just the mind games they put you through in acting class. Probably should've, though."

"Why's that?"

"My obvious emotional problems. Which is what you're here to establish, right?"

"I want to know as much as I can about you, Reed."

"That's kind of flattering." He smiled and flipped his hair again. He was in street clothes—a black T-shirt and jeans—but behind glass. A few days of incarceration hadn't hurt his looks, and his muscles were still huge and well-defined. Push-ups in the cell, probably. He was big enough to defend himself.

The deputy in the corner of the visiting room

turned toward us. Muscadine smiled at him, too, and he showed Muscadine a khaki back.

"How are they treating you?" I asked.

"Not bad, so far. Of course, I'm a model prisoner. No reason not to be—shall I tell you about my mother? She really was a piece of work."

"Eventually," I said. "But first, tell me about your love for animals."

The smile left his face and returned, stiffer. I could hear a director shout, "Loosen up, go with the feeling, Reed!"

"Well," he said, crossing his legs, "they do love me."

"I know. The reason I'm asking is the day I visited you I noticed how well you got along with Mrs. Green's bullmastiff."

"Samantha and I are good buddies."

"Mrs. Green said Samantha's very protective of her."

"She is."

"But not around you."

"I lived there," he said. "I belonged. But yes, you're right. I do have a special rapport with animals. Probably 'cause they sense I'm at ease with them."

"Did you have lots of pets as a child?"

"No," he said. "*Mom.*"

"She wouldn't let you have any?"

He shook his head. "Never." White-toothed snarl/ smile. "Mom was an extremely *neat* woman."

"And after you left home—how old were you, by the way?"

"College. Eighteen."

"Ever return home?"

"Not a chance. I—"

"Did you get any pets once you were living on your own?"

"Couldn't. The places I rented wouldn't let me. Then my job got in the way."

"Accounting."

He nodded. "The old nine-to-five. It wasn't fair to leave an animal alone all day. When I went back to school and got serious about acting, same thing. I did do some work as a groomer for a while."

"Really?"

"Yeah, just for a few months, one of those mobile van things. One of the many things I did in order to pursue my craft."

"Starving actor."

"Yes, I know I'm a cliché, but so what?"

"So am I, I guess. L.A. shrink."

He chuckled.

"So," I said. "Grooming must have increased your skills with animals."

"Definitely. You learn how to touch them, how to speak to them. With animals, ninety-nine percent is nonverbal communication. You feel right about yourself, they'll feel right about you. And working with them, you learn to read *them*."

"To know which ones are hostile, which are friendly?"

"Exactly."

"Nonverbal," I said. "Interesting. Was Hope Devane's Rottweiler easy to read?"

He looked at his feet. Flipped his hair. "We're going to get right into it?"

"Any reason not to?"

"I don't know," he said. "Oster says I should talk freely to you, but he's just a P.D."

"You don't have confidence in him?"

"He seems fine, but . . ."

"You don't trust him?"

"Sure I do. Twenty feet farther than I can throw him." Another white-toothed grin. "Which is about fifteen feet more than I'd trust most lawyers—actually, he's smarter than I expected from a civil servant. And what's my choice? I *am* a starving actor."

I jotted down notes, looked back up at him.

"The Rottweiler," I said. "How'd you handle her—she was a bitch, wasn't she?"

"Very much so." Smile. "Gave her some meat sprinkled with paregoric."

"Through the gate?"

He nodded.

"She just took it from you?"

"Just like that," he said. "Amazingly easy. Because I'd driven and walked by the house when she was out in the yard and she barked plenty. But she must have smelled the meat because the minute I started up the lawn, she quieted. And by the time I got to the gate, she was sitting there with her tongue out. Lapped it up."

"Was this during the day or at night?"

"At night. Maybe eight o'clock."

"The night Professor Devane was killed?" Use the passive voice, keep him at ease . . .

Nod.

"Was anyone home?" I said.

"They both were." Big smile. "That was the beauty of it. The street was so dark, those big trees, no one walking. I leaned my bike against the tree, walked up their front lawn, gave the meat to the dog, and just rode away."

Long silence.

Finally, he said, "So easy."

I nodded. "You came back later?"

"Yes."

"When?"

"Around ten."

"Because that was the time of her nightly walk."

The smile dropped off. "She walked between ten-thirty and eleven-thirty. Same route, black sweats one night, gray the next. Black, gray, black, gray. Like a machine. I didn't know if she'd walk without the dog or call it off. But she did—does that tell you the kind of person she was? The poor Rottie's barfing its guts out and she just goes about her routine? If she'd veered off-schedule, who knows, I might never have gone through with it."

"Really?"

He stared at me. Broke into the widest grin yet. "Nah, eventually it would have happened."

"In the script, huh?"

He looked down at his feet again. "Yes, that's a good way to put it."

"If you don't mind, let's back up a bit, Reed."

"To what?"

"Mandy Wright."

"Mandy who?"

I smiled, crossed my legs. "She bothers you? More than Devane?"

"No." He exhaled. "What do you want to know?"

"Tell me what happened. How she set you up."

He cracked his knuckles loud enough for the deputy to turn around. Flipped his hair, combed his fingers through it, let it cascade around his handsome face and flipped it once more.

The deputy turned again, frowned, faced the wall. Muscadine said, "Whew . . ."

"Still hard to talk about," I said.

454   *Jonathan Kellerman*

"Yeah . . . you hit the nail on the head. The basic issue *is* the setup. That fucking committee hearing."

"The blood test."

"Exactly. Devane hated my guts for whatever reason, must have decided right then to harvest me. Incredible, isn't it? Like a bad dream—for months I was walking around in a nightmare."

"Tell me about it."

"The nightmare?"

"Everything. Starting with Mandy."

"Mandy," he said. "Mandy the working cunt. She told me her name was Desiree."

"Did you know her before you met at Club None?"

"No, but I knew hundreds like her."

"How?"

"L.A. woman," he said. "Like that Doors song."

"Did she pick you up?"

"In retrospect, she must have. At the time I thought I was picking *her* up."

"Where?"

"Club None."

"You go there often?"

"Once a week or so. I was taking some night acting classes in Brentwood, used to drive home on Sunset. Sometimes I dropped in and had a beer. They must have been watching me. Stalking me."

He started to cry, covered his face. "Shit," he said through gigantic fingers. "To be *prey*—the *violation*."

"Spooky," I said.

"Sickening."

He looked up.

I nodded.

"The degradation," he said. "They *cheapened* me. I wouldn't treat a *dog* that way."

I let him compose himself. "So you went into Club None and saw Mandy—Desiree—and—"

"She was at the bar, we made eye contact, she smiled, bent over, showed me her tits. Luscious tits. I went over, sat down, chatted her up, we moved to a table. I bought her a drink, had myself another beer, we talked. Next thing her hand's on my knee, and she's saying let's go back to my place." Smiling. "It's happened to me before."

"Did you go to her place?"

"We never got there. She must have slipped something in my beer 'cause the last thing I remember is getting into my car and then . . . God, I still can't believe they *fucked* me like that!" Big shoulders shook.

Acting? Maybe, maybe not.

"Then what, Reed?"

"Then I woke up in an alley a block from my house with the goddamnedest pain in my back and the stink of garbage in my nose."

"What time?"

"Around four A.M., it was still dark. I could hear rats, smell the garbage—they *dumped* me like garbage!"

I shook my head. "Unbelievable."

"Kafka. I tried to get up, couldn't. My back was starting to hurt like hell. A throbbing, dull pain, right over my hipbone. And it felt tight, really tight, as if I was being squeezed. I reached around, touched something—gauze. I'd been *wrapped*. Like a *mummy*. Then my arm started throbbing, too, and I managed to roll up my sleeve and saw a black-and-blue mark—a needle stick."

He touched his inner elbow.

"At first I thought someone had screwed with my head, too—given me dope, though I couldn't figure

out why. Later I realized it was the anesthesia. I was
woozy, nauseous, started to throw up, heaved my
guts for a long time. Finally, I managed to stand,
made it to my apartment somehow and collapsed.
Slept all day. When I woke up, I was still in the dream
and the pain was unbearable and I knew I had a fever. I drove myself to the free clinic and the doctor
took off the bandage and this look came on his face.
Like how can you be walking *around*? Then he told
me, you've been operated on, man. Don't you remember? I started to freak out, he held up a mirror so I
could see the stitches. Like a fucking football."

He played with his hair some more, rubbed his
eyes, shook his head.

"Oh, man. It was like . . . you have no idea. No
idea, the violation. Fritz Lang, Hitchcock. This hippie
doctor's telling me I've had surgery and I'm saying no
way. He must have thought I was nuts."

"Hitchcock," I said.

"The classic plot line: innocent man gets caught up.
Only the *star* hadn't been told. The *star* had been *im-
provised* on."

"Horrible," I said.

"Beyond horror—splatter cinema. Then I started to
remember things. Desiree—Mandy. Us getting into
my car, her leaning over to me, kissing. Jamming her
tongue down my throat. Then fade to black. Boom."

He put the palm of one hand over his eyes.

"The free clinic doctor's saying calm down, man,
you've got a fever, better check into the hospital."

"Did the doctor say what kind of operation you'd
had?" I asked.

"He asked me if I'd had kidney disease and when I
said no, what the hell are you talking about, he took

an X ray. And told me. That's when he said I should be in the hospital."

"Did you check yourself in?"

"With what? I don't have insurance."

"What about County?"

"No," he said. "Place is a zoo . . . and I didn't want any more documentation. I didn't want to go anywhere. Because I was already thinking."

"About getting back at them?"

"About regaining my self-respect. It was only Desiree—Mandy—at that point. But I knew she'd just been the bait."

"Did you suspect Professor Devane?"

"No, not yet. I didn't suspect anyone. But I was damned well going to find out."

"So what'd you do?"

"Wangled a prescription for painkillers and antibiotics from the free clinic doc and went home."

"You weren't worried he'd report it?"

"He said he wouldn't. They're cool over there."

"So you went home to recuperate." Telling Mrs. Green it was a back injury. "What about the stitches?"

He winced. "I took them out myself."

"Must have been tricky."

"Dosed myself up with the painkiller, rubbed Neosporin all over and used a mirror. It hurt like hell but I wasn't going to have anyone else knowing."

"So you never saw another doctor?"

"Never. I should've, the scar's all fucked up—keloided. One day when I can afford it, I'll have it fixed."

I wrote some more.

"It's still tough to talk about," he said.

"I can imagine."

"Oster asked me if I'd experienced mental anguish. I had to control myself from laughing in his face."

"No kidding," I said, nodding. "Talk about under-statement—okay, let's move on. How'd you find Mandy?"

"A few weeks later—when I could walk—I went back to the club and saw the waitress who'd served us."

He put his hands behind his neck, flexed to the sides, back and forward. "Stiff. I stretch each morning but it must be damp in the walls."

"It's an old building," I said. "So you saw the wait-ress. Then what?"

He dropped his hands and moved closer to the glass. Smiled. Stretched again. "I waited until she was off-shift. She parked out in back—in the alley—poetic justice, huh? I was a regular alley cat. Meow, meow."

He scratched the glass partition. The deputy turned, looked at the wall clock and said, "Twenty more minutes."

"So she came out to the alley after work," I said.

"And I was there waiting." Grin. "Being the hunter is so much better than being the prey. . . . I put a hand over her mouth, a knee in the small of her back so she lost her balance, twisted her arm up behind her—hammerlock. Dragged her behind a dumpster and said I'm going to remove my hand, honey, but if you make a sound I'll fucking kill you. She started to breathe hard—hyperventilating. I said shut up or I'll cut your fucking throat. Even though I didn't have a knife, or anything else. Then I said, all I want is infor-mation about the girl I was with a few weeks ago. Desiree. And she said I don't know any Desiree. And I said maybe that's not her name but you remember her—remember me. 'Cause I'd left a big tip. I always do, waitering myself. She still tried to deny it and I said let me refresh your memory: She was wearing a tight white dress, drinking a Manhattan, and I was drinking a Sam Adams. 'Cause I know from waitering that sometimes it's the drink you remember, not the customer. She said I remember her but I don't know her. So I twisted her arm a little bit more and covered her mouth and nose—cutting off her air. She started to strangle and I let go and said, come on, honey, who's she to you to suffer for. Because I'd seen the way she and Mandy were acting—friendly, was sure they knew each other. She cried, stalled, got choked off some more, finally told me her real name was Mandy, she was from Vegas and that's all she knew, honest. I twisted the arm almost to the breaking point but all she did was whimper and say please believe me, that's all I know. So I said thanks, put my hand around her throat and squeezed."

"Because she was a witness."

"That and because she'd been *part* of it. The entire club was, contextually. I should've gone back and bombed the whole fucking building. Maybe I would've."

"If?"

"If I wasn't *here*."

The deputy consulted the clock again.

"Mandy from Vegas," I said. "So you went there."

"I had time," he said. "Nothing but. I'd dropped out of school to get the *Embassy Row* part, then lost it."

"Because of the scar."

"*Only* that. Before they saw the scar, they loved me. It was cable and I was just getting scale, but to me it would've been major wealth. I'd already been thinking of moving to a new place, maybe a nice rental near the beach."

His jaw clenched and his mouth tightened.

"So you went to Vegas," I said. "How'd you get there?"

"Took the bus, went from casino to casino. Figuring a whore that good-looking would be working out of one of them. And I was right—you know, that's the amazing thing about all of this."

"What is?"

"How *easy* it is."

"Finding people?"

"Finding and . . . taking care of them. I mean I'd never even come close to doing anything like that to anyone before I handled the girl in the alley." He snapped his fingers. "I've had harder parts to play."

"Was Mandy easy, too?"

"Easier. Because I had even more motivation. And she made it easy. Driving around in a *Ferrari convertible*. Ostentatious little bitch, right there in the open. I watched her park it at a casino, give the valet a big tip—Miss Hotshot. I followed her, watched her for two days, found out where she lived, waited until she came home alone, and surprised her."

"Same way?" I said. "Hand over the mouth, knee in the back?"

"Why mess with a good thing? She was stupid enough to have her keys out, so I just opened the door and got her inside her apartment. She was loopy to begin with—stoned on something. Probably coke because her nose was a little raw. I put my knife across her throat and told her I'd filet her like a monkfish if she made a peep—"

"This time you brought a knife."

"Definitely."

"It had to be a knife, didn't it?"

"Oh, yeah." Flipping his hair.

"Because . . ."

"Reciprocity—synchronicity. Like that Police song. They cut me, I cut them."

"Makes sense," I said.

"Makes perfect sense. All I had to do to remember how much sense it made was to try a toe-touch or a sit-up and feel the pain in my back. Thinking about *Embassy Row* and what might have been."

His eyes turned to slits. Moving closer to the glass again, he said, "They say you only need one kidney, I can live til a hundred. But having only one makes me vulnerable. What if I get an infection and lose the one?"

"So it was time to make Mandy feel vulnerable."

"Not feel, *be*."

"Be," I echoed. "What next?"

"She pissed her panties—Miss Tough Call Girl. I tied her up with some bicycle bungee cords I'd brought—hog-tied her, began the interrogation. She claimed all she knew was that a psychology professor from the U had hired her to pick me up, slip a Mickey in my drink. That she hadn't known why. As if that excused it. I said which professor and she tried to hold back on me. I covered her mouth and pinched her nose the way I'd done with the waitress and she blurted out the name. Which I already knew, because what other psychology prof hated me?"

"Did she say how she knew Devane?"

"Yes. She said Devane had hired her."

"For sex?"

"Games she called it. She said Hope was into kinky stuff—bondage. Had seen her dance somewhere up in

San Francisco and picked her up—sick, huh? A psychologist that twisted."

"Then what?"

"Then, I untied her and said thanks for being honest with me, baby. To disarm her psychologically. Then, I took her back outside in front of her house, told her I was going to let her go if she kept her mouth shut. She looked so relieved, she actually thanked me, tried to kiss me, showing tongue. It reminded me of how she'd kissed me in my car just before the lights went out. No one was on the street, so I took hold of her hand, held it still so she couldn't touch me. Then I gave her the knife."

"Where?"

"First in the heart, because they'd broken my heart by looting my body, robbing me of my entire future. Then in her cunt because she'd used her cunt to trap me. Then I put her on the ground and turned her over and stabbed her in the back. Just like she'd done to me. Right over her kidney."

He reached behind and winced. "Never really knew where the kidney was before."

"Still painful?" I said.

"Sitting is painful," he said. "How much more time do we have?"

"Ten minutes. So once you'd learned Hope's name from Mandy it was time to take care of her, too."

"You bet."

"And you used the same strike pattern. Heart, vagina, back."

"Absolutely," he said. "The only difference was that Hope tried to struggle. Not that it helped her, but it did mess me up. I'd wanted to get the fucking surgeon's name out of her but I was afraid she'd manage to break free and scream, so I just did it."

"When did you learn the surgeon's name?"

"Not until last week, when that kid attacked him and the news said he'd known Devane. Light bulb on. Two plus two. So I started watching him, too, and got a bonus. The punk."

"Casey Locking."

"My other *judge*. I was never really sure if he was in on the plan but I suspected because he was sucking up to Devane. Once I knew, he was history. I got his file from the psych department, learned his address. I already knew where Cruvic lived because that's where I'd seen him with the punk—his house up on Mulholland. So I started watching Locking."

"Saving Cruvic for last."

"You bet."

"Tell me about Locking."

"Another easy one—it's so easy."

"Probably harder to act it out."

"Definitely . . . where was I?"

"Locking."

"Locking. I followed him home, walked into the house, and shot him."

"Why a gun and not a knife?"

"Three reasons," he said, pleased to answer. "A. I know cops are into M.O. and I didn't want it to be obvious that the same person had done him and the girls. B. Stabbing was for the women, it just didn't feel right for him, and C. I'd already gotten rid of the knife."

"Where?"

"Tossed it off the Santa Monica Pier."

"You could have bought another one."

"Hey," he said, grinning. "Starving artist."

"What about the photos framing Locking's body?"

"Another bonus. Showing the world what she was

like—what they were all like. Do you *believe* that stuff? *Sick.*"

"So what was your plan? To get Cruvic?"

"Him and the asshole using my kidney. I figured to learn everything, eventually. Perform a little surgery of my own, take back what was mine."

The deputy said, "Two minutes."

Muscadine mouthed *Screw you* to his back and smiled at me. "So how're we doing?"

"Fine," I said. "I appreciate your forthrightness."

"Hey, only way to go. Tell the truth, it feels good to finally unload."

Oster was just outside the prison's main door. The line was still long.

"Well?" he said.

"Well what?"

"I instructed him to cooperate."

"He did."

"What do you think?"

"Gruesome."

"I'll say. So does it fit?"

"Does what fit?"

"Is there severe mental anguish?"

"Definitely," I said, shaking my head. "No shortage of anguish."

"Good," he said. "Great. Gotta go, we'll talk more."

He hurried into the jail.

Instead of returning home, I drove to a restaurant on Sixth Street where I ordered lunch—nice big one:

Caesar salad, T-bone steak medium rare, home fries, creamed spinach, their best burgundy by the glass.

While I waited for the food, I opened my briefcase and took out a yellow pad.

As I sipped the wine, I began.

PSYCHOLOGICAL EVALUATION:

REED MUSCADINE

PRISONER #464555532

EXAMINER: ALEXANDER DELAWARE, PH.D.

I wrote for a long time.

Read on for an exciting sneak preview of
Jonathan Kellerman's

RAGE

Available in bookstores everywhere
from Ballantine Books

On a slow, chilly Sunday in December, shortly after the Lakers overcame a sixteen-point halftime deficit and beat New Jersey, I got a call from a murderer.

I hadn't watched basketball since college, had returned to it because I was working at developing my leisure skills. The woman in my life was visiting her grandmother in Connecticut, the woman who used to be in my life was living in Seattle with her new guy—temporarily, she claimed, as if I had a right to care—and my caseload had just abated.

Three court cases in two months: two child-custody disputes, one relatively benign, the other nightmarish; and an injury consult on a fifteen-year-old girl who'd lost a hand in a car crash. Now all the papers were filed, and I was ready for a week or two of nothing.

I'd downed a couple of beers during the game and was nearly dozing on my living-room sofa. The distinctive squawk of the business phone roused me. Generally, I let my service pick up. Why I answered, I still can't say.

"Dr. Delaware?"

I didn't recognize his voice. Eight years had passed.

"Speaking. Who's this?"

"Rand."

Now I remembered. The same slurred voice deepened to a man's baritone. By now he'd be a man. Some kind of man.

"Where are you calling from, Rand?"

"I'm out."

"Out of the CYA."

"I . . . uh . . . yeah, I finished."

As if it had been a course of study. Maybe it had been. "When?"

"Coupla weeks."

What could I say? *Congratulations? God help us?*

"What's on your mind, Rand?"

"Could I uh talk to you?"

"Go ahead."

"Uh not this . . . like talk . . . for real."

"In person."

"Yeah."

The living room windows were dark. Six forty-five P.M. "What do you want to talk about, Rand?"

"Uh . . . it would be . . . I'm kinda . . ."

"What's on your mind, Rand?"

No answer.

"Is it something about Kristal?"

"Ye-ah." His broke and bisected the word.

"Where are you calling from?" I said.

"Not far from you."

My home office address was unlisted. *How do you know where I live?*

I said, "I'll come to you, Rand. Where are you?"

"Uh . . . I think . . . Westwood."

"Westwood Village?"

"I think . . . lemme see . . ." I heard a clang as the phone dropped. Phone on a cord, traffic in the background. A pay booth. He was off the line for over a minute.

"It says Westwood. There's this big uh . . . a mall. With this bridge across."

A mall. "Westside Pavilion?"

"I guess."

Two miles south of the village. Comfortable distance from my house in the Glen. "Where in the mall are you?"

"Uh I'm not in there. I kin see it across the street. There's a . . . I think it says pizza. Two *z*s . . . yeah, pizza."

Eight years and he could barely read. So much for rehab.

It took a while but I got the approximate location: Westwood Boulevard, just north of Pico, east side of the street, a green and white and red sign shaped like a boot.

"I'll be there in fifteen, twenty minutes, Rand. Anything you want to tell me now?"

"Uh . . . I . . . can we meet at the pizza place?"

"You hungry?"

"I ate breakfast."

"It's dinnertime."

"I guess."

"See you in twenty."

"Okay . . . thanks."

"You sure there's nothing you want to tell me before you see me?"

"Like what?"

"Anything at all."

More traffic noise. Time stretched.

"Rand?"

"I'm not a bad person."

**Don't miss this thrilling novel of
psychological suspense starring Petra Connor**

TWISTED
JONATHAN KELLERMAN

With her energies focused on a baffling, vicious gang slaying, and her personal life in shambles, Hollywood homicide detective Petra Connor has a full plate. The last thing she needs is a whiz-kid grad student claiming to have stumbled upon a bizarre connection between several unsolved murders. The victims had nothing in common, yet each died by the same method, on the same date—a date that's rapidly approaching again. And that leaves Petra with little time to unravel the twisted logic of a cunning predator who's evaded detection for years—and whose terrible hour is once more at hand.

"An **elaborate, tangled web** . . . with
unsuspected turns at every chapter break . . .
this **addictive** tale . . . is as intricately detailed
as it is **tantalizingly page-turning**."
—*Entertainment Weekly*

"[Jonathan Kellerman is] a
master of the psychological thriller."
—*People*

Ballantine Books • www.jonathankellerman.com

DR. DEATH

To some Eldon Mate was evil personified. Others saw the former physician as a saint. But one thing was clear: Dr. Death had snuffed out the lives of dozens of human beings and now someone had turned *him* into a victim. When Mate is found mutilated in a rented van, harnessed to his own killing machine, psychologist-sleuth Alex Delaware joins the hunt for the death doctor's executioner. But Alex harbors secrets of his own that threaten to derail the increasingly complex investigation into the most sinister corners of the human mind.

"Breathes new life into the crime genre...[A] roller-coaster plot...Just what the doctor ordered."
—*People*

"Intriguing...Stylish...A brazenly clever denouement."
—*The New York Times*

Published by Ballantine Books
Available wherever books are sold

Little girl lost...

FLESH AND BLOOD

Lauren Teague is a beautiful, defiant, borderline delinquent teenager when her parents bring her to Dr. Alex Delaware's office. Lauren angrily resists Alex's help—and the psychologist is forced to chalk Lauren up as one of the inevitable failures of his profession. Years later, when Alex and Lauren come face-to-face in a shocking encounter, both are stricken with shame. But the ultimate horror takes place when Lauren's brutalized corpse is found dumped in an alley. To find her killer, Alex plunges into the shadowy worlds of fringe psychological experimentation and the sex industry—and into mortal danger, when lust and big money collide in an unforgiving Los Angeles.

"Razor-sharp...A skillful piece of work."
—*The Washington Post Book World*

"[Kellerman] has shaped the psychological mystery novel into an art form."
—*Los Angeles Times Book Review*

Published by Ballantine Books
Available wherever books are sold

Who wrote the book of death?
Dr. Alex Delaware must find out—in the most
chilling *New York Times* bestseller yet
by Jonathan Kellerman.

THE MURDER BOOK

L.A. psychologist-detective Alex Delaware has received
a strange, anonymous package in the mail, containing
an album filled with gruesome crime-scene photos.
When homicide detective Milo Sturgis views the com-
pendium of death, he is immediately shaken by one of
the images: a young woman tortured, strangled, and
dumped near a freeway ramp—an unsolved murder that
has haunted him for two decades. Now, someone has
chosen to stir up the past. And as Alex and Milo set out
to finally break the case, their relentless investigation
reaches deep into L.A.'s nerve centers of power and
wealth...where the murder of one forgotten girl has
sinister ramifications that extend far beyond the
tragic loss of a single life.

"Dense plotting keeps the pages flying....
The outcome is one of perfect justice, which, like
revenge, turns out to be a dish most delectable
when served cold."
—*People* (Page-turner of the week)

"This may be the best Kellerman in years....A classic
puzzler to keep the most staid traditionalist gleefully
scratching his or her head until the wee hours."
—*Publishers Weekly* (starred review)